Except in Spring

Melanie Wyllie

1

1950

It would have happened.
It could have happened.
It should have happened.
But it did not happen.

Instead of sewing silk roses on her wedding veil, she helped her mother run up the blackout curtains on her old Singer.

When darkness fell, Edward was sent outside to inspect all the windows to make sure there were no visible chinks of light.

The mad dogs of war had gnawed through the last wilting strands of resistance — newly planted green shoots, destined to grow into unassailable thickets, now a pulpy mass, crushed into the sour black earth — and roamed the world in ravening packs, bringing terror and panic, and unimaginable horrors.

They had said goodbye in the driving rain, on the inadequately protected platform where the trains were always late, among other couples, anxious parents and uncertain children.
He had hugged her tightly against the bulk of his winter overcoat, and she had felt the warmth of his face against hers for the last time.

All that idyllic summer they saw each other as much as possible — lunch hours — after work — at weekends — sitting in the park — bumping down the country lanes on their bicycles, the hedges full of wild roses and flowering brambles — kissing in the long grass, and on the mossy ground beneath the beech trees in the wood that covered the hillside behind the town.
And when it rained they went to the pictures, or sat in steamy teashops, holding hands.
They made plans for their future — for their life together.

At home their father worried about the war that was bound to come.

There had already been men from the War Office looking at the factory. There were rumours it was to be adapted to make shells. Crates of equipment were arriving every day. As foreman he was to go on a course on handling explosives — a fortnight at some place in Somerset.

Her mother increasingly anxious, filling the store cupboards with homemade jam and bottled fruit — buying tins of salmon and baked beans — the cupboard under the sink crammed with boxes of soap and soapflakes.

Catherine would catch her —hands stilled on her mending, watching Edward doing his homework, knowing she was thanking God that he was too young to be called up, and praying that it would all be over before he was old enough. He was doing so well at grammar school, his best subjects maths and science, and was captain of the junior cricket team.

Her mother was obsessive about Edward. She had such big plans for him. Catherine was pleased when he went away to scout camp in the New Forest. It was good for him to get away for a while from their mother's perpetual fussing.

Catherine had not told her parents about Peter.
She knew her mother would start going on about 'knowing one's place', and 'heading for a fall'...
She would have liked to have confided in her father, but he was too preoccupied, studying manuals on explosives and safety... and Edward was too young to be interested.

At the library Miss Turnbull, the head librarian, remarked what a nice young man he was, and turned a blind eye when she came back late from her lunch hour.
Miss Turnbull had always been kind, making sure she had time to study for her librarian exams. In her forties, immaculate in a navy costume and white blouse. She lived with her mother in a bungalow on the outskirts of town. She seemed to have little social life. A keen historian, she liked to spend her holidays going up to London to the

British Museum. The Ancient Egyptians were her great love. They had a really good selection of books on Ancient Egypt in the library.

She was very strict about rules, but very fair and kind, particularly to people like Colonel Harding, who practically lived in the library. Since his wife died he was at a loss. Coming to the library gave him some sort of structure, a routine, a daily timetable. He arrived shortly after ten in the morning, and sat in one of the leather chairs in the window reading the newspapers, which were laid out daily on the low round table. At lunchtime he went to the Rose & Crown for a sandwich and a pint of beer before returning to the library for the afternoon to continue to read the papers and have a little nap. He went home just before they shut at 6, stopping at the Rose & Crown for a whisky and soda and a sausage roll, or one of Mrs Croft's Scotch eggs, before returning to his lonely house, still expecting Emily to greet him. They had had a maid, a nice girl, but she had left — gone home to London — wanted a more exciting life.

By the time war was finally declared the factory was churning out shells twenty-four hours a day — the employees swelled by young women who had given up their jobs as maids, waitresses, shop assistants, to contribute to the war effort.

Her father was on twelve-hour shifts, and her mother hung up her apron, and for the first time since she was married went to work, in the canteen, leaving notes on the kitchen table for Edward — 'Don't forget your gas mask' — 'Don't forget your Identity Card' — 'Don't forget your raincoat'…

Edward moaned about being too young. He wanted to join the navy.

And Peter joined up.
She knew he was going to join up but hoped it wouldn't happen, that none of it would happen, that the war wouldn't happen.
And he wanted her to meet his parents.
He assured her they would love her — 'How could they help it?'
Catherine was not at all sure.
She was hardly the sort of girl Peter's mother would be anticipating.

How could she be? A girl who works in the local library and lives in a street of terraced houses near the canal.

Ursula Tarrant drove a beige saloon.
Every Thursday morning she parked it outside Bella's Hair Salon whilst she had her hair done, emerging an hour-and-a-half later with neatly pressed light brown waves. A sturdy woman with thick legs and a heavy chin, sensibly dressed — expensive well-cut tweeds in winter, short-sleeved flower-printed rayon dresses in summer with, of course, appropriate shoes.
A well-to-do, middle class woman of unshakeable principles, very conscious of her standing in the community.
Peter was her only son — her only child.

His life had been carefully mapped out. A good, sensible nanny, prep school, then Harrow, Henry's old school, then Oxford, Henry's old college, and then the City with Henry's bank, and somewhere along the way, marriage to some nice suitable girl. The Blenkinsops, who were hugely wealthy, had a daughter who would be ideal — rather plain, but always cheerful, not very bright, but one couldn't have everything.

And now, when he was safely at Oxford, this awful war had come to disrupt everything.

Henry said not to worry, it wouldn't last long.
Certainly nothing dramatic had happened so far.
No massive air raids or invading armies.
Henry went daily to the City, the sun shone, and the garden flourished. The dahlias were magnificent this year.

And then Peter announced he had joined up.
He would not be going back to Oxford.
He had joined the army.
Henry's brother was in the army — a colonel, such a bore with his much recounted military anecdotes.

She had already had her sister-in-law on the phone, drawling away in her gin-sodden voice about how pleased Godfrey was that Peter had joined the army. Pamela, the elder of their two daughters — no son, much to their chagrin — had just volunteered for the ATS — 'Pamela was ready for anything'.

Ursula was not pleased.
She didn't want Peter to be in the army.
Marjorie was a fool.
Bossy Pamela was a fool.

Worse was to come.
Peter wanted to bring a girl home to meet them.
She had not known he was seeing a girl.
She thought he had spent most of the holidays playing tennis at the Carters'. Maybe he had met her there? Pleasant people the Carters, if a little left wing. But he had said no — she worked in the library.

Ursula had never been in the library. Their sort didn't go to public libraries. Not that she read much, ordering the latest best seller from the bookshop on the High Street, just to say she had read it, or was about to read it. She had never read any of the leather-bound books in the glass-fronted bookcase in the drawing room. Complete sets of Trollope and Dickens, the Romantic poets, and of course Shakespeare.

On further questioning she discovered that the girl lived in Bridge Street, near the canal, and that her father was foreman at the small parts factory on the road to Mecklenby.
'Working class,' she said to Henry that evening. 'Her father works in a factory...'
Henry said not to worry, she would probably have to meet a lot of girls before Peter settled down, and he thought tea was a good idea.

And then, to make matters worse still, Susan, the maid, gave in her notice. She was going to join up — everybody was joining up.
Thankfully Ethel, faithful Ethel, was too old to join up. They would just have to manage.
There was still Mrs Mount who came twice a week to do the 'rough'.

It was unlikely she would be called upon to contribute to the war effort.

Ethel would have to serve the tea.
If it was fine they could have it on the terrace.
It was still warm enough.

*   *   *

Catherine did not have much choice what to wear for this crucial meeting. Junior librarians were not exactly very well paid. She only had two dresses which could be considered suitable — a navy blue with tiny white spots, and a pale blue with a pattern of daisies and two pleats back and front.
She decided on the pale blue, and bought a new pair of white sandals at the Clarks shoe shop in the High Street.

The Tarrants' house was high above the little town, with manicured lawns and orderly flower beds, and, as if in defiance of all the well mannered neatness, a riotous herbaceous border, full of lupins, hollyhocks, delphiniums in all shades of blue and mauve, golden rod, ox-eyed daisies, and dahlias of all colours and all varieties. The herbaceous border was Henry's passion, the dahlias his particular pride. He liked to potter about, discussing the flowers with Hobbs, their gardener, who was also mercifully too old to join up, poking about with his trowel, clipping things with his expensive secateurs, and tying tall plants to stakes with green gardening twine. It was great relaxation after the stress of the City.

Ursula was not interested in gardening. She just liked everything to be neat, and to have enough flowers to cut for the house.

Tea had been set out on the terrace under a green umbrella, amid grey stone urns of trailing plants and borders of lavender.
There were wicker chairs with cushions, a white lace cloth and delicate, fluted china.

Mrs Tarrant did not rise to greet her, but Mr Tarrant did — a big

6

man with a hearty handshake, in casual slacks, white open-necked shirt and a dark blue cravat.

Catherine often thought of that afternoon, of the warm September sunshine, the tortoiseshell butterfly which had settled briefly on the crisp white cloth. The small square sandwiches of cucumber and salmon paste, the perfect sponge, Peter's tanned arms passing the plates, joking with his father about losing golf balls, and Mrs Tarrant stiff on her wicker chair. The stilted conversation — a polite, disdainful interrogation — the questions about her family — her job — her father's job…
She had a lump in her throat — she had wanted to leave —and then Peter had taken her hand, overwhelming her with his warmth, and he had said, 'Now I'm going to show Cathy the garden…', and he had led her away, across the soft grass, down the abundant herbaceous border, heavy with warm scents, to the rose garden and the summer house where he had kissed her. 'You mustn't take any notice of mother,' he had said. 'She's a terrible snob…'
And that was that.
She never met or heard from his parents again.

All through the golden autumn and the grey chill of winter the war held its breath.
She had letters from wherever it was Peter was — she didn't know where — writing back to anonymous box numbers — letters of hope and love.

But as the blossoms scattered their pink and white snow across the park, the daffodils danced by the river and the budding green woods were starred with white anemones and carpeted with bluebells, cold gusts of shivering wind began to reach them.

Down like ninepins the countries of Europe fell, tumbling dominoes spotted with blood.
Grim news crackled down the radio waves.
No more letters.
Did that mean Peter was in France? Was he going to have to fight?
Ice encased her heart. She prayed — 'Please God — Please God…'

It seemed always summer when things were at their worst.

The heat of the sun baked the blood into rusty abstract patterns on the sand, tanning the faces and limbs of the dead and dying soldiers, twisted bundles of ragged khaki cloth, strewn carelessly on the soft holiday beach where the breeze carried the whispering laughter of children, and the waves curled their toes where little feet had splashed with delight.

Lying within sight of the gleaming cliffs of home, almost able to stretch out and touch the short, rough clumps of grass growing on their white, shiny surface.

Peter might not have died on the beach.
She didn't know — she didn't know where he had died — perhaps on the long blank roads, in the dust of humiliating retreat.
She would never know.

She would not even have known he was dead if Miss Turnbull had not gone to try and get some fish.
On Thursdays MacFisheries sometimes had a delivery of fish — not every Thursday, but sometimes. It was never certain what sort of fish might be available — sometimes it was nothing but herrings or mackerel, or a mixture of smoked cod and measly dabs — occasionally plaice or lemon sole — very rarely real smoked haddock.

Sara Turnbull had taken an early lunch hour to get a good place in the queue, and had found herself in front of Ethel, wearing her habitual black cloth coat and black straw hat. She was usually good for a gossip, but today her face was uncertain — grey and puffy — the arm carrying her black bag listless at her side.
Sara Turnbull remarked on the lovely weather. 'So much sun — people will soon start complaining about the lack of rain…'
Ethel started to cry.

She stood in the fish queue clutching her worn black purse, the tears running down her face, unheeded. 'He's dead,' she whispered.

'Young master Peter. He's dead — at Dunkirk — at Dunkirk,' and she fumbled in her pocket for her clean white handkerchief.

The queue was moving forward.

Sara Turnbull was aghast. How could she think of buying fish? The slabs were almost empty — just a few herrings left — and some soft roes. How could she buy fish? But there was mother to think of — it was grotesque.
She took Ethel's arm. 'So sorry,' she murmured. 'I'm so sorry. Please go ahead of me. You have to eat…' What a feeble thing to say!
And then Mr Gibb was wrapping up the last three herrings in the newspaper for Ethel. 'Very tasty today…' He was always cheery. 'Very fresh — very tasty…'
And then she found herself with a package of soft roes — 'Very tasty on toast luv — very fresh — very tasty…' And the woman behind her complained that her husband didn't like soft roes — 'Nasty, sloppy things.' But there was nothing else left.

That afternoon the sun was shining — bright strips of light between the brown sticky tape that criss-crossed the windows. It had taken ages to do, and made the library perpetually dim.
The Colonel was snoozing in his chair by the table, a newspaper open on his lap.

She knew immediately there was something wrong when Miss Turnbull returned from lunch, and without speaking, went to put away her shopping.
There was a shelf in the passage that led to the back yard, where they kept the milk, lunchtime sandwiches, and any food they might have managed to buy.
It was always cool in the passage — the walls and floor were stone, making it always cool even on the hottest days. There was a sink with a cold tap and hooks to hang their coats.
She came back, abstractedly patting her hair.
'There were only soft roes,' she said. 'I expect mother will make a fuss, but what can one do…?'
She started tidying the already tidy pile of books on the counter.

'Let's have a cup of tea — I'm really thirsty. It was so hot in the queue…' She pushed the card file to one side. 'Go and put the kettle on — and see if there are still any biscuits…'

At Easter they had been given a tin of biscuits by Mrs King who ran the Tea Shoppe. Biscuits were a much sought after luxury, they were kept for special occasions, having only been opened so far when she had done particularly well in her librarian exams. They were locked in a filing cabinet in Miss Turnbull's small dusty office — she didn't like anything to be moved — with the precious sugar ration and the account books.
'Bring the sugar too — and another cup for the Colonel…'

Catherine knew then for certain something was dreadfully wrong —biscuits and sugar on an ordinary Thursday — and for the Colonel as well…

Waking from his snooze, he accepted the tea with pleasure.
'By Jove, that's kind,' he said. 'And biscuits! How very kind.' And he smiled, and Catherine suddenly saw how he must have looked when he was young. A good face, a kind face, a dependable face.
'Thank you,' he said again. 'And sugar — most kind…'

Miss Turnbull had insisted they sit down.
There were chairs behind the counter. She poured the tea carefully — she didn't look at Catherine. 'My dear…' she said.
There was not any way it could be said kindly. No way to lessen the numbing blow. No way to make it better. How could anything anybody said make it any better?

She heard what Miss Turnbull was saying as if she were drowning — the words a swirling undercurrent of incomprehensible sounds roaring in her ears.
The world went into slow motion.
Miss Turnbull's arm a heavy weight —her mouth slowly moving — her voice a run down record…
She felt herself being dragged down into a black whirlpool — the dark waters closing over her head.

So whether it was on the hot sand — in a waterlogged ditch — or on a wearisome road — it was all the same.

Time slotted into time — day into night — night into day — month into weary month — season into season — blossoming and withering. To put one foot in front of the other — just to put one foot in front of another — that was all that was possible.

They grew vegetables — everyone grew vegetables — potatoes and cabbages — spindly tomato plants — runner beans and straggly lettuce that went to seed.

Sometimes at weekends she would ride her bicycle out into the country to get some eggs from one of the farms that was not too far.

Mrs Craig, the farmer's wife, was always very bad tempered. She was fed up with the war — fed up that the young men had gone to war — fed up that her husband was too old to be much help — and stone deaf — fed up with the land girls who were worse than useless — 'Don't know one end of a cow from another. Eating us out of house and home…' — grudgingly selling her half a dozen eggs, and even more grudgingly, and very rarely, a pat of butter. She could make much more money selling to the Black Market, and Catherine, who once would have minded, have felt awkward and upset by her bad temper, now didn't notice, stood silently with her bike, listening to the stream of grievances, and thanking her politely as she paid for the eggs.
She didn't care about eggs — or butter. It didn't matter to her what she ate — if she ate. She came to please her mother. It would give her pleasure to have something nice to give them for supper.

Nobody had noticed her distress.
Her mother and father were too tired to notice anything much — working their punishing shifts and trying to get enough sleep. Her mother fretting about what they would eat, especially Edward.
'He's a growing boy,' she would say. 'He needs more food…'
Sometimes she managed to bring home some leftover rolls or scraps of ham or luncheon meat — but mostly she was too tired even to fret.

Mrs Tarrant's beige saloon was never seen now outside the hair salon. It was said that she had shut herself away, and would see no one.

Ethel continued to trudge up and down the hill from the house with her black shopping bag hanging limply at her side — queuing for whatever happened to be available — fish — sausages — carrots — a consignment of pickle, which almost caused a riot — anything — even tripe.

Miss Turnbull was very kind, as always, in her awkward, inarticulate way.
Her mother was not well and she worried continually about the inability to obtain proper food for her.
'There just isn't enough,' she said, arranging the index cards which she had just arranged. '2 ozs of cheese — it hardly makes a slice of Welsh rarebit. I couldn't even get any onions to make soup last week. And she's so fussy — has to be tempted.'

It had been another lovely summer afternoon when the devastating explosions reduced the factory to a mangled wreck — huge balls of flame and acrid black smoke blotting out the sun — blotting out the sky.

She had taken her sandwiches to eat in the park behind the library. Sitting by the pond in the shade of an old willow which bent over the water, brushing the surface with silvery fronds, watching the moorhens scuttle about in the reeds.
It was very peaceful.
There had been plans to dig up the park to plant vegetables, but the first experiment was not a success — people came in the night and took everything — so the plan was abandoned, so there were still flowers and shrubs, and the neglected tennis court with weeds growing through the asphalt, the trailing net broken and rotting, and old Johnson still swept the leaves from the paths in the autumn and planted the borders in the spring with geraniums and lobelia.

She had eaten her sandwiches slowly —cheese and lettuce. Mr

Turner had slipped her mother some extra cheese in return for a bar of soap she had given him for his elderly mother who was bedridden.

At last there had been some better news.
After so may setbacks and disappointments there had been spectacular successes in Africa. The Germany army was in retreat. At last it began to seem possible they could defeat this unmerciful, predatory enemy.

Everyone was working flat out at the factory. Production targets had been increased. Everybody was weary, but now the weariness was tinged with optimism.

She would have liked to have joined up — to have done something useful towards the war effort. Miss Turnbull had said they would be really pleased to have someone like her in the war office, particularly as she had been doing a Pitman's shorthand and typing course at evening class, and was already very proficient, but she knew her mother needed her help with the cooking and the housework now she was working twelve-hour shifts at the factory, and to keep an eye on Edward, even though Edward was now old enough to look after himself.
He had wanted to leave school this summer and join the navy, but his headmaster had persuaded him to stay to do his Higher School Certificate. His science and maths were exceptionally good, and Mr Lane said that people with his expertise were desperately needed, and that he could do more to help the war effort with his brains than on a boat, so he had reluctantly agreed, much to everyone's relief, particularly their mother, who became almost hysterical at the thought of Edward going to fight.

Catherine thought it would be best to wait until the autumn before she made a move. In the meantime she would drop hints.
It was not to be.

It was Wednesday, early closing day.
The Colonel was nodding off in his chair by the window, a copy of *The Field* open on his lap.

She was helping Miss Bone choose a detective story — Miss Bone worked at Cullens in the High Street, and always came to the library on early closing day. She was very fond of detective stories, and liked a bit of a gossip. Today she had brought two tins of tomatoes, one for Catherine and one for Miss Turnbull. They were delighted. 'We had a whole box,' she said, 'so I managed to put a few aside. Heaven knows when we'll get any more…'

They had just decided on a Dorothy L. Sayers, when a huge explosion seemed to lift the building off its foundations.

The glass beneath the brown sticky tape shattered, hanging in the windows like striped glass curtains.

The Colonel staggered to his feet, dazed and shaken, the copy of *The Field* flapping against his legs.

Miss Bone let out a small shriek and dropped the copy of *Murder Must Advertise* she was holding.

Miss Turnbull emerged from her office, her arms outstretched, but before she had time to speak, more devastating explosions shook the building and books were thudding all over the floor.

And Catherine knew — with a cold, terrible certainty — that it was the factory.

Her father's constant concern for safety — for not cutting corners — becoming increasingly worried at the demand to speed up production. There had already been accidents — girls who had been maimed, even killed. He didn't talk about it — couldn't talk about it. It was not to be talked about — safety — security — discretion…

As her brain tried to digest the horror of what was happening she also knew with terrible certainty that her mother was on the day shift.

Her mother was in the canteen at the factory.

Her father was sleeping at home — should be sleeping at home — he was on the night shift.

That day scarred her forever.

Even now, looking back, she could feel the chill that had enveloped her — the teeth chattering, shivering chill spreading through her limbs.

She could not remember how she got through the next hours — days
— weeks.
Images flickered in her mind — disjointed — unresolved — merging
one with another. Her father so rigid with shock she had had to
forcibly bend his knees to get him to sit down. Edward, white as a
ghost, repeating 'What about Mum…? What about Mum…?'
Trying to find the tin where her mother had hidden the sugar she
was saving — stirring heaped spoonfuls into the tea, trying after a
long and desperate night to get her father to drink some.

The unbearable funeral — another sunny day with cloudless sky — a
coffin that she doubted contained any of her mother's remains — so
little of any of the people who had been blown into unrecognisable
pieces had been salvaged.
Her father unable to walk. They had borrowed a wheelchair from
the hospital, and Edward had pushed him laboriously over the
rough ground to the graveside. He had said nothing, seemingly
unaware of his surroundings, of the service, the few hymns, did not
acknowledge the cluster of friends who stood heads bowed in the
bright sunlight as the crumbled earth rattled onto the coffin. And
after, back in the house, he had said, 'Why isn't Joyce here — where
is your mother?'
The frustrating difficulty of getting in touch with Aunt May,
her father's sister, in Yorkshire, who had been unable to come
— travelling was hopelessly problematical — and the gradual
realisation that her father was never going to be alright.
At first it was put down to shock.
The doctor thought with time he should recover, but as month
followed month he remained in a comatose state, sitting in his chair
all day by the empty grate — having to be helped to the table —
helped up the stairs — helped to bed — helped to cut up his food.

At first she didn't dare leave him, but she had to go back to work —
they needed the money.
Eventually their father received a small pension, and an even smaller
sum to compensate for their mother's death.
The catastrophe at the factory had affected so many people — so
many families had lost someone — half the workforce wiped out —

nearly all those unfortunate enough to have been on the day shift. There were a few survivors, and most of those were horrifically injured.
One of the boys in Edward's class had lost his sister, another his aunt. One of the younger boys had also lost his mother.

She felt she was sleepwalking in an unfamiliar, alien world. A world full of ghosts who vanished before she could reach them. She wanted to shout out, 'Don't go — please don't go...'

Before she went to work she would put her father's lunchtime sandwiches under a cloth on the table by his chair, with a flask of tea, his reading glasses, and the newspaper, and made sure he was near enough to switch on the wireless.
The sandwiches were often uneaten, the flask untouched, the newspaper still folded, but nearly always the wireless was quietly chattering away, keeping him company.

When term ended Edward took over. He had withdrawn into himself, spending most of his time in his room with his books.
Catherine persuaded him to continue to play cricket and meet his friends.
'Mum would have wanted it,' she said. 'You know she would have wanted it...'

The week before her death she had bought him a pair of cricket flannels at the school's second-hand shop — he had grown out of his old ones.
She had been so pleased.
'They're hardly worn,' she had said. 'And really good quality...'
And she had washed and ironed them ready for the Saturday match.

It was not until the following March that Aunt May managed to make the journey — travelling was still very difficult — so many disruptions and delays — but Edward's Higher School Certificate had been brought forward, and he was to go to a Top Secret location, to do Top Secret work, and it was very necessary to discuss what they should do now — what they should do about their father — his condition had not improved, just become more unpredictable.

He did manage now to dress and eat without help. He often went and stood in the much neglected garden — occasionally bending to pull up a weed, or poke about in what was left of the vegetables. He did not seem to notice if it was raining, just standing silent — staring — getting very wet. But mostly he sat in his chair, silent, staring at nothing — sometimes he would get agitated, wringing his hands and moaning, and then he would ask why their mother wasn't home…

'Why is your mother so late? She should be home by now… Where is your mother?'

And now he had started wandering down the street — as far as the corner shop — waiting outside — waiting for their mother.

Mr Turner said he had refused to come in, saying he was waiting for Joyce.

'I'm really sorry,' he said to Catherine. 'So sad. I'm really sorry…', and he slipped her a packet of end rashers of bacon. 'Such a nice lady, your mother…'

And neither she or Edward could bring themselves to say 'Mum's dead… She's never coming back…' — taking his arm, leading him home, making him a cup of tea — the words blocking their throats.

Catherine became aware of someone standing at the counter. It was Olive Fern, Lady Thornton's companion, wearing her drab brown mackintosh with the ugly buttons, her face anxious beneath her green felt hat.

She was carrying a shopping bag, and a dripping umbrella.

'I'm so sorry,' said Catherine. 'I was miles away.'

Poor Miss Fern. Lady Thornton was very particular. She never came to the library herself, sending Miss Fern with a list and explicit instructions on what she did not like — no Agatha Christie, too shallow, no Somerset Maugham, too decadent, no Ivy Compton Burnett, much too odd…

'I'm afraid Her Ladyship didn't like the Evelyn Waugh. She says he is a religious fraud,' Miss Fern said apologetically. Catherine had recommended *The Loved One*.

Miss Fern handed over the books she had taken from her bag — the

umbrella was making a puddle on the dark red library carpet.
'Oh dear,' said Catherine. 'I'm sorry…'
'She's very keen on this new recipe book by Elizabeth David. It's had wonderful reviews, and she thinks it would be nice to read about lovely places and lovely food, even if it isn't possible to go to the lovely places, or have the pleasure of eating the lovely food. They didn't even have lamb chops at Selfridges, and no red Cheshire cheese until next week… Everything is all so difficult…'
The drips from her umbrella were making an increasingly large wet patch on the dark red carpet.

It had been raining heavily the day Aunt May was finally able to make the journey from Yorkshire.
Edward went to meet her at the station as Catherine was still at work. It was a cold March day.
The following Monday Edward was to start his Top Secret job. He was going to go to London with Aunt May, and make sure she got her train back to York, before reporting to the War Office. They had arranged accommodation for him until he was taken to the secret location.

Catherine had sorted out his clothes, to make sure he had everything he needed.
They had saved their clothing coupons to get him a jacket, and a nice pair of grey flannel trousers. He would also need a tie. Catherine had gone to see Mr Cross who ran the gentlemen's outfitters in the High Street to ask particularly for him to find a jacket suitable for Edward. Nothing too stuffy, something really smart, but comfortable. It was, of course, very difficult to have much choice, but he said he would do his best, bringing out a book of cloth samples for her to look at. They pored over them together and made notes of the most suitable. Edward came to be measured.
The jacket Mr Cross managed to get was really nice — a light tweed. He had a friend who ran a shop in Burfield where there was a much larger clientele — it had an RAF base nearby, so he stocked more clothes for young men.
Edward made several trips on his bike to the woods behind the town to collect wood for the fire for the few days Aunt May would

be staying, and she went to Mrs Craig to see if there was any chance
of getting a chicken.

Since the accident Mrs Craig, though just as complaining, had been
gruffly kind. She no longer objected to selling Catherine eggs and
butter, and occasionally, like at Christmas, had found her a chicken.
'Only a boiler,' she had said. 'Cook it slowly — full of flavour.'
This time she also found her a boiler, and had put some carrots and
onions in the bag, and a big bunch of parsley.
'You can make a nice sauce with the chicken stock,' she said. 'And
the bones will make a nice soup.'
She only charged her for the chicken — waving aside Catherine's
attempts to thank her.
'So your brother will be going too,' she said. 'Doing something
important I hear...'

Catherine didn't know how she always seemed to know everything,
living as far away from the town as she did.
'I think so,' she said. 'He's rather clever...'
'Pity your mother isn't here to see it,' said Mrs Craig. 'She was very
proud of him.'
She had found her tears mingling with the rain as she cycled home
— for Peter — for her mother — for her father — for everything.
The war — the war — the dreadful, interminable cruelty of the war.

'And the *Diary of a Provincial Lady* — she has read it before, but she
found it very enjoyable...'
Miss Fern removed her gloves to fish in her bag. 'Oh dear,' she said.
'I've dripped all over the carpet...'
Catherine said that the Elizabeth David had been so popular that
there was a waiting list.
'Everybody is dreaming of lovely places and lovely food. I'll put her
name down, but it will probably be a couple of weeks...'
'Oh dear,' said Miss Fern again. 'She won't be very pleased...'
'Perhaps she might like Nancy Mitford's *Love in a Cold Climate*?'
suggested Catherine.
'Oh dear,' said Miss Fern. 'I really don't know. I better just take E.
M. Delafield.'

2

Yesterday the sun had shone. Elspeth had walked up to Regents Park, where waves of purple crocuses spread across the water-muddied grass. She had walked by the canal, enjoying the ducks and chubby-legged children throwing bread, and the round beds of pansies.

Today the sky was leaden, grey and cold.
Down below in Baker Street the wind tore at umbrellas and wrapped soggy newspapers round the legs of the people at the bus stop outside the tube.

Olive had burnt the breakfast toast.
She always burnt the breakfast toast, scraping it inexpertly — she did everything inexpertly — so that it snapped and crumbled when buttered.
Elspeth tried to hide her irritation. Fortunately Olive only did the breakfast on Paula's day off.
Olive's face was puffy and strained at the same time, her carefully set hair secure beneath a fine hair net, which made a red mark across her forehead.

Elspeth put a spoonful of marmalade on her plate — they had been lucky to get some lime marmalade — she was very fond of lime marmalade.
It would have been nice to have some proper toast to eat it with.

Now the long, wearisome, miserable war was finally over, it was like being convalescent after a near fatal illness.

Nothing would ever, could ever be the same again.
Jumbo, like so many others, did not return.
They sent his medals in a leather box with a brief note of condolence.

She was lucky to have Olive, although she considered her a poor substitute for what she had been used to before the war.

There had been so many servants, and their wonderful house, their home. Solidly comfortable in the evening sunlight, with the wisteria growing over the pillared porch, the sweeping drive, the avenue of beech trees, the scents of the garden filling the warm air.
Sitting on the terrace with Jumbo, ice clinking in glasses, delicious nibbles in cut glass bowls, watching the girls play tennis, listening to the satisfying springy sound of the ball — the occasional shriek — knowing that Mrs Dunstan was preparing a delicious meal — she made the most marvellous ice cream — and there was Penn, their invaluable butler, who looked after everything — so discreet, so effortless — parlourmaids and housemaids — Robert, the footman, so helpful when guests overimbibed — Ruby, her personal maid, with her unruly dark curls — Wilson the chauffeur — Meadows the head gardener, who knew all there was to know about growing things — sweet yellow tomatoes, new potatoes as small as a thumb nail, fatly podded peas, an abundance of flowers — and all the undergardeners.

During the war Martha, one of the older parlourmaids, had stayed with her in London keeping rigorously to the mistress-servant relationship. Martha behind the double doors in the servant's wing, emerging only to clean or serve the food, or to have the daily stilted discussion on the severity of last night's bombing, and what they were going to eat if it was available.

And now — now the war was over — although it hardly seemed to be over.
The City was in ruins. Everywhere you turned there were ruins — lives as well as buildings — so many people contemplating lives without their husbands and sons — fathers and brothers — so many houses bombed — mothers and children — sisters and daughters crushed — peppered with shrapnel — their worldly possessions shattered — bits and pieces among the rubble. The scars crossed and criss-crossed their lives — deep wounds that had hardly begun to heal, and all the time there were the shortages — potatoes now — and rationing — and power cuts.

And now she had to decide what to do about the house.

She would have to sell. It was impossible to keep up without staff — and there were no staff — and if there were she didn't think she would be able to afford it now.

Given so little time to pack up — to put everything in store — the servants to be dispersed — the younger ones to join up — the older ones to try and find a job elsewhere.
The girl's school had been evacuated to the Lake District — they had been quite excited — and she had moved into the flat.

It had been their pied a terre before the war — for when she came up to a matinee or company dinners — the Chelsea Flower Show — the opera. Jumbo had always bought her orchids in a round transparent box to pin on her dress. And for the girl's birthday treats and dental appointments — to get their school uniforms from Debenham & Freebody, or party frocks from Harrods.

At first it worked out very well. Jumbo was stationed at the Wellington Barracks, which was very convenient.
They had spent that first Christmas all together in the flat — the girls had gone to several shows and parties — certain that by the following Christmas they would all be home — safe in their beautiful house. By next Christmas it would all be over.

Nobody envisaged the awfulness to come.
When the bombing started, friends urged her to leave London — Jumbo had been posted abroad, and it wasn't safe for the girls in the holidays, but she had refused to budge.
It was unthinkable that she should leave for somewhere safer when darling Jumbo was in the stifling heat of the desert — the flies — the thirst — the tanks reflecting the sun on their sightless barrels as they ploughed laboriously forward, little flags flying, passing mounds of, well, whatever they were, mercifully buried beneath the all-enveloping sand.
Unthinkable that she should run away, when so many people were suffering so much.
She could cope with a few bombs and broken windows — and a little less food wouldn't do anyone any harm.

As a regular valued customer at Selfridges, she was luckier than most, getting extra bits of this and that.
Now, when things were just as difficult, she could sometimes get a chicken and even kippers, and once, last autumn, a really nice piece of salmon.

The flat below, now empty, had been taken over for some secret activity. The men from the Ministry came and went at all hours of the day and night. Bowler-hatted men in pinstripe suits, baggy-suited men with odd socks and heavily buckled briefcases, and pale well-born girls in ATS uniform, laden with files, puffing up the back stairs when the lifts were out of order — a frequent occurrence with the many power cuts.

Of course they were not supposed to know they were from the Ministry. It was all very Top Secret.

Silly really. One would have had to be completely dim-witted not to notice anything unusual, especially squashed in the lift with people so obviously foreign.

Martha once referred to them as those queer people wearing queer clothes, coming and going downstairs. She had just come up in the lift with a bearded man in a green tweed suit, and a very swarthy man with a navy blue overcoat and brown shoes — 'foreign if you ask me,' she had said sniffily.
Elspeth had told her sharply that they must never speak of them to anyone — everywhere there were 'Careless Talk Costs Lives' posters. 'We must just pretend we haven't noticed,' she had said.

So they endured burdensome day after burdensome day — anticipating the banshee wailing of the sirens cutting through restless sleep — dreading the telegram that would sever all hope.

It was the only time her courage failed her. She had actually gone into the kitchen and asked Martha to open it — holding grimly to the back of one of the rush-seated kitchen chairs — dimly aware of Martha pouring tea out of the brown teapot.

The worst of it all was there was no funeral — no proper formalities — no church service — no hymns or prayers — no lowering the coffin into the friendly earth — no proper mourning — no gathering of friends and relatives to offer support or sympathy.

The awful scrap of cheap, grey wartime paper bearing the curt, terrible message of finality.

Not knowing how or where he had died — hoping that he had had a proper burial, had not become another anonymous mound in the sand.

Not being able to say goodbye.

His last letter, months old, telling her of the amazing sunsets, and how the stars appeared to touch the earth, they seemed so close.

She had stood awkwardly in the sitting room with the girls.

Rosemary had been at the Admiralty since 1941, leaving school at the earliest opportunity to join the WRNS — no finishing school — no coming-out balls — everything was so grim…

For a while she had lived with Elspeth, but soon left to share a flat with two other girls in Cadogan Square. They seemed to manage to have a little fun…

She had just started going out with an American officer — Don — very handsome with excellent manners. He always brought Elspeth a bottle of whisky or gin, and kept Rosemary supplied with silk stockings, lipstick, chocolate — all unheard-of luxuries, all ordinary things had become luxuries, one got excited over an extra bit of cheese or a piece of fruit cake…

Rosemary was lucky that Don was stationed at the London HQ, and never had to go abroad.

Alison had only recently moved in with Rosemary, and was working as a secretary in the Foreign Office.

Both girls were very upset.

Rosemary said they should let Martha join them to toast Jumbo — 'Daddy would have liked that,' she said. 'She shouldn't have to sit alone in the kitchen…'

Elspeth had grudgingly agreed, after all, Martha had known the girls since they were toddlers.

Alison slumped down in one of the chintz covered armchairs that had come from the house — it was so important to have comfortable chairs — tears rolling down her cheeks. 'I do wish we could go home,' she sobbed. 'Will we ever be able to go home? Will this horrible, horrible war ever end? Why did Daddy have to die...?'

They had drunk a toast in his memory — his kindness and courage — and then they had to rush around seeing to the blackout.

The following year Rosemary and Don were married, at the end of May just before D Day and the last interminable dreadful year of the interminable, dreadful war.

They were married in the Marylebone Registry Office — hardly the wedding she and Jumbo had envisaged for their eldest daughter.

It should have been in the village church with Miss Carpenter at the organ — pulling out all the stops for the Wedding March. The church full of flowers and fancy hats, and Rosemary radiant in a white silk dress with Jumbo's mother's veil and her mother's pearls — everything beautifully arranged by Penn — and later still music and dancing — the young couple driving off, pelted with rose petals and confetti, for their honeymoon on the Riviera and Italy's magical coast.

Instead it was in the bare austerity of the Registry Office, minimally brightened with a vase of pinkish-purple asters and a colour photograph of the Lake District.

Nearly everyone was in uniform, including Rosemary and Don who, she had to admit, did look very smart, and they seemed ecstatically happy, and that was what really mattered.

Don had suggested a hotel for the reception, but Alison had got all weepy, and Rosemary said, 'No —she wanted it to be at the flat. It was their home now...'

The day before the wedding Don's driver Ivan — a small man, whose hair shone as brightly as his shoes and the buttons on his uniform — appeared with boxes of food and champagne, smoked salmon, potato salad, there seemed to be no end to the abundance of 'goodies'. It was quite overwhelming.

Martha was laughing and exclaiming as Ivan unpacked each box onto the kitchen table.

'Oh my goodness… Oh my goodness…', and then she had started to cry, and Elspeth had inexpertly tried to comfort her.

At least the sun had shone on the day of the wedding, and after the brief ceremony they walked back to the flat across Marylebone Road, and the living room was full of uniforms, laughter and flowers which she had managed to obtain, at great expense.

Alison wore a pale blue dress, clutching her sister's bouquet of pink and white roses and sniffing a lot, her fine blonde hair falling wispily round her face.

The dining room table was laden with all the delicious food — Elspeth thought it was better not to enquire how Don had managed to get hold of it all. There was even a proper wedding cake with silver bells and horseshoes and white silk ribbons. Somebody put records of Glen Miller and the Paul Whiteman band on the radiogram, which she had not played for years — somehow listening to dance music in these awful times had seemed inappropriate.

Of course there was no proper honeymoon — just forty-eight hours' leave at a hotel somewhere in Sussex.

It was already dusk when they all went down to the street to see them off. Someone had cut up a bagfull of paper, which they threw as make-do confetti.

Ivan drove them away in Don's official car with the American flag flying on the bonnet, the wind gusting the bits of paper along the pavement into the gutter.

It had been a successful but very tiring day.

The rest of the week they lived on ham and potato salad, and Alison came to help cut the remains of the wedding cake into slices to send to friends and relatives. There were no little silver boxes to be had, so

they could only wrap them in ordinary writing paper. She had some
blue Smythson paper left from before the war so they used that, and
hoped the cake would not be reduced to crumbs in the post.

Rosemary and Don lived in Los Angeles now, and had two little
boys, Hank and Murray. She hoped one day to be able to go and see
them — when things were more normal and travelling was easier.
There were still so many restrictions it was difficult to go anywhere.

The last year of the war had been particularly dreadful — the eerie
doodlebugs spluttering and chuntering across the sky, spurting
flames — and the unheralded destruction wrought by the sinister
V-2s.

The activity in the flat below became more and more frenetic, and
the occupants of the lift more and more obviously foreign.

And Alison had become such a worry — was still a worry.
She was involved with a married man — a very secretive relationship.
Elspeth had never met him, neither had Rosemary, but she thought
Rosemary knew who he was, and that she disapproved. It had been
going on for years now, and Alison was obviously very unhappy.
She was frightfully thin and peaky, unable to sit still, smoking
incessantly — practically lighting one from another — and topping
up her gin and vermouth before finishing what she already had, so
that it was difficult to know quite how much she had drunk…

Elspeth so wished Jumbo was still alive.
She missed him so much.
There was no one to talk to anymore.

Now she had the problem of what to do next.
She had to sell the house, but should she stay in this flat — which
was, after all, very convenient.
There was plenty of room — the sitting room was large, there were
four decent bedrooms, two bathrooms, and the servants' wing very
well separated with heavy double doors.
But it was rather dark — did not get much sun, if there was any —

the windows were not large enough.

It would be nice to have a small place somewhere in the country — with a garden. She so missed her beautiful garden, and the fresh smell of leaves and grass.

There was still the painful business of going back to the house and sorting out the sale.

She had already been to see their solicitor, Mr Green, of Green, Brook and Mildmay.

Mr Green had been the family solicitor when Jumbo's parents were still alive. He should have retired years ago, but the war had prevented that.

His son Anthony was to have taken over — an established, secure future after exceptional achievements in his study of law at Oxford. He had died in a Japanese POW camp.

His son — his only son…

Mr Green had become stooped and lined — his brisk confident form shrunken, the jacket of his Saville Row suit seeming a size too large. His habitual bonhomie a hollow sham, breaking off in mid sentence to shuffle papers abstractedly on his desk.

Jumbo's will had been very straightforward — a substantial sum for both the girls — the rest, apart from a few bequests — the village cricket club — the church — the local hospital — for her.

Mr Green agreed that she should sell the house. 'No alternative, really.'

It was also agreed that Meadows should keep his cottage on the edge of the grounds, that it should not be sold with the estate, but should be made over to him as a gift from herself and Jumbo.

Mr Green thought that was perhaps being rather too generous.
'It could be just for him to live in for his lifetime,' he said.
But Elspeth was adamant — that, she was sure, would have been what Jumbo would have wanted.
Her faithful Martha had left soon after the war was over — 'I'm

very sorry m'Lady,' she had said. 'But this terrible war has finished me off…' She also was well past retiring age. She was going to live with her sister, a widow, in Folkestone. 'Get some sea air — peace and quiet…'

Elspeth arranged that she should have a small pension, and then she had to start looking around for someone else to 'help'.
Fortunately Martha agreed to stay on until she found someone to replace her — the prospects had not been encouraging.

Rosemary was very insistent that she should have a companion.
Now she and Don were going to live in America, and Alison was worse than useless.
'Not just a maid,' she said. 'Somebody you can play cards with, and go to the theatre — even travel about a bit when things are back to normal…'

So now she had Olive who burnt the toast and made incredibly unappetising meals on Paula's day off — turning perfectly respectable ingredients into inedible anonymity — cheese a tasteless, elastic coating for Welsh rarebit or anything 'au gratin'. Such a waste of cheese. It was a good thing that today there was a chicken and mushroom pie from Selfridges and tinned peas — only a matter of warming them up…

Finding anybody at all to help had been hard enough. The agency had hardly anyone on their books, and among the few they had there was nobody remotely suitable — too old — too inexperienced — with minimal English — barely literate — quite impossible…

It was sheer luck that she had found Paula.

She had bumped into Amanda Petersen at a sale in aid of the Red Cross.
Inappropriately dressed in a red brocade jacket with gilt toggles, a brown tweed skirt which was much too short, white open-toed shoes and a mauve knitted shoulder bag.
Poor Hugh — Amanda had never really become accustomed to

being a diplomatic wife — serving ghastly food and completely unable to manage the staff. Goodness knows how she had got on in India…

In her customary clumsy way she had made herself evident by knocking over a complicated dried flower arrangement. 'Oh dear,' she was saying. 'I'm so sorry. Oh dear. Of course I will pay for it — how much was it? Oh dear…' and she fumbled in the woollen bag. 'Oh goodness — Elspeth — I didn't see you…'

After they had sorted out paying for the broken dried flowers — inexpertly gathering up bits from the floor — they sat down in the corner of the hall where a cheerful lady in the dark green uniform of the WVS was serving tea out of a very large aluminium tea pot. Elspeth felt quite sorry for Amanda, though she found her inadequacy really annoying.
How could a woman in her position be so hopeless?
She had even managed to slop her tea into the saucer — her over-powdered face flushed — and why was she wearing orange lipstick? It was a shame really. Amanda was, after all, very well meaning. A kind woman used to being overlooked, an unassuming shadow behind her husband, dispensing tea or sherry and social chit-chat with innumerable people she didn't know, and maybe didn't like…

She and Hugh were being posted to the Embassy in Stockholm.
'I'm so relieved,' she said. 'It could have been anywhere — it could have been somewhere in Africa — I don't think I could have coped with Africa — all those wild animals…'

Paula was her maid — Italian — she had been with them since before the war.
She had been interned briefly when Italy entered the war, but Hugh had used his influence, and she was soon back, complaining about the rationing and the weather.
She did not want to go to Sweden. The weather would be worse. She liked living in England. She was used to it. There was a thriving Italian community in London and she had many friends.
She refused categorically to go to Sweden.

So Paula came to work for Elspeth.
It was quite a change after the dutifully invisible Martha.
Elspeth was not used to dealing with temperamental servants, and
Paula was very temperamental…
She was a very good cook, but not at all happy cleaning.
Her mood could usually be judged by the vigour of her dusting
and the ferocity of her vacuuming. There were days when all was
quiet and she would be humming, patting the cushions and making
delicious wafer thin biscuits to go with the morning coffee.
Quite wonderfully Paula seemed to have lots of friends in Soho, and
came home with proper, juicy pork sausages, and translucent slices
of fine Parma ham, chunks of Parmesan and flasks of olive oil,
and joy of joys — real coffee — real coffee to go with the delicious
biscuits.

Rosemary had said she should give Martha some kind of present
when she left.
'After all these years Mum,' she had said.
Elspeth had no idea whatsoever what she could give her — she had
no idea what Martha liked or didn't like — as usual Rosemary was
insistent.
'You could give her something from the house — ask her to choose
something — when you get everything out of store…'

That was another thing — all the furniture — at least, all the
furniture that was left —the warehouse where most of the things
had been stored had been bombed — the rest had been stored in
Borehampton, the local town.
She had an inventory of everything, pages and pages, almost a small
book, the missing articles marked with a black cross — so many
things with a black cross — looking through it was like taking a
journey into another world — a painful reminder of how things
were and would never be again — so many things missing, believed
destroyed. The portraits of the girls in their new party frocks with
ribbons in their hair. Rosemary had just had her sixth birthday —
Nanny had had such difficulty stopping them from fidgeting. The
portrait of herself in the rose garden, the Singer Sargent of Jumbo's
mother in a dark green velvet ballgown, the Turner watercolours of

the park and the water garden — all had black crosses. The dining room table, the magnificent sideboard where Robert had laid out the silver breakfast dishes — Jumbo's favourite kedgeree and perfectly poached eggs... The Louis XV chaise longue and all the other furniture from her sitting room — and the library — all Jumbo's precious books. The desk. Persian carpets. On and on. Each item another barbed memory...

'Well, if you think so,' she had said. 'But she'll have to wait. I don't know when I shall be able to deal with all that...'

After Paula had settled in she really did not see the necessity of having a companion, but Rosemary continued to insist she should have someone with her — not just a maid. 'Pa would not have wanted you to be on your own...'

Elspeth supposed it would be useful to have someone to do the mundane everyday things — going to the post office —the dry cleaners — to pick up prescriptions — go to the library — and, maybe go to the cinema with. Elspeth enjoyed the cinema...

So she curbed her irritation as she attempted to spread the lime marmalade on the brittle toast, and tried to avoid watching Olive sucking up her cornflakes.

Olive wiped her mouth carefully on her napkin and said she thought she would go to the library this morning.
'It's very wet,' said Elspeth. 'Why don't you wait until later?'
But Olive said she had to pick up her shoes from the menders.

Elspeth took her second cup of tea to the window and looked down on the scurrying people crossing Baker Street — a mass of bobbing umbrellas.

She was to go to tea with Sybil this afternoon.
Olive had been recommended by a friend of Sybil, an elderly lady who lived in Richmond. 'Lovely place on Richmond Hill,' Sybil had said — she was now finding the house too much, and had decided to

go and live in a rather superior 'home' for genteel ladies.

'So much easier,' she had told Sybil. 'Everything done for you. And a proper restaurant…'

Olive had been with her all through the war. 'A bit dull, I think,' Sybil had said. 'But very reliable. Terrible cook — not that there had been much to cook. Completely honest. No fuss… Do you have anything decent to drink darling? I'm dying for a proper drink…'

She had settled herself in one of Elspeth's capacious armchairs — too big really for the flat, but so comfortable, and comfort was so important, and lit a cigarette.

Elspeth didn't smoke. Jumbo had smoked. Her daughters smoked. She pushed an ashtray across the leather-topped table between the chairs.

'I've got some gin,' she said. 'And some vermouth…'

'Oh marvellous darling,' said Sybil. 'I'll have a really big one.'

Sybil Anstruther, the Hon Sybil Anstruther — she was very particular about her title — would have been a Lord if she had been a boy — very unfair — had had her fortune dissipated by the war, and had been forced to sell her beautiful house in Eaton Square.

She had stayed in it throughout the war — living on the ground floor — sleeping in the elegant drawing room.

The rest of the house slumbered fitfully under voluminous dust sheets that before the war had kept the house free of dust whilst they summered on the Riviera — the windows shuttered and masked with cheap cloth curtains — the velvet and silk ones had been taken down and wrapped carefully in more dust sheets.

Thompson, her housekeeper, carried out daily inspections, taking a room once a week to strip off the dust sheets and give everything a thorough clean. Sybil's bathroom and dressing room remained open — a welcome sanctuary, polished and shining for her to bathe, even though the supply of hot water was sparse, relaxing in the depths of scented foam a distant memory. At least she had enough clothes in the glass-fronted wardrobes in her dressing room to last for a very long war.

It was a pleasant room. Here she had kept the curtains, multi-flowered chintz, bouncy and fresh, the ugly blackout curtains pulled back out of sight.

She could sit in her pink velvet chair and look out of the window at the magnificent plane trees in the square, and Thompson would bring her black market tea and biscuits on one of her favourite hand-painted trays.

Now it was not possible to run the central heating. She had acquired a few electric heaters to help keep off the chill in winter so long as there were no power cuts.

The only really warm room in the house was the kitchen — the coke-fuelled range a constant, comforting supplier of heat. Thompson had an arrangement with the coalman, as she had with various other tradesmen, managing to get cigarettes, tinned fruit and vegetables, macaroni, jam, extra large tins of Spam which fed them for at least a week. Thompson was very inventive, serving it in all kinds of different ways — fritters, stew, with precious eggs, with the macaroni, au gratin, in sandwiches, even Spam shepherd's pie. Sybil never asked where all this bounty came from, she just paid whatever Thompson asked for. It was a question of necessity. And, oh what joy to have a glass of sherry or port, or even whisky.

She also ate out a lot, mostly at the Ritz or the Dorchester, where she had so often lunched and dined before this dreary war. It was a very good way of having a reasonably decent meal without using one's rations. It was also very pleasant to be in the familiar opulent surroundings — and one sometimes encountered acquaintances, although most of the people she knew had left the city for their country estates, or hotels in suitably select places. The spacious rooms were full of uniforms — the occasional woman with an outrageous hat — the waiters wearily middle-aged — menus restricted — but she was still able to get a Champagne cocktail, and sometimes there was creamed chicken with mushrooms or Dover sole.

She had persuaded Elspeth to come a few times, but she was always reluctant. Since Jumbo had been killed she had become more reclusive than usual — hardly going out at all. She said it didn't seem right to eat in the civilised comfort of the Ritz when so many were dying — people's homes destroyed.

Anyway, Elspeth was really a country woman, happiest in her garden. She had never really enjoyed the society thing.

Thompson was the only one of her many servants remaining. She now lived and slept in her sitting room in the basement. The servants' quarters at the top of the house were completely shut off, creakily uninhabited.

All the paintings, ornaments and precious objects, including small pieces of furniture, had been stacked in the basement in the labyrinth of storerooms and pantries — the servants' sitting room and dining room. The stone larders and sculleries now mostly filled with crates and boxes.

Sybil and Thompson had labelled everything meticulously, which was essential when the time came when Sybil had had to start selling her precious belongings to raise money. Mr Pierce came regularly from Christie's to select items for sale as Sybil's financial situation became more and more precarious.

When the raids were at their worst Sybil would join Thompson in the basement, slipping one of her mink coats over her nightdress for warmth, and they would sit at the scrubbed wooden table and drink whatever was available.

All the wine from Pogo's carefully chosen cellar was gone.
Pogo had died in 1937, keeling over on the moors during a grouse shoot.
Sybil was sure Mason, the butler, had gone off with the remaining bottles when he left to join the Ordnance Corps, so they drank cocoa, unless one of Thompson's 'contacts' had managed to provide a bottle of contraband liquor.
They passed the night hours playing Monopoly and Bezique, ready, if necessary, to take refuge under the table, until the welcome wail

of the All Clear allowed them to go to bed in the cold, grey dawn, to snatch a few hours of suspended sleep.

'Olive found these little cheese biscuits,' said Elspeth. 'They're quite tasty…'
She put Sybil's drink on one of the table mats with old racing prints that Jumbo had been so fond of. She poured herself a small dry sherry. She only liked dry sherry.
'You're so lucky to have room to have someone to live in,' said Sybil. 'I only have this wretched woman who comes in three times a week and moves the dust around — totally useless…'

Her flat in West Hampstead was too small to have a proper servant, even if one could find one. It was really too small for anything. Her lavender silk upholstered chairs and sofa, which had been in the morning room in Eaton Square, took up most of the drawing room, with its curved legged little tables cluttered with Dresden figures and Chinese porcelain, silver boxes and table lamps with fringed pleated shades, the wires hopelessly tangled together on the Aubusson rug. Pictures covered the walls, and were unceremoniously stacked against the walls, spilling out into the hall and what was supposed to be the dining room. Oils and watercolours, sketches and pastels, the good, bad and indifferent all jumbled together, and over the miserable fireplace with the puny, ineffectual gas fire, hung the austere portrait of her father, painted by some eminent RA in the 1920s.

She lit a cigarette. She still smoked continuously, not so fussy about the brands now, it was almost impossible to get Sobranies — still using her many cigarette holders, inlaid with gold filigree and mother of pearl.
'I thought I should perhaps sell some of my jewellery,' she said.

Sybil said she was hardly likely to need her tiara again.
Gone were the glittering soirees, the intimate luncheon parties for a select few. She had dined several times with Edward and Mrs Simpson — tough and skinny — or more accurately, tough and stringy — like some old game bird — squeakily elegant — no sense

of humour — '*Pas sympathique du tout.*' Sybil liked to lapse into French. Before the war she had had a French maid.

Elspeth refilled her glass without asking if she wanted another.
Sybil always wanted another.
She would have like to talk to her about Alison, how she was afraid she was drinking too much — always refilling her glass before it was empty. She would really like to talk to someone about Alison, but Sybil was going on about her pearls.
'Pogo bought them from Asprey's — I think — I can't remember... They are supposed to be very good pearls. When am I going to need a tiara or a string of pearls? If I went around wearing strings of pearls I would probably be robbed — and as for the tiara — there will never be those sorts of occasions again...'

Elspeth said again that she should take some advice, and wrote the name of Jumbo's Oxford friend on a piece of her headed notepaper.

*   *   *

She finally had to go back to her house.

The train was slow and late and very cold.
Meadows met her with the old station wagon, damp and cold, jerky and creaking.

She had stood in the empty ruined hall of the home where she had spent so many happy years.
The bannisters hanging broken, fireplaces wrenched from the walls, the fleur de lys wallpaper black with scribbled obscenities, windows cracked and criss-crossed with sticky brown paper.
The urns on the terrace, which had trailed an abundance of flowers and plants, shattered into grey piles of stone.
And these had been British soldiers.
The enemy could not have done much worse, unless they had burned it down.
This was not her home anymore.
Would never be her home again.

Meadows held his cap against his chest as if warding off a blow, his weathered face stiff and sad.

'They got very excited m' lady,' he said, 'when they knew they were off to France…'

They toured the house slowly, going from shattered room to shattered room, and back out into the garden.

The sloping lawn in front of the house — the long herbaceous borders and round flower beds — nothing but churned earth, trampled by marching boots and the wheels of jeeps. The carefully trimmed privet hedges smashed by Bren gun carriers and lorries.

It had begun to rain, a fine persistent rain.

Elspeth couldn't speak.

She tried numbly to get herself together, to make some polite comment to Meadows.

'Well, that's that,' she said.

She sat at the meticulously scrubbed table in Meadows' kitchen.

His wife had worked in the house, helping Mrs Dunstan in the kitchen.

She had died of cancer in 1943, just after Elspeth had received the news of Jumbo's death.

Now Meadows' sister came and cleaned and cooked some meals.

She had made a cake, a jam sponge with a dusting of icing sugar.

Meadows put the kettle on the stove — opened the front and poked the glowing coals.

It was comforting to sit in the quiet, warm kitchen, so clean — floral cups hanging on the polished dresser, a hand-knitted tea cosy…

She knew very little about Meadows.

She had known very little about any of the servants.

She did know he had a daughter, who was married and lived in Norfolk.

Perhaps he had grandchildren.

She had sold the house to a stout man in a too-tight tweed suit of astonishing vulgarity.

3

It should have been a good summer, but after the euphoria of D-Day, it soon became clear that peace was still a long way away.
The armies bogged down in Normandy — ambushed and booby-trapped in the rustling orchards and on long dusty white roads — progress was painfully slow.
Berlin a distant mirage.

Now there were flying bombs ripping the sky — like tearing sackcloth — whining insects coughing fire.

There were queues for everything. People would ask each other what they were queueing for before getting in line.

Scrappy grey telegrams still brought their catastrophic messages of hopes snuffed out.
The war's rusty blade dragged its blunted edge across the scarred earth and black crows came in flocks to pick at the bones of those left behind.

It was so much harder after Edward had gone — leaving very early with Aunt May that dreary, cold Sunday morning. It had been foggy, and they had worried that the train would be late and Aunt May would miss her connection at King's Cross, and that Edward would be late for his meeting at the War Office.
She couldn't go and see them off. She had to stay with their father, trying to be cheerful as she waved them goodbye.

On the Saturday afternoon she had taken Aunt May to the church to show her where their mother was buried, and Edward stayed at home with their father. It was raining, a fine, misty drizzle, and the wind was cold.

There was no gravestone — there was not enough money for gravestones and also, the stonemasons' had only two elderly men to try and cope, overwhelmed by the amount of orders after the dreadful accident at the factory, so hardly anyone had yet received a gravestone.

Edward said now he was going to earn good money he would be able to pay for a really nice gravestone, as soon as it was possible.
He had planted a clump of snowdrops on the insignificant mound, and the delicate nodding green-veined bells were just beginning to open.
Aunt May stood and wept. 'Poor Joyce… Poor Joyce…'

There had been plenty of chicken left for their supper, and she added the remaining carrots and potatoes, and found a reasonable cabbage in the garden — there would even be enough over for tomorrow.

Their father ate a little better, and made sporadic, polite conversation with Aunt May. He was not sure who she was, so he spoke to her as if she was a stranger, asking her where she lived, and how long she was staying, and how sorry he was that Joyce was so late and wouldn't meet her. 'Such a nice supper too — such a pity…', and Aunt May started to cry again.

There was no pudding. Catherine had queued for some ginger cake, but had been unlucky — there wasn't even a currant bun in sight when she reached the head of the queue.

It had been decided that their father should go and live with Aunt May and Uncle Charles in Skipton. They had plenty of room, and their son Eric, who was in the Royal Engineers, was going to be married and would be moving to Scarborough.
'He'll enjoy the garden,' said Aunt May. 'He'll be able to potter about and sit out in the summer — and we'll be able to take him for nice drives once this awful war is over and we have some petrol…'

The only problem was how to get him there.
Nobody who had a car had sufficient petrol.
It was not possible to take him on the train — it was necessary to change trains in London and at York, and there were his things.

He could hardly go to live somewhere else forever with only an overnight bag.

She had felt so desolate after they had gone — so laden with luggage they could not turn to wave goodbye.
She went upstairs and stripped the beds, putting the sheets and towels into a bag ready to take to the laundry on her way to work in the morning.
Their father had gone to sleep beside the open grate — the glow of the fire a warm friendly presence.
Later she would have to take her bicycle and try and find some more wood.

Every day she worried about leaving her father when she went to work.
She was afraid he would wander off — get lost — fall in the canal — just get lost...
She could hardly lock him in, even though he would still be able to go into the back garden. He enjoyed the garden, and could now manage to weed and hoe, and plant a few things — some vegetables — some daffodil bulbs...

A job had come up in London at the Marylebone library. Miss Turnbull wanted her to apply for it.
'It's a wonderful opportunity,' she said. 'You would have a new life...'
But how could she apply for a job in London in the present situation? She could not leave.

She had difficulty sleeping.
When she closed her eyes her mind was filled with nightmarish images — Peter, his face bloody and disfigured, his body a ragbag of khaki... Her mother in her smart white overalls serving sausage and chips on thick white plates — engulfed in flames — with jolly music still crackling from loudspeakers on the exploding walls of the canteen... The huge, choking cloud of acrid black smoke that had hung over the little town, turning day into night...
She was always on the alert, in case their father stumbled down the stairs.

She would find him standing, fully dressed, in the cold kitchen.
'Joyce will want a cup of tea when she comes in…'

She had hidden the matches.
She didn't want him trying to light the gas.

She would make them both a cup of tea, settle him in his chair, and wrap him up in a blanket, with his tea on the little table by his side. Then she would take her tea upstairs, pull back the claustrophobic blackout curtains, and lie awake until the thick darkness gradually lightened into the washed-out grey of dawn.

Doctor Wheeler said he would try and get their father into a convalescent home. There was a nice one, with lovely grounds, not far from Bembridge, if only for a few days — there was a long waiting list — so that she could go for the interview in London.
'One step at a time,' he said. 'I'm sure we will find some way round the problem — something will turn up.'
He was very kind, and asked about Edward.
Edward didn't write very often.
He wasn't much good at writing letters. 'I'm well… How are you?… Everything fine here… Hope you are fine… Hope father is alright…'
Hardly very informative.

It was a miserable summer, wet and cold.
The day she went for her interview it was raining.
The train was delayed twice because of air raids — a V-1 had come down close to the line — but the interview seemed to go well.
They gave her tea and biscuits and were cheerfully dismissive about her being late — 'We're just glad you got here alright' — and wished her a safe journey home.

They offered her the job.
Miss Turnbull was delighted. 'I'm so glad — we'll miss you of course — but it's really wonderful — I'm so pleased for you…'

Catherine wrote to Edward explaining the situation — if only they could get their father up to Yorkshire — otherwise she couldn't possibly take the job. She didn't know what to do.

And then, as Dr Wheeler had said, everything was suddenly possible.

Edward telephoned her at the library.

One of his colleagues, Professor Miles, had a car and petrol, and they would take a 48-hour pass and come and fetch their father, and take him and his belongings to Yorkshire. It would be a bit of a rush, but they should be able to manage it.

She could come with them and go home on the train…

She cycled to the farm to get some eggs.

Edward had said they hoped to arrive mid morning, and that they would be very hungry.

Mrs Craig gave her some onions and potatoes as well, so that she could make a nice, substantial Spanish omelette.

'I'm pleased for you,' she said. 'This dreadful war, when will it ever end… very sorry to hear about your father… glad you have got it sorted out…', and she came out into the yard to watch Catherine cycle down the lane in the gathering dusk.

Professor Miles was very tall and gangly, his arms too long for his baggy brown tweed suit, displaying the frayed cuffs of his clean white shirt. The collar was frayed too, but he had a very smart striped club tie and highly polished brown brogues.

His handshake was warm and firm.

'Good to meet you,' he said, and then pumped their father's hand. 'Very good to meet you Sir. What a wonderful smell — we're ravenous!'

Catherine had already prepared the potatoes and onions, cooking them slowly to a golden brown, and had put them in the oven to keep warm. She had only to add the eggs.

Edward looked thin and tired.

Their father was overjoyed to see him — hugging him, and holding onto his arm..

'Your mother should be here,' he said. 'She works too hard — Cathy has to do all the cooking…'

Catherine had tried to explain to him that they were going to visit

Aunt May, and that he was going to stay with her and Uncle Charles for a while.

'It will be much nicer for you,' she said. 'You will enjoy the countryside…'

She didn't know if he really understood, but he seemed quite happy about it, although he kept saying that Joyce should come too.

'Perhaps she can come later…'

While she cleared the dishes and washed up, the professor and Edward loaded the car with their father's things.

It was a really lovely car — a grey Lagonda with plenty of room, and a welcoming leathery smell.

For the first time in many years she could actually stop worrying and relax — actually enjoy sitting in this comfortable car, looking out at the soft countryside. It was late September and the leaves were just beginning to change colour — glimpses of red and gold amongst the fading green.

Their father slept, and the professor and Edward chatted amicably in the front.

It was late evening by the time they reached Skipton.

They had stopped for petrol — the professor producing an impressive sheaf of papers — and also at a deserted hotel, where the professor had charmed a taciturn, elderly lady into providing them with tea and toast — with real butter and homemade strawberry jam.

Aunt May had prepared a thick vegetable soup.

They were all very tired — they had got rather lost finding the house. Catherine was to sleep in the little spare room, and Aunt May had arranged with a next door neighbour for the professor and Edward to stay with them. They had two bedrooms that were not being used. Both of their sons were away fighting the war, 'Heaven knows where… Such a worry…'

For the first time for a very long time Catherine slept through the night. She was completely exhausted.

Aunt May gave them eggs and bacon for breakfast.

'Under the counter,' she said. 'My butcher knows a farmer...'
'Excellent,' said the professor. 'First class... worth the trip... can't remember when I last had such a delicious breakfast,' and he had an animated conversation with Uncle Charles about growing vegetables — the importance of preparing the soil, choosing the right spot — and they wandered off down the garden to inspect Uncle Charles's parsnips, winter cabbage, and snow white cauliflowers.

Their father seemed quite calm and comfortable, and ate a good breakfast. After they had left Catherine felt a huge sense of relief that he was in such good hands, but the relief was mixed with an overwhelming sadness that all their lives had been so dramatically and irrevocably changed.

They left her at York station to get the train to London. She tried to thank the professor for his kindness — for his invaluable help.
'Pleased to be of use my dear,' he said. 'This war has gone on too long. I'm glad to have been able to help. Hope everything goes well for you — Edward will keep me informed...'
She could now accept the job in London.
Miss Turnbull brought the sherry from the filing cabinet in her office and invited the colonel to join them to toast her success and wish her well.

There were so many things to deal with.
The house felt so strange now — empty and sad.
Bridget, the girl she was replacing, was getting married, and had offered her her flat in Crawford Street, a very short distance from the library.
It was wonderful — a proper flat — two rooms, kitchen and bathroom on the second floor with carpeted stairs and a telephone.
She couldn't believe it was really happening.

She stood in the silent kitchen, seeing her mother rolling out pastry on the scrubbed wooden table and fussing about Edward — had he taken his gas mask? She didn't want him out after dark...

Her nights were still haunted by ghosts.

Running to catch up with Peter, always such a long way ahead among the jagged burning ruins — never looking back — her cries for him to stop — to wait — blown back in her face — vanishing into a grey swirling mist — horny hands grabbing at her clothes. She would wake, dry-throated, desperate, switching on her bedside light. Often she would get up and go and make a cup of tea, still unused to their father's empty chair with the neatly folded rug.

The house had to be cleared.
She would need some of the things to take to London, her dressing table and chest of drawers — the bookcase, the rugs from the sitting room — linen — china — cooking things…
There were fitted cupboards in the flat so she didn't need a wardrobe, and Bridget was going to leave the kitchen table and chairs.

She also had to find enough money to pay what was known as 'key money' for fixtures and fittings — and she had to get all her things to London.

She arranged for someone to come from the depot outside Bembridge, where they collected furniture to distribute among people who had been bombed out, to take the rest of the furniture.

A Mr Boyce, a large, bluff man in a crumpled grey suit with a bright yellow tie, came and made lists, and arranged to take everything including the lawn mower, garden tools and all her mother's flower pots. He was very friendly and kind. He said he would find her a brand new bed and take all her things up to London in his van when he made his next delivery to the depot at Chiswick.

And Edward was able to help with the 'key money'.

The last winter of the war was interminable. A slow movement of hours and days.
It was the end of October before everything was settled.

She locked the front door for the last time, feeling the silent weight of the house reproachful behind her, the small front garden and paved pathway already sprouting weeds.

There had been so much to do.

Every evening coming back from the library to sort and pack —
labelling boxes — for the depot — for London — to be thrown away
— hopefully to be sold — surrounded by memories, memories of
their quiet, ordered lives, finding the album of family photographs
— happy photographs of happy occasions.

She would give them to Edward. It was more than she could bear.

London, such a big city — a wounded city — an amputated city.
Bewildering after their little town with the one main street.

She was so lucky to have a nice flat. Bridget had decided to leave the
sagging sofa and chairs in the living room — much too shabby for
her new home — and she had her wireless to keep her company.

The blackout restrictions were beginning to be lifted — Doodlebugs
and V-2s were oblivious to street lighting.

She could come home from the library on lighted streets

The blackout had been so dreadful, intimidating and scary.

Edward had 36 hours' leave at the end of November.

It was good to see him.

He thought the flat was really good. He slept on the sagging sofa.

He was very thin and very tired. She left him sleeping while she went
to work.

They walked in Regents Park and found a small Italian restaurant
in Marylebone High Street where they ate spaghetti Bolognese, and
even had a glass of Chianti, at least that was what it was supposed
to be…

The last Christmas of the war was particularly bleak.

Edward had no leave, and she was unable to get to Yorkshire to
see their father. There was not enough time, only Christmas Day
and Boxing Day. The trains were hopelessly erratic and much too
expensive.

Aunt May telephoned on a crackling line — hardly audible — to
wish her a Happy Christmas. She was anxious and tearful. They
had not heard from Eric for months. They prayed that he was not

involved in the awful reversal in the Ardennes, or the shameful military miscalculation at Arnhem. Please God…
Catherine tried to sound encouraging, also praying. Please God. No more heartbreak. Please God. At least their father seemed reasonably settled. He still got agitated, trying to leave to find their mother, but Aunt May said he was eating and sleeping better.

It was not a very good start to the New Year. It was a very cold winter. There were frequent power cuts, and the gas pressure was often so low the fire wouldn't stay alight. She went to bed to keep warm, in a thick jumper, with a hot water bottle and a pair of Edward's old football socks.

She found it hard to adjust to her new job.
It was a wonderful library, much larger and better stocked than the one in Bembridge, and many more people to deal with, but much less casual and friendly.

Susan Milburn, the Head Librarian, was very different to Miss Turnbull. She was authoritative, and inclined to be bossy. She did not approve of people spending all day in the library.
'We're not a hotel,' she would say briskly, disapproving of the comfortable chairs and polished tables strewn with newspapers and periodicals.
'It just encourages the wrong type of people…'
She would never have let the Colonel use it as a second home, or offer cups of tea to the 'regulars'.

Catherine often felt like offering poor Olive a cup of tea.
'Why don't you sit down for a little while,' she said, indicating the sturdy leather chairs. 'I'm sure it will stop raining soon…' But Olive said she would have to get on. Lady Thornton would be expecting her back. It was the maid's day off and she had to get the lunch…

The head of the library, Mr Simms, and his wife Audrey, gave a small tea party at their house in Highgate to celebrate the end of the war.

It was raining, as it always seemed to be on such occasions, and

Catherine had difficulty finding it.

Mrs Simms, a cheerfully large lady in a mauve twin set and tartan pleated skirt had made a cake. She had even managed to secrete some candles from before the war. It was only a small cake which sat forlornly on an elaborate cake stand in a small lake of luridly pink icing. Mrs Simms laughingly announced that it wasn't real icing.

'It's cornflour with a bit of sugar and a lot of cochineal…'

The cake itself cut in small pieces had an unpleasant texture, tasting a bit like a wet sponge.

'I tried parsnip. I have a friend who grows them, mashed up with a bit of apricot jam. I have a friend who grows apricots, and semolina,' said Mrs Simms. 'Lord Wooten expects us all to be imaginative…'

There were also some rock cakes which did justice to their name, and thin sandwiches of grey wartime bread and unidentifiable paste. There was a glass of sherry for everyone and a lot of weak tea.

It did not feel like a celebration.

A few middle-aged women — herself and Beryl who did secretarial work in the office, were the only young ones. Beryl, a pretty girl, used too much Max Factor pancake make-up, her face orange above her white neck, and vivid, scarlet lipstick. She got it from a friend who was going out with an American soldier who was always giving her all kinds of things, stockings and chocolate and cigarettes and lots of make-up… She said she was fed up with the war — absolutely fed up. 'I don't suppose things will be much better now that it's over,' she said gloomily. 'Old Milburn will be just as sour — and when will there be some decent young men, instead of this miserable riff-raff?'

There certainly were not many men at this celebration. Apart from Mr Simms there were only two pleasant elderly men and two younger ones, one on crutches and the other with thick glasses, wearing a tweed jacket and corduroy trousers. Beryl said he suffered from asthma or something. 'I don't suppose they would have taken him anyway,' she said. 'He has terribly bad eyesight…'

Because of the rain they were unable to go into the garden, which looked invitingly green with bushy shrubs, and borders of lupins and bedraggled yellow daisies. Instead they sat on the faded chintzy sofa and easy chairs, or perched on the straight-backed leather-seated chairs which Mr Simms and the asthmatic young man — 'He's in Accounts,' said Beryl — brought from the dining room. Mrs Simms tried to jolly things along a bit by telling anecdotes about the neighbour's cat's reaction to the air raids, but one of the older women got very tearful and said they should all join in a prayer of thanksgiving.

Afterwards she and Beryl took a bus back to Baker Street and went to the ABC Café for poached eggs on toast.

Eric came home.
There was real rejoicing.
Aunt May said there were flags all over the fronts of the houses all down the street. 'It's so wonderful,' she said on the crackling phone line. 'So, so wonderful to have him home...' She said they had had a feast of roast chicken and apple pie — with the local farms and everybody growing their own vegetables and keeping chickens, they had never had a shortage of food. All the neighbours came. 'Now I shall be able to sleep again,' she said.

In the summer of 1947 Eric married his childhood sweetheart, Maureen.

Catherine managed to get a week's holiday so she could go to the wedding, and spend a little time with their father. Unfortunately Edward was not able to come. He was still in Cambridge, doing a PhD in astrophysics, whilst still working in the Research Laboratories.

It was such a happy day. Maureen had a lovely white satin wedding dress with a heart-shaped neckline and long sleeves, a long veil and a bouquet of white roses. She had two bridesmaids in pink satin dresses with full skirts and puffed sleeves. The little village church was full of flowers, family and friends.

The reception was held in the village hall.
Catherine had not seen so much food since before the war.
Long tables with white cloths, laid with platters of chicken and ham

— sausages — hardboiled eggs — cheeses — salads — crusty bread and butter — bowls of strawberries and cream and a really proper wedding cake with three tiers.
There was much laughter and singing.

But even this quiet leafy village, with its neat front gardens with hollyhocks and golden rod, bright geraniums and climbing roses — the village shop with its jars of boiled sweets, shiny tins of biscuits and jars of local jam, and the children playing cricket on the village green — even this place, so far from destroyed crops and shattered houses, had not escaped entirely from the rapacious, choking tentacles of the war.

There were sad people that day too, remembering those who had not come back. Those who had not been as fortunate as Eric. Eric's best man had lost a leg, the father of the young man who drove the bridal car had been killed in Italy, and their father, shrunken now and confused sat bewildered in his best grey suit, clutching the red carnation which should have been in his buttonhole, telling people he was sorry Joyce had been unable to come...

Catherine watched Olive gather her things together, fumbling with the books as she tried to put them in her shabby bag — fussing with the wet umbrella.
She wondered what it must be like to be Lady Thornton's companion — anybody's companion. Not quite a servant, not quite one of the family, an undefined position, uncomplainingly performing menial tasks whilst remaining unobtrusive and good humoured, the hope of a home of one's own — a life of one's own — a distant misty mirage further and further out of reach...
'We'll send you a card as soon as the Elizabeth David is available,' she said.
'Oh thank you,' said Olive. 'That would be most kind...'

In the November after Eric's wedding their father died, quietly, in his sleep.
Aunt May, her voice muffled with tears, phoned to say she had found him when she had taken up his early morning tea. 'I always took

him a cup of tea and biscuits first thing,' she said. 'He always liked his early morning tea. I thought he was still asleep, he looked so peaceful...' She tried unsuccessfully to control her voice. 'He hadn't touched his bed-time cocoa — he always liked his cocoa when he went up to bed...'

Catherine got the day off to go to the funeral.
The train was late. Uncle Charles was anxiously waiting for her. They arrived at the church as the coffin was being taken from the funeral car. Edward, who had driven up from Cambridge, was trying to comfort Aunt May. He was looking very well and very handsome. How proud their mother and father would have been. It would have been so good if their father could have been buried with their mother, but it was not possible — not practical. Aunt May said they would take great care of the grave, and that she shouldn't worry about it.

It was a crisp, bright day — the service comforting in its simplicity — the mossy graveyard, with clumps of mauve Michaelmas daisies and little birds searching for early berries in the surrounding hedge, such a calm, quiet place. At last her father could be at peace. At last he could rest.

Afterwards they had tea at Aunt May's — ham sandwiches, sausage rolls, fruit cake. Quite a lot of people came. 'Sad,' they said. 'So sad...' Aunt May cried a lot and a capable lady in a blue two-piece with tightly permed hair dispensed tea from a large brown pot. 'Here you are, pet. Help yourself to sugar. You sit down, May, I can manage...'

Edward drove her back to London.
She felt completely deflated — empty, overwhelmed by a jerking, flickering kaleidoscope of memories, choked with the sense of loss — what might have been — what should have been...

They stopped in a small town and had fish and chips in a café with a newly-painted sign and flowers in a window box. It was clean and welcoming with blue and white checked clothes on the tables and thick white plates. The fish and chips were very good, and Catherine was surprised to find how hungry she was.

'Aunt May was brilliant,' said Edward. 'She really looked after Dad. Do you want another cup of tea?'

It was very late when they got back to London. Edward had to go straight back to Cambridge.

'Come and see me soon,' he said.

She didn't manage to go very often.

There was little time, and Edward was always very busy.

He loved his life in Cambridge.

He loved his work.

He had bought a small house, and had a very uppercrust girlfriend, Harriet, who had a wonderful coil of thick blonde hair and beautiful clothes. She was an art historian. Both her parents were academics.

Catherine was always politely invited to their house.

She felt rather an outsider in this rarefied place, where thought and learning were so important.

It was a long way from Canal Street, from the towpath of broken stones and rusting moorings, to the daffodils and anemones cushioning the slopes beside the Cam, and the shiny punts sliding past the historic colleges.

A glimpse of civilised serenity in a disturbing, disturbed world.

The war had barely ruffled its surface.

Harriet's parents, both respected scientists, had had important and demanding jobs — Robert Cameron researching explosives and Felicity, nerve gases.

They had no son to lose, and were not very bothered by the rationing, rather enjoying the challenge of growing their own vegetables. Their gardener, Phillpot, whilst still growing his beloved sweet peas and floppy, old-fashioned roses, managed to produce an abundance of vegetables all year round, sweet sugary peas and fat, soft-podded broad beans in the summer, winter cabbage and kale, as well as parsnips and carrots. He had also provided them with eggs from his hens, and the occasional rabbit or pigeon which Mrs Phillpot would have already made into a tasty casserole — 'Just needs heating up.' Cooking was not their strong point, and their housekeeper Gertrude's cooking skills were, like her cleaning skills, practically non-existent.

Gertrude was Austrian. She had been stranded whilst on holiday in Cambridge when war broke out, and was unable to return to Vienna. She was Jewish and it was not known what had become of her family. It was not talked about, and now the war was over, she showed no interest in going back. The Camerons had taken her in and employed her as a housekeeper. Catherine thought she had wanted to be a poet, she certainly had no idea about housekeeping.

The downstairs cloakroom, hung with ancient mackintoshes and out-of-date calendars, could have done with a good scrub and a change of towels. The meals a haphazard mixture of odds and ends — cold tinned soup, jars of pickled gherkins, rollmops, maybe a few tinned frankfurters and undercooked potatoes, cheese so old that it had cracked and perspired with grease. Catherine didn't think the Camerons really noticed. The food was usually presaged with a number of gin and tonics or dry sherries. Mrs Cameron would occasionally remark vaguely that she had told Gertrude to get a tart or something from Fitzbillies — 'They do lovely tarts.' These, however, never materialised, maybe because Gertrude's English was still very poor, and communications were made in a disjointed mixture of German, pidgin English and a lot of gestures.

The Camerons lived in academic chaos. Every available surface covered with books, papers and files, jostling for space on tables cluttered with strange carvings, lacquered boxes and lopsided lights with broken lampshades and furry wires, and stacked on the floor by the sagging sofa and worn armchairs.

Outside the tall windows hung with rust red brocade curtains, their linings decayed with dust and age, the lawn of green velvet grass stretched down to the gently lapping waters of the stream winding its tranquil way at the bottom of the garden, brushed by fronded willows and paddled by curly-plumed ducks.

Gertrude, a heavy woman who wore a cotton dirndl skirt and open sandals regardless of the weather, or the time of the year, would appear with a tray of lukewarm, gritty coffee and stale biscuits, dumping it down unceremoniously anywhere she could find a space — muttering to herself in German.

The Camerons were tall and intimidatingly confident — distantly amenable — oblivious of their surroundings — completely immersed in their work.
They were obviously fond of Edward, who seemed totally at home, perched on the edge of a chair encumbered with books and overflowing ashtrays, chatting happily with Professor Cameron about obscure scientific theories, and joking with Harriet, who would sit cross-legged on the once magnificent Chinese carpet.
She thought they were unsure who she was, and had no idea whatsoever of her name — nor did they seem to be aware what their daughter was doing.

She saw Major Harding meet Olive as she was trying to negotiate the swing doors. Ever the gentleman he raised his brown trilby politely and, with a flourish, held the door open for her.
Catherine imagined Olive apologising effusively as she tried to get through the doors without dropping anything.
Major Harding was a regular, always smart in camel-hair coat, brown trilby, brown leather gloves and highly polished brown brogues.
Having extricated himself from Olive, he approached the desk.
‘Well young lady,’ he said (he always called her ‘young lady’). ‘Not a very good day — very wet…’
He gave her a suggestive smile and smoothed his sandy hair with stubby, nicotine-stained fingers.
‘Just the day for a good book.’
He was, in fact, a serious reader, mostly biographies and military history. She smiled politely. She thought he must be very lonely — no Mrs Harding — maybe there had never been a Mrs Harding. He

had probably done something very brave during the war. Now just a lonely middle-aged man.

She took the books he had put down on the counter, and stamped his cards. John Ruskin's *The Stones of Venice* that he wanted had come in. She went to get it.

'Excellent,' he said. 'Excellent. I suppose they won't let you out of this place to come and have a drink…?'

He always said the same thing — could she come for a drink — a coffee — lunch — he knew a really nice little place — Italian — just round the corner.

Thankfully she could truthfully say that unfortunately that was not possible.

So many different sorts of people came to the library. The well dressed — oddly dressed — poorly dressed — agreeable, disagreeable — patient and impatient — their choice of books constantly surprising. She had become quite friendly with some of them — some people liked to have a chat. London could be a very lonely place.

She was not lonely. She liked to be on her own. When she came into the flat and shut the door behind her, the weight of the day — of living, lifted, kicking off her court shoes with the sensible heels — not too high — hanging the strictly tailored coat and skirt in the wardrobe, changing into an old skirt and sweater, or loose-fitting dress, resting her tired feet in easy, welcoming slippers, having a cup of tea at the red formica-topped table which had one leg shorter than the others, and had to be propped up with a wedge of cardboard — quietly sipping her tea whilst she did the *Evening Standard* crossword.

All the day's niggles faded — the fusses, internal wrangles, the need to be endlessly pleasant and polite, agreeing with Susan Milburn's string of complaints — all the petty everyday things camouflaging the real issues that affected people's lives. The gradual groping back to normality in a city where walls leant precariously, gaping window frames mirroring nothing, where people picked their way with care along broken, pitted pavements sprouting weeds to work, and prefabricated huts sprang up amongst the rubble as temporary office space, and in the remaining, once imposing buildings of streaked grey stone primly suited secretaries took shorthand in boarded up, mahogany rooms, where once velvet curtains had swept thick carpets, and heavy-framed portraits had glowered disapprovingly from the now empty, grey crumbling walls.

There were still queues — and rationing — shortages of this and that — potatoes, bread, shoelaces, darning wool — still cardboard cakes in the posh patisserie shops in Marylebone High Street, and lurid joints of papier maché meat on the butcher's white slab.

In the winter the gas flames faltered — wavering and popping into nothingness — and cold marked the weary faces of people queueing at the bus stops.

Edward had bought her a refrigerator, an unheard-of luxury. It had changed her life — no more rancid butter, curdled milk or wasted leftovers. She could make a big stew of vegetables — cabbage and carrots, potatoes and onions, eking out a few sausages — meals for several days. Sometimes the butcher gave her some bacon trimmings, or a misshapen chop — mostly bone, but a good addition to her stew.

She wrapped herself in the safety of solitude, evading invitations, excusing herself from social gatherings, closing the door on possible entanglements — quiet with the radio and books.

When Beryl was still at the library, they had sometimes taken their lunchtime sandwiches to eat in the park, but Beryl had got a better job. She was engaged to a young man with curly hair who worked in a bank in the City, and they were saving to get married, so now she was quite content to go to the park on her own, and sit on a bench and watch the people, the children playing, and the ducks scuttling in the water. It was always a pleasure to go to any of the parks, and walk on the springy grass among the abundant trees and beautifully kept flower beds.

'You must speak to Miss Lazenby,' said Miss Milburn. 'Her books are always overdue — and is there nothing we can do about that person who comes every day to "read the papers"? I don't know why we offer this service. It just means anybody can sit here for hours — ANYBODY,' she reiterated, looking with distaste at the untidy man sprawled in one of the leather chairs by the polished table spread with the day's newspapers.

It was true that he did not give a very good impression — there every day in shabby brown corduroys and stained raincoat, shoes split and dirty. He did not seem to read the newspapers — just sat there with them spread out in front of him, sometimes turning a page.

'I've spoken to Mr Simms,' said Miss Milburn. 'But he says there is nothing we can do. Everybody has a perfect right to use the library…' she sighed. 'Anyhow, you could have a word — and don't forget to speak to Miss Lazenby about all the overdue books.'

Catherine wasn't sure what she was supposed to say to the untidy man who came to read the newspapers — he could be mentally ill — there were a lot of people like that now — he might have been a prisoner of war — anything. He was very unkempt, his hair hang limply on the greasy collar of his raincoat, and his hands shook when he turned a page.

As for Miss Lazenby, Miss Milburn had already had an altercation with her. Miss Lazenby was very shrill — her voice a thin shriek. 'You are only an employee,' she had shrieked. 'If it wasn't for people like me you wouldn't have a job…'

Catherine was tired. It did not matter if Miss Lazenby's books were overdue. She had to pay a fine, and she hardly read books anybody else was waiting for, having an insatiable appetite for romantic historical novels.

As usual Miss Milburn was making a fuss, just for the sake of making a fuss. The shabby man was not the only person who came to read the newspapers, or just sit and pretend to read the newspapers.

Of course she would do nothing, and Miss Milburn would find something else to make a fuss about.

It had at last been possible to have proper gravestones for their mother and father — plain granite, with simple inscriptions. Edward had paid for them — she never had any money left from her wages once she had paid the rent and other expenses, hardly enough to have her shoes mended.

Aunt May had written on flower-bordered notepaper to say how pleased they were with their father's stone — a lovely stone. Charles had already planted a rose bush on the grave — a Peace Rose — such a lovely pink and yellow flower.

Catherine had arranged to meet Edward in Bembridge, at the church. The vicar was going to say a few prayers at the graveside, where the stone had already been put in place.

She had had a problem getting the day off.
Miss Milburn was not pleased. 'It's most inconvenient Catherine,' she said. 'Elsie really can't cope on her own.'
Elsie was pretty hopeless. Not good with people. Easily flustered. Slow to find information on books, or where to find them on the shelves.
'And,' she continued. 'Have you done anything about *that man*?' indicating the shabby man in his usual chair, newspaper scattered untidily, half on the floor. He was asleep.
Catherine said he probably had nowhere else to go.
Miss Milburn said really that was not their problem, and drawing in her breath with a hiss of exasperation she made her way back to her office in her sensible black court shoes, stopping briefly to straighten a few books, which were not quite straight on a shelf in Crime Fiction.

It was a difficult day. She could hardly swallow her breakfast toast.
It was early March, grey clouds gusted low in a pallid sky — short bitter showers stinging her face, wrenching her umbrella.
The train was cold, and kept stopping unaccountably, and when it finally reached Bembridge, she was tempted not to get off at all.

It was exactly the same — nothing had changed — even the broken fence people had used as a short cut onto the platform was the same. Tattered posters, weeds pushing their way through broken stones, a dismal, neglected place.

She had to sit down on one of the old wooden seats, with rusty bolts, initials gouged in the peeling paint, trying to control the rising nausea — taking deep breaths — reliving the miserable night when she had stood, hand in hand with Peter, waiting for the train that would take him away forever, the defensive layers she had built up over the years cracking dangerously, exposing the raw pain that was still there. She closed her eyes, trying to shut out the surging images, but they remained, vivid against her eyelids — feeling the warmth of his hand — the roughness of his coat, damp from the persistent drizzle — the smell of damp cloth.

She rose slowly and left the station.

There was no one to take her ticket.

Outside she glanced down the street, almost expecting to see Mrs Tarrant's beige saloon parked outside the hairdresser's.

She crossed the road to the small florist's shop on the corner. There had always been a florist on the corner. There were green buckets of daffodils on the pavement, and hyacinths in pots.

The florist was a short woman with a dishevelled mass of hair. She wore a plastic apron over a striped jumper and black slacks.

Catherine chose some narcissi — their mother had loved narcissi — and asked if they could be arranged with some greenery.

'A sort of bunch,' she said.

'I'll do a spray,' said the florist. 'Sit down, dear, you look a bit pale. Myra—' she shouted towards the back of the shop. 'Myra — bring a glass of water.'

Catherine sat down gratefully on a green metal chair. She still felt giddy.

A tall, weedy girl in green dungarees appeared. She had secateurs in one hand, and a glass of water in the other. Catherine thanked her very much. She hoped there would be a taxi outside the station to take her to the church.

The florist made a lovely spray with the narcissi and greenery, securing it with some wide green tape.

'There,' she said. 'Will that do?'
Catherine said it was perfect.

There was a taxi outside the station.
The florist had said that old Martin was usually out there, in time for
the London train — 'He nearly always gets a fare from the London
train...'
A battered brown car with split seats.
Martin, himself somewhat battered in a shabby waterproof jacket,
tried to be chatty, but she could only respond with platitudes.
Very windy — cold for the time of year — hope it does not rain —
and so on and so on...

Edward was already at the church — his car smart and shiny — dark
blue.
He was talking to the vicar. A young man with a black raincoat over
his surplice, awkwardly clutching a prayer book — uneasy among so
many stones with the same date of death.
He would not have been there on that terrible day the acrid black
cloud had blotted out the sun — blotting out so many lives — the
world swivelling in slow motion — the endless moment of horrified
silence.

It was hard to believe in this tranquil place, with gently dripping
trees — soft moss amongst the springy grass.
Now, standing by their mother's grave, was he aware there could
be anybody buried here? There had been so little left amongst the
charred remnants — the twisted bits and pieces.
She was suddenly aware that she was shivering uncontrollably, and
had to reach out to Edward, standing rigidly by her side, to steady
herself. The sound of the vicar's voice a sea-sickly murmur — a
mumbled Amen — the shaking of hands — polite 'thank yous' —
turning their backs on the newly-placed stone — 'Much loved Wife
and Mother' — leaving behind the hidden secrets of this seemingly
tranquil place.

Edward helped her into the car.

They stopped at a hotel with flags flying over the porch — Waring Tennis Club — Waring Golf Club — green and white stripes, whisked by the brisk breeze.

There was an open fire in the red-carpeted foyer, and comfortable chairs. Edward ordered them both a sherry, something she very rarely drank, not since Mrs Turnbull had produced a bottle on her last day at the library in Bembridge, inviting the Colonel to join them to wish her every success.

The restaurant was almost deserted — two ladies in sensible hats, four men in dark suits and striped shirts and a woman on her own with wild hair and a vividly patterned cardigan.

There was steak pie, or fish and chips — choices were still very restricted. They had steak pie, which was really very good.

Edward had relaxed, the strain of having to appear calm and collected diminished — awful memories subdued.

He was telling her of his impending trip to Italy with Harriet — end of June — four weeks — Florence. Harriet was to do some research in the Uffizi. They were going to stay with friends of Harriet's parents who had a villa in the hills — they were hoping also to manage a short trip to Rome...

Among tumbling hills — knobbled olive trees — terraced gentle-leaved vines — peddled-dashed sunlight on rough stone paths... And Rome, of fountains and squares with elegant statues, and smart people drinking little cups of coffee in pavement cafés, the stones burnt white by the sun.

Last year Edward had paid for her to have a week's holiday in Brighton. It was a birthday present. He said the sea air would do her good. 'You never have a holiday...'

She stayed in a boarding house near the front, permanently wafted with a mixture of fried bacon and air freshener, but it was clean and comfortable. She had a wash basin in her room and a chair with two limp cushions. She could not see the sea from her window, only a dull side street, but it was only a short walk to the front. She liked to just sit and watch the surging sea. It had been quite stormy, and at high tide the salty foam-flecked water had come right up to the seawall — sucking the stones back in its rattling grasp. She walked right up to the boundary where Hove dwindled into drab Portslade, past the avenue with the statue of Queen Victoria stolidly staring out to sea, and liked to sit on the West Pier with its creaking boards, which was sedate — no slot machines or noisy music, just a few men in caps silently fishing.

Mrs Robertson, the landlady, did suppers as well as breakfasts. She was dismayed that Catherine did not eat her eggs and bacon — only toast and marmalade, insisting on making her egg and bacon sandwiches to take for her lunch.
The suppers were not very inspiring, but nobody expected inspiring food, grateful for whatever was provided — mostly stew — fish and chips — luncheon meat with lettuce, tomato and pickled beetroot — a really nice jam sponge pudding, let down by watery custard, and stewed fruit. Apart from her there were middle-aged couples who were pleasant, and a man of about sixty who spoke to nobody, and propped a book against the water jug to make it clear he wished to be left alone.

Catherine enjoyed everything. She wandered in the gardens surrounding the exotically domed Pavilion where George IV had entertained in lavish splendour, and along the winding lanes with the little fusty dusty shops selling fusty dusty bits and pieces — odd cups and saucers — decorative boxes whose decorations had been obliterated with use — brown-pocked pictures in chipped gilt frames…
One day she took a bus to Rottingdean, and had tea and a toasted bun in a café near the sea.

Edward had apple pie — but she was too full to eat any more.
Driving back to London he told her how well his work was going.
There was talk of a conference in San Francisco — probably in September — everything was really fine.

She was very tired.
She made a cup of tea and a hot water bottle — kicking off her shoes

— getting under her eiderdown — closing her eyes — shutting out the whirring images of the day — of the encroaching past. Maybe one day it would be over — maybe one day…

4

Olive had a terrible cold — confined to her room, her face unflatteringly swollen.

Paula produced thick, nourishing soups and strongly scented tisanes, tut-tutting about the poor Signora...

Elspeth was just irritated, her irritation compounded by the fact that she had told her not to go out in the rain, coming back dripping, making wet patches on the blue Chinese rug in the hall, one of two bought at Liberty's long before the dreadful war, the other one still in the warehouse in Borehampton waiting to be sorted out.

She would have to make some kind of decision soon — perhaps she would get a small place in the country — not too far from town — with a garden. She did so miss having a garden... but she could never make up her mind.

A card came from the library. At last the Elizabeth David was available. She would have to go and get it herself. She needed something to cheer her up.

She was very worried about Alison. She was concerned that she was drinking too much — her voice had been distinctly slurred when she had spoken to her on the telephone the evening before. She didn't know what she should do. It was best to pretend she had not noticed, or voice her concern. She wished, as she did so often, that Jumbo was here. He would have known what to do.

She had mentioned it in her last letter to Rosemary, and hoped she might give her some advice. She knew that Rosemary found Alison's behaviour exasperating, but Elspeth felt that things were becoming much more serious.

She decided to go to the library.

Paula was not pleased when she told her she might be late for her morning coffee. Paula did not like her routine interrupted, showing her displeasure by noisily banging the swing doors to the kitchen.

The girl behind the counter in the library was quite tall and very thin. She had short dark hair and delicate features.

She took Elspeth's card and went to find the Elizabeth David.
'My companion Miss Fern usually comes,' Elspeth said. 'But she has a terrible cold.'
'Oh dear,' said the girl. 'I am sorry. I'm afraid she got very wet the other day.'
'I told her not to go out in the rain,' said Elspeth. 'But she insisted…'

She thanked the girl, taking the book with its bright, cheerful cover. 'I'll just take a look around…'

Perhaps she could find a good novel. She liked a good novel. Sybil said the latest Nancy Mitford was very amusing — or there was a recent Elizabeth Bowen or even the latest Margery Allingham — her books were always diverting.
Her taste in books had become much lighter than it used to be. Life had become much more serious.
Jumbo had not really read novels — apart from Trollope, of whom he was particularly fond. His wonderful collection, bound in green leather and gold leaf, had gone with so many other things — the things on her list marked with a black cross.

She noticed the man in the shabby corduroys slumped in a chair by a round table covered in newspapers. He appeared to be asleep. He reminded her of Montague Selbourne who had played golf with Jumbo, permanently dishevelled. An amiable man with an impressive intellect — his wife Thelma — a bossy woman in heavy tweeds and crêpe-de-chine blouses — a keen gardener. They had peacocks, she remembered, fanning their wonderful tails, strutting on the lawns outside their house — a Palladian villa full of hideous furniture. She had been somebody important in the local horticultural society — an annoying woman — very opinionated. Elspeth had never cared for her.
She wondered what had happened to them. No doubt the Palladian villa had been requisitioned… They had had two sons — had the war destroyed their lives like so many others?
This man with his broken shoes and shabby corduroys — was he another casualty of the dreadful war which still cast its grim shadow over so much of life?

She found the Nancy Mitford, and took it to the counter for the girl to stamp her card. She noticed her long slender hands. There was a sadness about her, an indefinable feeling of sorrow. Elspeth had an impulse to reach out and pat her hand, to say, 'There, there, everything will be alright', but of course she didn't, merely remarking that at least it wasn't raining today, and that she was looking forward to a little escapism with the sun-drenched Elizabeth David.

Catherine had assumed, as Olive fumbled indecisively with the book list, that Lady Thornton was a demanding and autocratic employer — rather like Peter's mother, bossy and disdainful — but she was not at all like that. True, she looked rather intimidating — tall and bony — impeccably dressed in a pale blue and grey checked costume and dark blue hat — stern, chiselled features — an air of superiority, but immediately polite and friendly.
She watched her hesitate as she passed the shabby man, as if considering if she should speak to him, and then proceeding briskly through the heavy doors into the street.

Paula said the Signorina had telephoned and the Honourable Signora, Elspeth, was supposed to go to tea with Sybil this afternoon — but she had anticipated the usual excuses. 'I am feeling absolutely stifled — and there seems to be no milk…'

Really it was Paula's delicious little cakes, and an abundance of gin and tonic, and Elspeth's comfortable chairs which Sybil found preferable to her inadequate flat.
It was sad. Sybil, who had been used to her magnificent house in Eaton Square, now confined to the utilitarian three bedroom flat in West Hampstead — and, of course, no servants.
She was going to her friends Arlette and Maurice Legrand in Monte Carlo for the summer. They were at last back in their villa, which had had to be completely redecorated and the garden re-landscaped — so much wanton destruction. Elspeth was pleased that Sybil had something to look forward to. At least she still had some choices — Sybil didn't have many choices. Pogo had made too many disastrous gambles on the Stock Exchange, leaving her virtually nothing.

She would have to have a word with Paula, she was not expecting to have to serve tea today.

Fortunately she had a soft spot for Sybil, even though she always looked disapproving. Sybil always so elegant in her beautifully tailored clothes — clothes from before the war — a stark contrast to poor Amanda, whose clothes had always been haphazard and inappropriate.

Elspeth thought that Paula had probably been looking forward to going down to Berwick Street market, and also to the Italian delicatessen where she had Italian friends, to buy coffee and salami, Parma ham and mortadella, all so delicious.

Sybil did not require much to eat at teatime — it was only an interval before the cocktail hour. Biscuits would be sufficient.

If Olive had not been unwell she could have seen to the tea. It was most annoying.

Of course they could always go out to tea. There were several places in Marylebone High Street which had very good cakes.

However, she knew Sybil really preferred to come to the flat — so much more comfortable.

As for Alison, she would have to phone her this evening. It was not convenient to telephone her at work.

Elspeth was resigned to the possibility that Alison was in some kind of financial difficulty. Despite the fact that her inheritance from Jumbo had been very generous, paying for her flat with plenty over, and that she had a very good, well paid job, she still seemed to have problems paying her bills. She had not said anything the other day...

Elspeth put the books down on the little table by her chair.

She thought about the girl in the library. She had looked so sad.

Perhaps she would get her own books in future, have a little chat. It was nice to browse around and look at all the books — to choose at random, without a list...

She sighed, and went to find Paula.

Two small cutlets — two small mouthfuls — isolated in the centre of her gold-rimmed dinner plates.

Olive had appeared, wan and grey as her grey merino twinset. Elspeth only wore cashmere, difficult to find now, as everything seemed to be.
Sybil was on her second gin and vermouth.
Olive accepted a sweet sherry. She really only drank the occasional sweet sherry.
Sybil had been at her most voluble.
The usual extravagant entrance — greeting Paula effusively in Italian — Buon giorno! Buon giorno! — chucking her mink coat onto the chair in the hall, even though it was not really the weather for mink coats — settling herself in one of Elspeth's comfortable armchairs — her elegant feet shod in handmade shoes of the softest suede — stretched out, ankles neatly crossed.

She said she had to move from the stifling confines of the flat in West Hampstead. 'I can't breathe — I am suffocating,' she said, dramatically. 'I think I should move out, where there is more air…'
She had visited Esmé and Gerald Naughton at the weekend. They had recently bought a house in Harrow, unable to keep up their house in Ovington Gardens. It was impossible to run a house that size without staff, and staff were virtually unobtainable.
The house in Harrow was perfectly adequate — a pleasant house with a separate flat for a servant, and a small garden. It was not really far from town. Gerald went every day to the City on the Underground. They had also found a capable Polish woman as housekeeper — not much of a cook, but kept everything clean, and reasonable English. It seemed most satisfactory, and so near the countryside…
'Esmé says there are lovely walks, and she is going to join the tennis club…' Sybil broke off abruptly, leant her head on the back of the chair and closed her eyes, as if the idea of joining a tennis club was too dreadful to contemplate.

Elspeth was alarmed. She had always thought Sybil had been too hasty in taking the flat in West Hampstead. It was much too small. A friend had recommended it. But Harrow — good heavens!
Sybil had always considered the suburbs unutterably dreary, and the people who lived there as tediously boring bourgeois — 'small-minded', she would say, dismissively. 'Yawningly dull…'

And she positively disliked the countryside, never accompanying Pogo on his golfing holidays and grouse shoots. 'So uncomfortable — and ruins one's shoes. Freezing houses...'
'Why not a bigger flat? A proper roomy flat? A mansion flat — something like this?' she said. 'There are plenty to choose from — there are some really nice ones in Maida Vale — I'm sure you could find something really congenial...'

Sybil opened her eyes and reached out to take a cigarette from Elspeth's silver cigarette box.
'I can't say that I am particularly tempted by the thought of suburbia,' she said. 'There are still plenty of paintings I could sell — some of them I have never liked. Too many horses. Pogo liked paintings of horses... I'll contact some estate agents — have a look around...'

It was certainly true that Sybil had a great many paintings. What was supposed to be the third bedroom in her flat was crammed with paintings and bits and pieces of furniture that she had not wanted to put in store — a fragile table inlaid with mother-of-pearl — an Art Nouveau lamp of intricately entwined metal — a pile of silk tasselled cushions covered with a damask curtain to protect them from the dust...

Now, sitting opposite Olive at the dinner table, contemplating the two skinny cutlets, wondering when there would ever be an end to meat rationing, she felt her resilience had reached its lowest ebb. So good then to find, on lifting the gold-rimmed lids of the vegetable dishes — leeks in a white sauce, and crisp potato and carrot cakes. She rang the bell for Paula.
'I think we should have some wine,' she said. 'To accompany this delicious meal. Perhaps you would open the bottle of Valpolicella — and have some yourself...'

Elspeth had a letter from her friend, Tamarind Barclay from Scotland, written, as usual in purple ink on headed blue Smythson writing paper, an indecipherable scrawl of loops and dips.
Her nephew Alistair was coming to London — back from some terrible place — all terribly top secret. He was going to work at the

War Office, or was it the Foreign Office — could he possibly stay with Elspeth until he found a flat? She was sure his meat ration would be useful...

Elspeth was not pleased — apart from the fact that she didn't know this young man, of what she knew of young men, he would probably need all their meat rations.

She would have to go personally to Selfridges and speak to Mr Bowles, the head of the meat department, and see if she could wangle some sausages and offal, which was not rationed... Paula made very delicious braised liver — and kidneys sautéed with a little sherry.

It really was too much.
She hoped there were enough towels in a reasonable state.
She had not been able to replenish anything properly for so long.
Olive would have to help — make sure his room was in order, and help Paula with the bed.
Really, it was most inconvenient — and she had the continual worry of Alison.

After several attempts she had managed to speak to her on the phone.
She had seemed vague and incoherent, but categorically refused to let Elspeth come round to see her.
'I'm perfectly alright,' she had said. 'I think I've had the flu — I just need £200 to pay off a debt...'
Elspeth was horrified. How could she owe £200? She had a nasty feeling that things were not right — but Alison had cut her short, her voice rising hysterically. 'I just need it, that's all — as soon as possible...'
Again Elspeth wished Rosemary was not so far away — she had sent lovely photos of the two little boys — she was sure Alison was drinking too much.
She didn't know what to do.
'It would be good to see you,' she said. 'We could meet for coffee in Kardomah's if you are too busy to have lunch...', but Alison said she couldn't possibly at the moment — she'd ring later.

Elspeth wrote the cheque for £200 and put a little note in the envelope with it, to say she hoped all was well, and was looking forward to seeing her soon.

She hoped it wasn't anything serious. £200 was a lot of money. How could she owe someone £200? If only she could talk to her properly. She had never found it easy to talk to her properly — she was inclined to get defensive and upset…

Nanny had always said Alison was highly strung — so unlike Rosemary, who had inherited Jumbo's calm stoicism. Alison tended to burst into tears at the slightest thing.

She had twirled across this room in her new blue taffeta party frock — her pale hair tied with a blue satin ribbon. 'Look,' she had cried excitedly. 'Look how my dress swirls about — and my shoes — look at my shoes…' They were blue satin to match her hair ribbon — 'Aren't they lovely…'

It must have been one of the last parties the girls had gone to — the Christmas of 1938 — when the war was still hovering — a distant rumble — and Jumbo had laughed, and called Rosemary to hurry — the taxi was waiting. They were going to the Mortons' in Hyde Park Gardens. They always gave a big party for the young ones at Christmas.

It was almost the last Christmas they were all together. Before the distant rumblings became a terrible reality — before everything had started to fall apart.

She and Jumbo had gone to Gennaro's for dinner, and Jumbo had ordered champagne, and they had eaten little vol au vents filled with prawns in a creamy sauce.

It was hard to believe now that such a world had ever existed.

Olive came in to ask if she needed anything.

'Well, you could take my black jacket to the cleaners,' said Elspeth. 'And then get some stamps, and a few Air letters. I used the last one last week. Perhaps, after lunch we could go for a walk in the park — maybe the daffodils will be coming out. I shall go to the library — I enjoyed my visit to the library when you were not well…'

The shabby man was still in the same chair — this morning he had a newspaper spread on his knees, but he wasn't looking at it.

'He reminds me of a friend of my husband's,' she said to the girl. 'A very clever man. He looks as if he could do with a cup of tea…'
The girl smiled. A small, tentative smile. 'Where I used to work,' she said, 'the head librarian always gave people a cup of tea — but I'm afraid here Miss Milburn, my superior, just wants to get rid of him. She says he should not be allowed to be here.' She looked down at the counter in front of her, and moved some cards slightly to one side. 'I think he might have shell shock,' she said very quietly.
'Quite possibly,' said Elspeth. 'Poor man. Does he spend a lot of time here?'
'He comes every day,' said the girl. 'Stays a few hours — sometimes he sleeps…'
Miss Milburn was always furious if she saw him asleep. 'This is not a dosshouse — this is no place for tramps…', and she would go and complain to Mr Sims.
Catherine always ignored her.
She took Lady Thornton's book and stamped the card.
Elspeth had brought back the Nancy Mitford.
'I found it rather superficial,' she said. 'Quite amusing I suppose — but it's difficult to find anything slightly amusing nowadays — I shall go and look for something else…'
She would ask the girl's name when she came back.
Catherine — Catherine Bradley. She had been in the library for nearly six years.
Elspeth was sorry now that she had not bothered to come before.
It was much more interesting to choose something for one's self. Recommendations were always unreliable — and Catherine seemed such a nice young woman — *très sympathique*, as Sybil would say.
She chose *Brideshead Revisited* — on the whole she had always enjoyed Evelyn Waugh, despite his rather suspect religious beliefs.
She very much wanted to go and speak to the dishevelled man in his worn corduroys, but thought she better not…
This afternoon she would discuss Taramind's nephew coming with Olive. He would have to have the larger spare room. It had a wash basin, but he would have to share Olive's bathroom. The room

needed airing. Nobody had slept in it for years.

Of course, he might not be with them for very long at all.

Elspeth had another letter from Tamarind.

Alistair would be coming the following Thursday, the 4th of April — this heavily underlined with purple ink — his train should arrive at King's Cross at 5.24 — this also heavily underlined — and Hugo sends his regards, and says you should come and stay — perhaps in May.

Tamarind's husband Hugo was a nice person, rather bombastic but very well meaning. Too old for active service, he had done something with maps, or charts, she was not sure exactly what, but he had always been very interested in maps. Going to stay sounded a really nice thought — their house was surrounded by moorland — a wonderful fuchsia pink carpet stretching into the distance, dotted with clumps of saffron yellow gorse.

The train was late, of course — when were they ever on time — some problem outside York. He did not arrive until nearly 7 o'clock. Very thin — tall and dark with a livid scar stretching from his eyebrows right down the side of his face, and a jagged scar on the back of one of his hands.

He was wearing a navy blue gaberdine raincoat and had one large, battered brown suitcase.

Paula had managed to get a chicken, which she had roasted, with roast potatoes — and there was apple tart. They opened another bottle of Valpolicella, and even Olive managed half a glass, diluted with water.

Elspeth wanted him to feel welcome — goodness knows what horror he had experienced.

She shuddered inwardly — when would there be any end to it — how could there be an end to it when there were so many visible reminders — so much inner and outer damage.

Really, this won't do, she told herself — pull yourself together.

Paula brought in the apple tart, and Elspeth cut a large slice for Alistair — he looked as if he needed feeding up…

Sybil phoned in high spirits.

A charming young man had come from the estate agents, Brown and Saville, to look at her flat. 'He said there would be no problem selling it,' she said. 'A most sought after location — close to all the amenities…,' she laughed. 'They use such quaint jargon…' And, she had got Mr Carver to come from Sotheby's to look at two of her many horse paintings. 'Two I really didn't care for,' she said. 'He was delighted — Stubbs apparently — should be worth quite a lot. I told him I only wanted to sell one at present. He knows a keen collector — he positively chortled…' And she had made arrangements to view three large mansion flats tomorrow, and wondered if Elspeth might like to come along…

Elspeth said of course, it should be most interesting…

She had still been unable to contact Alison. She had not even acknowledged the cheque Elspeth had sent. It made her quite annoyed. After all, it didn't take much effort to make a short phone call.

She took a taxi to Sybil's flat, where the 'charming' young man, Mr Cochran, fetched them, in his extremely luxurious car, to view the flats.
The first one smelled unpleasant. An earnest young woman with messy, badly dyed hair and carpet slippers apologised for the rather untidy state of the quiet elegant rooms. There was a grey chandelier, in what was probably the dining room. It was certainly not very clean, but they were not there to judge the inadequacy of the young woman's housewifery skills. It was, in fact, rather dark, with a dismal area at the back containing the dustbins, and the front directly onto a busy street.

The second one was more promising — communal gardens at the rear, and a quiet treelined street in front. The rooms were high and light, rather spoiled by drab red curtains and matching upholstery.
A very talkative, middle-aged woman showed them round — draped in a long, fringed shawl, with old tennis shoes — opening the doors to each room with a dramatic flourish, the fringes of her shawl getting entangled in the door knobs. 'Dreadful furniture,' Sybil

said later. She offered them tea, which they refused politely, making appreciative murmurs over the lightness and loftiness of the rooms, the well kept gardens and the 'rather ghastly', as Sybil put it later, bathroom.

The third one was in a much larger block, but equally spacious and well placed. The owner was moving to Yorkshire — a short, terse woman in tweeds, smoking a cigarette. She was planning to join her daughter to run a stables. She said horses were much more congenial than people. Now her husband was retired, there was no reason to stay in London.

Mr Cochran drove them back to Elspeth's flat. Sybil said she would have to think about it, but it was definitely between the second and third one.
Sybil was keen to meet Alistair, but he was never home until about 6.30. He was really no trouble, leaving for work at about 8.30, and always said in advance if he was going to be out in the evening. He was keen on Classical music, and had already been to a performance of the Verdi Requiem at the Albert Hall.
She and Jumbo had a box at the Albert Hall. It had been Jumbo's mother's. They had seldom used it — the occasional performance of Handel's Messiah, or some Tchaikovsky — Jumbo had been very fond of Tchaikovsky. During the war she hadn't used it at all. Since the war she had been a few times — once to see Toscanini conduct, she couldn't remember what — it might have been Brahms... and there had been a recital by Gigli of operatic arias — that had been rather good. The girls never used it. Sybil used it quite often. She liked the occasion. Her knowledge of music of any kind was minimal. Pogo had had a positive aversion to any sort of cultural activity — retreating to his club. Sybil liked to be seen — she liked to invite her friends the Carmichaels when they came to London from their estate in Hereford. She liked the dressing up — the champagne and smoked salmon sandwiches in the interval. Elspeth hoped Alistair would use it often. He was delighted, saying that it was really wonderful, and hoped she wouldn't mind him using it a lot. Elspeth was equally delighted — pleased she could do something to help eradicate what were, probably, horrendous memories. She thought

of the poor man, so like Montagu, sitting alone in the library in his broken shoes.

That evening he was going to be out with his friends who might be able to help find him a flat.

Sybil was disappointed, but made up for her disappointment by having another large gin and vermouth.

They discussed the flats — dismissing the first one, and both agreeing that the second one was definitely the most appealing. They all had a separate bathroom and bed-sitting room for live-in help. 'If I can find somebody,' Sybil said. She would arrange to view the second one again. It was all most satisfactory.

Of course it would all have to be completely redecorated — new carpets and curtains — something serious done to the bathroom and kitchen. She could always sell another Stubbs. 'And there are all those gruesome pictures of dead birds and fruit and animals being torn to pieces we had in the dining room.' She waved her hand in disgust. 'Pogo thought they were marvellous.'

Elspeth thought sadly of the many lovely paintings she and Jumbo had had — most marked with a black cross in the book of what remained of their things still in store.

Pogo, of course, had been a great hunting, shooting and fishing man — liked nothing better than striding about the moors killing anything that moved. Rather ironic that that was where he died — but fitting…

Sybil had a third gin and vermouth.

'There are five large ones and two smaller ones — should keep me going for years…'

In the end she stayed for supper. Paula had made a wonderful rabbit stew with onions and mashed potato.

'Fabulous darling,' said Sybil. 'I can't remember when I had anything so delicious.'

They opened another bottle of Valpolicella — even Olive perked up. 'If only I could find someone like Paula,' said Sybil. 'This is so good — I'll have a little more wine, Elspeth. We must drink a toast to my new flat. Maybe it can all be settled before I go to France…'

*　　*　　*

Still no word from Alison. Elspeth was now very annoyed that she had not even bothered to acknowledge the cheque. It really was too bad.

She decided to telephone her at work and risk her getting into trouble. She would telephone before she went for her hairdresser's appointment in South Kensington. She went regularly to Albert's for a shampoo and set, even though Albert had retired some time ago. His successor, Maurice, was very pleasant and capable.

The woman who answered was positively chilly — Alison was not in the office — she was off sick… She said this in the sort of tone to suggest she did not think that this was actually true — that Alison was not sick at all, but was just taking time off. Elspeth thanked her politely, and apologised for troubling her. She then tried Alison's home number, but there was still no reply. She rather tended to agree with the woman in Alison's office — she had probably gone off somewhere for a few days — she had done that before — feigning illness. As a child she had inclined to be deceitful. Nanny had called her 'over imaginative'…

She had just settled herself against her pillows and prepared to look at the latest issue of *The Field* — the April issue which had arrived that morning. Jumbo had always had a subscription to *The Field* — everything about the countryside. She had kept it going — it gave her a comfortable feeling — even though now it was completely irrelevant. Spring seemed irrelevant, continuing to sprout and blossom each year — oblivious to battles — new grass — the clotted cream of orchards — bluebells — slopes of wild daffodils crushed and bloodied.

She closed her eyes. Really this would not do at all. She was becoming positively morbid.

And then the telephone rang — shrill and demanding — so late — who could it be?

It was St Mary's Hospital. A curt woman's voice asked to speak to Lady Thornton.

Alison had been admitted as an emergency. It seemed that she was quite dangerously ill.

Elspeth said she would come straight away — suddenly shrinking cold, making it difficult to breathe. 'Straight away', she repeated, already half out of bed, pulling on her dressing gown — knocking on Olive's door. 'I will have to ask you to go with me,' she said, as Olive sat up, startled, reaching for her bedside light. 'Of course,' she said. 'Of course — oh dear, what a thing…'

As Elspeth put her coat on and waited for Olive in the sitting room, she was surprised to see Alistair coming through the swing doors from the kitchen carrying a cup of tea. He looked equally surprised to see her.

'I couldn't sleep,' he said. 'I've just made myself a cup of tea — I hope you don't mind…'

'No — no, of course not,' said Elspeth, and it suddenly occurred to her that she had never made herself a cup of tea — or anything else for that matter — in all the many years of using the flat. Before the war when they only came on brief visits, Penn would send one of the servants — usually Martha — to prepare the flat for them, and do everything necessary. During the war it was just herself and Martha, and now it was Paula and Olive. In all that time she had rarely been in the kitchen, and then, except for the dreadful day the telegram came, only to discuss some domestic matter.

She looked at the young man standing across the room holding the cup and saucer — so gaunt and pale, wearing a tartan dressing gown and brown leather slippers.

'My daughter has been taken ill,' she said. 'Olive and I have to go to St Mary's Hospital.'

He said could he help, but she told him to go back to bed.

'Olive and I will manage,' she said. 'You get some rest…'

It was well after midnight when they got back.

Olive went to make tea.

Elspeth sat down without taking off her coat.

She felt chilled right through — empty and hopeless — her eyelids ached with fatigue.

After waiting some time in the miserable hospital waiting room —
grubby and dimly lit, smelling damp and musty, the chairs hard
and shabby — a sister finally appeared — brisk and sallow faced
— coldly disapproving. Elspeth asked what was wrong with Alison.
The sister said septicaemia, annunciating very clearly and repeating
it slowly — septicaemia — and noticing Elspeth's bewilderment
added, 'I suppose you didn't know. Botched abortion.' She paused,
and then continued. 'You can see her for a few minutes — but she is
hardly conscious...'

Leaving Olive sitting on the edge of one of the hard chairs, Elspeth
followed the sister along long brown linoleum corridors, and up
several floors in a dark brown creaking lift. It was a long ward with
about eight beds. Alison was in one near the door. Her eyes were
closed — whey-faced — her fine hair damp and wispy on the pillow.
A nurse who had been sitting at a central table brought over a metal-
framed chair for her to sit on. She had a slightly more sympathetic
air than the coldly contemptuous sister.
'She has a very high fever,' she said. 'I don't think she will know who
you are...', and she turned away to exchange a few words with the
nurse. They went together back to the central table, leaning over to
study some papers which were laid out.

Elspeth sat down and took Alison's hand. It was dry and hot. She
moaned slightly but did not open her eyes.
Somebody further down the ward started making noises, and the
nurse went to see to them.
Elspeth only stayed a little while. She could feel the sister's animosity,
and Alison showed no sign of waking.
She left reluctantly, thanking the sister with her usual politeness.

Olive had spilled the tea on the tray. She had overfilled the teapot.
'Don't fuss,' said Elspeth. 'Don't fuss — it doesn't matter...'
Her mind was swirling with disjointed thoughts.
This sort of thing didn't happen to them — botched abortions — any
sort of abortions.
Once one of the servants had got herself in trouble — a parlour maid
— a pretty girl — Beatrice something. Penn had dealt with it — of

course she had to go. Jumbo had said to give her two months' wages instead of one.

It had all been most unpleasant.

And this man — was he the same married man that Alison and Rosemary had quarrelled about? The man responsible for Alison's drinking? And now this — this humiliatingly dreadful situation. So that was what Alison had needed the £200 for.

It was all too much.

'Don't wait up for me,' she said to Olive. 'I shall just sit here a little while. Just pour me another cup of tea. Leave the tea things — Paula can see to them in the morning…'

Tomorrow she would telephone Rosemary — and better go to Debenham & Freebody to get Alison some sensible nightdresses.

She placed a personal call to Rosemary for 7 o'clock that evening — that would be late morning in Los Angeles — so hopefully she would be there.

Her surprise and pleasure to hear her mother's voice quickly changed to shock and disgust.

'Oh ma,' she said. 'I'm so sorry — how could she be so stupid?' Saying she wished she could be more helpful — that she was not so far away.

Elspeth found the hospital disconcerting.

In her limited experience of hospitals she had found them places of soft carpeting and a great many flowers — calmly serene with deferential nurses in pristine white uniforms — not dismal corridors with dark brown paintwork, scuffed yellowing walls and old brown linoleum billowing unevenly on the floors. The ward with the high metal beds, dispirited patients, mute or moaning in unsuitable nightwear — the nursing staff casually disinterested.

It had been really difficult to persuade the sister in charge to let her visit in the afternoon. She was told severely that visiting hours were 6–8. Finally she had grudgingly said Elspeth could visit between 3 and 4, but she must not stay long.

She had taken a taxi to Debenham & Freebody in the morning, and managed to get two surprisingly pretty, practical nightdresses — one blue with sprigs of flowers and white with sprigs of flowers — there was still very little choice. She had also bought a pair of slippers and some Elizabeth Arden toiletries in a smart zip-up bag.

Alison had a drip in one arm. She was still the colour of curdled milk, with purple circles under her eyes, her fine hair matted damply on the pillow. She avoided looking directly at Elspeth, and fiddled with the sheet.

It was not a satisfactory visit.

Alison obviously didn't want to talk, saying she was very tired — and no, she didn't need Elspeth to go to the flat to get anything. She had given her keys to her friend Heather. She seemed pleased with the nightdresses and the toiletries — that was that.

There was no one about to ask how she was getting on.

When she came out it had started to rain, and she had to wait quite a long time for a taxi.

It had been the most depressing day.

Rosemary's voice was faint but clear. 'I'm so sorry, ma,' she repeated. Elspeth said she did not know what to do — what should she do — was there anything she could do...'

Rosemary said there wasn't anything she could do. 'She's grown up, ma,' she said. 'She will do what she wants — she knows you are there if she needs you...'

'But her drinking,' said Elspeth. 'What about her drinking? She's making herself ill. And now — now — this awfulness...'

But Rosemary only repeated that there was nothing she could do. If Alison wanted help she knew where to come.

'Perhaps when she is better, she could come over here for a holiday,' she said. 'It would be a complete change. We've plenty of room, and it would be nice for the boys to meet their English aunt...'

'That is a wonderful idea,' said Elspeth. 'We will arrange it when she is better.'

She felt immensely relieved. Alison would talk about things with Rosemary — and all that wonderful Californian sunshine would do her the world of good. She might even meet someone nice... It was really good to speak to Rosemary — to hear her reassuring voice.

Maybe she could go herself sometime — see her grandsons.

Alistair was not going to be in for supper. He was going with a friend to see a possible flat. So no need to make small talk.

Paula had got some plaice fillets, and a cauliflower with parsley sauce, the cauliflower and parsley fresh that day from Berwick Street market.

She reluctantly said goodbye to Rosemary, and poured herself a large gin and vermouth.

The spring sunshine had disappeared, and in its place dark clouds and intermittent drizzle.

Alison had been discharged from hospital, which was a relief. Elspeth had not enjoyed her nightly visits. Alison had remained obstinately uncommunicative, and Elspeth could think of nothing to talk about.

Alison had reacted negatively to the suggestion that she should go to visit Rosemary in Los Angeles, saying she had no desire to go to America. Elspeth said how nice it would be for her to see Rosemary and the children — and all that lovely sunshine — but Alison had reiterated that she didn't want to go to Los Angeles, so that was that.

Elspeth was also anxious how she was going to explain her lengthy absence from work, but Alison said she had got a letter from her doctor to say that she had had an urgent gynaecological problem which required immediate surgery. She seemed quite calm about the whole thing, saying it was not necessary for Elspeth to come round to the flat — that she could manage perfectly well...

It was impossible. She wondered if she could talk to Sybil about it all, but it was not the sort of thing she felt she could talk about to anybody except Rosemary. Anyhow, it might not be very helpful — Sybil had always considered Alison to be rather airy fairy, as Nanny used to call her, little miss head in the clouds...

In any case, Sybil was very occupied with all the arrangements entailed in buying and selling flats. Everything seemed to be going really well. She had already had offers on the flat in West Hampstead, and had put down a deposit on the flat in Maida Vale.

She had had to sell another Stubbs. 'It's a relief really,' she said. 'Now I don't have to worry about where to hang them…'
The befringed lady was very pleased, and had invited Sybil round for a glass of sherry to discuss what, if anything, she might wish to buy — for instance, did she want the hideous mirrors in the hall — would she like to keep the antiquated stove in the kitchen or the unpleasantly zigzagged carpet in the dining room.
'Mrs Stein asked if I wanted the nasty red velvet three-piece suite,' said Sybil. 'I had to be quite firm — without being rude — really everything was unimaginably ugly. Perfectly ghastly…'

5

Really she should take the Elizabeth David back to the library. She was not in the mood for nostalgic escapism. It was almost painful to remember the abundance of fruit and vegetables — the glistening colours and soft fragrance — heaped on the stalls in the market in Nice…

She should take it back — other people would be waiting for it, when things had settled down — a rather dim prospect at the moment — she would order a copy from Hatchards.

Catherine saw Lady Thornton come through the glass doors of the library — so smart in a dark navy double-breasted coat and matching hat with a slight brim. She saw her pause as she passed the shabby man in his usual chair — today he had spread a newspaper on his knees and appeared to be reading it.

Catherine smiled and said 'Good morning…'

'Good morning,' said Elspeth. 'I see he is still here — poor man…'

Catherine said he was always there. What was there to say — each day she thought the same things — had he had anything to eat — did he have somewhere to go — and Miss Milburn eternally tut-tutting, frustrated in her inability to tell him to leave.

Elspeth said she had brought back the Elizabeth David.

She took off her gloves and placed them on the counter, whilst she took the book from her bag.

Catherine said she hoped she had enjoyed it.

'I'm afraid I have hardly looked at it,' said Elspeth. 'I haven't felt like it.' She paused. 'Too many memories of happier days…'

She stopped, feeling rather foolish. She was not in the habit of talking about her feelings.

Catherine took the book, and put it to one side.

'It's difficult,' she said. 'Sometimes it's difficult to pretend to be normal.'

Elspeth sat down on the chair that was placed by the counter.

'Yes,' she said. 'Sometimes it is very difficult... I do wish we could do something about him,' indicating the shabby man, who now looked as if he had gone to sleep. 'So like my husband's friend — but I suppose one cannot interfere.'
She sighed, and got up.
'I'll go and find another book — maybe a biography — something interesting...'

Miss Milburn emerged from her office carrying a pile of books which she placed carefully on the counter. One of the few good things that could be said in Miss Milburn's favour was her commitment to the library. She was enraged if books had been damaged in any way, and positively apoplectic if they had had been scribbled in.
She would really prefer it if nobody came to the library — handling the books, replacing them in the wrong place, disturbing the peace and quiet — sometimes even bringing drinks, which was strictly forbidden. She had had an unpleasant altercation with a young man who had a small bottle of something, which had become so heated that she had threatened to call the police. She considered the public to be an irritating intrusion.
Now she complained about Elsie. 'Sometimes I wonder if she even knows her alphabet,' she said. 'And her knowledge of authors is minimal...'

Catherine knew why she had recently been complaining more often about Elsie's inadequacies. It was true that she was not very efficient, made worse by Miss Milburn's constant criticism. It was because Catherine had asked for a day off in June. Harriet's parents were giving a garden party at the end of June, and she had been invited. It was on a Thursday so she had to have a day off. Of course she had not told Miss Milburn about the garden party. She had sighed. 'You know Catherine how awkward it is. Elsie is not really capable of taking charge. She's really quite hopeless...'
Catherine said she was very sorry, but that it was important.
Miss Milburn sighed again and reluctantly said she supposed it would be alright. So this morning she was complaining again about Elsie, just to emphasise how inconvenient it was for Catherine to have a day off. She looked around her, the pale, thin mouth in

disapproval, wincing visibly at the continued shabby presence of the shabby man, and viewing with suspicion a middle-aged woman with flowing grey hair seemingly engrossed in the Classics section. She noted Lady Thornton in the Biography section — obviously someone of class.

'What will someone like that think of us allowing that sort of vagrant to lounge about in here?'

'That is Lady Thornton,' said Catherine. 'She says he reminds her of a friend of her husband's...'

Miss Milburn made a kind of choking noise and stalked off back to her office, stopping to straighten some books in Science Fiction.

Elspeth had chosen the first volume of Osbert Sitwell's autobiography, *Left Hand, Right Hand.*

'My husband thought the Sitwells were extravagantly eccentric — but so very talented,' she said. And then not knowing quite why she added, 'My husband was killed in the war... in the desert.'

'Oh, I'm so sorry,' said Catherine. 'So very sorry. It was all so dreadful, so dreadful...' She stopped, uncertain how to continue.

This was the first time Elspeth had mentioned Jumbo's death to anyone — never able to articulate her grief. At the time it had seemed self-indulgent to grieve.

Then something deep inside her had quietly died — a silent crumbling of all things hoped for...

She picked up the Sitwell, put it in her bag, and pulled on her gloves. 'It should be quite entertaining,' she said. 'The whole family is rather bizarre...'

Catherine watched her go — glancing at the shabby man, who still seemed to be reading the paper, and out into the drab, grey morning.

She thought of her husband being killed in the desert. She too would never really know what happened — could only imagine the interminable stretches of sand — gritty wind stinging the eyes — the thirst — the blood drying brown in the white hot sun...

Desert — beaches — sand — contaminated by death — squandered lives.

There was not much difference between the beaches of Dunkirk and the empty expanse of the Sahara.

She thought she had seen Peter walking ahead of her in Baker Street — tall and fair, straight and slim — walking with an easy stride. Her throat had gone dry — constricted. She had tried to catch up before he crossed the street — trying to call out — halting, gasping and stupid.

She had gone into the little park off Paddington Street and sat down on a wooden seat under a comforting tree, curled with new green, to steady herself.
It had happened before — a glimpse of someone in a crowd — the heart-stopping moment, and then the weary loneliness of grief re-establishing itself.

She picked up the Elizabeth David and put it on the shelf behind her. She would have to check the waiting list to see who would have it next.

At last the sun was shining.
So far April had been a miserable month. A month of grey skies and drizzle, with intermittent, unconvincing sunshine.
Today would be a good day to go to the park in her lunch hour. She often just came back to the flat, if she had nothing special to do, and had tea and toast and listened to the wireless.

She made her sandwiches — marmite, lettuce and a bit of left-over cheese she had grated to make it go further.
It would be good to go to the park and sit by the canal — the daffodils were finished now, but there were always lots of other flowers and plants.

She had been feeling very unsettled since the visit to Bembridge to see the stone on her mother's grave — the smell of the black, acrid cloud still a pervading memory.
She had tried to put all the difficult, painful times behind her — to never think of her life in Bembridge — except for Miss Turnbull who

had been so kind and supportive. They still exchanged Christmas cards.

Miss Turnbull's mother had died a few years ago, just after the end of the war, and she now had more freedom. She went on holiday, visiting Scotland, Cornwall, the Lake District, sending Catherine cards of the places where she had stayed — 'Having a lovely time. Such beautiful views…'
Catherine was very pleased that she now had a life of her own — she certainly deserved it. She often thought of her in the library, and wondered if the Colonel still came every day.

Elspeth had a really good walk in the park.
She went almost as far as the Broadwalk, and then back through the Rose Garden.
It was such a nice day — so good to have a little sunshine — a chance to distance herself from the continuing worry of Alison, who steadfastly refused to meet her or let her go to the flat, in fact, to do anything at all for her. It was very worrying.
She had had a letter from Rosemary, who said she had written to Alison to try and persuade her to come to Los Angeles for a holiday, but had so far no reply.
'You should come, Ma,' she had said.
Elspeth would like to go to see Rosemary and the two little boys, but she felt so unsettled — Jumbo should be here — always so sensible — she missed him so much…
Also she had had a letter from Phipps and Sons in Borehampton, where her things were still in store, informing her that regrettably they had to increase their charges.
What on earth should she do about that?
Was she ever going to have a house again — did she want to have a house again — where would she want to live — did she want all the upheaval… Otherwise what was she going to do about her things still in store in Borehampton?

She saw Catherine sitting on a seat by the stream, which flowed among reeds under the little bridge. She was quite motionless.

Elspeth approached her, and greeted her warmly.
'Such a nice day,' she said. 'Can I join you?' and she sat down beside her on the seat. 'I've had a really nice walk.'

Catherine had not noticed Elspeth approaching — so smart, as usual, in a brown tweed coat and skirt, and jaunty brown hat.
She had been pondering how she was going to tell Miss Milburn that she wanted another day's holiday.
Edward wanted her to stay the night after the garden party — to have another day in Cambridge. She loved staying in his little house, and was not able to go very often. She was so looking forward to it — to have some time to wander about and relax. Of course there would be a fuss, but she would have to stand firm. If necessary go to Mr Simms for permission…
'It's good to see the sun,' she said, really taken aback that Lady Thornton wanted to come and sit with her.

There were small children playing by the stream, kicking a red ball and laughing.
'I've got two little grandsons,' said Elspeth. 'I've never seen them — my daughter married an American — a soldier — stationed in London during the war. They live in Los Angeles…'

Catherine said that must be really lovely — envisaging endless stretches of white sand — glistening sea — warmth — lots of fruit. She thought they must have lots of wonderful fruit in Los Angeles…

'I've never seen them,' said Elspeth, again watching the small boys with the red ball. 'I will go one day — travel is getting easier now.' She paused. 'I have another daughter who has not been very well… and there are other things to deal with here…'

Catherine wondered what Lady Thornton's daughters were like — hearty and horsey — dainty and waif-like — lazily posh, like some of the students at Cambridge — or earnestly academic…

Elspeth said she shouldn't be too long. 'Olive is getting the lunch — it is my housekeeper Paula's day off — she will have left some soup

— she makes wonderful soup — she is a wonderful cook. Poor Olive gets in a fuss over heating some soup — cooking is not her forte I'm afraid… It is very nice to see you — I expect I will see you soon in the library… I'm really enjoying the Sitwell…'

She got up then, straightened her skirt, and held out a gloved hand for Catherine to shake.

It was strange that she found it so easy to talk to this young woman. She was not in the habit of talking to people… She was, as Sybil would say, *très gentil*… which reminded her that tomorrow, she was to go to Harrods with Sybil, who had phoned excitedly to say that they had had a new delivery of furnishing fabrics from Italy, and she must come with her to see if there was anything suitable for her new flat. They could have lunch in the restaurant there.

Elspeth was pleased that everything seemed to be going so well for Sybil. She had managed to get the price of the flat reduced because of the poor state of both the bathroom and the kitchen — 'Rust marks in the bath,' Sybil had said, scandalised. 'And all the things in the kitchen will have to be thrown out — embedded in grease — disgusting — the cooker is positively dangerous…'

And she really must try to see Alison.

Alistair had found somewhere to live.

The two upper floors of a house in Spanish Place. A large and a small room and a kitchen on the lower floor and a large and a small room and a bathroom on the top floor.

Unfurnished.

Paula had made a wonderful casserole of pigeon with mushrooms.

'That's very good news,' said Elspeth, trying not to notice Olive had managed to drip sauce on the white damask cloth.

Alistair looked exhausted. When he was tired or stressed his scars seemed more prominent — the lurid gash slicing down the side of his face, an angry purple pathway — the bones of his hand more fragile, with the edges of the scar unevenly cutting it in two.

'Well,' said Elspeth, forcing herself to be cheerful, 'it sounds extremely nice.' Suddenly she wanted to scream — to stop being polite, and carrying on as if nothing had happened.

'We should have a toast', she said. 'Pass the wine please, Olive…', mentally adding, and don't spill it on the cloth. 'You'll always be welcome to come and enjoy some of Paula's delicious cooking…'

She did not sleep well — thinking — thoughts were not a good idea, did not promote sleep — finally dropping off near dawn.
However, during her sleepless hours she had had a good idea.
She would offer Alistair some of the remaining furniture in storage with Phipps and Sons in Borehampton.
She had not studied the inventory for some time, not since Alison had taken some things for her flat. She had managed to get a decent bed and a small sofa that had been in the morning room — quite a lot of things — occasional tables, a table and chairs that had been in the small sitting room, a bookcase, and the dressing table from Alison's room. Most of the larger furniture and the valuable things had been in the warehouse in the City which had been bombed.
After breakfast she took the inventory out of her desk, and sat down in her chair by the window, where she could watch the people in the street below hurrying and jostling.
It was always depressing to see pages and pages of things crossed out with heavy black lines.
Really nothing had survived amongst the things that had been in the warehouse in the City.
Jumbo had made some kind of arrangement with the authorities in charge of the requisition over all the furniture in the servants' quarters, which had been left in the house — no doubt all the beds would have been very useful, apart from all the other things.
As she turned to the page headed Phipps and Sons, she noticed at the bottom of the last page 'Black Bechstein 6ft Grand Piano' scored through with black ink.

Jumbo had thought it would be nice to have a piano.
It would be good for the girls to learn to play the piano. Neither she nor Jumbo played any musical instrument — neither of them was the slightest bit musical.
Miss Carstairs had come every Thursday afternoon — with smart bobbed hair and knife-pleated skirts, in her sporty little car. She had done her best but neither of the girls had shown any aptitude at all — Rosemary plodding dutifully through her pieces, oblivious of any

wrong notes, Alison tearfully resentful. They had hoped she might enjoy it — she loved her dancing class.

Jumbo's nephew, Richard, who visited occasionally, played very well. He knew all the popular dance tunes. It was always jolly when he came. Such a nice boy with thick fair curly hair.
He joined the Navy at the beginning of the war — his ship was torpedoed — there were no survivors.

Sometimes it was hard to cope with the weight of all the memories. She was never sure whether Jumbo had ever received the news of the young man's death…

She must pull herself together. She was supposed to be looking for possible furniture for Alistair's flat.

There were a great many beds — they had had a great many beds — they had had a great many bedrooms — there were quite a lot of bedside tables, and several chests of drawers of different sizes…

She would make a list — or maybe just let Alistair have a look and see what might be useful.

Sybil stayed to supper. Paula was making a risotto — she made a wonderful risotto with kidneys and mushrooms. She had been to see her Italian friends in Soho, bringing back risotto rice and a large piece of parmesan.

Elspeth had met Sybil at Harrods for lunch.
It was not a success. The choice on the menus in restaurants was still very limited, and having noticed the thin grey slices of meat that were served to a neighbouring table, decided against the roast beef, and chose the savoury flan. It was actually quite nasty. Sybil had a mouthful and immediately called the waitress — a dejected young woman with a crumpled apron — and ordered a double martini.

'What do you suppose these green things are,' she said, poking at the pastry with her fork.

Elspeth said she thought they were supposed to be asparagus. She took a long drink of water. 'This pastry is really rather dreadful...'
'Sort of hard and soggy at the same time,' said Sybil. 'Not very nice — and the asparagus, or whatever it is — has to be tinned...'

They did not attempt a dessert, finishing with a rather bitter coffee. 'You would think they could at least serve decent coffee,' said Sybil. 'Do you think they sell this sort of horrible coffee in their world-famous grocery department?'

The furnishing fabrics were not a success either.
Sybil did not like the designs or the colours — complaining about the quality — not what she was used to.

When they came out it was raining, and they had a long wait for a taxi.

Olive made tea — managing as usual to slop it on the lace-edged tray cloth — and they sat and talked — Olive tactfully excusing herself to go to her room.

The work on Sybil's new flat was going well. It was almost ready for her to move into. The sale of the flat in West Hampstead was completed, and the young couple who had bought it, both civil servants, were anxious to move in as soon as possible. Sybil said the young woman's hair was a fright — cheap hairslides — uncombed — but they seemed very pleasant.
'What I need,' said Sybil, 'is a proper servant. Somebody who can cook, somebody who understands bed linen, somebody like Thompson or your Martha...'
Elspeth said she didn't think there were people like Thompson or Martha anymore — and then remembered guiltily that she had not asked Martha if there was anything she would like from the things still in store in Borehampton. It was nearly all the furniture, and she really didn't think that Martha would want any furniture. She had liked the Dresden lady with a beribboned bonnet — pretty things — Elspeth had never really cared for them. She would have given them to Martha when they left the house, but who was to know

what was going to happen. They had been packed up with all the many ornaments and precious objects which had been destroyed in the bombing.

Nobody could have known.

She always sent her a cheque at Christmas. Perhaps she would send her a note if she was going back to look at things with Alistair.

'They are nearly all foreign,' said Sybil. 'I have to have someone who speaks English — and someone who can cook. Or someone incredible like your Paula...'

'Perhaps Paula might know someone,' said Elspeth. 'She has a lot of Italian friends...'

'What a wonderful idea,' said Sybil. 'Absolutely wonderful... We should have thought of that before...'

Alistair came in quite early. He looked exhausted. Elspeth said he must join them for a quick drink before supper — 'Paula has made delicious cheese straws...' — and then she could suggest the furniture.

Alistair was genuinely surprised and pleased by Elspeth's proposal. Things were difficult to find, not very nice and very expensive. He said of course he would pay for whatever he took, but Elspeth waved that aside. 'I am never going to need them again,' she said. 'And the more things I have in store the more I have to pay. I have been wondering what on earth to do about it. It would be pleasing to know that some of the things are being useful... We will have to arrange to go down there so that you can choose what you would like...'

Olive had quietly joined them, perching unobtrusively on a chair by the door.

'Don't hover, Olive,' said Elspeth. 'Come over here and pour yourself a sherry — and have some of Paula's delicious cheese straws, before they have all gone...'

It was a most festive meal. Alistair was more relaxed than Elspeth had ever seen him. Sybil, who by this time was quite tipsy, was even more voluble than usual, telling Alistair about the dish-rag quality

of the curtain material in Harrods — 'So disappointing' — and bemoaning the general lowering of standards of everything since the war.
Even Olive managed not to spill anything and had a second helping of Paula's wonderful risotto.

*   *   *

Miss Parker had come to collect the biography of Garibaldi she had ordered. As she was enthusiastically telling Catherine that he had fought in South America, Uruguay, Brazil, Catherine saw the shabby man suddenly sit stiffly upright, throwing out an arm, and collapsing forward in the chair. Cutting Miss Parker short, she lifted the flap of the counter and rushed to his side. He had slumped forward, half in and half out of the chair. He was a terrible colour — a dirty grey — and didn't seem to be breathing.
As she tried to move him, she was aware of a young man in a dark blue gaberdine raincoat kneeling beside her, gently easing him onto the floor.
'Something to put under his head,' he said.
There were no cushions — plenty of chairs and tables, but no cushions. A small group of people had gathered — other people in the library. Somebody offered a rolled up jacket, someone else a folded shopping bag...
Miss Milburn appeared from her office. 'I knew something like this would happen,' she said accusingly, glaring at Catherine. The young man said 'Call 999 — get an ambulance...' He was doing artificial respiration, rhythmically working on the shabby man's chest. Catherine got up and hurried to the phone, pressing the number for an outside line, and dialling 999. She felt very dizzy and weak. 'It's coming,' she said, as she knelt beside the young man. He had dark hair — a lock had fallen over his forehead — a livid scar running down the side of his face.

In her mind the images clashed. He must have been wounded in the war. Everything came back to the war — the shabby man — this young man's face — and she was back in the library in Bembridge as the black cloud of acrid smoke blotted out the sun, and the books tumbled from the shelves, and then the terrible silence as the town held its breath before the sirens — the clanging fire engines — the frantic ambulances.

She sat down heavily on one of the chairs and closed her eyes.

She was dimly aware of Miss Milburn on the interphone, shrilly summoning Elsie to come immediately, and bring a glass of water, and then, in her best modulated tones, asking Mr Simms if he could come straight away as there was an emergency.

The ambulance men had arrived. One of them was speaking to the young man in the raincoat.

Elsie appeared with a glass of water.

Catherine wondered how she always managed to look so untidy. She was wearing a perfectly proper skirt and blouse and a sensible cardigan, but she still managed to look a mess.

She drank some of the water, assuring Elsie that she was alright.

'Just a bit dizzy…'

Mr Simms arrived precipitously, striding stork-like across the library to join the little group surrounding the shabby man's inert body. The ambulance men had put a rolled up blanket under his head, and one of them was fixing on an oxygen mask. The other one, who had been talking to the young man in the raincoat, turned to speak to Mr Simms.

Elsie, who was standing stiffly by Catherine's side, said, 'He looks really bad — oh dear,' her small, sallow face puckered with concern. Catherine patted her arm. 'They'll know what to do,' she said, trying to sound reassuring, and started to get up, but her legs gave way, and she sat down again. She felt sick, and drank some more water.

They were lifting the shabby man onto a stretcher — the little crowd made way for them — somebody holding the doors open — and then Mr Simms and the young man started coming towards her.

This time she did manage to stand up, holding firmly to the side of the chair.

'Don't get up Catherine,' said Mr Simms. 'I think it best if you took the rest of the day off — Elsie, go and get Miss Bradley's things —

and I'll have a word with Miss Milburn...'
Miss Milburn was at the counter stamping Miss Parker's biography
of Garibaldi. She was gesticulating, but Miss Milburn merely
nodded dismissively.
'I'm sure I shall be alright in a minute,' she said.
'No — no,' said Mr Simms. 'Go home and have a rest. This nice
young man has offered to go with you...'
Catherine looked at the young man. He had a good face — but tired
and tense. He smiled, and the tension eased.
'Mr Simms says you live very near here,' he said — and she had a
sudden feeling she wanted to put her arms round him, and bury her
head against him, and weep all the tears she had never wept...
'It's very kind of you,' she said. 'I'm sure I shall be perfectly alright...'
'Nonsense,' said Mr Simms. 'Mr — er...'
'Sinclair,' said the young man. 'Alistair Sinclair...'
'Yes — yes,' said Mr Simms. 'Mr Sinclair will make sure you get
home safely. I'll go and speak to Miss Milburn...'
Alistair stood quietly and looked at her. 'I was about to join the
library,' he said. 'I'll go and fill in the form and have a look around...'

He suggested taking a taxi, but Catherine said it was only a short
walk.
He took her arm in a comforting grasp — she was still very shaky —
and they went out carefully into the street.
He said perhaps they could stop somewhere for a cup of tea.

They went into the little Italian café where Catherine sometimes
came in the evening for a spaghetti Bolognese — between the
newsagent and the laundry where she took her sheets and towels
once a week.

They sat opposite each other at a table by the window.
Catherine put a lot of sugar in her tea — cafés had a special
allocation of sugar — she felt she really needed a lot of sugar.
She stared at her cup — disconcerted — very conscious of Alistair's
presence. She noticed the dreadful, jagged scar on his hand.
'Did you know him?' he asked.
She shook her head numbly. She wanted to say just another casualty

— we are all casualties — all wounded — but she just said 'He was so alone. He came every day. So alone…'
He saw her to the door of the flats — hoping she got a good rest — hesitating — waiting until she was safely inside before walking away.

*   *   *

Olive came in, more flustered than usual — wearing that dreadful hat — green felt — misshapen. Surely she could buy herself a new hat — she had a good salary, and things were much easier to find now — more choice. Anything would be better than her present hat.

She had gone to the library after lunch — corned beef rissoles — to get another Agatha Christie. She had a great liking for detective stories, and Elspeth had asked her to go down to the Classic Cinema and find out what times they would be showing *Frenchman's Creek*, which she fancied going to see. She was trying to make an effort to do things. She had always enjoyed reading Daphne du Maurier. She had particularly enjoyed the film of *Jamaica Inn*, which she had seen with Jumbo just before the war took hold — a blackout curtain on life.

'That poor man has been taken ill.' Olive was breathless with concern. 'This morning — he collapsed — they had to call an ambulance. The young woman, I think it's Elsie — who never knows where anything is, was there. Catherine had been sent home — apparently she fainted…'

Elspeth folded the *Daily Telegraph* which she was making a pretence of reading, and placed it carefully on the table by her chair. She felt suddenly nauseous. 'Is she alright?' she said. 'Is she alright?'
'A nice young man took Catherine home,' said Olive. 'I don't know about the poor man — Elsie wasn't very clear, kept going on about oxygen masks…' She sat down without taking off her coat. 'I do hope he will be alright — poor man…'
Elspeth said they should have tea early. 'Go and tell Paula,' she said sharply. 'We'll have it now…' She could not stand dubious sentimentality — the pricking excitement at bad news.

Afterwards she went to rest.

Maybe if she closed her eyes she could control the haphazard fragments of memory, jagged splinters, like sharp shards of broken glass.

She saw the shabby man, so like Jumbo's friend Montague Selbourne — his split shoes and stained coat — Catherine, thin, pale face taut with anxiety — Jumbo hailing a taxi after seeing *Jamaica Inn* — dinner at Pruniers — dover sole — a single white rose in the vase on the white tablecloth. Alison — cheesey-faced in the iron-framed hospital bed with a drip in her arm — the staircase of her old home smashed — the broken bannisters leaning drunkenly — obscene graffiti on the walls — Martha holding the dreadful telegram — the brown teapot on the kitchen table...

It was better to have her eyes open.

She should concentrate on things that were relevant now.

She had spoken to Paula about finding someone for Sybil. 'She would not have to live in,' she said. 'But there is a very nice room — and a bathroom, of course...'

Paula had remained impassive — only nodding slightly, and saying she would see. Elspeth had never seen Paula smile. She remained coolly aloof, maintaining a strict distance. She had softened slightly towards Alistair, even putting a tin of her special biscuits by his bed, without relaxing her stern demeanour.

Also there was Alison.

She had finally rung her office — the superior woman who answered said that Miss Thornton was on holiday, without divulging any further information. Of course she had every right to go on holiday. After all she was a grown up, independent woman. All the same, it would have been nice to be informed. She just hoped it was true...

Olive and Alistair were standing by the window — they turned as she came in.

Olive, her face unattractively shiny — why on earth didn't she use a little face powder? And so drab in the unbecoming beige twinset — Alistair really too thin, and so pale...

Olive said, 'It was Alistair — in the library — Alistair took Catherine home...'

'I was on my way to the estate agents,' said Alistair, 'and I thought I would go in and join the library. I arrived just as the poor man collapsed.'
'Do you know who he is?' said Elspeth. 'And Catherine?' She felt unaccountably relieved that Alistair had been there. There was a certain quiet strength about the young man that was very steadying.

He said he didn't know if the shabby man was alright. 'It looked rather bad.'
Catherine had been very shaken. Her boss, Mr Simms, had insisted she went home to rest. 'He seemed very decent, said he would phone the hospital later to find out about the man. It seemed he was there a lot...'
'He was always there,' said Olive. 'Poor man...'
'Get Alistair a whisky, Olive,' said Elspeth, stopping her before she could start sentimentalising. 'And I'll have my usual — and sherry for yourself of course...'
She didn't want to think about the shabby man. Maybe he had relatives somewhere — hopefully — and she would go herself and speak to Catherine. It would be nice to invite her to tea — she must have time off sometime.

Over supper — fillets of lemon sole, mashed potato and frozen peas — after her initial reluctance to use frozen peas, Paula had decided they were an excellent idea. Peas all year round — what could be better? — baked apples stuffed with precious scarce sultanas. They discussed Alistair's flat and the furniture.

*   *   *

The Major said, 'Good morning, dear lady.'
He unbuttoned his gloves, carefully removing them and tucking them into his coat pockets. 'So pleased you're back...'
He made it sound as if she had been away for weeks instead of one afternoon. 'Your colleague was not able to be of much help — I was enquiring about a possible biography of Jan Masaryk — I don't believe she knew who I was talking about...'

Catherine said she was sorry about that, and that she didn't think there was one at the moment, but that she would make enquiries.

'She said you were not well,' he added.

Catherine said she had felt rather dizzy, but that she was quite alright now — remembering with a sudden surge of warmth the comforting support of Alistair's hand on her arm.

'I understand there was quite a drama here,' said the Major. 'Your permanent visitor — a crisis...?'

'Yes,' she said. 'I'm afraid he was taken ill and we had to call an ambulance...'

Mr Simms had been down to tell her that he had finally managed to get a very small amount of information from the hospital. The shabby man's name was Thomas Gardner, and he was still in intensive care. Mr Simms said they had been very reluctant to tell him anything at all — not family members. He'd try again later.

The Major said he would go and look for something else. 'Perhaps a biography of Jan Smuts — a remarkable man...', and with a small bow, made his way to the Biography section.

And then there was Olive — breathless — her green felt hat askew.

'Lady Thornton is really sorry not to have been able to come herself,' she said. 'We were so sorry to hear about...' She glanced briefly at where the shabby man had always sat. 'Poor unfortunate man.' Then she explained about Alistair. 'Such a nice young man — did something terribly secret in the war...' Her voice trailed off.

Catherine felt her throat constrict — seeing the livid scars on his face and hand. She could not contemplate it, what he must have suffered. 'He was very helpful,' she said. 'And very kind.'

It was quite a shock to find out he was staying with Lady Thornton. It made her feel rather foolish. Obviously he was not going to be interested in her. She had hoped she would see him again, that he might come into the library...

Olive said she'd just go and find another Agatha Christie whilst she was there. ' I prefer the ones with Miss Marple.'

'Oh yes,' said Catherine. 'They are most entertaining...'

It had been a silly thought — that she might see him again — that she might get to know him — that he might like to see her again. Automatically she began to sort out the library cards, smiling vaguely at a young woman with untidy red hair and a red jacket, who asked where she could find Rosamund Lehman's *Invitation to the Waltz*, that a friend had recommended.

6

Elspeth made an appointment to see Dr Myers. They had always had Dr Hartmann, but he had retired. In the country they had had the local doctor, Dr Barnes. A large, bluff man with large square hands and a transparently fake, jovial manner. Slightly wheezy and flushed, Jumbo said he drank. However, he had been perfectly adequate for run of the mill ailments. For anything of a more serious nature they went to Dr Hartmann.

She felt quite relieved that he had retired. It would have been rather embarrassing discussing Alison with him. He had known her since she was a small child. She had always gone with Nanny. She made such a fuss, and Nanny had been so good at managing her.

She had been very surprised to receive a telephone call from Alison's friend Heather. At first she had no idea who it was — hesitant and apologetic — so sorry to bother her.
It seemed that she and Alison had had a few days' holiday in Brighton — 'Alison had really not been at all well'. She had to go to hospital. There was a pause.
She had been drinking, thought Elspeth. She had had too much to drink. She waited for Heather to continue. 'The thing is, I think she needs some special help.' There was another pause. 'She has been really unwell recently…'

Elspeth said she was so difficult to get in touch with. 'I never seem able to speak to her — and she never wants to come to the flat.'
Heather said she would try and persuade her to get in touch. Or perhaps they could meet on neutral ground. 'We often go to the Dorchester after work. It is very relaxing there. They have a marvellously comfortable lounge…'

Elspeth was slightly taken aback at Alison and her friend frequenting the Dorchester — unescorted. Unescorted young women would be regarded with suspicion in such an establishment — the staff on the look out for any of the smart 'ladies' who patrolled the pavements of Park Lane. Perhaps they were escorted. What about Alison's man? She felt it would not be suitable to question Heather about him.

It was agreed that they should meet in the lounge of the Dorchester on Thursday evening, at about 6 o'clock, and try and persuade Alison to agree to some sort of treatment.

The lounge certainly was very comfortable. Deep armchairs, tall vases of flowers, a young man in evening dress unobtrusively playing a white grand piano, screened by luxuriant greenery.
Elspeth vaguely recognised the music he was playing — she wasn't very good on music, it all sounded much the same, but this music was very familiar — and then she remembered it was Ivor Novello, from a musical before the war. Something rather silly with elaborate glitzy costumes and a hopelessly improbable story... *Glamorous Night*. Very popular at the time. Jumbo had loved it — had even bought gramophone records of all the songs. The radiogram had a particular smell when you opened the lid — a woody, fusty smell — the records plopping down one by one, with a scrapy thud as the needle arm swung over. There was certainly a black cross next to that. It was good to hear the tunes again. She seemed to remember she had worn a midnight blue dress and diamond necklace.

Heather and Alison were almost on time.
Elspeth had never met Heather. Alison never introduced her friends. She was about the same height as Alison — pleasant faced, rather short in the leg, smartly dressed in a light grey coat and skirt with medium heeled black shoes. She was holding Alison's arm as she teetered uncertainly in very high heels on her twig-like legs. She was wearing a misshapen tweed coat with the hem hanging down one side, her fine fair hair straggled limply on the collar. Elspeth was shocked. Surely she did not go to work like that — she must have better clothes...

Making an effort to smile, she got up to greet them, shaking Heather's hand, making polite exchanges.

A waiter appeared. Alison ordered a bottle of white wine. Heather smiled and nodded. 'That would be nice…' Elspeth asked for a dry sherry. 'And a plate of sandwiches.' She wasn't sure what sort of sandwiches you got nowadays. She had not been in a place like this for years — had no idea how rationing affected them.

Conversation was slow. She asked about their holiday. Heather said it had been very windy — it always seemed to windy in Brighton — and Elspeth said yes, she seemed to remember Brighton was always windy. Alison said nothing, waiting impatiently for the waiter to bring the wine. Another waiter came with an oval platter of sandwiches, small plates, proper napkins. The sandwiches looked very good — chopped chicken and mayonnaise, smoked salmon, egg and cress, smoked cod's roe — appetisingly arranged with sprigs of water cress.

The young man at the piano was now playing a selection of other familiar tunes. Heather said she loved the music — so relaxing. Elspeth agreed. Alison said nothing, and poured herself another glass of wine. Elspeth said 'Do have something to eat, dear — these sandwiches are really delicious…' Heather said she really ought to try them. She pushed the platter towards Alison, who carefully picked one and put it on her plate.

It was a slow, laborious meeting. Alison didn't object when they suggested she needed a really proper rest — somewhere nice — in the country perhaps. She drank some more wine and nibbled at the sandwich. Heather encouraged her to have another. 'Try the cod's roe,' she said. 'It's really good…'

Elspeth's appointment with Dr Myers was at 11 o'clock.
She had got there early.
The waiting room was light and airy, as she remembered, but had been completely redecorated. The chairs were rather uncomfortable, shiny white leather — the carpet an unfortunate shade of green with black squiggles. She could almost hear Sybil saying, 'Quite dreadful, darling. Quite dreadful. Makes one feel quite bilious…'

It would be good to be able to confide in someone about Alison, but there really was not anybody. She had already discounted Sybil. Rosemary was too far away.

How could she tell anyone about Alison's drinking — she did not even like to admit it to herself. And then the dreadful humiliation of the abortion. That was another thing that could never be discussed with anyone.

Of course Olive knew, but it had never been mentioned since the awful night they had had to go to the hospital. And Olive was very discreet. There was a rather large cubist painting on the wall opposite — thick black and orange zig-zags — not very soothing. The languid receptionist sat at an imposing desk, pretending to be busy, sorting out papers with long scarlet nails.

Dr Myers did not keep her waiting. On the dot of eleven he came out of his consulting room, holding the door open for a short, dumpy woman in a mink coat.

He was a small, wiry, dapper man, with shiny black hair — looking ridiculously young. However, he was easy to talk to, to explain about Alison.

He said it would really be better if she came herself, to ascertain the state of her health, but Elspeth said that was out of the question. 'She absolutely refuses to come herself,' she said. So Dr Myers gave her a list of names and addresses of several reputable clinics in easy reach of London, and said to please call on him if he could be of any assistance.

Elspeth walked home from Harley Street, cutting through into Marylebone High Street, vaguely looking at the shops. She stopped in front of a rather nice dress shop. There were some very pleasant dresses in the window — florals in pinks and mauves with little matching jackets — but she wasn't really looking at the clothes.

She remembered a sobbing Alison bursting into the morning room where she and Jumbo were having their breakfast, closely followed by Nanny and a resigned looking Rosemary.

Nanny said, 'She won't go to school. She says she is feeling sick and has a stomach ache.' Jumbo pushed aside his plate of eggs and bacon to ask her what was the matter, patting the chair beside him. 'Come and talk about it,' he had said.

Rosemary had said, 'she doesn't want to go swimming. It's swimming today. She doesn't want to go swimming...' And Jumbo had talked quietly to Alison to find out why she didn't want to go swimming. The teacher shouted. She wasn't any good at swimming. She didn't like swallowing the water. The sobs gradually subsided.

'Miss Mills is a bit fierce,' Rosemary had said. 'All the gym teachers are a bit fierce...'

'I won't jump in,' Alison had said. 'I won't jump in,' and had started crying again.

Elspeth couldn't remember exactly how it was resolved, but somehow it was smoothed out.

She was sure that Alison would not have got herself in such a mess today if Jumbo had not been killed.

She must try and be positive.

She would phone the clinics — arrange appointments — as soon as she got home.

She sat at her precious walnut desk — such a perfect size — elegantly unobtrusive.

What a good thing she had insisted on having it in the flat. Jumbo had wanted to put it in store. He hadn't thought she would really use it. After all, they were not expecting her to be staying in London very long. 'We'll probably be home by Christmas. Easier to keep things together.'

How wrong they were. How very wrong.

Now it would just be another one of the things marked with a black cross... Better not to think about it — much better not to think about it.

She spread the list in front of her and started to telephone the clinics. They were all at a reasonable distance from London — St Albans, Hertford, High Wycombe — which was a bit further — Amersham, Aylesbury and Stanmore — which was almost too near. Alison might be tempted to leave and get on the Underground.

She tried to feel hopeful that at last this would really help Alison. She hadn't managed to speak to her since they had met at the Dorchester. She never seemed to be at home. And what had happened about this man — this married man? Rosemary had been witheringly critical. 'His wife has probably found out,' she had said. 'So he has dropped Alison like a hot stone…'
If only she could talk to her about it. She sighed inwardly.
Lately she had been doing a lot of inward sighing.
She started to make the telephone calls.
They all sounded pleasant and efficient, and would send brochures and information.

She had just put the list away in the desk drawer when Sybil phoned, indignant that the telephone had been engaged for so long.
She was coming straight over.
She had just received samples of curtain material from Liberty's — she had given up on Harrods — most disappointing — miserable selection.
'There are at least two which I really like.'

The new flat was almost ready. Completely redecorated. A new bathroom and kitchen had been installed. Her wonderfully comfortable, capacious sofa and armchairs taken out of storage and re-covered. She had been able to take most of her things out of storage. The flower-painted dressing table and chest of drawers, the shell-shaped headboard for the bed. She had bought a new bed from Heals. The old one had been damaged. The lavender silk sofa and chairs fitted easily into her bedroom and she had found a lovely curtain material — creamy silk with a pattern of mauve irises. She was still trying to find something suitable for the other rooms. There were the Chinese porcelain table lamps, the Crown Derby dinner service, highly polished dining table, chairs, a great deal of other china and expensive crystal glasses in all shapes and sizes.
So many things emerging from crates and packing.

Sybil was in raptures. She had sold another couple of pictures — one of the hunt in full gallop, which had fetched quite a lot, the other a conventional depiction of snow-covered mountains, which Sybil had

never liked. She said the mountains looked unreal, and the sky was a strange colour. So everything was going very well.
However it did not prevent her from appearing at mealtimes, at very short notice.

Elspeth was not pleased. Paula might not have enough for an extra person.
Olive would be back soon.
She had gone to the hairdressers — would come in with her hair pressed in flat waves — her forehead red-rimmed from the edge of the hot hairdryer — breathlessly anxious not to be late for lunch.
It was most inconsiderate of Sybil.
She rang the bell for Paula.
After a lengthy pause she appeared in the doorway, wiping her hands on her apron.
Elspeth said that Signora Anstruther was on her way. Could she manage an extra person for lunch? She was sorry it was such short notice.
Paula shrugged. An eloquent shrug, as if to say, 'What, again!' and said she would see, and then as she turned to go she said she thought she had found someone for the Signora.
'Oh Paula,' said Elspeth, 'how perfectly splendid!'

It seemed this friend, Francesca, was not happy with the family she was working for — non felice — molto dificile — Signora dificile — Signor dificile — tutta la famiglia dificile — the children. She shuddered. 'I think she would like the Signora.'
'Oh splendid,' said Elspeth. 'That is good news.'

Olive was almost late — flustered and apologetic. There had been so many people in the chemist.

Elspeth had given her a list — toothpaste, Elastoplast, aspirin, and a box of Elizabeth Arden's Blue Grass bath soap. Very expensive, but a long awaited indulgence. Another huge step forward. The end of soap rationing. At last one did not have to be careful not to use too much washing one's hands — or bathing — squashing odd little bits into a ball to make it go further.

Years ago it would have been difficult to imagine having to accept so many privations in one's life — to be overcome with delight at the sight of a box of soap.
Elspeth's irritation at Olive's effusive apologies was almost completely dispelled by the sight of the once familiar pale blue-green box of bath soap.
She cut her short. 'You are not late, Olive,' she said. 'In any case we have to wait for Mrs Anstruther, who has just telephoned to say she is on her way.'

Sybil arrived in her usual flurry of scarves and bags, wearing a really attractive perky purple hat and camelhair coat.
'Darling, I'm gasping,' she said, removing the perky hat, smoothing her hair, and dropping the bags on the nearest chair.
Elspeth wanted to say that she was too late to have a pre-lunch drink — that lunch was already on the table.
Elspeth did not serve wine at lunchtime unless it was a special occasion. However, as a good hostess she told Olive to get Mrs Anstruther a gin and vermouth — if Sybil didn't mind bringing it into the dining room.

Paula had produced a really nice meal. A salad of crisp cos lettuce sprinkled with chopped hard-boiled egg, a glass bowl of sliced beetroot, a platter with two different kinds of salami, and a substantial piece of Dolcelatte, thanks to Paula's wonderful Italian friends, and a crusty loaf of proper bread — how good it was to have proper bread again after the nasty grey stuff they had had to put up with through the interminable war.

She wanted to tell Sybil about Paula's friend Francesca, who sounded very promising, but Sybil was babbling on about the difficulty of getting anything done, and the workmen kept failing to turn up — so inconvenient…

So it was not until they had finished, and Paula brought the coffee into the drawing room — with a plate of her special thin biscuits — that she was able to say something.
'Thank you, Paula,' she said. 'I was just about to tell Mrs Anstruther

about your friend Francesca. Sybil, Paula thinks her friend Francesca might be someone who would come and work for you.'

Sybil was delighted. She threw her arms dramatically in the air. 'Paula, you are an angel. And the best cook in the world.'

'I'm sure if you think she would be alright — she must be alright…' Paula almost smiled.

It was decided she should speak to Francesca and find out when she would be able to meet Sybil at the new flat.

It was most satisfactory.

Sybil was so pleased she almost forgot about the curtain material.

Elspeth asked Olive to find Mrs Anstruther an ashtray (before she started dropping ash everywhere).

Sybil took the samples out of the smart Liberty bag and spread them out on the coffee table.

Elspeth was not at all sure.

She did not think either of the ones Sybil liked — a heavy plum red damask and a cerise and cream striped satin — would be suitable. She had had brocade and velvet curtains in the spacious rooms of her beautiful house in Eaton Square, but similar curtains would completely overwhelm the rooms in her new flat.

'I think they are rather too heavy,' she said. 'You really need something lighter. Maybe a plain linen…'

She suddenly realised that her own curtains were hopelessly dingy and out of date. It had been impossible to renew anything during the war. She had simply put it out of her mind.

Perhaps she should think about getting something new.

Perhaps she should get some plain linen curtains.

Sybil left in a flurry of scarves, gathering up the scattered samples — there had been several others — one with dizzying red zigzags, one with large red roses, and a few more which were totally unmemorable. She had to go to her flat in West Hampstead — she still hadn't moved out properly — because the young couple who were buying it were coming to measure things. They were getting more and more impatient to move in, so they would be very pleased to hear that at last she would be moving out.

'Very pleasant, but no taste whatsoever,' she said, adjusting her perky hat in front of the hall mirror. 'She wears the most dreadful clothes and those awful hair slides. No grown-up woman wears hair slides. And they want maroon carpets. Maroon. Right through the flat. How could anyone live with maroon carpets...?'

Elspeth felt completely drained.

She asked Olive to make some tea, and said she was going to lie down.

There were so many things to think about.

She had got to try and get in touch with Alison. She wished she was easier. She never seemed to be in, and she hesitated to phone her office. She didn't even know if she was still going to work.

She had to telephone Heather to tell her what she was doing. Maybe she could tell her how Alison was getting on.

She should think about arranging to go with Alistair to Borehampton for him to choose some furniture.

So many things.

Maybe if and when Alison was comfortably settled in a clinic she could go and stay with Tamarind for a week or so — such lovely countryside. She had not seen her for such a long time...

But Alison might change her mind. Refuse to go after all.

She remembered her refusing to get in the car and go and have tea with the Robertson's children. Perfectly agreeable people, with a lovely garden.

Nanny had said, 'Now, now Alison. Don't be silly. You know you'll enjoy it when you get there...' And Alison, sobbing, 'I won't go. I hate them. Dorothy pinches...' And Rosemary saying, 'Oh come on, Alison. We can play croquet. And they always have egg sandwiches and chocolate cake for tea...'

She had finally got into the car — with much sniffing — and had sulked all the way.

'Highly strung.'

Jumbo had been better at coping with her. Always so calm and reasonable. Better not to think about that either.

Olive brought the tea on a little tray. She had managed as usual to spill some on the tray cloth, apologising. 'I'm afraid I filled the teapot too full.'

'Oh never mind,' Elspeth said in exasperation. Why did she always have to spill something? 'Just put it down...'

Olive put it down on the bedside table. 'I think I will go to the library,' she said. Perhaps there would be some news about the poor man, and she thought she might try something by Nevil Shute. She had heard his books were very good.

Elspeth said, 'Yes — yes — ask about the poor man.' She saw him again in the shabby corduroys and broken shoes — his resemblance to Montagu Selbourne — they had had box hedges — she loved the smell of box hedges. 'And see if the girl, Catherine, is alright...'

She wished Olive would hurry up and go.
She was too tired.
Later she would telephone Alison.
Later she would telephone Heather.

*   *   *

She settled herself comfortably in the armchair by the window. She had poured herself a dry sherry, and put it on the table by her side next to the telephone.

There was no reply from Alison. There was never any reply. She really did not know what to do.
Heather answered fairly quickly.
Elspeth said she was telephoning to tell her what progress she had made finding a clinic for Alison. There was a long pause, and then Heather said, 'Alison said she would tell you...'

Elspeth felt herself stiffen — involuntarily holding her breath. What now? What was Alison going to tell her? 'I'm so sorry,' said Heather. 'I really thought she had told you. She has lost her job. She's been given a month's notice...'
Now she really felt unable to breathe — Heather's voice a distant murmur. She made a big effort to remain calm — to sound calm.

· 'Could you repeat that?' she said. 'I did not really hear you properly.'
Heather said Alison had been warned several times about her
lateness, and for appearing to be inebriated at work. And then she
had come in after lunch one day last week completely...' Heather
searched for polite words to describe it. 'Well, really drunk. And
then she was sick and passed out.' She paused, and then continued.
One of the other secretaries had revived her and cleaned her up, and
then they had put her in the sick room until she was fit to go home,
and the next morning the Head of Personnel had called her in and
said she was very sorry but they had to give her a month's notice, and
not to bother to come in again. Her voice trailed off.
Elspeth struggled to take it all in. Coming into work drunk and
being sick over everything...
Alison with her fine fair hair full of sick after gorging herself on
meringues — jelly and cream all over the white damask tablecloth
— the assembled nannies aghast — Lady Marsh's footman fetching
hot water and towels — her granddaughter's sixth birthday party a
shambles. It was all too ghastly.
'So where is she?' she asked. 'I have tried so many times to phone.'
Heather said she had gone away. 'She didn't say exactly where. She
has some friends who live near Salisbury, so I think she may have
gone there.'
Elspeth told her about the clinics.
'As soon as I get the brochures I will go and see which one would be
best. I do hope they will be able to help,' mentally thinking, if she
agrees to go, but she didn't say that aloud.
She told Heather she would let her know as soon as possible, and
asked her to let her know if she heard from Alison, and then she
thanked her very much for all her help.

Well, she supposed, if Alison had lost her job, she would not have
to ask for extended leave to attend a clinic, so at least that was
something.

Olive had come in earlier and gone to her room. She now appeared
to say that she had been to the library, and that Catherine seemed
to be alright if rather pale, and that there was not more news about
the shabby man.

And then Alistair — his scars more livid than usual. Elspeth thought he was finding things rather difficult. She must arrange to do something about the furniture.

They had a rather silent meal. She didn't have the effort to make polite conversation.
Paula had prepared rigatoni with a thick tomato and onion sauce, using a small amount of mince, which was a great way of eking out the meagre meat ration.
Elspeth had asked Paula never to serve spaghetti. The thought of sitting opposite Olive whilst she tried to cope with eating spaghetti was just too much to contemplate.

7

Catherine worked every other Saturday.

Miss Milburn worked every other Saturday.

Elsie did not work on Saturdays as she was still studying.

Miss Milburn was disdainful — she did not think much of Elsie's ability to do anything, and considered it a waste of time.

Catherine remembered how encouraging Miss Turnbull had been when she was taking her librarian exams. 'I'm sure she will do well,' she said. 'She's just rather shy…' But Miss Milburn made one of her deprecating noises. 'Those cards look very untidy,' she said. 'I hope they are being properly filed…'

Catherine had still not asked her about having the extra day off in June to go to Cambridge. There had been so much going on, and she needed Miss Milburn to be in a good mood.

She didn't like working on Saturdays — no proper end to the week — an extra effort — and then only Sunday to sort oneself out.

People on Saturdays were more fussy and demanding — and she felt immensely tired.

The shabby man's collapse had really upset her. She couldn't help thinking about him — wondering how he was. Mr Simms had telephoned the hospital several times, but they were not very forthcoming — 'As well as can be expected' — and that very reluctantly. Mr Simms was not family. And where would he go if he was discharged from hospital? Did he have a family — a home somewhere? He had looked like someone who had had a home and a family. Now maybe just a bed-sitting room with a gas ring, and a bit of grubby rush matting on the bare floor. There were so many lost and lonely people — some half-crazed — sitting in doorways. There was a bedraggled woman who wandered up and down Baker Street talking to herself. And the man in an old army greatcoat outside the Tube, who tried to sell you sticks of chewing gum. So many people had lost everything — all familiar things gone — their homes piles of rubble…

Olive had come into the library on Wednesday afternoon. She hardly ever came in the afternoon — more flustered than usual — fiddling with the tarnished gilt clasp of her ugly handbag — putting it on the counter whilst she took off her brown knitted gloves. She was really anxious for news of the shabby man.

Catherine said there really wasn't any more news, explained about Mr Simms' efforts to get information from the hospital.

Olive said she was so sorry, and sat down abruptly on the little chair by the counter. 'So sad,' she said. She looked as if she was about to cry, fumbling in her handbag for a handkerchief.

Catherine wished again that she could offer her a cup of tea and a biscuit like she would have done at home — and thought of the Colonel who had many cups of tea. Of course the small library in Bambridge was hardly comparable to the imposing building of the Marylebone Library — perhaps not suitable for offering tea and biscuits — but everybody needed a little comfort sometimes…

She wanted to say that she was sure the shabby man would be alright — but she didn't really think so.

Olive blew her nose discreetly on a small embroidered handkerchief. 'Lady Thornton wanted me to find out how you are,' she said. 'She was very concerned about you…' Her voice trailed away.

Catherine said it had all been very upsetting. 'We'll just have to hope for the best.'

Olive said she was going to look for something by Nevil Shute — she'd heard his books were very good. She got up and picked up her gloves from the counter. 'Take my mind off things…'

Catherine wished suddenly — achingly — for the green, leafy woods on the hill behind Bembridge. The gentle rustling of the lofty branches — the scented sea of bluebells that carpeted the mossy ground every spring, the starry wood anemones clustered by the knotted roots of the trees — striped sunlight piercing the thick canopy of green. She closed her eyes — remembering.

A boy came in with his mother — his school tie askew, and an ink stain on the sleeve of his grey blazer. His mother smart in a black and white checked coat, with a shiny handbag, propelling him forward. She said she needed a book about the Vikings — he was doing them

at school — 'With pictures.' His school book only had one or two blurry pictures of a Viking ship. 'They will be going to the British Museum,' she said. 'A special school trip. He is supposed to read up about them...'
The boy shifted uncomfortably from foot to foot — eyes on the floor. Catherine said she was sure they had something suitable, and directed them to the right shelves.

A woman with her hair tied up untidily with a long multicoloured bit of scarf, complaining about the limited selection of books on medieval French architecture — so fascinating. She was most disappointed that what was supposed to be such a good library was so badly stocked.
Catherine said she was sorry about that, and made a note to investigate what had been published on the subject, and order what was available.

At least Major Harding never came on a Saturday. He had been genuinely concerned about the shabby man. 'Poor chap,' he had said. 'Must've had a heart attack...'

And then Alistair in his dark blue raincoat, smiling.
'I thought I'd come and see how you are,' he said. And she had the same overwhelming feeling that she wanted to hold on to him — just hold on. She had really thought she would not see him again, and now he was here — smiling — near enough to touch...
'I wondered if you have a lunch hour,' he said. 'We could go somewhere and sit down — have something to eat — perhaps where we went before...'
She said her lunch hour was not until half past twelve.
He said that was fine. He would come back.

She wished she'd put on a better blouse this morning — she never bothered much on a Saturday. At least her shoes were quite smart. She always liked to wear smart shoes.
She was hardly aware of a large man in a business suit, tapping impatiently on the counter. He wanted something on the Visigoths — nothing too demanding — he did not have much time for reading.

They ate cheese on toast.

He asked if there was any news of the poor man who had collapsed — and Catherine explained again about Mr Simms' not very successful efforts to find out how he was. All they knew was that his name was Thomas Gardner, and that he was 'as well as can be expected'.

Alistair said he hoped he would soon be back in the library annoying the woman she worked with.

Catherine said Miss Milburn hated him being there — but that she was always fussing about something. 'I think she likes to have something to complain about...'

Alistair told her about his new flat — and how there was still a lot of work to be done, and how good it was of Lady Thornton to have let him stay for so long.

Catherine felt completely at ease — eating slowly — listening to him — warm and contented.

'She is very kind,' he said. 'She and my aunt are very old friends. They visited each other a lot before the war...' He stopped suddenly, and put down his knife and fork.

Catherine's feeling of contentment drained away — aware of the jagged scars on his face and hand. What depths of darkness had he suffered?

She pretended not to have noticed, and said his flat sounded really nice — and yes, Lady Thornton was very kind, although she seemed rather forbidding at first.

Alistair drank some tea — stirring the cup slowly, and replacing the spoon carefully in the saucer. He said she had this marvellous Italian housekeeper who cooked great meals — 'You wouldn't think there was any rationing.' And then he told her how Elspeth had offered to let him have some furniture.

'She still has a lot in store,' he said. 'My aunt says they had a really magnificent place with wonderful grounds. Requisitioned of course. I believe it was left in rather a mess...'

He drank some more tea. 'Everything still seems so strange.'

Catherine wanted to reach out and take his hand — to say she felt the same — that her life seemed like a patchwork quilt with torn pieces that did not fit — that would never fit.

They walked back to the library together not touching — but
touching.
He said perhaps they could go out one evening — for dinner or to see
a film — and she said that would be very nice.

*   *   *

The brochures started arriving quite promptly.
All glossily splendid.
The first ones to arrive were Hertford and Aylesbury.

The Hertford Clinic looked like someone's rather grand house — red
brick covered with Virginia creeper — a secluded drive bordered by
rhododendrons, pictured in full bloom — a large chintzy lounge — a
library with brown leather armchairs and sofas — perfectly proper
bedrooms with private bathrooms — well kept gardens…

Aylsebury was quite different. A low white building with a great
deal of glass — steel chairs of strange shapes and white leather sofas
— in fact nearly everything was white — with an occasional large
abstract painting on the white walls — immaculate lawns — two
tennis courts.

Then came Amersham, St Albans and Stanmore.

Amersham was mock Tudor, with a rose garden, also pictured in
full bloom — comfortable looking rooms, if rather dark — and the
promise of locally grown fruit and vegetables.
St Albans was grey stone — square and solid — large vases of flowers
in the lounge and dining room — a large leisure room with a grand
piano, a radiogram, piles of magazines and chairs with a lot of
cushions.

She hardly looked at Stanmore. She had already decided it would be
much too near.
High Wycombe came last.
It was the most impressive. Indoor and outdoor swimming pools
— tennis courts — horse riding — miniature golf. There were

121

photographs of people dancing and doing gymnastics — buffet style meals.

Of course they all had information on the treatments they provided. They were all fairly similar. One to one talks with highly qualified staff — group discussions — special diets — plenty of rest — gentle exercise. They encouraged movement to music — creative activities such as painting and pottery — everything, of course, tailored to each person's individual needs.

She thought she would start with Hertford and St Albans, and then maybe Aylesbury, which looked very stylish, and emphasised creative arts and relaxation. She didn't think Alison would care for mock Tudor, and High Wycombe was almost too much. Alison didn't like any sort of sport, except, perhaps, tennis, so most of their facilities would be of no use — might even put her off — it was also the most expensive.

At intervals she phoned Alison — no response.
She telephoned Heather again to tell her about the clinics, and find out whether she had heard from Alison.
Heather said she was planning to go round to Alison's flat. She was rather worried as she had had no news. She still had the keys, so she could let herself in. She would let Elspeth know.

The next thing was to visit the clinics.
She should be able to manage it in one day. Hertford and St Albans in the morning and Aylesbury after lunch.
She would hire a car.
Before the war they had always used Ladbroke Cars — they had Daimlers and reliable chauffeurs. They had seldom brought their own car into London — Jumbo had liked to give Wilson extra time off. Of course they might no longer exist — so many things no longer existed — and then there was the question, should she go alone? It would be nice to go with someone. Sybil was out of the question. She did not want to take Olive. She had had to tell her briefly why she was receiving so many brochures, although she had studiously pretended not to notice. She told her she was trying to

find Alison somewhere to go to have a really proper rest, as she really was not at all well. Olive had clucked sympathetically — 'Poor little thing,' she had said. 'Such a shame…' — which had irritated Elspeth considerably. 'Somewhere in the country would do her the world of good…' Elspeth had said tartly, 'Yes, yes, I hope so…'
No. Going with Olive was not a good idea. She would do a lot of sighing, and would agree with her about everything, and she needed someone else's sensible opinion. So going with Olive was definitely not a good idea. Heather was possible — a nice enough young woman — but apart from Alison, she didn't feel they had anything in common. And then she thought of Catherine. She felt she would understand — properly understand — and although she hardly knew her, she felt at ease with her, able to talk about things.

Perhaps she could ask her to supper, and they could discuss it — tomorrow — Wednesday. Alistair would be out. He was going to a concert at the Albert Hall — some pianist or other — Beethoven, she thought he had said.

She asked Olive to go and find out if it was possible, and then Heather phoned to say that Alison's flat was a fearful mess, but she wasn't there. She said, 'I'll stay and tidy up a bit, and leave a note in case she comes back after I've gone.'

*　　*　　*

Olive looked quite excited, almost tripping on the heavy doormat inside the swing doors, in her sensible lace-up shoes of indeterminate colour — not really brown — or black — or grey. Catherine smiled and said, 'You're late today.' It was nearly lunchtime, and she knew Lady Thornton was very particular about mealtimes — or maybe it was the wonderful Italian housekeeper that Alistair had mentioned who didn't like people to be late.

Olive sat down on the chair by the counter and explained.
'I think she wants you to go with her,' she said. 'Her daughter Alison has got herself into a lot of trouble, and Lady Thornton is going to look at these places to see whether they might be able to help. Such a

problem. So I think she would like you to go with her…'

Catherine was completely taken aback.
Surely Lady Thornton should go with Olive — after all, Olive was
her companion, and she had only seen Lady Thornton a few times.
And apart from that time when they had met in the park, it had only
been here in the library.
Olive said, 'She wants you to come to supper tomorrow so you can
discuss it. She said to apologise for it being such short notice, but
it is rather urgent — about seven, if that's alright.' She fished Lady
Thornton's card out of her handbag. 'You better have the telephone
number — just in case. I don't have much time to look for books this
morning — I shall be late for lunch…'

Catherine wondered what was wrong with Lady Thornton's daughter.
It must be quite serious if they were going to visit clinics. She might
be having a nervous breakdown — a broken love affair — maybe she
was drinking too much.
She wondered if Alistair would be there.
Last Saturday had been so very, very nice. She knew he worked
long hours, and she hadn't given him the number of her flat, or her
telephone number.
'I would love to come,' she said. Please thank Lady Thornton very
much.'
'I'm afraid Alistair won't be there,' said Olive, as she got up to go.
'He's going to a concert. I think Lady Thornton wants to speak to
you alone.'
Catherine watched her make her awkward way out, and felt a surge
of sympathy. There was something really sad about Olive. So self-
effacing — accepting everything without fuss. As she had thought
before, it must be very difficult to have to be unobtrusively available
all the time. She must feel very hurt that Lady Thornton preferred to
go with a young woman she hardly knew on such a sensitive occasion
— or maybe she was relieved not to have the responsibility of giving
an opinion. She would always have to have the same opinion as Lady
Thornton, even if she did not have the same opinion. But if Lady
Thornton wanted her to go with her, she must want someone else's
opinion.

It was all so unexpected — hard to take in.

She was really sorry Olive had said Alistair would be out. It would have been so very good to see him again. She thought about him a lot — his quiet strength that made her want to put her arms round him. It would be nice to see where he was living.

She didn't know if Lady Thornton was aware that they knew each other — well, knew each other a little... She hoped so much to see him again.

Elsie appeared to take over so that she could go to lunch. She said she was finding the exam work very difficult.

'I'm no good at writing essays.' She tucked her blouse into her skirt where it had come astray. Catherine said she was sure she would be fine.

She would just go back to the flat and have some tea and toast, and listen to the radio.

She would have to decide what to wear tomorrow. She would have plenty of time to come home and have a bath and change. She only had one suitable dress. She thought it was a really nice dress — grey wool, with a V-neck and three-quarter sleeves, which she wore with a black patent belt. And she had a pair of black patent shoes with reasonably high heels. Edward had given her the money to buy them as a Christmas present.

8

Elspeth said, 'I am having a guest to dinner this evening. Could you manage something a little special?'
Paula came into the drawing room every morning after breakfast to tell Elspeth what she was planning for the meals that day.

Elspeth had always given Penn the week's menus to give to Mrs Dunstan, who sometimes made suggestions, which she conveyed via Penn — perhaps different vegetables, or a new sauce — she was very good at sauces, and she made a wonderful Yorkshire pudding. Jumbo liked good, plain food. Jumbo carving the roast, which Penn had placed on the sideboard in the silver-domed dish. Was that something else marked with a black cross? She must check the list. Alison had always been a fussy eater, but she was very fond of roast potatoes. Rosemary would eat anything. Always hungry…

During the war, it was just whatever Martha could find, and now she left it entirely to Paula.

'Mr Sinclair will be out, so there will be just three of us.'
Paula said she would go down to Selfridges Food Hall, and see what she could find — she had friends who worked there. Elspeth thanked her and said she knew that anything Paula prepared would be absolutely delicious.

She thought she would not try to find about hiring a car, or phoning the clinics to ask when it would be convenient to visit, until she had spoken to Catherine.

Later in the morning Sybil phoned — thankfully not to say she was on the way — but to tell Elspeth that Francesca was coming tomorrow afternoon at about three o'clock, and that she would like Elspeth to be there.
'You're so much better than I am at this sort of thing.'
Elspeth wasn't sure about that — apart from Paula, who she had

126

inherited from the Petersens, and, of course, Olive, who Sybil's friend had recommended, Penn had always dealt with the staff — informing her if someone new had been taken on — or if someone was leaving — which happened very seldom. They had never really had much trouble with their servants. Anyhow, she told Sybil that of course she would come. She was looking forward to meeting Francesca.

They had a really good thick vegetable soup for lunch — Paula was so very good with soups — and fresh rolls with some of the Dolcelatte. Paula was in a particularly good mood. Elspeth hoped it was because her trip to Selfridges had been successful.

Catherine was very punctual. She hated to be late.
It was only a short walk up Gloucester Place, across Marylebone Road and up Glentworth Street to the entrance to the flats. A uniformed porter, sitting in a glass-fronted office by the door reading the paper, acknowledged her with a polite nod, as she went across the thick-carpeted lobby to the lift.

Olive greeted her effusively — a little flushed — actually wearing an olive green dress — a colour that really did not suit her pallid skin.
Lady Thornton rose to greet her — shaking her warmly by the hand. 'So good of you to come,' she said. She was wearing an elegant slate blue dress with a diamond brooch in the shape of a flower on the shoulder. Catherine had never seen her without a hat — her dark hair was beautifully cut with a slight wave.
She sat down in one of the very comfortable armchairs.
The room was furnished with quiet good taste — light brown velvet curtains — Chinese rugs — discreet watercolours of pleasing landscapes — carefully placed lights on little tables — all slightly worn in a tired upper class way.

They had sherry and delicious cheese straws. 'One of Paula's many specialities,' said Lady Thornton.
Olive perched nervously on the edge of her seat, and Catherine thought again how difficult it must be to be Olive. Unfortunately it was a bit late for her to be whisked off by a dashing Laurence Olivier

figure, like Joan Fontaine's down-trodden companion in *Rebecca*.

'Olive has probably told you that I am hoping you might be able to accompany me when I go to inspect these places for my daughter,' said Elspeth.

Catherine said yes she had, and that of course she would be very pleased to.

'I feel a younger person's opinion would be very helpful,' said Elspeth. 'After dinner I will show you the brochures, and you must tell me what you think — and I'll try and arrange some visits.' She really liked this young woman — neat and smart in the grey woollen dress — her dark hair short and a little curly.

Paula had surpassed herself.
There was smoked salmon — chicken wrapped in Parma ham with mushrooms and a red wine sauce — scalloped potatoes and peas — caramelised oranges with thin crispy biscuits. A feast.

The dining room was furnished in the same understatedly classy way as the drawing room. Light brown velvet curtains — attractive oil paintings of fruit and flowers — a highly polished table set with crystal glasses — gleaming silver — lace mats — starched napkins and a bowl of yellow primroses.
Catherine felt completely at home. It was all so calm and untouched — very reassuring.

After they had finished the sumptuous meal, Elspeth told Olive to go and fetch the coffee. 'I think Paula has done enough for the evening — and do tell her how much we enjoyed the excellent meal.'
She had had to become more accustomed to being less formal with servants. The world had changed so much. There were no longer the strict rules of behaviour there had been before the war — and really she could not treat Paula as a servant — that would be ridiculous.

During dinner the conversation had been fairly general — the usual moan about the continued rationing, the vagaries of the weather — a really miserable spring, and how lucky Lady Thornton's friend Sybil was to be going to the South of France for a whole month at the end of June.

Catherine was going to say something about Edward's forthcoming trip to Italy with Harriet, but she didn't. After all, Lady Thornton didn't even know she had a brother.

Whilst they drank their coffee Elspeth spread the brochures out. She said she had selected four possibles — passing them to Catherine. 'I think we could do them all in one day...'
Catherine said she could only manage the weekends, as it was very difficult to get time off — (she must do something about Cambridge) — and that she worked every other Saturday — the next one was free — but that might be too soon. But Elspeth said, 'Good — good. I'll try and arrange it. I don't see why there should be any difficulty. The sooner the better...'

And then Alistair came in. His look of surprise and delight at seeing Catherine there was evident.
Elspeth was quite taken aback by his obvious pleasure, and by Catherine's immediate, equally delighted reaction.
Elspeth said, 'Of course — you know one another. You met in the library when that poor man collapsed.'
She saw him again with his split shoes and shabby clothes, and thought of the peacocks on the Selbournes' lawn, fanning out their wondrous tails. Had they all survived the war?
'Come and sit down and have some coffee,' she said. 'Did you enjoy the concert? I hope you've eaten. I'm sure that Paula could find you something if you need...'
Alistair thanked her and said yes he had eaten, and the concert had been very good indeed.
She then went on to tell him about the brochures for the clinics, passing them over to him to have a look.
'I thought Catherine would be able to give an unbiased opinion, so I have asked her to come with me to inspect them. I have to find somewhere really congenial where Alison would feel comfortable...'

Catherine found it difficult to go to sleep — her head so full of the impressions of the evening.

Alistair had insisted on walking her home — so good to feel him so close.
He said she must come and see his flat. He was very pleased with it, and was looking forward to going with Elspeth to choose some of her furniture.
He was very pleased that she had asked Catherine to go with her to inspect clinics for Alison.
'I'm afraid she has got herself in rather a mess,' he said. 'Of course Elspeth never really says anything — I think she finds it very difficult — but I know she has been very worried.'
Catherine said she had been very surprised to be asked, and hoped she could be of some use.
They said goodnight quite formally, and he walked away, a tall thin figure in his dark navy blue raincoat.

Elspeth also found it difficult to sleep.
She thought the evening had gone extremely well — a truly wonderful meal — she must remember to thank Paula in the morning — and she had felt so at ease with Catherine — a really charming young woman — and Alistair's delight at seeing her — that had been a surprise — there was definitely a rapport there — very pleasing.

She phoned the clinics after breakfast, and arranged that she would visit on Saturday.
She found the number of Ladbroke Cars in her old address book. They did still exist. She said she wanted a really nice car for the whole of Saturday, and explained where she was going, and in which order she thought best.
She tried again to speak to Alison without success.
She would phone Heather this evening — she would be at work now.

It was Paula's day off, so Olive was in charge. Paula had left a quiche Lorraine — a good way to eke out the meagre bacon ration — and a salad — all ready prepared. Elspeth asked Olive to serve it early as she had to be at Sybil's flat by 3 o'clock.

It was going to be interesting to meet Paula's friend, and to see what Sybil had been doing with the flat.

Francesca was short and plump, very neat and tidy, dressed entirely in black, keeping her hands folded primly on the black handbag on her lap. Her English was quite good, if somewhat faltering, and she spoke firmly in a pleasant voice.
Sybil had made some tea. Elspeth was amazed. She had never seen Sybil do anything remotely domesticated — hardly capable of folding a dinner napkin.
She had assembled the tea things on a tray, with a plate of biscuits, and paper napkins with a design of blue leaves, which went well with the willow-patterned china. She had even remembered a tea strainer. She placed the tray on a small round table with spindly legs — Elspeth thought it must be an antique — Sybil had so many valuable things.
'Perhaps you could pour it out,' she said to Elspeth, as if the unaccustomed effort of making the tea had worn her out.

Whilst they drank their tea Sybil went through the things she would like Francesca to do.
Shopping — cooking — cleaning — dealing with the laundry.
'I am out quite a lot,' she said. 'I shall be away at least a month from the end of June, so I should want you to look after the flat whilst I'm away.'
She had opened accounts at all the local shops, and there were, of course, accounts at Harrods and Selfridges. The laundry would be collected once a week…
Francesca had put her handbag down beside her chair, and accepted a biscuit — Sybil had managed to find some ginger nuts — which she nibbled, wiping her mouth discreetly with a napkin. She nodded, and took a sip of tea, replacing the cup carefully onto the table.
'I like simple food,' said Sybil. 'If I am going to be in I will discuss it with you. When you have finished your various jobs, you are free to do whatever you want.' She then went on to say that, of course, she would have a proper day off once a week.
Sybil was a generous employer — the salary she suggested was very generous.

Francesca said that was very good — all very good.

When they finished their tea they went to inspect her quarters.
The kitchen was gleamingly new, and very well equipped.
Francesca seemed delighted.
Her own rooms led off from the kitchen — sitting room — bedroom and bathroom.
The rooms were not very large but looked very comfortable.
Sybil enjoyed doing this sort of thing.
The sitting room had two easy chairs, and a table and chairs by the window where Francesca could eat her meals, a bookcase and cretonne curtains with a pattern of pale green ferns.
Elspeth thought it was very nice.
The bedroom had a divan with a blue bedspread, a dressing table, a wardrobe, a small chair upholstered in blue, and a bedside table with a pretty lamp. Elspeth recognised it as one Sybil had had in her dressing room in Eaton Square — a flowered china base and pleated dark blue silk shade. The curtains, also of cretonne, had a pattern of dark blue cornflowers.
The bathroom had blue linoleum on the floor, and a new white bathroom suite.
Francesca said *bene* a lot.
It was agreed that she should start at the end of the following week. She would give her present employers a week's notice. It was all most satisfactory.
They all shook hands, and there were a lot of *benes* and *arrivedercis*.

Sybil pushed the tea tray aside, and went into the dining room to fetch drinks from the sideboard.
At present, her 'help' in West Hampstead was coming to clean up and do a bit of cooking. Sybil fetched her in a taxi. 'Better than nothing,' she said. She sat down with a sigh of relief, and poured herself a large gin and vermouth. Elspeth had a small one. It was a bit too early for her. 'She seemed a very nice woman,' she said.
'Marvellous,' said Sybil. 'Really marvellous. What a relief. Now all I need is to get the rest of my curtains sorted out...'

Elspeth said she would get Paula a box of chocolates to thank her.

She never used her sweet ration. She had never cared for sweets or chocolate. She used to give her coupons to Rosemary and Alison, but now she saved them up so that she could get a really nice box of chocolates for such an occasion.

Olive greeted her in great agitation.
Heather had phoned. She was at Alison's flat, and wanted Elspeth to phone her back as soon as she came in.
Olive said, 'I think Alison is very unwell.' She had phoned Heather at work — quite hysterical — so she went round as soon as she could.

Elspeth dropped her coat on the nearest chair, and went to the phone.
Heather said Alison was in a bad way — I think you should come. I got her to have some tea and toast, and helped her to have a bath. She is sleeping now… but she is really not well…'

Elspeth said she would come at once. 'What about food? Has she got anything? This wretched rationing, it made everything so difficult. Anyone would think they had lost the dreadful war. Heather said she had managed to get bread and milk. 'I found some marmite…' She sounded as if she was about to burst into tears.
Elspeth said she would be there as soon as possible. 'Don't worry,' she said.
She told Olive to go and see if there was anything in the kitchen that she could take. Paula would not be back until late. She often went to the cinema on her day off, and then had supper with her friends. Olive found two tins of leek and potato soup, three eggs, some margarine, some of Paula's biscuits, a jar of cherry jam that someone had given Elspeth last Christmas, and two apples.
There were other things in the store cupboard and fridge, but they were not really suitable. Alison was a fussy eater at the best of times, and wasn't going to eat things like salami or tins of corned beef.

'I'll take the rest of the quiche,' said Elspeth. 'Although I don't suppose she will eat it. Heather said she had got some bread and milk.'

Olive wrapped everything carefully, if rather untidily, and put it all into a Harrods shopping bag.
Elspeth said not to wait for supper — she had no idea how long she would be — and explain to Alistair, 'Paula has left some soup…'

She had no trouble getting a taxi outside Baker Street Station, but the traffic was very heavy — they crawled most of the way, and the lights always seemed to be red.

Heather looked anxious and dishevelled. She was wearing a grubby blue and white checked apron and was holding a teacloth.
'I'm just trying to clear up a bit,' she said, following Elspeth into the sitting room.

This was such a nice flat — light and airy — looking out on a tree-filled square.
Alison had been so thrilled — her very own flat — furnishing it with care, fussing over the cushions and curtains — carefully positioning the lamps and ornaments, and the watercolours of bowls of roses salvaged from one of the guest rooms of their old home.
Now there were stains on the pale mushroom-coloured carpet, and the arms of the sofa and armchairs — the coffee table covered with dirty cups and saucers, glasses, an overturned wine bottle — overflowing ashtrays — a vase of dead flowers by the window.

'I was in the kitchen,' said Heather. 'I thought I'd do some washing up.'

The kitchen was worse. It smelt of old grease. There seemed to be a thin film of grease on everything. The floor was filthy, the sink full of dirty dishes. 'I've out them in to soak a bit,' Heather said, removing a plate with the congealed remains of something from the table, and adding it to the pile in the sink.
'I've had to throw away some stuff from the fridge. It had all gone mouldy. I'm afraid I haven't had time to do very much.'

'I didn't know whether to call a doctor, but I don't know if she has a doctor. I got her to eat a little, and gave her a bath. She was in an awful state.' She paused. 'She'd been sick. I think her clothes will have to be thrown away. She's sleeping now...'

'Oh dear,' said Elspeth. 'Oh dear. I'm so sorry you have had to deal with all this.' Her voice trailed away. What could she say? The situation seemed to get worse and worse. Alison so meticulous with her appearance — matching bags and shoes — outfits for every occasion — clean clothes every day — now a hopeless drunk wondering around covered in vomit. It was too too dreadful.

She put the bag of food she had brought on the kitchen table, pushing aside dirty crockery, a half-eaten apple that had gone brown, a few crusts, old newspapers and more overflowing ashtrays.

'This is all Olive could find,' she said. 'The soup will be useful. I don't suppose she will eat the quiche. Maybe you would like some. It would be a shame to waste it. Paula, my housekeeper, is very good with quiches...'
Heather said that would be great. She was absolutely starving.

Elspeth went to have a look at Alison.
She was fast asleep — rather a nasty grey colour — wearing one of the nightdresses Elspeth had bought her — an arm flung across the none too clean pink eiderdown. She would have to get it cleaned. There was a place in Marylebone High Street — a really good specialist cleaners. The room was a real mess — the dressing table strewn with open pots and tubes — scrunched up paper handkerchieves — bits of dirty cotton wool — another overflowing ashtray, and a half empty wine glass. There were clothes everywhere. She picked up a skirt and some stockings off the floor and put them on a chair.
It was all too much. And for the first time ever she was glad that Jumbo was not there. Not there to see his daughter in this state.

She went back into the sitting room and sat down.
Heather brought in some tea.
'I did my best to clean the tray,' she said. 'I couldn't find much cleaning stuff. There was a packet of soap flakes, but it was

practically empty.' She said she might have some quiche, if that was
alright.
Elspeth said of course. 'I won't have any,' she said. 'I shall be having
something later.'
She felt at a loss. She took a sip of tea, which was very weak and not
very hot, and asked Heather if she knew where Alison was registered
for her rations.
Fortunately she did know. There was a grocer round the corner, and
a butcher on the next street — they knew her — she had picked up
rations for Alison in the past. Her ration book was in a drawer of the
little chest in the corner with the lamp on it.

It was beginning to get dark. Heather got up to close the curtains —
dusky pink velvet — Alison was very fond of pink — now they were
grubby, and the lining of one was torn. Alison had been so proud of
her lovely new flat. Elspeth took another sip of the weak tea, trying
to avoid looking at the cigarette burns on the polished surface of the
coffee table.

Heather said that, of course, she would stay the night, but that she
would have to go to work in the morning.

The spare bedroom was the only clean room in the flat, apart from
being very dusty.

The bathroom was quite disgusting.
The laundry basket overflowing — dirty towels — scummy bath —
smelling of damp and dirty clothes — really unpleasant.
'I couldn't find any clean towels,' said Heather. 'But at least I got her
to have a bath…'

Elspeth thanked her again. 'You've been wonderful,' she said.
The whole flat would have to be properly cleaned. She remembered
that Sybil was getting a firm of professional cleaners to give her flat
in West Hampstead a thorough clean before she handed it over to
the young couple. She had had the same firm to clean up after all the
decorating and building work in her new flat.

She asked Heather if there was a laundry nearby. 'All those things in the bathroom should go to the laundry...'

Heather said she thought there was one not very far.

Elspeth said she would get Olive to find out, and take everything to be washed. 'I'll send her very early in the morning to take over when you go to work, whilst I get in touch with Dr Myers. Maybe he can arrange for Alison to go into a nursing home to recover a bit — I'll definitely arrange for him to visit...'

While Heather ate some of the quiche, Elspeth told her about the clinics. 'I was going to phone you this evening,' she said. 'I am going with a friend on Saturday to have a look at some, and try and fix up something as soon as possible. Hopefully we will find somewhere nice. I will discuss it with Dr Myers in the morning. She could always come and stay with me, but I'm sure she would refuse.'

How sad that she would refuse to come home. Of course now with Olive and Alistair it might be rather difficult — but she would have refused anyway. Elspeth couldn't remember how long it was since she had come to the flat — not for months.

She wished so much that Rosemary was here.
She would try and telephone her tomorrow.
She couldn't put all this down in a letter.

She insisted Heather took some money.
'You've done so much,' she said. 'And you've had to buy so many things. I'll get Olive to get some more keys cut, we should all have a set.'

Before she left she went and had another look at Alison. She was still sleeping soundly — still a nasty sickly colour, like a fading bruise.

Heather said she would telephone during her lunch hour, as it was frowned upon to have personal calls at work, and find out what was going on.

By the time she got home it was quite late.

Olive was listening to the wireless and knitting. She was always knitting — some unidentifiable garment, which she never seemed to finish. Wool had been almost impossible to find during the war, apart from khaki wool for knitting scarves and mittens for the soldiers. Some more accomplished knitters made more ambitious things, like socks and hats. Now it was much easier, there was a choice, if limited, of colours. Olive's knitting was a shapeless length of rusty brown. Elspeth didn't knit. She considered it tediously unappealing.

She asked Olive to go and warm up some of the soup.
'I'll have it in here on a tray,' she said.

The soup was very good — and Olive had, for once, managed not to spill any.

Elspeth told her, as briefly as possible, what she was proposing to do. She was reluctant to discuss her private affairs with anyone. Certainly not Olive, but she had no choice.
'You'll have to get to the flat by 8.30 at the latest,' she said. 'Heather has to go to work — the whole situation's is...' She couldn't find an appropriate word. 'I'll telephone Dr Myers as early as I can, and arrange for him to go and see Alison — and hopefully get her into a nursing home.'

Olive clucked sympathetically. 'Oh dear,' she said, rolling up her knitting and putting it into a well-worn floral knitting bag. 'Oh dear.'

Elspeth ignored her, trying to hide her irritation. 'You'd better leave Paula a note to say you will get your own breakfast, as you will have to have it very early — and I will have mine with Alistair at 8 o'clock...'

She and Olive normally had their breakfast at 8.30 after Alistair had gone to work.
She would have a word with Paula and explain about them having to take the food yesterday. She didn't like people poking around in her

kitchen. They would probably not be in for lunch tomorrow either. She would not be able to phone Dr Myers until at least 9 o'clock.

*   *   *

Dr Myers was very sympathetic.
He said he would try and be at Alison's flat at about midday.
She told him about the clinics, and which ones she thought might be suitable.
He said they were all excellent, and he was sure she would make the right choice.
He certainly had an exemplary bedside manner. She hoped he was as good a doctor.

She and Alistair had had a very silent breakfast. She had no wish to try and make conversation — he looked exhausted. Elspeth wondered if he had difficulty sleeping — too many nightmares — so apart from passing the marmalade, and a few trite remarks about the weather, they hardly spoke.

She telephoned Olive, who had arrived in plenty of time for Heather to leave for work.
Alison had woken, and was very displeased to find her there. She had actually been quite rude, but Olive just said she was rather annoyed. 'I told her I had to stay until you came,' she said. 'I don't think she wants you here either, she's shut herself in the bedroom…'

Elspeth booked a call to Los Angeles for 7.30 that evening, and rang for Paula. 'I'm sorry about all this upheaval,' she said.

'My daughter is unwell, and we were trying to find something for her to eat. Miss Fern has had to go early to be with her, and I shall be going shortly…'

Paula said she was sorry the signorina was unwell.
Elspeth said she didn't know how long she would be, but not to worry about lunch, and then she remembered she had said nothing about Francesca. All this business with Alison had put it completely

out of her mind.
'Your friend was a great success,' she said. 'Mrs Anstruther was absolutely delighted — she's going to start next week — we can't thank you enough. I'm sorry, I should have said immediately, but all this worry over the signorina has put everything else out of my mind…'

Paula said she quite understood, and that she was very pleased that the signora was happy, and that she would try and make something very good for supper.

Elspeth reached the flat well before 11.30.
Olive was anxiously waiting. She had been trying to tidy up.
She vacuumed the sitting room, and had done some dusting. She said Alison was still in her room.

Elspeth had tried to think what she could say to Alison. She had decided not to mention Jumbo — to say 'what would your father have thought about all this?' was almost to blame him for not being there — as if he had been killed on purpose to avoid all these difficulties. Dear Jumbo, how she missed him. All the same she was glad he could not see Alison in this pitiable state.
Perhaps she should have tackled Alison about her drinking a long time ago, but she would not have listened — would have got all huffy and told her not to fuss. Rosemary had tried to talk to her without success. Alison was very stubborn and would do exactly as she liked. It had been impossible to intervene…

She told Olive to go and buy some cleaning things — find out where the laundry was, and see if there was somewhere they could get keys cut — there must be a shoe menders nearby — they nearly always cut keys.

Alison was propped up on her pillow. She looked unnaturally flushed, with purple rings round her eyes, as if she had been punched. Her fine hair a matted mess.
The room smelt sour and unwashed. Elspeth opened the window a little. She was embarrassed by the thought of Dr Myers coming into

this dirty smelly room. As she looked for somewhere to sit amid the piles of discarded clothes, she noticed a half empty bottle of gin on the floor by the bed, and a smeared glass on the bedside table with a packet of aspirin and a plate of half-eaten toast.

'De Myers is coming very soon,' she said, perching gingerly on the side of the bed. 'I hope he will be able to find somewhere nice for you to go for a few days...'

Alison fiddled with the sheet. 'I'd rather see Dr Hartmann,' she said. Elspeth knew that Alison was perfectly well aware that Dr Hartmann had retired, she was just being contrary. 'Dr Myers seems very competent,' she said. 'I'm sure he will be very helpful...'
Alison shrugged — she had this annoying habit of shrugging when she felt threatened — a dismissive shrug, as if to say, 'What do I care?' Elspeth said she'd just tidy up a bit, putting out a hand to grasp the gin bottle.
Alison said, 'Leave my things alone. He's not coming to see if my room's tidy...'

Alison stamping her foot in defiance when caught out in some misdemeanour, or when she didn't want to do something — 'I won't — I won't — I won't.'
Nanny had always said it was best to take no notice.
Elspeth found it profoundly irritating — making a big effort not to tell her to stop being so childish, and that it was hardly appropriate to have a half empty gin bottle on the floor by the bed when you were expecting the doctor — or at any time for that matter — so she suggested she might like to comb her hair, to which Alison replied that she was not competing in a beauty contest.
Not a very good start.
She decided she wouldn't mention going to see the clinics the following day — one thing at a time — things were shaky enough as it was.

Dr Myers arrived just after midday — suavely immaculate in a pin-striped suit and snowy white shirt, with a dark blue tie patterned with gold fleur de lys.

He examined Alison briefly — taking her pulse and temperature, listening to her chest, inspecting her eyes with a small torch.
The usual procedure.
He asked her various questions about her general health, and whether there were any particular problems. He was very calm and reassuring. He said she had a slight fever, and that her chest was slightly congested — generally a little run down. He thought it would be a good idea to have a few days complete rest somewhere where she could be looked after. He would arrange for her to go to a very nice small convalescent home in Weymouth Street — just off Harley Street.

He made no sign that he had noticed the gin bottle, closing his bag with a snap, and said he would arrange it straight away, asking Elspeth if there was somewhere to wash his hands.

Alison had started to cry — making no attempt to wipe away the tears that ran down her face. Elspeth wondered if she had any handkerchiefs — or rather any clean handkerchiefs.
Better not ask.
She showed Dr Myers to the bathroom — apologising for the state of the towels — but he said not to worry, emerging, wiping his hands on a spotlessly clean white handkerchief.

He then telephoned the convalescent home, and arranged for Alison to go that afternoon. Elspeth said an ambulance was not necessary, they could take a taxi.

In the midst of all this Olive returned with bags of cleaning materials. She had found a laundry that would collect and deliver, and had had several sets of keys cut.

Elspeth introduced her to Dr Myers, who shook her hand politely. He told Alison not to worry about anything. He was sure she would be very comfortable in the convalescent home, and that he would come and see her as soon as she was settled. He said he thought a mild sedative would be a good idea, so that she could get a proper rest.

Elspeth had to send Olive out again to get some bread and eggs. They all needed something to eat, Olive could just about manage to scramble a few eggs. She found Alison's ration book where Heather said it would be, in the drawer of the little chest where they had found the keys. She knew nothing about ration books. Martha and Paula had always dealt with the rations.

She was sure that Alison would have quite a lot of points that she had not used. 'Try and get some butter and tea and sugar as well,' she said.

She was right. It turned out that Alison had not collected any rations for some time, so Olive had come back, quite triumphant, with a decent supply of butter, sugar and tea, as well as eggs and bread.

Between them they got Alison out of bed and into the bathroom to have a bath, ignoring her protests, and stripped the bed, adding everything to the rest of the dirty clothes. Elspeth put the eiderdown to one side to take to the specialist cleaners in Marylebone High Street, and then they tipped the contents of the overflowing laundry basket out on the floor. Olive sorted it out and Elspeth made a list. She would arrange for the laundry to pick it up from the porter, and deliver it back when it was ready.

They did manage to get Alison to eat some scrambled egg on toast. The eggs were rather solid, but at least Olive had not burnt the toast, and, for once, there was plenty of butter — and tea with plenty of sugar.
During the meal Heather phoned. Alison answered — huddled on the sofa — turned away — murmuring inaudibly — a short call.
Olive managed to persuade her to come back to the table and finish her tea, and eat a little more toast.
Elspeth hoped she would be able to talk to Heather later this evening, and let her know what was going on.

They had found some clean underwear screwed up at the back of a drawer, and a creased blouse, also a passable skirt and cardigan for Alison to wear, and packed a few things — toiletries, nightdress,

dressing gown and slippers — into an extremely expensive small leather suitcase, with Alison's initials embossed in gold leaf. Elspeth thought it must have been a gift — from Alison's married lover? She must try and see if Heather would tell her anything…
Olive helped Alison do her hair, carefully combing the tangled mess, whilst Alison began to sniff tearfully again.

Elspeth telephoned the laundry to arrange collection and delivery, and spoke to the porter, saying that Miss Fern would bring it down on her way out, and thanked him for being so helpful.
She then phoned for a taxi to take them to Weymouth Street.
She left Olive to clear up, and try to make some headway with the washing up and the filthy state of the kitchen, and to take the rubbish out to leave by the service lift.

They stood together silently whilst Alison put on her coat and found her handbag.
Elspeth said nothing about the fact that she had noticed the gin bottle by the bed was now empty.

By the time she got home it was 5.30.

They had not spoken in the taxi. Alison had turned her head away, and stared steadfastly out of the window. There was really heavy traffic, and they were held up for quite a while at Marble Arch.

The Weymouth House convalescent home occupied two adjoining houses in Weymouth Street, with the name in tasteful blue lettering over the double doors. The panelled foyer was soothingly furnished in pale green with large vases of flowers and abundant foliage, a sofa and chairs…
A smart young woman at the reception desk said they were expected, and perhaps they would like to sit down whilst she informed Sister Flynn of their arrival.
They sat down on the pale green sofa whilst she made a brief phone call. She said Sister Flynn would be with them in a minute. Elspeth wished she would hurry up before Alison decided she didn't want to stay after all, and was very relieved when a tall bony woman in a

spotless white nurse's uniform appeared. After a brief introduction she took them up to Alison's room in a rather cramped panelled lift. Elspeth thought it was a good thing they were all quite slim.

The room had two windows overlooking the street, with a double bed and two small armchairs covered in the same flowered chintz as the curtains. There was a low table with a bowl of fruit — there was even an orange — and an adjoining bathroom with a great many towels.
Nurse Flynn said if there was anything else Alison needed she could just ring and ask — there was a phone on the bedside table.
'I hope you will be comfortable,' she said. 'Dr Myers said he will be coming to see you at about six o'clock. Would you like me to send up some tea…?'

Alison sat down on the edge of the bed and kicked off her shoes.
She said she was perfectly alright and didn't want any tea, adding a rather belated thank you.
Elspeth hoped she had not managed to secrete any alcohol into her case whilst she and Olive were not looking.
She also thanked Nurse Flynn. 'Most kind,' she said. 'But I think we have all we need for the moment…'
She made sure that Alison had everything she needed before she left. She had declined an offer to help her unpack, and threw herself back onto the pillows and closed her eyes.

Elspeth took another taxi home.
Normally she would have walked. It was not very far, and it was good to get some fresh air, but she was too exhausted.

Olive was not yet home.

She would have to telephone Heather — and there was the call to Rosemary — and she should confirm with Catherine about the morning… Paula said the Signora had telephoned. She had been very pleased — most happy… Elspeth couldn't face speaking to Sybil at the moment, she was too tired. It would have to wait. She would have to ask her about the cleaning firm, and she would expect some explanation. She would also have to make sure she had enough money available to cover all these extra expenses.

She poured herself a large gin and vermouth, and sat down to wait for Olive.

9

Catherine had had a very tiring day.

Miss Milburn was in a particularly dreadful mood.

Elsie had inadvertently put a volume of Dostoevsky's *Crime and Punishment* in the Legal Section.

Catehrine said it was just a mistake.

'Just a mistake,' said Miss Milburn, her voice rising alarmingly. 'Just a mistake… Really Catherine, that is not good enough.'

Poor Elsie was understandably crestfallen, apologising profusely. 'I don't know how I got it mixed up,' she said. 'I'm really sorry…'

Miss Milburn refused to be mollified, and stalked off muttering darkly about consequences.

Catherine told Elsie not to worry. 'She'll calm down,' she said. 'You know what she's like. She loves something to complain about.' She wanted to say, how could she have been so careless? It had been a really incomprehensible blunder. She really could not be that ignorant.

Elsie fished a crumpled handkerchief out of her cardigan pocket, and blew her nose. 'I never seem to do anything right,' she said tearfully. Catherine said again that Miss Milburn always wanted to find fault with everything. 'You just need to be a bit more careful. Come and ask me if you are not sure about anything, and try and keep out of her way.'

Later in the morning Mr Simms had come down to say that he had telephoned the hospital, and that, sadly, Mr Gardner was now on the danger list. 'That's all they would say,' he said. 'Not communicative at all. I had to insist…'

She was so glad to get home.

In her lunch hour yesterday she had bought vegetables to make a stew which would last her for a few days — cabbage — carrots — onions — and the butcher, Mr Gough, a small wiry man with large red hands, raw from cutting meat, had given her a couple of chump ends. There was very little meat on them, so they did not affect her ration. 'Couple of nice chump ends today,' he had said, wrapping them up briskly in the heavy white paper. 'Very tasty.' She would warm some up for supper.

Lady Thornton had said she had arranged for the car to pick her up at a quarter to ten in the morning, and then to come and collect her. She would wear her navy blue coat and skirt, which had inverted pleats, her white blouse with the bow at the neck, and her best navy court shoes.
She hoped it would not rain, but that would not matter much as they would be in the car for most of the time.

She was really sorry about Lady Thornton's daughter — drink problems were so very difficult to solve. Her daughter must have been very unhappy to get into such a state. It seemed there was a man involved somewhere — married probably.
She hoped they would be able to find somewhere where they could help her.

Edward phoned. He was coming up to London next Wednesday, for a conference at the Science Museum. He was very sorry but he didn't think he would have time to meet her.
'It will go on until at least six o'clock, and then there is a reception and dinner…'
Catherine was really disappointed. It would have been so good to see him.
'Have you asked about your time off?' he said.
Catherine said not yet, there had been so many things going on, she hadn't found the right moment.
Edward said that he and Harriet were very excited about the Italian trip, and they were also looking forward very much to the garden party. 'They're having proper caterers, which is a relief,' and he laughed.
The thought of Harriet's parents organising the food for a garden party was really quite hilarious. She could see Gertrude in her dirndl skirt and sandals, grumpily cutting up stale bread, and smearing it

with anything she could find — aged cream cheese, questionable pate, marmite, gritty bits of rollmop — dotting them all with sliced pickled gherkin. She laughed too. 'A very good idea,' she said. 'It should be really lovely...'

She said she would really get it sorted out next week, and told him briefly about Lady Thornton, and where they were going tomorrow. It was a good call.

Later Lady Thornton phoned to confirm the arrangements for the morning, and then, later still, Alistair phoned to say he hoped everything would go well, and that maybe he would see her when they got back.

She had a nice big plateful of stew, and listened to some music on the wireless. She didn't know much about classical music. Alistair had been at a concert the other evening. She had never been to a concert. There were all sorts of things she had never done.

The car was coming at 9.30.

Elspeth had had a restless night.

Her phone call to Rosemary had not been very satisfactory. The line was very bad, buzzing and faint, Rosemary's voice fading away at crucial moments. She had, however, agreed that all that Elspeth was doing was very good, and hopefully would prove successful.

Heather was pleased too. She said she would visit Alison tomorrow as Elspeth would not be able to, and Catherine said she would be ready in the morning.

She didn't phone Sybil. She knew she was going to dinner with Lord and Lady Paterson.

They had an estate in Norfolk where Sybil occasionally stayed.

Andrew Paterson had been an old friend of Pogo's. They had always gone shooting together.

Elspeth didn't think Sybil cared much for Myrtle. 'Frightfully stiff,' she would say. 'No sense of humour, and very mean with the heating...' All the same, she enjoyed going to stay, and they always invited her to dinner at Rules or Simpson's when they were in London. Elspeth remembered that they had two sons and a daughter — had they all survived? Andrew had been a brigadier —

she couldn't remember what regiment. Hopefully their children had been too young. She vaguely remembered their daughter, a plain, skinny child…

Anyhow, Sybil would be out this evening, and there was no point phoning in the morning. Sybil never surfaced before 10.30. Elspeth wondered, as she had done many times, how she managed. The one thing that Sybil really missed were the servants — just pressing the bell and everything immediately done. Her personal maid, Sabine, a delightful French girl, who kept all her clothes immaculate — who helped her dress, and choose her jewellery — brought her breakfast in bed on a tray with a lace cloth and a single flower in a cut glass vase — a perfectly boiled egg, triangles of toast, delicate rose-patterned china.
These were the things Sybil really missed. The loss of her husband, which she had treated as unfortunate, the inevitable sale of her beautiful house in Eaton Square, both paled into insignificance with the departure of Sabine and all the inconspicuous staff who kept her life in order.
Sabine had been whisked off by the War Office — a native French speaker, very much in demand. She had wept profusely when she had had to leave. Sybil had given her a valuable brooch of diamonds and sapphires as a parting gift.

Finally surfacing after the war, when the dust sheets were removed and the blackout curtains taken down, when one no longer dreaded a moonlit night, making London a sitting target for the enemy bombers, she still sometimes woke in the night, instantly alert, expecting to hear the whistling hiss and crump of bombs.

It had taken some time to adjust to the stark reality of a servantless world.
Of course she had to cope with the same sort of difficulties as Sybil. The difference being Jumbo's death had been completely devastating, outweighing any kind of deprivations.
Selling the house had been traumatic and upsetting, but there had been no alternative. But she already had the flat, and Martha didn't leave until Paula had arrived, so she had never been without

domestic help. And she had Olive who did all the boring things, like collecting the cleaning and going to the post office.

She had never even had to make herself a cup of tea, and as for cooking, the only cooking she had ever done was at school, when they had learnt to make fairy cakes in the domestic science class.

And dear Jumbo had left her very well provided for, whereas Pogo's unsuccessful ventures on the Stock Market had left Sybil in a rather precarious position.

Thank goodness for Francesca. She hoped it would all work out well.

The Hertford clinic — The Elms — was in a residential part of the town, on a tree-lined road.

It looked very much like the picture in the brochure.

A short drive, bordered by rhododendrons, just coming into bud. A large red brick house covered with an abundant Virginia Creeper sprouting new growth. The paving and stone steps which led down to a sloping lawn were cracked and broken in places. There were clumps of shrubs, and a row of elms along the fence.

It had a very old-fashioned feel. Like something out of a nineteenth-century novel. It even had two small lions each side of the porch, their features completely worn away.

Two men were walking across the far end of the garden, heads bowed in conversation. One was wearing shorts, the other a blue and white striped jersey.

The chauffeur parked the Daimler in front of the porch.

The car had been very punctual.

A black Daimler. They always had a black Daimler.

The chauffeur was wearing a smart grey uniform. Wilson had had a grey uniform — Jumbo preferred grey. He said it seemed less formal. She thought Wilson had joined a tank regiment. She tried to imagine the quietly deferential Wilson in command of a tank — a great lumbering, cyclopsed-eyed monster, crushing everything in its path. He could have been killed in the desert with Jumbo… She hoped he had not been killed.

Really this would not do. She must concentrate on finding somewhere for Alison.

She had told Olive to explain to Sybil, if she telephoned, that she would be away all day.

She had phoned Weymouth House to find out how Alison was. They said she was sleeping. Dr Myers had seen her last evening, and would be coming later in the morning.
Elspeth was very relieved that she was in good hands. At least that was something less to worry about.

They did not speak much during the drive.
Elspeth thought how nice Catherine looked. She liked the way she dressed, and she had such pretty, slightly curling light brown hair. Catherine though how Elspeth always had such classily expensive, tastefully understated clothes. Today she was wearing a lightweight lovat green tweed costume with matching hat and gloves.
It was a pleasant, sunny morning, a few high white clouds moving slowly in the light breeze.

Elspeth said it was good to get out of London — to see some green fields — the trees were particularly lovely at this time of year.

Catherine thought again of the serene, luminously-leaved beeches in the woods behind Bembridge.

Such a short summer. Just a few months of warmth and hope — trying to ignore the ominous shadows, the approaching threat.
Her whole life shaped by a distant summer.

Sitting in a café during the sudden shower, drinking tea — Peter staring at his cup — telling her he had joined up — that his mother was furious — his father resigned. 'I can't sit about as if nothing is happening,' he had said, and they had fallen silent, watching the raindrops sliding down the window, as if weeping for what was to come.

Elspeth told Catherine briefly about the events of the day before.
'I just hope she stays there,' she said. 'It seems a very nice place, but there is nothing to stop her leaving.' She then told her about going

with Alistair to pick out some furniture for his new flat from the storehouse in Borehampton.

'There are still quite a lot of things left,' she said. 'Mostly bedroom furniture.' And then impetuously — 'Most of the things were destroyed in the bombing — the storage firm had all their big warehouses in the City.' She sighed inwardly — did anybody really care anymore? So many people had lost so many things in the bombing…

Catherine said he wondered whether things would ever be normal again. Could the irreplaceable ever be replaced…?

She then told her that the poor shabby man was on the critical list, and that Mr Simms had done his best to get more information. Elspeth said it was so sad, so very sad, and they fell silent.

There was nobody at the reception desk.

The hall was tiled with a few hessian mats strewn about.

There was a small polished table with two large, ugly Chinese-style jars beneath a large, gilt-edged mirror, and a pot of sickly-looking ferns.

Elspeth rang the bell on the reception desk, and after a short interval a young woman appeared. She had a lot of bushy hair and bright orange lipstick. She was wearing a green polo neck jumper and a brown skirt.

She apologised for keeping them waiting. 'Dr Taylor is expecting you.'

She fiddled with the interphone and then said loudly, 'Lady Thornton is here…' She made a vague gesture and said, 'She'll be here in a minute…'

Catherine had suggested that she would wait outside whilst Elspeth had her meeting with Dr Taylor. After all she didn't know Alison, had never met her, and only had a vague idea what she was like. She felt awkward about being there whilst she was being discussed, but Elspeth said she wanted her to be there, to hear what was said and to give her opinion.

Dr Taylor did not keep them waiting long, her high heels tapping loudly on the bare tiles. Probably in her forties — neat brown hair, glasses, wearing a blue twinset and pleated grey skirt, carrying a large number of folders which prevented her from shaking hands.

'So sorry,' she said, leading them down a dark passage to her office. It was a large, comfortably, if shabbily, furnished room with a bow window overlooking the garden. The grass needed cutting. At the far end there was a lopsided pagoda and a broken stone seat.

Dr Taylor gestured for them to sit down, placing the files on her desk, already cluttered with piles of papers, notepads, and a collection of pencils in an old jam jar.

Elspeth explained about Alison — that she was in need of help.

'I'm afraid it has become quite serious,' she said. 'And now she has lost her job.' Her voice trailed off. It was embarrassing having to discuss Alison — to have to admit that one's daughter was a hopeless drunk.

Dr Taylor took notes and asked a few questions — how long had she been drinking — did she live alone — was her health affected? She said that they had experienced psychiatrists and nursing staff who were used to dealing with all sorts of problems, which were often deep-rooted. She twisted her pen in her fingers, and shifted some of the papers into a tidier heap.

'We do have a number of people from the armed forces here,' she said. 'Unfortunate casualties of the war.' She paused. 'In fact our patients are predominantly male. However that shouldn't make any difference — I'm sure I can help your daughter.'

Whilst she spoke Catherine stared at the corner of the desk. Featureless they trudged, an endless procession, dragging weary limbs, heads bowed — the haunted — the bereaved — the disillusioned — nursing hidden wounds — and trailing behind them those unable to cope with their lives, like Alison.

Elspeth was uncomfortable and angry. Angry that she had such a weak, hopeless daughter. She felt she hardly knew her. As a child, Nanny dealt with her — and then school, where she hardly shone — mediocre — not like Rosemary who seemed to be good at everything. Alison was very pretty in a blonde waif-like way — much prettier than her sister. And then the war. The war, cutting short any normal life. No coming out parties — no presentation at Court — no suitable young men for a suitable marriage. She was sure Alison would have met and married somebody very suitable. All the same, she had a great many advantages — good education — privileged family — her own flat — no money worries — until recently a very good job. No excuse for being a total mess. Fortunate that she could go to an expensive clinic to get help. She should be ashamed.

Elspeth was ashamed. Ashamed that Alison, apart from her father's death, had had nothing more life-shattering to deal with than a sordid affair with a married man — she really must ask Heather if she knew who he was — should be among people who had had unspeakably horrific experiences, their lives irrevocably changed forever.

Dr Taylor got up abruptly from her desk and said briskly that she would show them round.

It was very much like the brochure.
The bedrooms were quite small, but adequately furnished with private bathrooms.
The chintzy lounge, the library — there were several men in the library, sitting on the brown leather armchairs, reading.
Catherine would have liked to have a look at what books they had, but didn't think it would be appropriate.

The dining room was a good size, with a low ceiling, overlooking a lumpy lawn with a rather scruffy hedge separating it from a neglected-looking vegetable garden — a stretch of brown, weedy earth dotted with a few sad-looking cabbage stalks. There was someone digging at the far end, maybe about to plant some new vegetables.
The tables were laid for lunch. There were a few young women with blue aprons putting out jugs of water.

Dr Taylor said they managed to provide a varied diet despite the rationing. 'We do grow a few of our own vegetables, and we are lucky to be able to get a lot of local produce.'

She took them to see the studio, a spacious room with a glass ceiling. There was a tall man with a red beard standing in front of a half-finished oil painting, a mass of lurid-coloured swirls. Another man was drawing a jug and bowl on the table in front of him. They were totally engrossed, and did not even acknowledge their presence.

Dr Taylor led them back up the passage to the dismal hall.
The untidy young woman had disappeared. Dr Taylor said they were much in demand. 'We do our best to help everyone who comes here. Of course we are not always successful. Everybody's problems are very different.' She stopped as if it was all too much — too difficult to talk about.
'I hope you can let us know as soon as possible what you decide. We don't get many vacancies… If you would excuse me now,' she was looking at her watch, 'I have a meeting.'
They shook hands, and Elspeth thanked her.
They made their way across the hall and out into the sunlight.
Suddenly from somewhere inside they could hear shouting. Angry shouting and then silence again.

On the way to St Albans they had hardly spoken.
Catherine didn't really see the newly sprouting hedgerows and young-leafed trees, her mind full of flickering images. Peter laughing, hand in hand as they walked among the beeches. The crunching underfoot of the empty beechnut shells. Clumps of starry white anemones in the soft brown earth. The mossy graveyard where her mother was buried — someone's bones were buried — a coffin full of salvaged bones — her father still expecting her to come home — 'Why is Joyce so late?' The livid scar down the side of Alistair's face. The people in the clinic struggling to beat their demons, or perhaps they didn't want to — didn't want to face reality. Reality was perhaps too difficult — or perhaps reality was too unreal.

Elspeth was still angry. Maybe she should just let Alison get on with it. She didn't seem to want any help.
She wondered what Jumbo would have done. Of course he would never have abandoned Alison, however irritatingly impossible she was, or whatever stupid situation she had got herself into.

The whole experience of the Hertford clinic had been immensely depressing. In her mind she had already ruled it out as a possible place for Alison.

'Not very encouraging,' she said.

And Catherine agreed.

The clinic at St Albans looked much more like a clinic.

Also very much like the photograph in the brochure. Square and grey and solid. The gardens were extensive, with tennis courts round the side. There was an energetic mixed doubles in progress. The players were not exactly dressed for tennis — no pristine whites — just an assortment of casual clothing. But they were obviously enjoying themselves.

Elspeth remembered the girls playing on the court at home — at the far end of the rose garden, bordered by shrubs — she could never remember their names. Meadows had been very good with shrubs. The games were always contentious. Alison hated losing — made a frightful fuss. Rosemary was a so much better player. They had worn white Airtex shirts and short white pleated skirts, and had looked very nice.

Jumbo had not been keen on tennis. He was a golfer. They had had a good local golf course — a wonderful place for a nice long walk — she did not play herself. She had never been interested much in games — couldn't get excited in hitting balls about — seemed rather pointless — maybe a quiet game of croquet on a summer's afternoon… Jumbo had belonged to the golf club. They had a lot of social events which she had felt obliged to attend. Rather dull affairs. She had never cared for the club — too much drinking. The bar was always packed. Too cliquey — a lot of gossip. She did not care for gossip. Some of the women had been really insufferable, putting on airs and graces — awful snobs. Jumbo had always enjoyed going to the club. It seemed such a very long time ago — in another world.

The gardens in front of the clinic were very well kept. There were beds of tulips of all colours — almost finished now — and well pruned rose bushes which should have a lovely display later on.

The house had large picture windows and a glass-fronted entrance.

The hall had parquet flooring scattered with Persian rugs, and a large watercolour of sailing ships above a cane sofa with pale green cushions, two chintz covered armchairs, and a tall treelike plant with glossy green leaves reaching nearly to the ceiling in a wooden tub by the front door.

There was a young woman at the reception desk. Very blonde wearing a pink angora jumper with matching lipstick and nail varnish. She said she would ring for Dr Phillips. She thought he'd gone into the garden, and would they like to sit down.

They had hardly time to sit down on the cane sofa when Dr Phillips appeared.
A distinguished-looking man with silver grey hair, very smartly dressed in a slate grey suit, pale blue shirt and dark blue tie. He acknowledged the receptionist with a smile. 'Thank you, Shirley,' he said. 'Would you ask Brenda to bring some coffee to my study?' He then turned to them, shaking them warmly by the hand.

His study also had a big window with a view of the garden.
A large ornately framed oil painting of a wooded landscape hung on the wall behind an impressive leather-topped desk — there were several smaller pictures on the other walls. There were comfortable chairs and a beautiful arrangement of flowers in a square glass case on a table by the window.

Elspeth told him briefly about Alison, and he took notes — nodding — asking the occasional question.
He said it was their aim to rehabilitate all the people in their care. 'We work at building up their confidence, so that they feel able to cope with their lives without the prop of alcohol or drugs.' He paused. 'The biggest problem is when they leave here, and go back to the same situations that they needed to escape from. Unless there is a considerable alteration in their circumstances, they are highly likely to slip back into their old habits...'

There was a brief knock at the door, and a short young woman in a white uniform came in with a tray, which she put down on the desk.

'Thank you, Brenda,' said Dr Phillips. 'Very nice.'

She nodded and smiled, leaving the room as quietly as she had come. Dr Phillips poured the coffee. The china was fine white porcelain, edged with silver. There were brown sugar crystals in a round bowl. Elspeth wondered where on earth he had found the sugar. She thought it was unobtainable.

There had always been a bowl of brown sugar crystals with their after dinner coffee that Penn had brought into the drawing room on a round black lacquered tray inlaid with mother of pearl flowers, and a dish of peppermint creams. Jumbo had loved peppermint creams. She had stopped taking sugar during the war, saving her ration for emergencies, when it could be very helpful.

Catherine had her coffee black with sugar, also noting the sugar crystals. Dr Phillips also took his coffee black with sugar, and carried on talking.

'We do our best to prepare people for going back to their ordinary lives. Some go back to university or college to finish their interrupted degrees or training. There are lot of people struggling with the aftermaths of marital breakup — the loss of home and family. The war was responsible for a great many broken marriages — and so much grief — so much grief...' He paused, and drank some coffee. 'We try to do practical things. We have arranged secretarial courses with a secretarial college in the town — accompanied, of course. It can be very helpful, especially for women who have never had a job — never had to earn any money. Here we encourage all kinds of activities. A very competent lady comes once a week to take dancing and movement classes. We have a very well-equipped studio — pottery is very popular — some people have made wonderful pots and dishes — and we get them fired at a local pottery. We have a resident artist to give any help or instruction. There is a lot of music — chamber groups, an excellent choir, sometimes even a small orchestra. We can hire instruments, if necessary, from the music shop in town. Anybody can help in the garden, or in the kitchen. We had one man who was a marvellous pastry chef. We all benefited from his cakes and pies. And of course there is personal and group therapy, which some people find very helpful. All our staff are very well qualified and very experienced.'

He finished his coffee, placing the empty cup carefully on the tray. 'Anyhow I must show you round — if you are ready.'

All the rooms were light and airy, comfortably furnished and welcoming. The bedrooms had easy chairs and bookshelves. Dr Phillips said they liked everybody to feel at home.
At the back there was a large kitchen garden. A tall woman in Wellington boots and a waterproof jacket was standing in the middle of newly dug earth, talking to a man leaning on a spade.
'One of our regulars, I'm afraid,' said Dr Phillips. 'She comes and goes. She is a very keen gardener — only content in the garden. Unfortunately she now lives in a flat — lost her house in the war — an impossible situation. We are trying to find a solution...'
There were several greenhouses. Dr Phillips said they grew tomatoes, cucumbers, salads, marrows, most of their own vegetables. 'We also have chickens, so we always have plenty of fresh eggs.'

Elspeth thought of Meadows, and the sweet-smelling greenhouses full of red and yellow vined tomatoes he had been so proud of, and the surrounding wooden fence covered with large flowering purple and white clematis.

Dr Phillips said he would just show them the hall and dining room. As they started to walk down the corridor, a young man in a tweed jacket and beige corduroys came rushing towards them, obviously distressed. 'I can't find Dr McPherson,' he said. 'I have to speak to Dr McPherson — I can't find him.'
Dr Phillips put out a restraining hand, and took his arm. 'It's alright Stewart,' he said. 'I'm sure he's around somewhere. Come into the lounge and I'll see if I can find him...'
Stewart said 'I have to speak to him now — I have to speak to him now...'
Dr Phillips led him slowly towards the lounge, talking reassuringly.

He came back quickly. 'You'll have to excuse me while I sort this out,' he said. 'The hall is just at the end of the corridor on the left, if you would like to go and have a look.' He hurried back up the corridor towards the reception.

The hall was spacious, rather dusty, with high windows and a platform at the far end with a grand and an upright piano, and a collection of music stands. There were chairs stacked against the walls, and several large portraits of severe-looking men with starched collars.

Dr Phillips did not take long. He appeared accompanied by Shirley.

'It seems that Dr McPherson is not on duty this weekend, and he has gone out,' he said. 'So I shall have to take over myself. Shirley can answer any questions you might have.'

He shook hands, thanking them for coming, and strode off quickly towards the lounge.

They had gone back to the entrance with Shirley. Elspeth asked about the meals — how did they know if people had actually eaten anything — thinking of Alison's aversion to eating anything…

Shirley said that everybody had to tick a register when they went into the dining room.

'Of course they can have meals in their rooms, but Dr Phillips prefers them to come to the dining room. There are members of staff in the dining room who make sure people are actually eating something — so we do are best.'

Elspeth thanked her, and said that was very reassuring.

Shirley accompanied them to the door, and waited for them to get in the car, giving them a cheery wave.

Elspeth said what a charming girl, and Catherine said it had all seemed very nice and well run.

Elspeth told their driver, Collins — she remembered that Ladbroke Cars had told her their driver would be a Mr Martin Collins when she had confirmed the booking for the car. It had slipped her mind with all the fuss about Alison — to drive into the town to see if they could find somewhere to eat. She wasn't really hungry, but it was lunchtime.

The town was crowded with Saturday shoppers. They passed two rather rundown looking pubs — one had a billboard outside with

"Steak and Kidney Pud with 2 Veg" written on it in large black letters. The other had a broken sign and a rusty bike chained to the railings. They also noticed a classy looking restaurant called La Belle Epoque, but neither of them felt like eating in a classy restaurant, and then they spotted an Olde Worlde Tea Shoppe on a corner.
'They should do things on toast,' said Elspeth. 'If that is alright with you.' Catherine said that was fine, she really liked things on toast.
Collins dropped them off. He said he had brought his own sandwiches so he would just go and find somewhere to park, and come back and pick them up. Elspeth said about 2 o'clock should be fine, or perhaps a little later. 'Thank you, Collins.'

There were lots of things on toast — cheese, baked beans, mushrooms, plain toast and butter. There was soup of the day with roll and butter, and scones and jam…
They chose cheese on toast and a pot of tea for two. It was such a treat to have proper cheese on toast without having to worry about the rations.
'Very nice,' said Elspeth. 'Most appetising.' And Catherine suddenly found she was very hungry. 'Perfect,' she said. 'Couldn't be nicer…'

They ate their lunch slowly. The café was very full — bustling and friendly. They both relaxed, enjoying their food and the general atmosphere. It was good to have something nice to eat. Elspeth said 'Just what we needed.' She took the remaining brochures out of her bag and pushed them across the table for Catherine to look at. She said she thought they really only needed to go to Aylesbury. 'Amersham looks so old fashioned, and High Wycombe looks much too high-powered with lots of sports, and Alison hates sports.'
Catherine said Aylesbury looked very modern and chic, more like a posh hotel. She agreed that Amersham looked old-fashioned, and the small windows would make it rather dark inside, and the High Wycombe did seem rather energetic, offering fencing, gymnastics and Scottish dancing, as well as two swimming pools and a squash court. 'Also,' Elspeth said, 'I am getting rather weary.' Catherine said she was also feeling rather weary, although they both agreed that the food had made them feel a lot better.

The Aylesbury clinic was on a high piece of ground outside the town, surrounded by fields, with sloping lawns, and poplars lining the road.

The afternoon sun reflecting on the long walls of glass accentuated the building's whiteness.

As they turned into the drive, Elspeth leant forward, sliding open the glass partition that separated them from the driver.

'Could you stop here a moment Collins,' she said. She felt suddenly unable to continue.

The house reminded her so much of the Berniers' villa in St Tropez — on the terrace — the gardens leading down to the cliff edge dotted with magical umbrella pines — the murmuring of the sea below where it curled frothing against the rocks. Claudine in her flowing gowns, glass in hand, and Jumbo trying out his halting French on Michel. There was much laughter — much laughter... Their housekeeper, Marianne, severe in her black dress with the little white collar, producing trays of delicious titbits to go with the champagne — so much champagne. The stars so large — so close — the air so soft and warm.

They had never taken the girls with them to the South of France — they were safely at home with Nanny.

They had once all gone together to Trouville, where Jumbo played golf, whilst she and Nanny and the girls had gone to the beach. It had not been a success. Alison had not liked the sand — had sat and screamed to go home — finally persuaded with much hiccupping to join Rosemary who was building a sand castle. She had enthusiastically dug a moat around it, and it had promptly collapsed, and Alison had started crying again.

She had been so relieved to have been invited to dinner with Jumbo's golfing friends, leaving Nanny to battle with the girls' bedtime.

'Well,' she said. 'This looks almost continental. Thank you, Collins, we'll go on now...'

Catherine had never been abroad. It had, of course, been impossible during the war, and then it was just too expensive. She would love to go to France. It looked so lovely in films and magazines. The sparkling Mediterranean with fashionable ladies in beach pyjamas and huge floppy-brimmed hats lounging under sun umbrellas, or sauntering along the promenade. Paris with the Eiffel Tower, and the treelined Champs Elysees. Croissants and hot chocolate at little cafés in the Tuileries Gardens. Perhaps one day she would go… Peter had been to France several times. He had friends who had a villa near Antibes. He had told her how great it was — surprisingly mountainous and rocky. He had a marvellous time swimming and sailing — his friends had a yacht. He told her of evenings sitting on the deck with his friends drinking funny coloured cocktails and then going ashore to eat freshly caught fish in one of the many seaside restaurants.

He said his mother did not approve, considering all this cavorting about on yachts with scantily dressed young women, and drinking too many cocktails was the height of decadence, and Catherine had thought of Ursula Tarrant with her neatly pressed waves, mouth pursed, disapproving of practically everything. But Peter said that when she discovered the owners of the yacht were Sir and Lady Carpenter, the Wiltshire Carpenters, her attitude changed completely, and she had been very keen to encourage his friendship… He always said she was a frightful snob, and they burst out laughing. They had laughed a lot before life had become devoid of laughter.

He had taken her to tea at the Excelsior Hotel, a very grand establishment just outside Bembridge. There had been an orchestra playing dance music — so many lovely tunes — some people were dancing. They had not danced, just sat and held hands. Peter had talked about their future, their life together. He said they would go to the South of France as soon as this awful war was over. And they drank tea, and ate scones and jam and pretty little cakes with different coloured icing. He had leant across the table and kissed her cheek. It had been a truly blissful afternoon — a chink of light before the onset of enveloping darkness — of grief — of a world with no laughter.

There was a lily pond with a small slurping fountain outside the wide glass-doored entrance.

The hall had a floor of black and white tiles.
There was an aquarium along one wall full of wavy green fronded plants and darting multicoloured fish.
On the wall behind the reception desk was a film poster for *Top Hat*, starring Fred Astaire and Ginger Rogers, with a notice pinned beside it with coloured drawing pins, announcing it was to be shown that evening at 8 o'clock in the Small Hall. 'Everybody Welcome'.
The young man behind the reception desk got up and came towards them. He was wearing a navy blue blazer with a red and gold monogram on the pocket, and grey slacks. He had a pleasant, open face, and a lot of fair wavy hair. He greeted them effusively — shaking them warmly by the hand. 'You must be Lady Thornton,' he said. 'I'm Luke. Dr Carruthers is terribly sorry, he has been called away, so he asked me to show you around.'

He proceeded to conduct them down long corridors — throwing open doors. It was all very spacious and light, with floor to ceiling windows, and white walls, with an occasional large violently coloured painting, and strange, contorted black and bronze sculptures on little plinths.

There were quite a few people in the white lounge, playing cards and chess, or reading newspapers.
They interrupted a group therapy session, with people sitting round in a circle looking very stressed — one woman was crying.
The dining room had white tables and chairs. There were staff in white uniforms preparing tea behind a long counter. Luke said, 'They can just help themselves to whatever they like. Tea is served between 4 and 5.30.'
He was only able to show them a couple of bedrooms. 'Some people like to have a rest in the afternoon,' he explained.
The ones they did see looked very comfortable, with white carpets and curtains. Luke said, 'Dr Carruthers says white is soothing — unchallenging — helps people relax...' He also said that Dr Carruthers did not encourage visits. 'He thinks it best to have very

little contact with the outside world — too unsettling...'

When they got back to London it was nearly 6 o'clock.
Luke had been very thorough, showing them the Sports Hall, where
he said they played a lot of basketball, and did gymnastics —
'Dr Carruthers is very keen on exercise...' — and the smaller hall
where they were going to show the film tonight. 'We try to put on a
film at least once a month. Dr Carruthers thinks it is good to have
some entertainment.'
He then took them on a brisk tour of the well kept gardens,
apologising for the overgrown tennis court. 'We hope to have it
ready for the summer...'

Elspeth dropped Catherine outside her flat.
She invited her to come back for tea or a drink, but she said she was
very tired and had things to do.

They had discussed the two clinics in the car.
Both had seemed excellent — well run — plenty of activities —
positive treatment — comfortable rooms.
It was really difficult to decide.
In the end they had both agreed that St Albans would probably be
the best. They had both liked Dr Phillips. It was a shame they had
not had the opportunity to meet Dr Carruthers — he had sounded
extremely competent. They thought that all Dr Phillips was trying
to achieve was really impressive, and the clinic had seemed more
homely and not so challenging.
Elspeth thought it would be more suitable for Alison.

Elspeth said she would phone Dr Phillips on Monday, and hoped
there would be a vacancy very soon — 'Before Alison has time to
change her mind.'

Olive was in the sitting room listening to the wireless and doing
a crossword. She was very fond of doing crosswords. She got up
quickly when Elspeth came in, smiling anxiously.

Elspeth sat down gratefully in her favourite armchair. She took off her hat and put it on the little table by her side. 'I suppose it is too late for tea...'

Olive said she would go and see. 'I'm sure it will be alright.'

Paula was very fussy about people coming into the kitchen, particularly if she was preparing a meal.

Elspeth said, 'Thank you, Olive, that would be really wonderful — I'm completely parched...' Goodness, she thought. I sound just like Sybil.

Olive was not long bringing in the tea. 'She grumbled a bit,' she said, 'but I was as quick as possible.'

Elspeth moved her hat so that Olive could put the tray of tea-things on the table.

Olive said that Heather had phoned. She had visited Alison. She said she had seemed very comfortable. She thought she must have been sedated because she was rather groggy. She had managed to have some tea and a slice of cake. Olive hesitated. 'She said she didn't want you to come and see her...'

Elspeth drank her tea. She was not surprised Alison didn't want to see her — really she was relieved. She never knew what to say to Alison. Whatever she said was wrong.

'And Mrs Anstruther phoned,' Olive continued. 'She was very agitated. She said she is booking herself into the Hyde Park Hotel until Francesca comes on Thursday. Apparently she had set fire to several pieces of toast, and broken one of her best plates. She said she couldn't cope anymore. She wants you to go to lunch with her tomorrow at the hotel...'

Elspeth said, 'Oh dear. You better go and tell Paula. Hopefully she will not be too annoyed. She knows how unpredictable Sybil is. Perhaps she can postpone Sunday lunch until Monday. Alistair will not be here. He is going to spend the day with friends in Wimbledon, and you can look after yourself. I can tell Paula to take the day off. We shall only need a light supper.' She finished her tea. 'I would like you to go on Monday and get her a really nice box of chocolates to thank her for finding Francesca. Could you speak to her now?

I'm going to change and have a bath before supper — and I have to telephone Heather…'

They had a very quiet evening. Paula had taken the sudden alteration to tomorrow's plans quite well. She was fully aware of Sybil's idiosyncrasies. She said the 'joint' was so small anyway, it was hardly worth roasting. She was pleased to have the day off, and would make mushroom omelettes for supper.

This evening she had made one of her delicious rabbit stews with mashed potatoes. They ate in comparative silence. Alistair had come in looking pale and drawn, his scars more obvious than usual. Elspeth sent Olive to fetch a nice bottle of wine. She hoped he was alright. Tamarind had been evasive about his health, all she had said was, 'I think he's fine now…'. At least he was getting plenty of good food, although she thought he was still much too thin.

She really did not want to discuss her day, or talk about Alison. She did not really want to even think about her. She just hoped she was doing the right thing. She didn't really know what else she could do. Olive talked about the weather — quite nice for this time of year — and Alistair hardly said anything at all, except how good the stew was.

She had telephoned Heather, who had just said the same things as Olive. Alison seemed comfortable, but probably sedated, and that all the staff were very friendly and helpful.
Elspeth told her about the clinics.
'I'm going to telephone St Albans on Monday and try and get a place as soon as possible.'
She said she hoped Heather would be able to go with her. 'She won't go with me. And she can't go alone…'
Heather said of course, she would do all she could to help. It was awful to see Alison like this…

Catherine did not go straight into the flat.
She went round the corner to the newsagent to get a paper, and treat herself to a *Woman's Journal* — she felt she needed a little light relief.

The Express Dairy was still open so she went in and bought a pint of milk and a pack of four current buns. It had been a very stressful day. She had found visiting the clinics quite disturbing — especially Hertford. Dr Taylor had been so edgy and distracted, as if she wanted to jump up and run away. It must be such a difficult job. Dr Phillips had been most caring and positive, calmly reassuring. She wondered how many people really did recover, and she wondered about Alison — what sort of young woman she was. Lady Thornton didn't seem to know her very well at all.

She would have liked to have gone back with Elspeth to her flat. She might have seen Alistair, but she felt awkward. Just because he had been friendly did not mean he would like her to keep popping up. Despite his friendliness and warmth, she felt he was struggling to be normal — to be calm and competent — managing to conceal any inner distress — to be as he was expected to be. She did not want to make things worse.

Tomorrow she would take the bus to Hyde Park and walk round the Serpentine and Kensington Gardens, and then go and have something to eat in the Lyons Corner House at Marble Arch.

Elspeth was glad that it was Monday.

Now she could get on with arranging things.

She telephoned Dr Phillips, who was most friendly, apologising for cutting short their visit on Saturday. He said there might be a vacancy in a few weeks' time. An ex-commando who was making excellent progress — 'very supportive wife' — should be ready to go home — and a young woman who had decided to emigrate to Canada and start a new life — 'We always have people waiting.' He would let her know as soon as possible.

She phoned Weymouth House and was told that Alison was fine, but getting rather restless. Dr Myers would be in later to see her.

Elspeth was concerned. What was she to do? Alison could not be kept sedated until there was a place for her at the clinic…

She would just have to come here — whether she liked it or not. There was really no alternative. She couldn't go back to her flat on her own. Anyway, Elspeth was just about to try and arrange for the whole place to be thoroughly cleaned. She would speak to Heather. Perhaps she would be able to persuade her, and she would send Olive to see her this afternoon and try and get her to agree to come. Alison didn't mind Olive. They seemed to get on quite well. She'd better see if there were enough sheets — she might have to order some more.

Sybil hadn't been able to remember the address of the cleaning firm she had used. She thought they were called Supreme Cleaners — she would have to check — she had been very satisfied with their work. Elspeth had looked them up in the telephone directory. She wasn't going to wait for Sybil. She had probably forgotten about it already. Their receptionist was very polite. It sounded as if they were efficient and well organised. She said they might be able to start by the end of next week — this was rather a busy time — spring cleaning... Of course they would have to see the flat first — see what had to be done — before they could say how long it would take.

Elspeth said everything would have to be cleaned — including carpets and curtains. It might even need redecorating.
They arranged that a Mr Anderson would meet her at the flat that afternoon at 3.30.

She had had a very civilised lunch with Sybil the day before. They had arranged to meet at 12.30 in the lounge of the Hyde Park Hotel. Very opulent and comfortable. Sybil was only slightly late — elegant as always in a pale blue tailored dress with a diamond brooch on the shoulder — matching hat and high heeled shoes. Elspeth was wearing her favourite pale blue and grey checked costume — she felt she would always look rather dowdy next to Sybil.

Sybil slid into one of the capacious armchairs, stretching her long legs in front of her and neatly crossing her ankles.
'This is almost like pre-war,' she said. 'I had breakfast in bed this morning — coffee and croissants — proper croissants...' She beckoned the waiter who was standing by the door beside a giant fern, and ordered two large martinis.
'Perhaps I could just come and live here,' she said, and laughed.

They had a friend, Clarissa Fearweather, who had spent the entire war living in Grosvenor House — never having to worry about rationing — the laundry — cleaning — everything unobtrusively managed for her. She had returned to her house in Somerset, which had been requisitioned during the war as a hostel for land-girls — 'Left it in a frightful mess.' She complained ceaselessly about everything — even objected to the cows in a neighbouring field. 'There were no cows before the war…' Looked after by a faithful parlourmaid, who had come out of retirement especially, but who was now very arthritic, and was finding all the domestic tasks an increasing problem — and was not much of a cook. 'Can't even make a decent custard,' Clarissa had said despairingly.

Elspeth sighed. She didn't think she would like to live in a hotel, however grand…

They had roast beef. The Head Waiter had recommended it. It was excellent. Very tender, with proper Yorkshire pudding and roast potatoes. They declined wine — too much after the very strong martinis — and drank sparkling water. They did not have dessert, but said they would have coffee in the lounge.

Sybil said the evening with the Pattersons had been a pleasant diversion.

They had gone to Wheelers.

She had had a nice piece of salmon with creamed spinach — very good. Andrew had oysters. Pogo had always had oysters — impossibly messy things. Myrtle had lobster.

Elspeth remembered going to Wheelers with Jumbo — he used to have oysters. She had never really got the hang of them — all that throwing one's head back and swallowing. She much preferred a nice Dover sole.

'Wonderful stuff,' Sybil continued. 'A bit ancient — but the whole place is a bit ancient.' Elspeth said it had always been a bit cramped, but such a nice atmosphere.

Sybil said poor Myrtle was stultifyingly dull. 'She has such a boring

life. I felt quite sorry for Andrew, although he spends a lot of time in the City, and of course there is the shooting and all that sort of thing. Myrtle just sits at home and fusses whether the "help" has done the dusting, or has used the wrong vases. The big thing at the moment is her daughter's wedding. She is getting married in July — there is to be an excessively extravagant wedding and reception. She showed me a photograph of her daughter. Plain little thing. Marrying a solicitor — so endless fussing about that. She'll probably have a nervous breakdown. I shall be in France so I will not be able to go. Thank goodness...'
Elspeth said it could be very nice — rather fun — thinking of Rosemary's wedding, which had, in fact, been a really happy occasion.

She needed to talk to Sybil about Alison.
She had thought a lot about what she would say — whether to prevaricate — say Alison wasn't very well — needed a rest — and so on and so on — but in the end just told her what had happened.
'I am having a lot of trouble with Alison,' she said.
Sybil lit a cigarette and leant back in her chair, blowing a waft of cigarette smoke up to the ornately decorated ceiling.
'She has a serious drink problem.'
'I shouldn't worry,' said Sybil. 'Probably having a messy love affair...'
'No,' said Elspeth. 'It is very serious. She has gone completely to pieces — has lost her job — her flat is, to put it mildly, absolutely disgusting — she wears filthy clothes, never seems to wash — refuses to discuss it...'
She told Sybil about Weymouth House, and the search for a suitable 'drying out' clinic, and how she didn't know what to do. Sybil said she was very sorry. Alison had always been rather 'sensitive'. She was sure it could be sorted out — and the clinic sounded an excellent idea. 'And then, perhaps, she could go and visit Rosemary in Los Angeles — that would cheer anybody up.' Elspeth said that was what she was hoping...

Paula came in and said she was going to pot roast the 'joint'. She had just been to the Berwick Street Market and bought some really good, fresh vegetables. She would make a leek and potato soup for lunch, and she had also been to the Italian shop and bought some Mortadella and salami. Elspeth said 'splendid', and to wait to serve coffee until Olive came in. She had sent her to get the chocolates.

She came in, more breathless and flushed than usual, putting her bag down by the door, and removing her awful hat.
She had been to Selfridges and had managed to get a lovely round box of chocolates tied with a blue satin ribbon. 'It used up most of your coupons,' she said. 'I think it is a really nice assortment. I bought some wrapping paper as well — silver and white stripes. I'll wrap it up later.'
'That is excellent Olive,' said Elspeth. 'Thank you. I'm sure Paula will be delighted — we can have coffee now...'

She took her coffee to the window, and sat in the small armchair looking down on the street. So many people rushing about — or just sauntering — a group of young women gathered at the entrance to the underground, two men arguing on the corner — everybody busy with their lives.

'Come and sit over here, Olive,' she said.
Olive sat down opposite her — nervously apprehensive — putting her coffee cup down carefully on the little table between them.
'I would like you to go and visit Alison again this afternoon,' she said. 'I want you to try and persuade her to come here until there is a place for her at the clinic. There is really no alternative — she can't go back to her flat on her own — and anyway I am planning to have it all thoroughly cleaned — should be fumigated — so there is really no alternative to her coming here. She can't be sedated indefinitely...'

Olive put more milk in her coffee.
'I'm sure she won't listen to me,' she said.
'Well, she certainly won't listen to me,' said Elspeth. 'I shall phone Heather this evening, and ask her to try — and I will speak to Dr Myers. She seems better with you,' she sighed. 'I would like you to try anyway...'

Dr Myers was not in his consulting rooms. The receptionist said he was out on calls, and she was not sure what time he would be back, so Elspeth left a message, and said she hoped to speak to him later.

10

The sky was grey and overcast when Catherine left for work, and her coat, which was getting rather threadbare, did not protect her from the chilly wind. She would have to start saving up now to buy a new one for next winter — coats were very expensive. She liked to get to the library early — to let herself in, and stand for a moment in the enveloping stillness — with the comforting smell of books — and paper — of polished shelves — surrounded by millions of words waiting to be discovered. She loved books. She loved handling books. The wonderful anticipation of opening a new book. At least that was one thing she and Miss Milburn had in common, their mutual love and respect for books. But she still liked to get there first, before Miss Milburn arrived in an irritable flurry of scarves and bags, and moans about the traffic.

This morning she stood a little longer, breathing in the familiar atmosphere, before she went to the pokey room downstairs where they hung their coats, and made the mid morning and afternoon tea. The library didn't open until 10 o'clock, and there were never many people on Monday morning. She fetched the pile of newspapers the cleaning staff had left on the counter, and took them to place on the round tables by the windows, passing the chair where the shabby man had always sat — she couldn't think of him as Mr Gardner — just the shabby man. She hoped Mr Simms would be able to get more news — to find out how he was getting on…

By the time Miss Milburn arrived, making an unaccountable fuss of negotiating doors, she had installed herself behind the counter, putting her handbag in the drawer, and was already sorting out the post. They received frequent lists from publishers of new and reissued publications. At the moment there were quite a lot of books on gardening. Late spring, early summer was a good time to think about gardens — Catherine doubted there would be much scope for gardening in Marylebone, but people liked to daydream. There was always a demand for books on travel — the exotic and beautiful places to visit — blue seas and expanses of white sand — towering snow-covered mountains and deeply green forests — journeys on the Orient Express — the Trans-Siberian Railway — the Blue Train to the South of France — so these books on gardening — *The Secret of a Perfect Cottage Garden* — *A Garden for All Seasons* — *Making the Most of Shrubs* — would all be just as popular as Elizabeth David's *Mediterranean Food*. There was even one on growing your own vegetables.

Miss Milburn reappeared carrying a pile of books. 'Isn't Elsie in yet?' she said. 'She's very late — she's always late.' She put the pile of books down on the counter. 'These all need putting back...'
Catherine said she'd do it. She liked putting books back in their proper places.
'We will have to get a new copy of the Margaret Irwin. It has been quite badly scribbled on with green ink...'
Catherine said there were at least two more copies — *Young Bess* seemed a popular choice...
Miss Milburn said she couldn't understand how people could deliberately spoil books — she was about to launch into a tirade about the careless and boorish behaviour of people nowadays when Elsie arrived, causing her to break off to demand why she was so late, and they disappeared together down the stairs.

Catherine looked through the pile of books that Miss Turnbull had left on the counter. A History of Medieval England — a copy of Rosamund Lehmann's *Weather in the Streets* — Catherine had loved that book — so evocative — so well written. Aldous Huxley's *Point Counter Point* — a battered copy of Rabindranath Tagore's *Collected Poems and Plays* — the latest Margery Allingham, *More Work for the Undertaker* — *Latin for Beginners*...

Mr Simms emerged from the glass doors at the back of the library which led to the staircase to the offices, and came towards her with his stork-like stride. He looked very serious, but he always looked serious — maybe it would not be bad news — but it was bad news. 'I'm afraid our Mr Gardner has died,' he said.

Catherine felt suddenly chilled and somehow defeated. She had hoped he would not die — after all, lots of people survived heart attacks.

She gripped the edge of the counter to steady herself.

Miss Milburn appeared from her office carrying a stack of papers, and approached them purposefully. Before she could say anything Mr Simms said, 'I have just been telling Miss Bradley that sadly, Mr Gardner has died. I did manage, finally, to speak to someone in authority. They told me that he was, in fact, a Commander in the Royal Navy — so even more sad that his life ended as it did.' He paused. 'They managed to locate a sister, who is going to deal with everything — I have obtained her address. I have drafted a letter of condolence,' he went on. 'Miss Palmer will type it up for us all to sign…'

There was a long silence. Elsie, who had quietly joined them, and was standing behind Miss Milburn, started to cry, hunting for a handkerchief in her cardigan pocket. Mr Simms said again how sad it was, and then, 'Well, we'd better get on — Miss Palmer will bring the letter down later.'

Miss Milburn started to speak. 'I have some things I need to discuss,' she said. Mr Simms said he would see her later — perhaps she could come up to his office after lunch, and he turned and made his stork-like way back across the library.

Catherine sat down on the chair behind the counter. Somehow she had always known he would die. What would have happened to him if he had recovered? They knew so little about him — where had he lived? Would there have been anyone to look after him? Just another casualty. They trouped through her mind — Peter — her mother and father — the people in the clinics — Alistair — the shabby man. Maybe they were torpedoed — maybe he had seen young sailors drowning — choking on oil — unable to save them — young men whose lives had been in his charge — feeling guilty to still be alive — not even wanting to be alive — sitting day after day in his chair, staring unseeingly at the newspapers — and so many others — so many others…

Miss Milburn snorted — she was at daggers drawn with Miss Palmer, Mr Simms' opulent secretary with her peroxide blonde perm, her high heels and frilly blouses, jealously guarding any access to him.
'Well I suppose that's the end of that,' she said tartly. Catherine could almost hear the added 'Good riddance', and she stalked back to her office. Catherine said nothing — there was nothing to say. Elsie said, 'Poor man. What a shame. A Commander. In that state.' She picked up the pile of books from the counter. 'I'll put these back,' she said.

*   *   *

Graham Anderson was waiting for her in the lobby of the flats.
A young man of medium height with gingery hair, wearing a brown suit and knitted yellow tie, and very shiny brown shoes.
They shook hands, and took the lift to Alison's flat.
'I'm afraid it is in rather a state,' she said, and Mr Anderson said cheerfully that that was what they were there for.
He took a clipboard and a business-like tape measure out of his shiny brown briefcase and started making notes.
He crouched down to inspect the stains on the carpet, running his hand over them. 'Wine,' he said. 'Coffee — some sort of food — very engrained. I don't know whether we will be able to get rid of them completely.' He got up and went to the window. 'Nice garden,' he said. 'Nice trees.'
Elspeth agreed, the garden in the square was very well kept, with trees and flower beds — even a little round summer house and a play area for children. She thought it highly doubtful if Alison had ever used it.

The bedroom was just as disgusting. Worse really. Elspeth had not gone in again after Olive had stripped the bed. The mattress was badly stained, and the pillows were really unpleasant. There were stains on the wallpaper by the bed — Alison must have knocked something over — and the carpet was almost as bad as in the living room.

She felt very embarrassed. 'This is really dreadful,' she said. 'The mattress and pillows will have to be disposed of. I think it probably best to throw away the eiderdown as well — it is almost impossible to get rid of smells.'
Mr Anderson assured her that they would see to everything. He agreed about the eiderdown, inspecting the stains on the wall, and said the room would need redecorating. He made notes.

The kitchen was not quite as bad.
Olive had managed to finish the washing up, and had put the various cleaning materials on the kitchen table. Elspeth had forgotten to tell her to empty the refrigerator — a very handsome American model. She must ask her to come and clear it out.
Mr Anderson said he would make sure that everything was properly cleaned, inspecting the floor which was caked with dirt and grease round the cooker, and a large unidentifiable stain by the sink.
'This will probably clean up alright,' he said. 'The linoleum's very good quality — practically new...'
Elspeth was hardly surprised. She couldn't imagine Alison had done much cooking — just spilt things — everything was dirty.
Mr Anderson said his only real concern were the carpets.
Elspeth said to just do his best. 'I quite understand.'

The bathroom was just messy and dirty, with more mysterious stains on the floor, and a very scummy bath and basin.
Mercifully the spare bedroom was neat and tidy — rather dusty, but otherwise unspoilt.

They agreed that everything was to be cleaned and redecorated, and to do the best with the carpets. The sofa, which had come from their old home had loose covers — she had always insisted on loose covers which could be laundered. The easy chairs, which were new, fortunately also had loose covers.

Mr Anderson was not sure when they could start, perhaps by the end of next week. They were working on a house in Ealing, which needed much more work than they had anticipated — rotten window frames, and broken floorboards. He would send her a fully itemised estimate for approval, and start as soon as possible…

They shook hands amicably, and he crossed the road to where he had parked his car — a sleek black saloon — and she went to find a taxi. She had decided to go to the library to see how Catherine was, and to tell her about the latest developments.
It had started to rain.

Catherine felt weighted down, wishing she could go home, trying to focus on what she was supposed to be doing — carry on as normal, always having to carry on as normal.
She was quite relieved to see Mrs Turner come into the library. A short, jolly woman — very talkative — always with a lengthy moan about something — trouble with the neighbours, their wireless was always too loud — 'don't have to bother turning ours on, we can hear everything through the wall' — unaccountable power cuts — in the middle of ironing — the inefficient postal service — a whole week to get a letter from her sister in Norfolk — a whole week — the length of time she had had to queue for a small piece of smoked haddock — people's lack of manners nowadays — her husband Harold worked in the ticket office at Marylebone Station — 'hardly ever a please or thank you.'
She dressed haphazardly, as if she had been thinking about something else whilst she was selecting what to wear.
Today she was wearing a lime green hat, a long yellow and red scarf wound several times round her neck, an ankle-length beige mackintosh with large buttons, and high-heeled scarlet sandals.
She had brought back two books, one on the Desert Campaign, which her husband had requested — 'Harold found it very interesting' — and the latest in Mazo de la Roche's Jalna series.
Catherine had introduced her to them. She was an avid reader — always looking for something new. She had just finished the third one and had come to get the fourth, *The Master of Jalna*.
She put the books on the counter. 'There was nearly a fight in the butcher's this morning,' she said. She had gone early to get some liver — Harold was very fond of liver — pity there was no bacon. She supposed that one day they would be able to have bacon as well again, if there was ever an end to this dreadful rationing.

There was already a small queue, there was an elderly lady in front of her, very well dressed with a fur coat — 'It looked real' — and beside her a smart young woman, all peroxide hair and a lot of make up, inspecting what was on offer. 'She sort of slid in front of the elderly lady who looked very annoyed. I thought she was going to bash her with her stick,' said Mrs Turner. 'She told her to get back in the queue. The young woman said she was in the queue, and refused to move. The elderly lady threatened her with her stick, and the young woman called her an old cow, and then the butcher — Gordon — a really nice man, intervened and said "Ladies, please — let's all calm down — you'll all be served..." Other people were getting impatient. The woman behind me said some people had to get to work, and there was a lot of muttering. In the end Gordon served the elderly lady first, and then she made it worse by taking ages finding her ration book — she had this really large, expensive handbag. Snakeskin. A beautiful thing...'
'So what did she manage to get?' said Catherine, visualising with some amusement ladies nearly coming to blows in the butcher's over their meagre meat ration.
'Half a shoulder of lamb,' said Mrs Turner. 'Quite a small one. The young woman had to put up with a fatty piece of pork belly — there was no lamb left — just a bit of scrag end. She wasn't very pleased. I got my liver — a really nice piece. Goodness me I mustn't stand here talking. I must go and get the book. I'm really enjoying them...' And she hurried off to find it.

She had certainly created a much-needed diversion — lifted the mood of regret and sadness. Catherine felt a great deal better — not so guilty and hopeless. At lunchtime she went to the Italian café and had a nice bowl of minestrone.

Miss Palmer came down after lunch with the letter for them to sign. Elsie got all tearful again. Miss Milburn bristled, signing her name with a flourish. 'Mr Simms says he can see you in about half an hour,' said Miss Palmer. She was wearing a very frilly white blouse, grey pleated skirt, high-heeled black patent shoes, a gold necklace, several gold jangly bracelets and vibrant mauve lipstick. Miss Milburn bristled some more and stalked off to her office.

Catherine was glad to see Elspeth come into the library. She was looking quite pleased. Elspeth never really smiled — she just didn't smile — but she was looking pleased.

'I've just come to see how you are,' she said. 'And to tell you what is going on.'

Catherine was glad that she could tell her now about Commander Gardner, that she would not have to telephone.

Elspeth sat down carefully on the chair. 'I was afraid he would not recover,' she said. 'Poor man. I always knew he was someone reputable — so like my husband's friend...' Sitting in Thelma's uncomfortable drawing room, drinking weak tea, whilst Jumbo and Montagu discussed the intricacies of cricket — something about spin bowling — and Thelma telling her how much her dahlias were admired. They were quite magnificent, and Elspeth had thought rather sourly that that was absolutely nothing whatsoever to do with Thelma, but the work of her excellent gardener. She wondered if they still had dahlias, or had their pillared mansion been taken over by the Armed Forces and smashed to pieces. And now the shabby man — a Commander — dying alone — a broken man. Was there ever going to be an end to all the misery — the dreadful aftermath of the dreadful war.

'So sad,' she said. 'At least they were able to locate a sister...'

Olive brought in the tea. They had it by the window.

It had stopped raining. Down below in the street there was a long queue at the bus stop outside the underground station, and the pavement was still wet and shiny from the rain.

Elspeth had already told Olive about Mr Gardner — Commander Gardner. She was very upset — poor man — poor man, she said — oh dear — oh dear, how sad — and she had made some excuse to leave the room.

Now she put the tray down on the table between them.

Elspeth asked her to pour the tea. She suddenly felt completely demoralised. She was tired, and she really didn't want to confront the problem of Alison.

Olive said she had seemed better — dressed and reading magazines. She thought she must be having some kind of medication — very vague. A nurse had brought in tea and biscuits — quite nice assorted biscuits. Alison had eaten two, very slowly. She seemed quite calm, and she hadn't objected to the idea of coming home — didn't seem to react at all.

Elspeth realised that she had not considered the full implications of Alison coming to live here. What had seemed a good idea in the small hours of the morning after a sleepless night now seemed utterly unrealistic. What would Alison do all day? Should she be allowed to go out? How on earth would she occupy herself? And the drink. Her eyes strayed to the well-stocked drinks cabinet on the other side of the room. It would have to be kept locked. She wasn't even sure if there was a key, and if so, where it was. No wine with meals. Constant surveillance.

Alison really needed other people to be with. They did not get on. Olive was hardly a scintillating companion, and Heather would be at work all day. And then there was Alistair, who seemed more tense and withdrawn than ever. She hoped he was alright — she must arrange to choose furniture — she must telephone Tamarind.
Alison might have to be here for weeks.
The whole thing was ridiculous.
Abruptly she said, 'I don't think it will work. We don't know how long she might have to be here.'

Olive wiped her mouth carefully with the corner of her napkin.
Elspeth tried not to be irritated. Why did Olive always have crumbs, or bits of whatever she was eating stuck around her mouth?
Olive said, 'Oh dear — it is going to be rather difficult.'
'It won't work,' said Elspeth. 'I have to speak to Dr Myers.'

She tried phoning again. The receptionist said he was with a patient, but she was sure he would phone her as soon as possible.

Elspeth took some aspirin. She had a splitting headache.
She would have to write to Rosemary and tell her what was going on.
She didn't want to telephone. The line was always so bad — fading in and out, making conversation very difficult. Not at all satisfactory.
Rosemary had sent photographs of the two little boys — tanned and

laughing — lovely little boys — playing in their swimming pool. The water so blue — the sky so blue. It all looked so idyllic. Pity Alison didn't like swimming — but she could always sunbathe.

She must tell Olive to go and empty Alison's refrigerator. And the laundry. She would have to bring the laundry here. Alison would need some clean clothes. She only had a few things with her. No wonder she had a headache.

Dr Myers was very apologetic. He had had a really hectic day. He thought Alison had settled down well, although she was still very fragile.

He was pleased to hear about the clinics, and very pleased they had chosen St Albans — 'Dr Phillips has an excellent reputation.'

Elspeth explained their predicament. Alison couldn't stay in Weymouth Street indefinitely, and it might be weeks before she could go to St Albans, and they never got on very well…

Dr Myers said he didn't really think her coming home was a good idea.

'She needs company,' he said. 'Stimulus — things to occupy her…'

He knew of a convalescent home on the cliffs outside Bournemouth. 'Wonderful position. Mostly people recovering from operations or serious illnesses. It would be ideal for Alison. Of course it would not address her drinking. Drink would be available, but at least she would be supervised, and the nursing staff are all very experienced.'

Elspeth felt guilty about being so relieved — relieved at not having to try and cope with her daughter — not having their lives disrupted.

It was agreed Dr Myers would arrange everything as soon as possible.

Elspeth poured herself a large gin and vermouth.

She would have to transfer some money from her savings account. All this was going to cost a lot of money.

She must phone Heather and tell her what was going on — such a nice girl. Perhaps she would be able to visit Alison in Bournemouth — she would offer to pay the train fare — insist on paying the train fare. She just had to hope that things would turn out alright, that the clinic would be able to help Alison, that she would go and stay with

Rosemary — a complete change of scene — that she could turn her life around. She might even meet someone nice…

Paula had made a really good pot roast with the joint.
Alistair was much more relaxed — enjoying his food. He had had a good day yesterday with his friends in Wimbledon, and Olive managed not to spill anything on the newly laundered tablecloth. Things seemed slightly more optimistic.

Elspeth managed to speak to Heather, and gave her all the news. She said she would try and visit Alison tomorrow evening, and that Bournemouth sounded a great idea. She was also pleased to hear about the clinic. 'It has all been so awful,' she said.
Elspeth was tempted again to ask about the man who had behaved so very badly. She was sure that Rosemary also knew who he was, but neither she nor Heather were prepared to tell her anything about him — just that he was married.

If Jumbo had been here everything would have been different. Alison might have confided in him — she had always taken her problems to her father. He could have helped her — prevented her from becoming a drunken wreck. And the abortion — she preferred not to think about it. As Heather rightly said, it had all been so awful. She just had to hope that things might be better now. Try and stay positive.

Her mother, a remote, stern figure, had regarded any sign of weakness with contempt. She wondered what on earth she would have thought about Alison. Her behaviour would have been considered utterly reprehensible. She had to admit that she was finding it increasingly difficult to be sympathetic.

In Rosemary's last letter she had written about a friend of Don's who had a serious drink problem. He had never recovered from his experiences in the war. He had been at D-Day, and all through the interminably frightful last year of the war with all its horrors. He had lost his wife and family — in and out of clinics — unable to hold down a job. He had been a promising architect — now a broken man.

Elspeth had found this very disturbing, and had found it even harder to be sympathetic about Alison, who really had no excuse whatsoever for her behaviour. One could hardly equate her situation with the appalling suffering of war. Again it made her feel very angry and ashamed.

11

Catherine was glad it was Friday, even though she would have to work tomorrow. It had been a very tiring week — the sad news of the shabby man's death casting a miserable shadow.
She had finally asked Miss Milburn about having an extra day off in June — that was giving her plenty of notice.
Edward had phoned on Tuesday evening to say he was sorry he would not be able to see her the next day, but the meetings would be going on all day, and had she asked for the extra day off yet.
Miss Milburn had not been pleased. 'Really Catherine,' she said, 'you can't keep having days off. It is most inconvenient.'
Catherine did not remonstrate, or point out that the only other day she had had for a long time was to go to see about her mother's gravestone. She just said 'It is rather important.'
If necessary she would go to Mr Simms and tell him about the garden party. She wasn't going to say anything to Miss Milburn.
'I'll speak to Mr Simms,' continued Miss Milburn. 'But you really must not make a habit of it...'
At least that was something she had done.

She saw Alistair coming towards her, and felt a jolt of pleasure.
He was smiling. 'I'm a bit late,' he said. 'I thought I would catch you before you left work, and see if we could go for a drink.'
Catherine said that would be really good.
He said he knew quite a nice little pub in Marylebone High Street, which didn't get too noisy.
Walking together down the street, she felt the same close warmth as she had before touching without touching. She felt another jolt of pleasure when he took her arm to cross Baker Street.
The pub was on a corner — dark and smoky, with small round tables. It was busy. She asked for a gin and lime, and Alistair had a whisky and soda.
Elspeth had told him about the shabby man.
They didn't say much — just how sad — what a shame...
Neither of them wanted to think about the reasons for him being

there — anonymous — irreparably damaged by his experiences — a broken man — another casualty of the war.

Alistair said he had looked pretty bad, and they sat quietly for a moment staring at the table.

He said Elspeth had told him she was hoping to go and stay with his aunt in Scotland later in the summer — 'when she has got her daughter sorted out.' He was lucky to have his aunt and uncle. His parents had gone to live in Canada before the war — his mother had relatives there. 'I believe I have a lot of Canadian cousins,' he said.

He had been at Cambridge — doing modern languages — French and German and a bit of Spanish. 'People with languages were very much in demand during the war. I was encouraged to finish my degree, and also had extra intensive language courses. Whole weeks living French and German. Total immersion.' He laughed. 'I also had to have a good knowledge of Russian. Sometimes it was rather confusing...'

He finished his whisky and went to get another. Catherine was still sipping her gin. She didn't want to get tipsy.

He told her he had extra training as a radio operator, before he was drafted into the RAF as a Flight Lieutenant. He looked down into his glass.

She said she had always been a librarian. She also told him about Edward — lucky to escape being called up, although he had been so keen to join the Royal Navy. 'They said his scientific expertise was more important.'

Alistair had another whisky.

He suggested they went and had something to eat — there was a really good fish and chip shop further down the street.

He said he was hoping to move into his new flat soon.

The fish and chip shop was almost like a real restaurant. It had a large seating area with white tablecloths on the tables. It was very busy. They had to queue. Catherine had plaice and Alistair had cod — the portions were generous with plenty of chips — very appetising.

It was a cheerful, bustling place.

They sat in a corner by the window. Alistair talked about music. How lucky he was to be able to use Elspeth's box at the Royal Albert

Hall whenever he wanted. He asked if she was interested in music.
Catherine had never been to a proper concert. She had gone with
her mother to the church hall a couple of times to concerts to raise
money for the war effort. Her mother had worn her best print
frock and little straw hat for the occasion. They had sat on hard
slatted folding wooden chairs in the dusty hall. One time there had
been a very amply built middle-aged lady, wearing an overtight
blue satin evening dress exposing a large amount of flabby flesh,
who had hooted and warbled her way through a variety of songs,
accompanied by a very thin woman with wild hair and glasses
on the tinny upright piano, and another with a lady cellist who
had attacked her instrument with much heavy breathing, also
accompanied on the tinny piano by an older woman with very thick
glasses which kept sliding down her nose.
Later there had been quite a famous violinist, a young man, who
played to raise money for the families of all those killed and injured
in the disaster at the factory.
She had not gone to that. It was more than she could cope with, and
in any case she couldn't leave her father.
She said she liked to listen to music on the wireless — there was a
lot of good music on the wireless — but had never actually been to
a proper concert.
He said she should come with him.
There was a really good programme next Tuesday — all Brahms —
one of his favourite composers. Perhaps they could go together…
Catherine said that would be really lovely.
They agreed to meet at the Albert Hall.
It was easier to go straight from work.

It had been a wonderful evening.
He walked her home.
They stood awkwardly on the pavement outside her flat.

Catherine started to thank him for a lovely evening, when he
suddenly hugged her — holding her briefly, his face against her hair,
and then saying goodnight, he walked away down the street without
looking back.

It had been such a long time since she had had any real physical contact with anyone — apart from the occasional polite handshake. The last time anyone had put their arms around her was Aunt May's tearful embraces at their father's funeral.
She felt quite shaken.
Wishing he had held her longer.
Wishing she could have held on to him.

*　　*　　*

Elspeth took Alison to buy some new clothes at Debenham & Freebody's. It had been arranged that she should go to the convalescent home in Bournemouth on Friday. Dr Myers had seen to everything. Alison was to share a car with a lady recovering from a serious operation.

Olive had been to the flat and emptied the refrigerator — very little in it — a bit of stale bread, half a pack of margarine, an egg and two bruised apples — and dealt with the laundry. She said there were several blouses and some underwear which were in good condition. The rest of the laundry was bed linen and towels. The skirts and dresses in the wardrobe all needed cleaning — she thought everything had been rather neglected — she didn't know if some of the garments could really be salvaged. There were, however, a great many pairs of shoes — very expensive shoes — most of them practically new.
Elspeth told her to bring all the decent blouses and underwear, and to take anything she thought recoverable to the cleaners. Alison would have to decide what to throw away. She would ask her about the shoes.

Alison was reasonably cooperative — chiefly, Elspeth thought, due to medication — and the trip to Debenham's was quite satisfactory. Alison chose two skirts, a rather nice woollen dress, and two cashmere twinsets in different shades of blue. Elspeth had insisted on her having a lightweight summer coat. It could be chilly by the sea.

Sybil had arrived unannounced on the Wednesday morning, in time for coffee. She had found a small painting among all the stuff she was sorting out from the move — really quite small — of an ugly old man wearing a ridiculous hat, sitting in a chair. Mr Carver had got quite excited — said he thought it could be very valuable.
She didn't remember it at all, or where it had hung. 'Probably in the servants' quarters. I'm sure I didn't want it anywhere in the house.' She said she hoped it was valuable — her stay at the Hyde Park Hotel was costing a lot of money — she was being much too extravagant. She stayed to lunch. Paula had made a mushroom quiche, so there was enough. She was not at all pleased at the short notice though — and was quite huffy.

Elspeth thought this might be an appropriate time to give her the chocolates. Olive had wrapped them up very nicely. Sybil didn't know about the chocolates. 'What a splendid idea!' — how good of Elspeth to think of it — and to have had enough coupons. 'I am ashamed to say I always use all mine...'

Paula was very pleased — she almost smiled.
Elspeth said, 'Mrs Anstruther is so grateful to you for finding her Francesca — and this quiche is absolutely delicious,' and Sybil said, 'Wonderful Paula — really wonderful.'

Catherine had been very worried that she might be late — hurrying home to change into her grey dress. She hoped her coat didn't look too shabby.

As usual the traffic was gridlocked at Hyde Park Corner.

He was waiting in the foyer — the familiar tall thin figure, standing out among the many people milling around — smart and not so smart — cheerful and grim — moving towards the doors to the hall. She felt again the jolt of pleasure at seeing him, wanting to rush up and hold on to him.

Since Friday she could only think of going to the concert on Tuesday. On Saturday she had been very busy in the library — everybody seemed particularly demanding. Sunday it had rained most of the day. She had done mundane jobs — washing and cleaning — and read the paper.

On Monday there had been another fuss with Miss Lazenby over the overdue books. As Catherine was stamping her new choices — a Georgette Heyer and Nevil Shute's *A Town Like Alice*, Miss Milburn appeared. 'We would appreciate you returning your books on time,' she said. 'We have had to send out two reminders.'
Miss Lazenby sniffed and put the books in her bag. 'Some people's lives are too busy to have time for constant visits to the library,' she said.
'It is just as inconvenient for us,' said Miss Milburn. 'We have better things to do than keep sending out reminders.'
'Rubbish,' said Miss Lazenby, and stalked off, leaving Miss Milburn fuming. 'Really,' she said. 'What a dreadful woman...'

Later Olive had come in. She looked very tired, and even sat down on the chair by the counter. She said there had been so many things to do. Lady Thornton was so busy trying to arrange things for Alison. She told her about Bournemouth. 'Lady Thornton thinks it will be possible for Alison to go to the clinic next week. She is talking to Dr Phillips today, so I suppose I shall have to go and fetch her. There is supposed to be a good train service from Bournemouth — if she is fit to travel on a train...' She sighed. 'She is not a very easy person.' She sighed again. 'And then she will have to stay for a few days.' There was an uncomfortable pause. 'I'm afraid they don't get on at all well... And then I suppose I will have to go with her to the clinic. Lady Thornton says they would only end up having some awful argument. And then there has been all the business with Alison's flat. Dealing with the laundry and the cleaners, deciding what to throw away — such a mess... Lady Thornton is having it completely cleaned and redecorated. Such a nice flat...'

Catherine was really sorry. Sorry that Olive had to deal with all these problems, and that Lady Thornton had such a bad relationship with her daughter. And Alison — what about her behaviour? Seeking to escape her problems by drinking.

'Oh dear,' she said. 'It all sounds very difficult.'

And then Tuesday morning there was the Major. 'Good morning dear lady,' he said. 'Looking as delightful as ever. No chance of a coffee I suppose…? I think it is going to be a nice day. There is a really nice place close by…'
Catherine said she really couldn't get away.
'Oh well,' he said. 'Perhaps another time.' He picked up his brown leather gloves that he had put on the counter. 'I think I fancy something on the Napoleonic Wars…'

Lady Thornton's box was in the centre of the hall — there were little gilt chairs with red velvet seats — the feeling of excitement and anticipation as the orchestra filed in to take their places — the wonderful music.
She had not expected to be so overwhelmed by the music. It was all-enveloping — cutting through the bleakness — the weary struggle — unlocking long suppressed feelings — banishing the ghostly outstretched hands — all swept away by the tumbling waves of sound — flooding the darkest places with light.
In the interval a waiter with white gloves served them champagne and smoked salmon sandwiches.
Alistair talked enthusiastically about the music — the violinist 'a real talent' — 'a great Brahms conductor'.

They took a taxi.
They held hands — it felt so natural to be holding hands, as if they always held hands.
A magical end to a magical evening.
Outside the flat they said goodnight. She thanked him for a wonderful evening. He said they must go again.
They stood a moment in silence, and then he walked away.
She stayed, watching him go — still feeling the warmth of his hand in hers — before going up the steps and letting herself in the front door, giddy with so many new sensations and long buried emotions.

*　　*　　*

Mr Phipps said that they did not normally open on Saturdays, but, of course, for her, they would make an exception.

Alistair had taken her to see his new home on Sunday. She thought it was absolutely splendid — light and airy — spacious, with views of the magnificent trees in Manchester Square — still recovering from bomb damage. Fortunately the bomb which had landed on Manchester Square had caused minimal damage to Hertford House with the impressive Wallace Collection, which had, in any case, been evacuated during the war. Jumbo had always enjoyed visiting it. He had always been fascinated by museums, spending many hours in the British Museum, among the Greek and Roman sculpture and the Egyptian tombs. She had never cared for Greek and Roman sculpture, or Egyptian tombs — finding them all rather tedious. The Wallace Collection had some quite nice paintings, but she definitely did not find the portraits remotely inspiring. She had frequently made excuses not to accompany him.

Alistair's flat was really finished now. The carpets, a pleasant creamy colour, had been laid — a sparkling new bathroom and kitchen, with sensible dark grey linoleum, were excellent.
They assessed what furniture might be required. Beds — a double and a single — bedside tables — hopefully a sofa — chairs — a table…
Elspeth knew there were plenty of beds.
She made the arrangement to go down to the warehouse the following Saturday.
Alistair said he would hire a car. He would enjoy the drive.
Elspeth was very pleased that at least something had been sorted out.

She seemed to have spent most of Monday morning on the telephone. First she phoned Mr Phipps, who was easiest to get hold of early in the morning, to arrange about Saturday. She then spoke to Dr Phillips' secretary, who assured her that he was going to telephone her later in the morning, and that there would definitely be a place for Alison the following week. Then Mr Anderson's office telephoned to say they could start on Alison's flat on Wednesday. Mr Anderson had already told Elspeth he thought the work would take at least two weeks — maybe three... She then phoned the convalescent home to find out how Alison was settling in. She spoke to the matron. It was not good news. Alison had managed to consume a large amount of alcohol. Dr Myers had said alcohol was available — this was not a drying out clinic. Alison had spent a lot of time in the bar. The staff had been told not to serve her alcohol with her meals, but this had not extended to purchasing drinks at the bar. Also it was not advisable to consume alcohol whilst on medication. She had become quite ill, and was being cared for in the sanatorium. 'We are not really accustomed to dealing with this kind of problem.' Elspeth was alarmed. She would have to speak to Dr Myers as soon as possible.

His receptionist said he was with a patient, but would certainly call her as soon as he was free.

Then Olive came in, almost late for lunch — more flustered than usual.

Elspeth wondered if she would be capable of going to fetch Alison — if she was able to travel.

Dr Myers phoned back quite promptly.

He said he had spoken to the matron at the convalescent home, and he was quite concerned.

Elspeth told him that there should be a place for Alison at the clinic in the following week. He said he was very pleased to hear that as Alison obviously needed proper help.

'I only prescribed her a very mild sedative — I thought that would be sufficient, but I'm afraid that alcohol is too readily available — almost encouraged...'

It was decided that she should come home until she went to the clinic. 'I know it's not easy,' Dr Myers said. 'These sorts of problems are very difficult to deal with.' He said he had a patient being taken down to Bournemouth on Thursday, and the car could bring her back.

Elspeth was very relieved. She had already dismissed the idea of Olive bringing her back on the train.

Olive seemed very relieved too. Elspeth thought she had probably been apprehensive about bringing Alison home on a train.

Paula had made an egg and bacon flan for lunch with a green salad. Elspeth felt more able to enjoy it now that something had been settled.

As they were finishing their lunch, Dr Phillips phoned.
He sounded cheerful and reassuring. There would be a place for Alison next Wednesday. They were looking forward to welcoming her.

Elspeth went for a walk in the park.
She needed some fresh air, and although it was overcast, it was not raining.
She walked as far as the rose garden. It was still too early for the roses to be in full bloom — here and there spots of colour, soon it would be a mass of fragrant flowers.
The garden was beautifully kept.
Meadows had been so proud of their rose garden. She had always had bowls of roses in the house. She was particularly fond of the old-fashioned cottage roses with their abundance of petals and wonderful scent — and sweet peas — masses of sweet peas.
Long ago, when life was tranquil and orderly.
Nobody had taken any notice of the impending catastrophe — heeded the warning signs — the threat padding stealthily across Europe. Czechoslovakia did not seem very important — a place of little significance — and Austria — well, they were all really German anyway, so it would probably not make much difference.
Jumbo, though worried, was convinced nothing would happen. 'There really cannot be another war with Germany...' The shadows of the First World War still hovering — blood-saturated soil hardly dry — even when the nice young officer from the War Office had come to look at the house — he had assured her it would be alright. 'It won't happen — it can't happen...'

She got up.
There were things to do.

Tomorrow they would have to go to Alison's flat, and collect her things to bring back to Baker Street. She would have to sort them out when she got back from Bournemouth, and she had to telephone Heather.

Heather had been very sympathetic and helpful. She said she would come and spend the day with Alison on Saturday, so that Elspeth would not have to worry about not being there. She couldn't manage Sunday. She would try and think of something nice they could do… at least get her to go to the park.

Elspeth had tried to telephone Catherine on Tuesday evening, but there was no answer, so she didn't speak to her until Wednesday. She thought it would be a nice idea if she came to tea on Sunday and to meet Alison, although she could not guarantee that Alison would appear. Paula was going to make a Victoria sponge. Alison had accumulated quite a lot of coupons, so she would be able to make a proper pre-war cake…

Catherine was very pleased. She said it would be really nice, and she hoped very much that Alison would appear, as she would really like to meet her.

She had been disappointed the call had not been from Alistair. She had really hoped it might be him — breathlessly hopeful. She had so enjoyed the concert — so enjoyed being with him — cautiously hopeful that they would get to know each other better — that maybe the long, lonely slog would be over — a feather-palmed oasis almost within reach — but she was fully aware of his need to keep a distance, afraid, as she was, of allowing himself to feel too much — or maybe unable anymore of allowing himself to feel at all, or maybe she was just overestimating the mutual attraction — one brief hug, and holding hands in the taxi — she was just being rather stupid.

He telephoned late on Friday evening — it was nearly midnight. He sounded weary — said he had had a tough day. There was another Brahms concert on Wednesday, if she would like to come. Tomorrow he was going with Elspeth to the warehouse to choose some furniture.

She said she would love to come to the concert, and was pleased about the furniture.

She would have liked to have kept talking, but he just said he would see her on Wednesday. She was going to say that Elspeth had invited her to tea on Sunday to meet Alison, but he had already rung off.

Alistair drove very fast.

Elspeth was not accustomed to driving fast — not accustomed to driving — in the petrol-less misery of the war years there had not been much opportunity for driving.

Wilson had always maintained a steady speed.

Alistair seemed very assured. She was sure he was a very good driver. She really was too tired to care. It had been an exhausting week.

She and Olive had brought all Alison's things — so many shoes and handbags — expensive designer shoes and handbags — back to Baker Street, with an assortment of clothing.

She had given the keys to the porter, and explained about the cleaners, who would be coming in the morning. She had tipped him generously — Jumbo had always believed in tipping generously — with a crisp, new, five pound note — and asked him to let her know if there were any problems.

They had had to get Alison's room ready. Elspeth sent Olive to buy some flowers — a really pretty bunch of pink and blue lupins, with some sort of fern.

They had had to clear out the drinks cabinet. Olive had taken all the contents, apart from the whisky, which Elspeth gave to Alistair, saying he must only drink it in his room, for Paula to put in one of the kitchen cupboards. 'No wine with dinner, I'm afraid,' Elspeth said.

Alistair had hardly been in all week. He had gone to a concert on Tuesday, and had been out both Thursday and Friday. Elspeth thought he was being tactful — to make it easier — in case there were any problems with Alison, who arrived on Thursday evening looking like a ghost, and had gone straight to bed, refusing supper.

On Friday Dr Myers came — so very spruce in a pinstripe suit and

perfectly laundered white shirt — washing his hands carefully.
He had a quiet talk with Alison.
He told Elspeth it was best that she have plenty of rest, and that he
was not going to prescribe a stronger medication. 'Just enough to
keep her calm.' He said he would be back on Monday, unless there
was an emergency.

Later they managed to get Alison to sort through some of her things
— and choose clothes she might want to take with her to the clinic.
There was a lot of sniffling and throwing things about.
Elspeth had to leave Olive to deal with it. She was good at making
soothing noises and putting things in neat piles. She could not cope
with this pathetic, snivelling creature — petulant and complaining.
Shameful — so utterly shameful.
Alison refused to join them for dinner. Olive took her a tray — she
barely touched the food — messing it about on the plate. It was
disgraceful.

Sybil had wanted to invite her to lunch — Francesca was a great
success, and it seemed that, as she had not used any of her meat
ration for at least a month, it might be possible to get a crown of
lamb. She would order one from Harrods. She was thinking of
inviting Lilian and Mathew Thompson to lunch as well. 'She is
rather a bore. Mathew is thinking of standing for parliament. He
hasn't a hope of being elected. He is a fearful stick in the mud… but
they have invited me so many times. They have a rather ugly house
in Somerset — all beams and chintz… They were lucky that it was
not suitable for requisitioning — too pokey…'
Elspeth said she could not arrange to do anything until Alison
was safely in the clinic. She had met the Thompsons once at one
of Sybil's cocktail parties before the war. She had found them very
tiresome. Mathew was particularly pretentious — holding forth on
the inadvisability of getting involved in anything remotely foreign.
'Asking for trouble.' Lilian blowsy with too much makeup — too
much jewellery — rather tipsy — rather foolish. She really did not
want to meet them again.

She still hadn't written to Rosemary to tell her what was going on.

She was glad to be away from everything for a few hours.
She had been dreading going to the warehouse — of seeing her things again — fearful of stirring up too many memories.
Reliving those days when all that was normal ceased to be normal.

They were given so little notice — just over three weeks.
A letter arrived from the War Office with the official date they had to vacate their house.
Two officers and a stiffly correct man came with forms to be filled in, and papers to sign. They went round the house with Jumbo, making notes and asking questions.
Then they had to arrange for the removal of all their possessions. Jumbo and Penn sorted everything out, labelled and ready for the removal men. They had chosen the most well-known removal firm, Leversons, with warehouses in the City, where the most important and valuable things were to go — and the rest went to a relatively unknown firm in Borehampton, which a friend had recommended — Phipps and Sons. She had only dealt with her personal things, which she packed with the help of Ruby, who was hoping to join the ATS, and was quite excited, and the things they were going to take to Baker Street.

Everything seemed so unreal. Jumbo reassuring, 'It won't be for long — we'll soon be having to bring everything back…' Had they really believed that? They had wanted to believe it — not wanting to look back at her home — so solid and comfortable in the afternoon sun — saying goodbye to Penn and Ruby — going to find Meadows, busy with his tomatoes — Mrs Dunstan so different out of her kitchen, in a smart navy blue two-piece and matching hat, clutching a shiny handbag — the whole of her safe world tumbling…

And then there was the bombing. The dreadful news that the warehouse in the City had been completely destroyed — reduced to ashes by firebombs.
All their things gone. It had been so difficult to pretend it did not matter. After all, it was only furniture…
Shrugging one's shoulders — braving the blackout to go to dinner at Pruniers — lobster and champagne — with Thérèse and Jean

Jacques Colbert, newly arrived from France, leaving their house in Paris just before the reptilian columns of German troops and squat cyclopean tanks snaked their way down a deserted Champs Elysées, taking a long circuitous route down through France, staying with various friends, who themselves were dithering about whether to leave or not, to Marseilles, where after a very long wait, and many expensive transactions, they managed to get on a boat to England.
They had rented a furnished flat in Kensington. It was easy to find somewhere to rent. Everybody was leaving London. Jean Jacques had transferred money to his bank in London when things had begun to look bad, so they would be alright financially. Thérèse said they had just had to leave everything behind — what would happen to their beautiful house, her collection of miniatures — she had just had new silk curtains for the salon…
Jumbo tried to sound reassuring, but his cheerful 'I expect it will be over soon' was becoming less and less convincing.
Incongruous in their evening clothes, searching for a taxi on a darkened Haymarket.

No good getting maudlin. Nothing would ever be the same again, but that was how it was. No good dwelling on it…

It was time she came to a decision about the remaining things in Borehampton.
She had dismissed the idea of buying a small house in the country. It would be very impractical — what sort of life would she have? She couldn't drive, and the days of having one's own car and chauffeur had gone forever, which would mean hiring cars all the time. Very inconvenient.
She had never cared for a life of coffee mornings — tea parties — cocktails — inane social chit-chat — petty disputes — local politics — and most importantly, Paula would certainly not want to live in the country.

She had considered a seaside flat, but how often would she use it? Better to take holidays when she felt like it.
She was so out of the habit of doing anything, going anywhere, if she managed to visit Tamarind and Hugo in Scotland this summer

it would be a major achievement. All this made it even less likely she would ever need any of her remaining furniture again.

She was glad she was going with Alistair — it made everything easier.

They did not speak much during the drive. She asked how he had enjoyed the concert, and he said it had been excellent, and that he was looking forward to going again next week. She said she had invited Catherine to tea on Sunday to meet Alison — hopefully — she might refuse to join them, and apart from commenting on the weather, which was quite fine, there did not seem much else to say. Alistair did not go in for small talk, and at the speed they were going, it was probably better he concentrated on the driving.

Mr Phipps was short with slick-backed hair, middle-aged, wearing an ill-fitting suit and striped tie. Elspeth thought he was probably unused to wearing a suit. He was amiable and unhurried. Elspeth's things were at the far end of a vast warehouse — an older man and a youth in blue overalls were waiting for them. They all shook hands. Mr Phipps had a folder with lists of everything, and where the various things could be found. She tried to be objective — after all, if was only furniture — but it was difficult not to remember the rooms where it had been. A small sofa and glass-fronted bookcase from the morning room — standard lamps and a coffee table from the small drawing room — a pine table and four chairs from the breakfast room — another bookcase, side table and small sewing chair from her sitting room — and then there were the beds and bedside tables, two table lamps and a small Persian rug...

Everything was carefully labelled and it was arranged that everything would be delivered by the end of next week.

Elspeth asked Mr Phipps if he knew of a local salesroom where she could sell the remaining furniture. 'There is no point in keeping it any longer.' Mr Phipps said there were monthly sales at a very reputable place in Borehampton, and he could arrange everything for her.

They went back to his office and she signed various papers authorising him to arrange the sale, and all other things that were necessary.

Elspeth felt immensely relieved. It was time to stop holding on to vestiges of the past. It served no purpose, and was just another depressing reminder of how things once were.
She was glad that some of the things would be of some use to somebody.

They were much more cheerful on the way home.
Alistair was really pleased — thanking her profusely for her generosity, saying how much he was looking forward to moving into his new home, and thanking her very much for putting up with him for so long. Elspeth said it had been a pleasure, and that he must continue to come whenever he felt like it to have one of Paula's marvellous meals.

They stopped at a large, old-fashioned, red brick pub for something to eat, darkly panelled with worn brown leather chairs, and had a rather dubious steak pie with sloppy cabbage and lumpy mashed potato. Alistair had a whisky, and she had a sherry, and they drank a toast to Alistair's future.
They got back to the flat at teatime. It was completely silent. Alistair said he was going to make a couple of phone calls, and have a bath before supper.
Elspeth was about to ring for Paula and see if she would bring some tea, when Olive appeared bleary-eyed, smoothing her skirt, and adjusting her cardigan. 'Oh dear,' she said, 'I must have dropped off...'
Elspeth said that was quite alright, and could she get some tea.

Olive poured the tea, spilling some on the clean tray cloth.
Elspeth pretended not to notice as she tried to mop it up inexpertly with a paper napkin. She said Heather had come at about half past eleven and had spent some time with Alison in her room. Whilst Alison was dressing she had told Olive that she had managed to get tickets for a matinee of *Oklahoma*. 'Such a nice girl,' said Olive. She said they would go for a meal afterwards — she had everything planned. Alison had appeared looking quite decent — 'She had even brushed her hair' — and they had gone off together. Heather said they would get a snack somewhere before the performance.

Elspeth was immensely relieved and pleased. Now they could have a relaxed evening, without having to deal with Alison. Of course she would reimburse Heather for all the expenses — a cheque in an envelope, with a little note would be best.

Catherine was looking forward to going to tea with Elspeth, and meeting Alison. She hoped very much that Alistair might be there, but she thought it unlikely. She wore her navy blue skirt with the knife pleats and a flowery blue blouse, and arrived punctually at four o'clock.

It had not started very well. There was no sign of Alison. Olive was visibly anxious — more nervously awkward than usual.
Paula wheeled in the tea trolley with the perfect Victoria sponge, and plates of small square sandwiches, and wafer thin biscuits.
Alison didn't appear...
Lady Thornton coolly implacable. The perfect hostess apologised for her daughter's non-appearance — 'She seems to have a headache' — and asked Olive to pour the tea.
She was quietly furious. Heather had brought her home the night before in a very bad state. Olive had had to help Heather put her to bed. She had made Heather stay for a cup of tea to thank her for all she had done. Heather said she was very sorry. 'It is very difficult to stop her...' They had gone to a very nice French restaurant in Old Compton Street, which they had been to before. 'She had two martinis, and nearly a whole bottle of wine — I only had one glass. I managed to stop her ordering more, but she ordered a cognac with the coffee...'
Elspeth said not to worry. 'I have to apologise to you for Alison's disgraceful behaviour, and I have to thank you for all your help and concern, it has been invaluable. We just have to hope the clinic will be able to sort her out.'
Now she passed the sandwiches to Catherine. 'Egg and cress, I think,' she said.
The conversation was stilted. Catherine said how lovely the park was now — so many flowers. Olive said, 'Shall I go and see? Maybe she is feeling better now?', but Elspeth just shrugged. 'I don't think that will be necessary, Olive,' she said. She turned to Catherine. 'It's such

a pity her sister is so far away. She would be able to talk to her...' And then, as it if was an afterthought she asked if she had any brothers or sisters. Catherine said she had a brother.
'Oh that's nice', said Olive, and asked where he was.
Catherine started to explain — to tell them about Edward — not to seem to be boasting. 'Gracious,' said Olive, 'that's wonderful. You must be so proud.'
Elspeth said, 'Really Catherine, why did you not say anything before? That is splendid. Really splendid.'
Catherine told them about the garden party, and what a problem it had been getting enough time off.
After that everyone cheered up — really enjoying Paula's Victoria sponge — Alison's absence not mentioned. Elspeth said it was a real pity Alistair was not there. 'I believe he was at Cambridge. I am sure he would be most interested...'
Catherine was sure that Elspeth did not know about her going to the Albert Hall with Alistair, or that she was going again. She said, 'He very kindly invited me to a concert. It was very good...'
Elspeth carefully hid her surprise. 'That is nice,' she said. Olive did not attempt to hide her pleasure. 'Oh how very nice,' she said. 'Such a nice young man...', tailing off, embarrassed that she had said too much.
Elspeth said she was very pleased, she hoped they might become friends. 'I think he is finding it very difficult to adjust to ordinary life.' She then went on to tell them all about the visit to Borehampton, and how it had been very successful.

In the end she had had to go with Olive to take Alison to the clinic on the Wednesday morning. Heather had been unable to get time off work, and Olive was really not capable of managing on her own. Dr Myers had come on Monday. He spent quite a lot of time with Alison. He said he was very glad she would be getting some proper treatment soon — she seemed very disturbed.

On Tuesday they went to Dickens & Jones to get her some summer dresses — they were less fuddy duddy than Debenham & Freebody's. There was still not much choice, but they were able to find some which were quite pretty — floral prints with full skirts, and a pale green linen shirt dress, and she managed to keep her temper while Alison made a big fuss about trying them on.

They had the same car and chauffeur — Collins — as they had had before. She had told Paula not to worry about supper — one of her lovely soups would be quite sufficient. Alistair was going to a concert. She wondered whether he was going to take Catherine. It would be most satisfactory if their friendship developed, but she was unsure of Alistair's ability to cope with a normal relationship. He had obviously been very damaged, and Catherine seemed very vulnerable — her calm air of dependability hiding goodness knows what… It was good to know she had such a successful brother.

Halfway to the clinic Alison said she felt sick. Elspeth had to ask Collins to stop the car. Alison got out, collapsing weakly on the grass verge. Olive said 'Oh dear… Oh dear…', and hurriedly got out as well. Collins produced a bottle of water. He said he always carried a bottle of water in the car. He also had a thermos of tea. He said his wife always made him a thermos of tea. He took the beaker off the flask and filling it with water handed it to Olive. Olive made sympathetic noises, and persuaded Alison to drink some. Elspeth half got out of the car. There was no point adding her presence. Collins was standing by the car holding the bottle of water, and Olive was crouched by the huddled figure of Alison, urging her to drink some more water.

She felt unaccountably annoyed.
It was really pathetic.

Dr Phillips was very cheerful and sympathetic, greeting Alison warmly, saying he hoped she was feeling better now. Her room looked over the garden with its smooth lawns and beds of flowers. Elspeth was particularly pleased to see a really impressive display of delphiniums in all shades of blue and mauve. She had always loved delphiniums. Meadows had been very good with them. Alison's room was quite spacious — comfortably furnished with a spotless bathroom. 'Nurse Walker will look after you,' he said, introducing them to a tall pleasant-looking woman in a pristine white uniform.

They shook hands. Nurse Walker had a firm handshake and seemed genuinely pleased to see them. Dr Phillips said that unfortunately they were too late for lunch, but that Nurse Walker would go and see if she could bring something up on a tray. Alison said she was not hungry. She turned her back and went to look out of the window.

Elspeth did her best to control her exasperation. 'I think it best if Miss Fern and I left now,' she said, 'and let Alison settle in.' Olive gave Alison a hurried pat on the arm, and they followed Dr Phillips out of the room, leaving Nurse Walker with Alison. He assured them she would be quite alright. 'I am sure Nurse Walker will find her something tasty to tempt her, to eat a little. We had delicious strawberry tarts for lunch — early strawberries from our greenhouse…' He said they shouldn't worry. 'She will be very well looked after.'

The concert had been wonderful — the whole evening had been wonderful.
They had had drinks in the bar before the performance. It was impressively opulent, with red velvet seating and glittering chandeliers. It was very crowded — quite a lot of people were in evening dress — everyone talking loudly, and jostling each other to get the barman's attention.
Alistair told her about the visit to the warehouse with Elspeth, and choosing the furniture. 'It was a bit weird,' he said. 'I think Elspeth found it rather difficult, seeing all her things after so long. She kept saying things like, oh, that was in my dressing room, or that was in the breakfast room…' He said they had found all the things he wanted, and that it had been arranged for them to be delivered by the end of the week. 'And then I can really move in…' He was very relaxed.

The music was as inspirational as before — perhaps even more so. Alistair said he thought the Fourth Symphony was his favourite… Going out he took her arm.
A little way in front of them a group of young people in evening dress were standing together, smoking and laughing. Suddenly one of the young women detached herself from the group. She was wearing a

beautiful strapless dress of some kind of silk — a hazy blue — with a diaphanous scarf round her shoulders — a really lovely girl. She called out 'Alistair — darling!', and rushing towards them she flung her arms round his neck and kissed him. 'Where have you been? We are all going to Freddie's. You must come. Do come...'
Alistair's grip tightened on her arm. She felt him stiffen — withdraw. 'Sorry Cass,' he said. 'Some other time...'
The young woman gave Catherine a quick, disdainful glance, as if to say who is this dowdy woman? 'Don't forget,' she said. 'I'll be expecting you...'
One of the young men called out, 'Hurry up Cass! Jeremy has just got us a cab...'
Catherine tried to swallow the sudden, choking lump in her throat. They walked round to the main road facing the park to get a taxi. Alistair was still gripping her arm. 'Rather silly people,' he said. 'Very silly people.'

They sat side by side in the taxi, without touching — without speaking.
The euphoria of the evening draining away, surrounded by the glowing throb of a big city. Stopping at the traffic lights alongside another taxi. A woman with a fox fur stole stole had turned on the overhead light and was applying lipstick.
Alistair had turned his head away, his scar lividly prominent in the light from the street lamps.
She wanted to say something — something to make things feel better.
'It was a lovely concert,' she said. 'Wonderful music...'
He turned towards her, and took her hand. 'Yes,' he said. 'The music was wonderful...'

<h1 style="text-align:center">12</h1>

Elspeth was going to lunch with Sybil. She suggested to Olive that she should take the day off. 'Why don't you go down to Brighton,' she said. 'You could take the Brighton Belle and spend a day by the sea. I think we deserve a bit of a treat...'

So far everything seemed to be going very well. She had left it some days before phoning to ask how Alison was getting on. Dr Phillips' secretary said that after some initial difficulties she had begun to settle down, and had started to join in with some of the activities, and had been playing a lot of table tennis. There seemed to be a lot of enthusiasm for table tennis at the moment. Dr Phillips was thinking of arranging a tournament.
Elspeth was really surprised. Alison rarely showed any interest in anything. She vaguely remembered the girls playing table tennis during the time their school was evacuated, and that they had really enjoyed it. Rosemary had even won a cup. 'Well that is good,' she said.

So this morning she was looking forward to going to lunch with Sybil. The sun was shining. 'It is such a nice day for once,' she said to Olive. 'I'll tell Paula to take the day off too...'

Sybil wanted her to help choose the clothes she should take to the South of France.
They had a delicious lunch. Francesca had turned out to be an excellent cook. They had Coquilles St Jacques with asparagus, and a dense jelly full of raspberries.

Sybil had a large cabin trunk packed with clothes, all individually wrapped in sheets of tissue paper. She unpacked them carefully, one by one, and spread them out on the bed in one of the spare bedrooms. An astonishing array of beautiful clothes.
Sybil said she didn't know what to take. 'They used to entertain a lot before the war. Cocktail parties, wonderful luncheons and dinners

on the terrace,' she sighed. 'But of course everything is so different now…'

Elspeth thought how everything was defined by the war — before the war — after the war — with a vast black hole in between — a gigantic painful pause in everyone's lives.

It was a very pleasurable afternoon sorting through all the lovely things — fine linens and silk, dresses and slacks, beach clothes, evening clothes, clothes for all occasions.
It took a long time. Everything reminded Sybil of something. A reception. A holiday. Lunch on a friend of Pogo's yacht, when a rather inebriated, scantily clad young lady had almost fallen over the side. 'One of the amazingly good-looking members of the crew had rescued her… So many important people. Well, they all thought they were very important. Pathetic really…'
She couldn't decide. Elspeth suggested she should start by choosing one of everything, and then eliminate anything she felt she would not need.
'I don't suppose you will want anything black,' she said. 'Or a great many evening dresses…'
Sybil said she would have to think about it. 'Perhaps I should make a list,' she said.
And then they had tea and almond cake, and Sybil had a large martini.

It had been raining all day.
It was so dark in the library they had to have the lights on.
Miss Milburn had quickly taken refuge in her office. The sight of so many people with dripping umbrellas and mackintoshes, leaving wet footprints all over the floor — despite the extra mat that had been put down by the door — made her very agitated.
Quite a few people came in to escape the rain, sitting at the tables, reading the newspapers.
She had got very wet during her lunch hour. She had gone to the Italian café and had a warming bowl of vegetable soup. Her shoes were soaked through. She couldn't wait to go home and take them off.

She had not heard from Alistair since the concert, which was almost two weeks ago. She felt rather low and despondent. She supposed he was busy with his flat, and his glamorous friends. Just as the library was closing he appeared, closing his dripping umbrella as he came towards her. 'Just in time,' he said. 'I can escort you now — this umbrella is very large — should be big enough for us both...'
They left arm in arm close together under his umbrella, and she felt her spirits lift. She was even glad it was raining. He said they could go for a drink, and then, perhaps, to that nice fish and chip shop — if that was alright...
Catherine said she had to go home first and change her shoes and stockings. He said that was fine, he would like to see where she lived. As they went up the stairs he told her he had moved into the flat, and Elspeth had been really helpful, organising all the bedding. Olive had bought him new towels. 'She's a really good sort,' he said. 'Utterly cowed by Elspeth...' Catherine said she could be rather intimidating. Poor Olive. 'And Paula gave me a tin of her special biscuits. I feel very honoured.'

She had left him in the sitting room whilst she went to dry her feet. She found him looking at a photograph of Edward. It was a very good photograph, taken in Cambridge outside his house. 'It's a lovely little house,' she said. 'He has done so well.' She told him about Harriet. She also had a really good photograph of Edward and Harriet in the garden of her home. 'She is a really lovely girl — very clever.' She then told him about her parents — brilliant scientists who had done incredible things during the war. Alistair said he knew all about them — highly respected, whose work had been invaluable. 'I never met them,' she said. 'But I heard a lot about them.'
He sat down on the sagging sofa. 'I haven't been to Cambridge for years,' he said.
She told him about the garden party. She said he should come. 'I'm sure it will be fun, and you would probably know some of the people there.'
He said he could hardly turn up uninvited.
Catherine sat down opposite him on the old wicker chair with its dilapidated cushions. 'I'm sure it would be alright,' she said. 'I'll talk to Edward. Harriet is arranging it all — her parents never know

what is going on. They're always too busy with their work.'
She thought of them sitting amongst the shabby, valuable clutter that
filled their drawing room, drinking cold coffee and gin and tonics,
and the books piled everywhere, the holes in the Persian carpet from
carelessly dropped cigarettes. She laughed. 'Anyway, I'm sure they
would be delighted if you came…'
Alistair said he would like to meet Edward, and see Cambridge
again.
He got up and went to the window. It had stopped raining.
He said he thought they could go out now. 'The sun is even trying
to come out.'

She showed him the rest of the flat. 'I was so lucky to get it,' she said.
He said he thought it was great. He particularly liked the pictures
in the bedroom, and the flourishing plants on the windowsill in
the kitchen. Catherine liked to have plants. She had tried to grow a
tomato plant but it had not survived.

They made their unhurried way to Marylebone High Street — not
touching — but touching — joined in some undefinable way. Again
it was a pleasurable shock when he took her arm to cross Baker
Street.

Elspeth was particularly pleased with Alison's progress. Heather
had been to see her and said she looked so much better. 'She actually
showed me around, and we had lunch together in the dining room
— they have flowers on all the tables.' And she had eaten a whole
fish cake and some peas, and had introduced her to this nice, rather
shaky woman who goes to the same painting class.
Elspeth said it all sounded excellent — table tennis, and now
painting. Alison had never been remotely artistic, and had never
shown any interest in art. It was all extremely satisfactory. Perhaps
they would be able to persuade her to go to California. Rosemary
had written to say she had sent her photographs of the boys by
the pool, and of herself and Don in their garden. 'I hope they will
encourage her to come…' Things were looking much more positive.

Mr Anderson's secretary had telephoned to say that Alison's flat was now finished. She made an arrangement to meet Mr Anderson there the following afternoon.

She took Olive with her. She felt in need of some moral support.

They had done a really impressive job. The whole flat was transformed, even the stained carpet looked like new. Olive made appreciative noises, and went round patting the cushions. Mr Anderson said they had had to replace the linoleum in the kitchen. There had been several quite serious burn marks, and blistering from spilled boiling water, and the grease round the cooker had completely solidified.

Elspeth thanked him very much for all his hard work, and said it was an excellent job, and that she was delighted with the result.
Surely this would help Alison to sort her life out, make a fresh start. On the way out she thanked the porter for all his co-operation, and gave him another large tip.
Perhaps now she could really start thinking about visiting Tamarind and Hugo.

They had not heard from Alistair since he had moved into his new home. She and Olive had gone for tea. He had bought a walnut cake. It was strange to sit on her chairs at her table, but rather pleasing. Her furniture had fitted in really well, even the chintz-covered sofa — he could always get different covers later on.
Olive admired the gleaming kitchen, breaking her customary, dutiful murmuring to say she thought it was lovely.
She had brought him some wine glasses, and Olive had brought some tea towels with a pattern of sailing ships.
He had not yet had his telephone connected. It took so long to get anything done. It would probably be months before he had a telephone. She expected him to come sometime to collect the rest of his things — a few books, and some shirts which had come back from the laundry.

Alistair opened the door wearing an open-necked blue shirt and dark grey slacks.
Catherine had never seen him in casual clothes before. He looked

much younger, and somehow rather vulnerable. She had become accustomed to the jagged scar down the side of his face. Today it did not seem so prominent.

He had thought it was a good idea for her to come and see his new home on one of her Saturdays off — around teatime, so they could go out for a meal. 'I'm not much of a cook,' he said. 'OK with toast and eggs, and anything in a tin, but I think it would be nicer to go to the Italian restaurant in Marylebone High Street.'

Catherine thought the whole place was lovely. Very light with high ceilings, pale carpets and curtains. Even Elspeth's floral chintz-covered sofa, with its pattern of pink roses, did not look out of place. There was dark grey linoleum on the floors of both the bathroom and the kitchen, which was very smart. Alistair said he was really pleased with everything. The bed was exceptionally comfortable. 'Elspeth said they only had beds from Heal's, which were the best beds you could buy...'

They sat by the window where they could just see the trees in the square. Alistair fetched a bottle of champagne from the kitchen. 'We must drink a toast to something,' he said. Catherine could not remember when she had felt so good — sitting here in Alistair's new home, drinking champagne. She wished she could touch him — hug him — hoping nothing would happen to spoil it all.

She had written down both Edward's and Harriet's addresses and telephone numbers, which she gave him. They discussed the garden party. She would be going to Cambridge in the morning. Alistair said he would be able to get there about half past four, certainly no later than five o'clock.

They drank another toast to the success of the garden party, and another just for everything, and then they went to the Italian restaurant in Marylebone High Street and had lasagne and salad and a bottle of Chianti. Catherine was not sure she should have any more to drink after all that champagne, but she had a glass anyway. They arranged to go to a Beethoven concert the following week. Alistair said it should be really good — the pianist was amazing...

He reached across the table and took her hand, and they sat there for
a while without speaking.

They stood on the pavement outside the restaurant. He put his arms
round her, holding her close, and they stood there just holding onto
each other, oblivious of the people passing by.
He said, 'I better get you a taxi…'
She said she could walk, it wasn't very far.
He said it was too late. There were plenty of taxis.
He did not let go of her hand whilst he gave the driver her address,
and some money for the fare. Catherine started to protest, but he
gave her another brief hug, standing aside as the taxi drove off.

The night before the Beethoven concert he phoned.
It was very late — almost midnight. He said he was very sorry but he
would not be able to take her to the concert. He sounded very tense
— he didn't want to talk — just repeated that he was sorry.
He did not give an explanation.

As the day of the garden party approached, she sent him a short note
saying how much she was looking forward to it, with the addresses
and telephone numbers again, just in case they had got mislaid.
He was still waiting to have his telephone connected, so it was not
possible to call him.

Elspeth phoned to tell her about Alison's progress — 'I hope she
keeps it up' — and said she must come and have tea again soon…

Catherine wanted to ask her if she had seen Alistair, but she didn't
like to. He would suddenly appear like he had done before, and
everything would be alright.

Olive came into the library. She said Lady Thornton would like the
second volume of Osbert Sitwell's autobiography — she had really
enjoyed the first one. 'She is so pleased that Alison seems to be
getting on so well — even joining in with things,' she said. Then she
said they hadn't seen Alistair since he moved. 'We really miss him.
We had got used to him being there. Such a nice young man — very

troubled…' she sighed. 'Dreadful war.' And she sighed again.

Catherine felt her throat constrict — staring down at the counter. Would they always live in the shadow of past horrors? Would there never be an end to it — the choking black smoke — the blood-soaked beaches — the columns of living skeletons. She wanted so much to alleviate Alistair's pain — to make things better… What could she say? There was nothing to say. Nothing at all.

The day of the garden party was fine, after days of murky skies and drizzle. The sun was shining.

She had hoped, right up until late the night before, that Alistair would get in touch — telephone, or appear as he often did — but there was nothing. She resigned herself to the fact that he had changed his mind about coming and, for some reason, did not want to tell her. She felt sad — not let down — just sad.

She arrived at Edward's house at lunch time. They sat in his little garden and ate salad and fresh, crispy rolls. Edward said there would be a lot to eat at the party. 'Harriet is really enjoying seeing to everything. Robert and Felicity were very reluctant about the whole thing. Robert said alright if she really had to have a party, and Felicity said it was going to be very disruptive, and that she was much too busy for parties…' Edward laughed. 'Harriet always gets her own way. And she is very good at organising.'

Edward's garden was beautifully kept — a real cottage garden. The Cameron's gardener, Phillpot, looked after it. There were borders of lupins, delphiniums, stocks and pinks — filling the air with summer scents. There were apple trees, and a pear trained against the far wall.

Mrs Phillpot came once a week to clean, and deal with the laundry. She usually brought one of her meat pies for him to warm up.

Catherine thought how proud their mother would have been. How proud she had been when he had got into the grammar school — so anxious that he had everything he needed — a clean white shirt every day…

He was full of the forthcoming trip to Florence. He showed her photographs of where they were going to stay, a beautiful place in the hills above the city. A grey stone villa, serene and mellowed by the sun, amid an abundance of shrubs and climbing plants, with steps leading down to a pond with waterlilies, and a fountain of dancing fishes spurting water. An idyllic place.
He said he would have to take some work with him — there was so much to do at the moment. Harriet would be busy with her course in Florence. They thought they would be able to spend a few days in Rome. 'Robert has friends in Rome,' he laughed. 'Robert has friends everywhere…'

After lunch she changed into her new blue linen dress, and Edward drove them in his smart dark blue car to Harriet's.

Long tables with white cloths had been laid out on the terrace. Harriet had thought it wiser to have the food under cover, in case it rained. She was looking particularly lovely in a lavender-coloured dress with a very full skirt — flushed with pleasure, darting around to greet people. Edward was in deep conversation with a man in a beige suit with a red bow tie, further down the garden by the stream. He had got her a drink — a Pimm's — very decorative with sprigs of mint and slices of orange — there were large jugs of Pimm's on the table — and found her a seat in the shade. She sat quietly thinking about Alistair. Her tentative attempt to feel for someone again abruptly rejected. Harriet's mother came towards her across the lawn, rather unsteady in white high-heeled sandals, and a sari-like garment in shades of brown. She had a glass in one hand and a cigarette in the other in a long ebony cigarette holder. Her hair was as thick as her daughter's, but in a wispy tangled bundle, vaguely held in place with a velvet hairband — not a lustrous shiny coil like Harriet's.

'I don't really care for this sort of thing,' she said, as she sat down next to Catherine. 'I'm no good at small talk, but Harriet was so enthusiastic — she loves parties. We are so delighted with Edward. They are looking forward to their trip to Italy…' Catherine said it sounded wonderful.

This was really the first time Harriet's mother had actually talked to her. She was usually so distracted with her work or whether Gertrude had remembered to get something for lunch.

Gertrude was standing in the veranda by the tables of food — wearing the habitual dirndl skirt and open sandals with the addition of an elaborately embroidered peasant-type blouse — solid and unmoving, holding a plate with what looked like a large slice of cake.

Harriet's mother said, 'She doesn't want to go back to Austria. We suggested she should just go and see — just a short visit — she might still have some family there.' She paused. 'Of course she might not — and that would be very distressing. Robert and I are almost as busy as when the war was on, otherwise we might have taken a holiday.' She laughed. 'I can't remember the last time we went on holiday. Anyway, Robert is never happy unless he is working…' She got up. 'I suppose I'd better circulate. I thought you were bringing a friend?' Catherine said he had been unable to come after all. Harriet's mother said that was a pity — and do make sure she had something to eat — 'There's masses of food' — and made her rather unsteady way back across the lawn to speak to some other people.

She was glad to be home.
The day after the party Edward had had to go into work. She spent the morning wandering around Cambridge. She walked by the Cam and looked at some of the lovely college gardens bordering the river, and then went into King's College Chapel, and sat for a long time in the calming stillness.
She always tried not to think of disturbing things — reliving the moments that had left such deep scars — not visible scars like Alistair's — but hidden, internal scars.
She wondered what would have happened if Peter had not been killed — if he had survived the war — would they have ever been together? Looking back now it seemed very unlikely. He would have gone to Oxford to finish his degree — a changed person — a

stranger. It was fanciful imagining to think that one magic summer would last forever. His life would have been so different.

The thought of the beach strewn with the shattered remnants of so many lives — discarded heaps of bloody rags — still made her feel sick, and then all the undiscovered horrors that emerged — moaning winds shuddering over the polluted earth... And her mother — always doing her best — never thinking of herself. She had always hoped that she had died instantly — not buried among mounds of burning rubble unable to escape. In a way her father had been lucky — living in his own world, still believing that their mother was still there, about to come home — rather late — working too hard.

She then continued her walk. She went into Heffers and spent some time browsing among all the books, before meeting Edward for lunch in a very crowded café, where they ate Welsh rarebit. Edward had to talk really loudly to make himself heard over the din.

That evening they had been invited to dinner with friends of Edward's and Harriet's, Imogen and Toby — Toby was a research scientist, and Imogen was doing a PhD on something rather obscure — Romania in the twelfth century — at least that was what Catherine thought it was. They had invited another couple, Damian and Sonia. Damian was a mathematician. She didn't know about Sonia...

Their house was modern — square and white — on a street of square white houses — the gardens laid out in squares of grass and paths — some more unkempt than others — the rather characterless uniformity broken up by several magnificent chestnut trees — now in full heavy leaf.

Imogen and Toby's garden was immaculate with a few carefully-placed shrubs. Inside almost everything was white. White carpets, covers and curtains — lamps — glass occasional tables — a white bowl of oranges — a mauve orchid in a white pot. One long room with French windows leading onto a paved terrace. There was one large painting of red and black squares.

It reminded Catherine of the Aylesbury Clinic — nothing out of place — everything very impersonal.

Imogen was a striking young woman with short black hair, wearing a Grecian-style white dress with a necklace of large blue glass beads. Toby casual in a white open-necked shirt with a blue silk cravat and blue linen trousers. Damian and Sonia cheerfully crumpled — Damian in an old brown corduroy jacket and twill trousers, and Sonia, wild-haired with long dangling earrings which swung as she talked, and a great many rows of beads, wearing a washed-out cotton frock and scuffed white sandals — untidily out of place on the white sofa, messing up the carefully arranged cushions.

Everybody was very jolly.
They drank colourful cocktails with little umbrellas and cherries, and ate little twisted things and nuts from white bowls, and then they had dinner at a white table with white china. Vegetable lasagne and apple tart.
Imogen said that they had this Polish woman, Magda, to clean and do some cooking — very gloomy, but a good worker. 'Her cooking is rather limited, but she makes a reasonable lasagne…' Catherine thought there couldn't be much to be cheerful about working for Imogen. Not much fun at all.
Nobody took much notice of her. Edward was at the far end of the table talking to Toby. Harriet and Imogen giggled a lot with Sonia who just sat and smiled, and Damian filled his glass continuously and helped himself to more food.
She was quite relieved not to have to make conversation — glad that nobody asked what she did.

Next day they had lunch with Harriet's parents.
The usual haphazard meal. There were leftovers from the party — squashed sausage rolls, soggy sandwiches, broken fruit tarts.
Gertrude had made no attempt to arrange anything — just piled everything on plates and dumped them on the table.
Harriet's father took his food to eat in his study. He was in the middle of something. Harriet's mother said maybe they should have had some soup — everything seemed rather dried up. Harriet said the sausage rolls were fine, just rather squashed.

It was good to be home.

<h1 style="text-align:center">13</h1>

August was a dismal month — wet and mild.
Families on their annual holidays shivered on beaches behind wind breaks. Anyone brave enough to venture into the sea emerged blue with cold, teeth chattering, hands and feet numb. Seaside cafés, their windows dripping with condensation, served weak tea, rock hard scones, and a runny red liquid that passed for jam, luridly iced cakes of an unpleasant texture, and greasy fish and chips.

Sybil had returned from the South of France euphoric. It had all been absolutely wonderful.
'They don't seem to have any shortages like we have,' she told Elspeth, settling herself in her favourite armchair with a large martini. 'They seem to have plenty of everything. Of course there is plenty of fish, but we had fillet steak, and wonderful desserts with real whipped cream, and of course, plenty to drink.'
She had met a lot of old friends — some, however, had not survived. 'Ruth and Ivor were deported with their daughter — a fragile child. I think she was about ten. They never came back. Their lovely villa is derelict. Completely overgrown. There were German officers there during the war, but now the war is over nothing can be done without the owner's permission, only, of course they are never coming back. Such a cultured couple. Ruth was always so chic — beautiful clothes —everything meticulous. They gave wonderful dinner parties. I don't like to think what happened to them…'
Elpeth didn't want to think about it either. All those dreadful pictures in the papers, and the ghastly newsreel she had seen on one of her rare visits to the cinema — to see *The Wicked Lady* with James Mason. Jumbo had always like James Mason…
Sybil sighed. 'The same with the Brandts,' she said. 'Always so hospitable. He had an impressive collection of rare books. All the rooms were lined with books. I think she had been an actress — very theatrical — wore too much makeup — probably very lovely in her youth. They have some American cousins who have come over to deal with everything — the whole place had been ransacked. They

were very upset. They didn't want to talk about it. We didn't see much of them.'

There had been lots of parties. Somebody had a yacht. It had all been great fun.

She had brought Paula a large decorative box of sugared almonds, and Elspeth a box of Roger & Gallet soaps, and two tins of foie gras.

She had been stopped at Customs. 'This ridiculous man thought I might be smuggling cheese. Can you imagine? I said did he really think I would have cheese hidden among my clothes. The smell! I told him it was ridiculous. He didn't react at all — remained absolutely impassive — asked was I sure I had read the list of prohibited articles. Finally marked everything with a white cross. Of course I did have rather a lot of luggage. Really Elspeth, me, smuggling cheese...'

Elspeth was really pleased Sybil was back. A little light relief was very welcome. Even Olive brightened up.

Despite the miserable weather, she had decided to go and visit Tamarind and Hugo. The weather in Scotland was never very good anyway. At the moment things were reasonably alright. Alison seemed to be getting on well. There had been one rather unfortunate incident. On a supervised visit into town she had managed to evade the others and had found a bar, where she consumed several vodka and tonics before she was found. She had become quite hysterical, saying she was going to leave, but they had calmed her down, and now she was finishing a painting for an exhibition the art teacher was arranging in a hall in Aylesbury. Alison was quite excited, and had even written to Rosemary to tell her about it.

Sybil came to lunch.
Paula served some of the foie gras on little squares of toast, and then they had egg salad and strawberry jelly.
She said she had arranged to go and stay with the Carmichaels for a couple of weeks. 'London is so depressing with all this rain.' She hadn't been for years. 'They really have such a lovely place —

beautiful grounds.' It was just outside Hereford, so there would be plenty to do. 'Of course, now I can invite them back,' she said. 'I can take them to a concert. They so enjoyed going to the concerts...'

Elspeth said she would have to get the tickets back from Alistair. They hadn't seem him at all since he had moved into his new place. 'Still no telephone,' she said. 'It takes months and months to get anything done...'
She hoped he was alright. He was probably busy settling in, and his job was very demanding. She must invite Catherine to tea. Maybe she would have some news of him.

Sybil said she had suggested to Francesca that she should take a holiday whilst she was away in Hereford. 'She was very pleased. She is going to go to Italy to see her family. I believe she has a sister and some nieces and nephews. She hasn't been there since just after the war. She went back then and found everything very upsetting — a lot of destruction — very little food — power cuts — disruption on the railways — her family home destroyed in the bombing. Anyway she is looking forward very much to going. Hopefully things will have improved.'

Elspeth had suggested to both Olive and Paula that they might like to take a holiday whilst she was away in Scotland, but neither of them were at all enthusiastic. Olive said she was happy to stay here. She might go to Kew Gardens, or take a boat trip down the river to Greenwich. Paula just shrugged, and said she was not interested in holidays, and was quite disagreeable all day.

The journey to Scotland was long and tiring. The last time she had visited Tamarind and Hugo was with Jumbo before the war. Jumbo had driven the Bentley, and they had stopped somewhere nice overnight. There was a particularly good hotel outside Durham. Jumbo had never really liked going to visit Tamarind and Hugo. He thought their house immensely uncomfortable, and that Tamarind talked too much. He used to go for long walks with Hugo that always seemed to end up at the golf club, where they could have a peaceful whisky and soda. They had only stayed a few days. Jumbo had a lot of things to do, and there was the looming worry over the requisition of their house. Even Tamarind had been subdued. It was as if they were all waiting for the dreaded inevitable.

She had been very angry that her brother Edwin and his wife Estelle were about to leave for Canada. Estelle was Canadian. Tamarind said she was neurotic, totally neurotic, becoming increasingly disturbed about the prospect of war, and when it was announced that everybody was to be issued with gas masks it was the last straw. 'You would have thought she was deranged. Said she was not going to sit around waiting to be gassed. When I asked her about Alistair, she just said he was old enough to make up his own mind. It was really dreadful, and Edwin just gave in. Anything for a quiet life. As a doctor he could easily find work in Canada, but he would also be needed here. If there is a war, we shall need all our doctors.'

Hugo met her at the station with the same old station wagon, even more jerky and noisy. Hugo said he was afraid the side window didn't shut properly anymore. 'It seems to have got stuck…'
He had hardly changed at all. Short and skinny, wearing a green knitted waistcoat and rough tweed jacket. An erratic and absentminded driver, as if expecting the old car to drive itself.

Tamarind hadn't changed much either. A tall, angular woman — taller than Hugo — bony hands sticking out of the sleeves of her polo-necked sweater, her rather unmanageable frizzy hair turning grey. She wore a tweed skirt and heavy brown brogues. Elspeth wondered what they wore in winter. Probably two layers of everything.

Their house was perpetually cold. Years of fine Scottish rain and mist had penetrated the walls, making them damp and cold to the touch. There was still no central heating, just a few very old electric fires. In the dining room only two of the three bars functioned, and there was one with a single bar in her bedroom — totally inadequate.

They had had a live-in maid, a scrawny, uncomfortable girl who always forgot to take her apron off when she came into the drawing room. Her name was Marlene — her mother was a great fan of Marlene Dietrich. Unfortunately, her daughter bore no resemblance whatsoever to the exotically beautiful actress. She was a miserable little thing. Elspeth thought she was probably miserable with the cold.

Mrs Melrose, a capable lady from the village, came every day to cook. She didn't want to live in. She had a husband and a comfortable and, no doubt, warm cottage in the village. She was a good plain cook, very good with roasts and pies. Dinner was always served punctually at 7.30. She didn't like to work later than 8 o'clock. Marlene did the clearing up.

Meals were taken in the gloomy, freezing dining room, dimly lit, with heavy dark furniture. A heavy dark sideboard, heavy dark table, heavily carved dark chairs, even the silver was heavy, and the crystal glasses. Tamarind kept up an endless flow of inane conversation. Hugo just drank a lot of whisky, and agreed with everything she said.

In the evening a small fire would be lit in the old black grate in the drawing room, and Marlene would bring in a rattling tray of coffee.

Marlene had left to do war work, and Mrs Melrose had retired. Now they had a rather fierce cook-housekeeper — Mrs Foster, a middle-aged lady who always wore her carpet slippers.
'I just let her get on with everything,' said Tamarind. 'She doesn't like to be told what to do. I do suggest things from time to time, but she completely ignores me. I don't want to upset her. It is so difficult to find anybody nowadays, particularly as we are so far away from everything...'

Supper was no longer served on the dot of 7.30. Mrs Foster was more 'flexible', as Tamarind put it. There was now a serviceable easy-iron servants' tablecloth on the heavy table, and the silver needed cleaning. Also the heavy crystal glasses had been replaced by a somewhat cheaper variety. The food was also more varied. Sometimes it was very good — fresh salmon trout and juicy pork chops from a local farm — sometimes not so good — tough liver and bacon, uneatable pastry, underdone or overdone vegetables, lumpy custard and sour stewed fruit.

Neither Tamarind or Hugo had ever been particularly interested in what they ate. Elspeth was no longer fussy. The war had made everyone uncomplaining — years of dried egg, hard margarine, and substitutes for practically everything had dulled their expectations.

On the whole it was quite a pleasant visit. Tamarind had lent her Wellington boots, and they trudged across the wet heath behind the house, and into the nearby woods, knee deep in bracken. One day they did go to tea at the golf club. Elspeth was thankful for the warmth and the comfortable chairs.
It rained nearly all the time, but that was to be expected.

Hugo spent most of the time in his study, working on his maps. Tamarind said he was only really happy when he was working on his maps. 'We had couriers on motorbikes coming and going all through the war...' She said he had not heard from Alistair for some time. 'He stayed here for quite a while,' she said. 'He had been in hospital in Glasgow for some time, and then in a special convalescent home. I am afraid he had had some dreadful experiences during the war — doing something terribly Top Secret...' Elspeth said it had been a pleasure to have him staying with them, and that she had no news of him either.

She supposed it had been a good thing to get away for a few days. Tamarind and Hugo had been very welcoming, but everything was so strange without Jumbo. She had hardly ever been anywhere without him, and on the rare occasions she had been on her own, she had been chauffeured everywhere by Wilson. She had never had to negotiate strange railway stations — changing trains at Glasgow had been very confusing — or try to find a porter. Somehow she felt Jumbo's absence even more — an aching, empty space.

Mrs Foster had grudgingly made her sandwiches for the journey. The bread was unevenly sliced, but it was very fresh — the local baker still made his own bread — generously buttered and filled with plenty of excellent local ham.

Tamarind said she didn't know what the food was like on trains nowadays, so it was best to be on the safe side.

Elspeth was glad to have the sandwiches, but she did venture to the restaurant car for tea and a small square of rather stale fruit cake.

The train was of course late in arriving in London, nearly an hour for no apparent reason.

It was such a relief to be home, to have a really hot bath. The water in Scotland had been somewhat erratic, from a rusty trickle to a gurgling rush of tepid water. The bathroom had been freezing, and the towels old, thin and scratchy.

Catherine had also been away.

Edward had, again, very generously, given her the money to have a holiday.

She thought of Bournemouth, or Eastbourne, or maybe even Torquay, but ended up deciding to go back to Brighton — so easy to get to, unchallengingly familiar, with plenty to do in case it rained, which seemed highly likely.

Mrs Robertson seemed really pleased to see her, greeting her effusively, giving her a better room, with a small armchair as well as a wash basin, and a little table by the window, from which the sea was just visible.

The food was much the same, as were the people — a middle-aged couple, two elderly ladies who had their own bottle of wine, and a younger woman with her daughter — a peroxide blonde in her twenties, who seemed very bored.

It rained most of the time.

She walked along the front, battling the wind — the heavily rolling sea a curdled khaki, slopping biliously on the slippery shingle.

There were hardly any other people about, most dispirited holidaymakers taking refuge on the Palace Pier.

She went to the cinema to see *The Third Man*, and took a bus to Lewes, looking in the little shops, almost buying a pair of shoes prominently displayed on a velvet cushion. They had high heels, and a metallic sheen — very smart. They were much too expensive, and there would never be an occasion when she could wear them.

She had egg and chips in a pretty café with hanging baskets of geraniums and floral curtains.

She tried not to think too much about Alistair, like in the song. It had been 'Just One of Those Things'…

Elsie had passed her exams, much to Miss Milburn's astonishment. She suggested there must have been some lowering of standards. She came back to say goodbye. She had smartened up, her blouse tucked into her skirt. She was going to work in Westminster. Miss Milburn made an effort to appear pleased — wishing her well — and Catherine had bought her a box of Cusson's soap.

Her replacement, Diana, was completely different. A pretty girl with fair curly hair, very neat and tidy — sensible court shoes, pale pink lipstick — very attentive and polite. She lived at home with her parents in Enfield, and had a boyfriend who worked for an electrical goods supplier in Tottenham Court Road.

Miss Milburn viewed her with suspicion, but had to admit she could find no fault with her work.

Edward and Harriet had extended their trip to Italy. Edward had been given access to the university in Florence, so had been able to get on with his work. She had had cards from Florence and Rome, where they had had a wonderful time with Robert's friends, and were now going to visit Pompeii.

Olive came into the library to tell her that Lady Thornton was back from Scotland. 'I don't think she enjoyed it very much,' she said. 'She is going to telephone you and ask you to tea, but she is rather preoccupied at the moment sorting things out for Alison…'

She didn't mention Alistair.

Elspeth had a very long conversation with Dr Phillips on the telephone. He was pleased with Alison's progress, and thought she should be well enough to return home by the end of September. However, he didn't think she should go straight to Los Angeles to visit her sister — she needed time to adjust, to get used to 'ordinary' life again in her own home, but should not be on her own.

Elspeth had given this problem a lot of thought. She knew she would not be alright on her own — that she shouldn't be on her own — but that she would not come here.
Dr Phillips said maybe there was a friend who could stay with her — temporarily of course — until she felt able to cope.
Elspeth said she was sure she could arrange something, and she had thought maybe she could do a little temporary work. 'She is a very proficient secretary…'
Dr Phillips said he thought that was an excellent idea. She should have something to occupy her, and temporary work would be completely flexible — no serious commitments. Yes, he thought that would be an excellent idea.
Elspeth said she would speak to Alison's friend Heather, and see if she would agree to come and stay with Alison for a while.

Since she had come home from Scotland she had felt restless and unsettled. The flat looked drab and tired.
She decided to have the carpets, curtains and covers cleaned.
They had not been cleaned since just after the war.
It had been one of the last things Martha had seen to before she left.
She remembered the euphoria of getting rid of the abominable, claustrophobic blackout curtains.
Sybil had insisted they toast the occasion, and had brought two bottles of champagne to celebrate. That was when there was just her and Martha, and Sybil had taken her a glass in the kitchen, and went round putting on all the lights.

She had gone to stay at the Mostyn Hotel for a few days, until the carpets had dried out.

It was one of those things she had never had to bother with.
Penn had always dealt with everything.
She told Olive she was going to get Supreme Cleaners to come in.

They had done such a good job on Alison's flat. She would have everything cleaned, including Paula's quarters.
She would go and stay a the Mostyn Hotel for a few days. It was very convenient, and quite adequate. Olive and Paula would just have to manage.

She telephoned Heather and told her what Dr Phillips had said, and asked her if she could possibly go and stay at the flat, temporarily, of course. She thanked her again for all she had done already, and suggested they meet for lunch to discuss it.

They met in Heather's lunch hour, at an old-fashioned, dark-timbered pub in the City, hazy with cigarette smoke, full of men in smart City suits, loudly guffawing. The noise level was extreme, making polite conversation rather difficult. They had mushrooms on toast, which were very tasty. Heather declined a drink, sticking to soda water, and Elspeth had a martini.

It seemed that Heather lived in a bedsit near Gloucester Road. It was quite poky, and she had to share the bathroom and the cooker which was on the landing. She said she would be delighted to stay in the flat with Alison for as long as was necessary. Elspeth said of course it would be rent free and she would happily pay for any extra expenses. She said she would ask Alison if it was alright for her to move in straight away. 'It seems a shame it is sitting there empty...'

It was such a relief to have got that settled.

She contacted Supreme Cleaners and arranged for Mr Anderson to come and give her an estimate for the things she wanted done. The girl in the office said he could manage that evening at six o'clock if that would be convenient and Elspeth said yes — yes, that would be perfectly alright.

He looked very tired. They went round the flat, and he took notes. She invited him to sit down and have a whisky and soda, and told Olive to go and see if Paula had any of her delicious cheese straws. He sat down gratefully. He said he had had a very tiring day. She thought how strange it was to be sitting here with someone who was effectively an employee. It would have been inconceivable before the war. Penn would have dealt with everything as usual. She would probably have never encountered Mr Anderson, and Jumbo would have settled the bill.

She asked if he had any children. He brightened up immediately. Yes, he had a son who was six years old. Olive came back with a bowl of Paula's cheese straws. Elspeth told her to get herself a sherry, and they sat together, comfortably relaxed, talking about schools, and the importance of learning to read.

14

Diana said there had been a young man asking for her — tall and dark, with a horrible scar down the side of his face. He had wandered around a bit, and then had come and asked if she was there. 'I told him you had gone to lunch,' she said. 'So he just left.' Catherine's mouth went dry, and she suddenly found it hard to breathe. 'Did he leave a message?' she asked, trying to sound casual. Diana said no, he had just said thank you, and then he left.

Catherine had taken the bus to Oxford Street to have a quick look for a new coat. She thought maybe grey or black — camel hair did not suit her at all. There had been quite a nice one in the window of D. H. Evans. She hadn't had time to go down Regent Street. Dickens & Jones usually had nice coats.

Perhaps he had gone round to the Italian café to look for her. Perhaps he would leave a note at the flat. Maybe he would come back…

She went down to the staff room in the basement to take off her coat, and sat down on the rickety chair in the narrow passage with the strip of rough matting, next to an equally rickety table with the dusty First Aid box, which contained aspirin, antiseptic cream, plasters, and a pair of very blunt scissors. It smelt of damp coats and mould. She felt choked — near to tears. He could at least have left a message.
'I hope you are not feeling unwell.' Miss Milburn had appeared from the staff room — a cheerless place, sparsely furnished with two wood-framed easy chairs with sagging, beaten-up cushions, a couple of spindly upright wooden chairs with uneven legs, a much-scratched table, and a lop-sided cupboard for the tea things, lunchtime sandwiches, and various odds and ends — old magazines, several glass ashtrays, and empty biscuit tins. There was an ineffective gas fire, and a gas ring for boiling the kettle. It was windowless. Hardly a place to raise one's spirits, but in some ways comfortably familiar.

'There is a lot to do,' she said, looking at Catherine suspiciously. 'There is a list of new publications to check.'

Catherine got up. 'I think I will just make myself some tea,' she said. She thoughT Miss Milburn was going to say that it was not time for tea, but she just said 'Well, don't be long...'

Catherine had still not taken her coat off. She felt choked and miserable, and wished she could just go home.

'I'll take Diana a cup as well,' she said.

Elspeth went to lunch with Sybil. She was very pleased with Francesca — a good cook — not as inventive as Paula — not so good with fancy things — but good basic cooking, and an excellent cleaner. Everything was always spotless.

She had acquired an admirer whilst she was staying with the Carmichaels — a widower with two grown-up daughters and three grandchildren. He was very keen...

'He keeps sending me flowers,' she said, waving her hand airily towards a magnificent bouquet on the table by the window and a large vase of red roses on the table by the sofa. 'And chocolates. An extravagantly large box from Fortnum's. I hardly eat chocolate, it tends to give me a headache. Nice to have to offer guests... I don't think we are really used to having all these things yet. I would rather have a larger butter ration.'

Elspeth agreed. It would be nice to have a larger butter ration — and a larger meat ration. Nice to have more of everything really. She said it must be rather flattering to be showered with gifts.

Sybil said it was completely absurd. 'I'm not the slightest bit interested. Of course it's flattering — but really...'

She poured herself a generous gin and vermouth. Elspeth declined. She did not really care to drink at lunchtime. A glass of wine with her meal was quite sufficient.

'He was a brigadier during the war. I don't think he did much fighting — sitting in an office in Whitehall most of the time. Very proper. What one calls an upstanding figure of a man...'

She sat back in one of the deeply comfortable armchairs and lit a cigarette.

'He has invited me to the opera next week. As you know, I don't really care for opera. I suppose it would be an opportunity to dress up. I have a rather lovely silver-grey frock.' She sighed. 'But people don't dress up anymore…'

Jumbo had loved opera — particularly Italian opera. Verdi had been his favourite. They had had a lot of operatic records. All gone now. She had never been that keen and, unlike Sybil, she had never cared for dressing up. They had always had a box so it was all very comfortable. And there was always the champagne and smoked salmon sandwiches. The sopranos taking such an interminable time to die. The champagne was especially welcome. Jumbo had often had to invite business associates. There had even been a German couple. A difficult evening with war looming, and barrage balloons floating monstrously over Hyde Park. They had been very polite, very smartly and expensively dressed, the wife in bottle-green satin with an impressive diamond choker and earrings. They both spoke impeccable English. She remembered it had been a performance of Tosca — very dramatic. Afterwards they had had a late supper in the Italian restaurant they always went to after a performance. Conversation had been difficult — nothing at all controversial — Jumbo urging them to fit in a visit to the British Museum before they went home. 'Fantastic collection…' The restaurant had been destroyed in the bombing.

Sybil said she didn't think she would go. 'I will think of some excuse…'
They had salmon and spinach and apricot tart for lunch.
Sybil said Cedric wanted to show her his house in Hampstead Garden Suburb. 'Very grand I believe. I really don't want to be bothered. I don't want to seem to be encouraging him. I don't want any attachments — I'm perfectly happy as I am. And he has all this family. I don't like children — too sticky — too noisy.' She shuddered, and poured herself more wine, refilling Elspeth's glass. 'He's very persistent…'

It had always surprised Elspeth that anybody as elegant and charming as Sybil had remained an unattached widow for so long. There had been a few mild flirtations over the years, but nothing serious. She and Pogo had really lived separate lives. Pogo's filled with masculine pursuits — hunting and fishing, riding to hounds, polo, golf, a good port at his club, and, of course, a great many disastrous gambles on the Stock Exchange — but he was nevertheless very gratified to have such an extremely attractive wife by his side on formal occasions — whilst Sybil happily pursued the social round she enjoyed. Elspeth thought she had hardly noticed Pogo's death. She had had a stunning black outfit at his funeral. She had, in fact, often expressed her distaste for anything remotely physical, shuddering at the thought of anybody slobbering over her. 'Damp hands.' She had a horror of damp hands. 'Wet mouths.' They were a worse horror.

Elspeth thought how desperately she missed Jumbo. Their comfortable caring life. Always there to support each other. The circumstances of his death making it even more unsupportable. Seven years ago — seven painful years — an empty space that would never be filled.

Sybil said, 'He's quite good-looking, and really quite jolly, but all the same, I'm really not interested.'

Elspeth telephoned to ask if she would like to come and keep her company for supper at the Mostyn Hotel. 'Not up to Paula's standards of course, but perfectly acceptable...', and went on to explain about the carpets.

When the telephone rang, Catherine had so hoped it might be Alistair. Not many people had her telephone number. She had still heard nothing, and the sadness she felt was like a weight — a continuous aching pressure.
She did not know why he had not said he had changed his mind about coming to the garden party. Maybe he had not wanted to meet people he had known — not wanting them to pretend not to notice the livid scars — aware that they were wondering how he had got them — exposing him to silent scrutiny. But he still could have told her he wasn't going to come. And now the continual silence. His brief appearance at the library. No word since.
She did not wish to make him feel obliged to be kind to her.

She would just like to be there in case he needed someone to talk to. She had felt so safe beside him, like the first time she had seen him, and wanted to hold onto him. Just hold on.

Her feelings were quite irrational. Why should she feel this way about someone she hardly knew? Someone who was so obviously still fighting his own demons. And yet she felt so safe when she was with him. It was foolish. There were other people in his life — glamorous people, like the beautiful young woman at the Albert Hall.

Perhaps Elspeth might have some news of him. After all, she had been staying with his aunt. It would be good to go out, and she liked Elspeth. Despite her rather stiff upper-classness, she found her very easy to talk to.

She wondered how her daughter was getting on in the clinic. She hoped it was being successful.

Elspeth was pleased she was going to see Catherine. She found her very sympathetic.

Olive had said she had looked very pale and peaky when she had last visited the library. She wondered whether it was something to do with Alistair. He seemed to have vanished. Unfortunately there was still no telephone. She had written him a note to say she hoped he was well, but there had been no reply. She supposed it had been foolish to hope he and Catherine might have got together — two lost souls. Life never worked out as one would like.

The hotel was genteelly shabby.

Perhaps slightly shabbier than when she had been before. It was still so difficult to get anything done. Then the windows were still boarded up — shattered by the bombing. They had been lucky to escape — so many of the surrounding buildings had been completely gutted.

She had wondered how they had managed to keep open during the war — probably occupied by people who had been bombed out — or refugees... Now there was the gradual rebuilding going on. At least the hotel windows had been replaced. The hot water and heating was still erratic, but that was the same for everyone — one was grateful to have any heating at all. The food was unmemorable — but it was food.

She suggested they had a sherry in the lounge before dinner. Somebody had thought to put a large vase of bronze chrysanthemums on the table by the door, which distracted one's attention from the worn carpet and over-used furniture.

Catherine was very punctual. Elspeth liked people who were punctual. Alison was never punctual. It had used to really annoy Jumbo. She had always lost something, or forgotten something. Olive was always early, afraid she might be late.

Catherine chose fish. The menu was very basic — lamp chop, fillet of plaice, steak pie. Elspeth said she would have the same. 'The chop will probably be very tough, and rather miniscule, and I'm never sure about steak pie. One is never sure about the steak being steak...'
She ordered a bottle of red wine. She said she hoped that it would be alright. 'I really can't drink white — too acidic....'
Catherine was just pleased to be there.
Elspeth asked about the garden party — had it been successful?
Catherine tried to sound positive. She felt unaccountably embarrassed and moved quickly on to tell Elspeth about her holiday in Brighton. 'Very wet...'
Elspeth said everywhere had been very wet, and told her about her own visit to Scotland. 'I suppose you have had no news of Alistair,' she said. 'Tamarind had had no news. He hasn't been to pick up his things. I can only presume that he is away somewhere. He was sometimes sent away to do with his job — he never said where — and, well, of course, one never asked.'
She didn't look at Catherine — just felt her sadness.
'Such a nuisance to have no telephone. I suppose one day things will get back to normal. Sometimes it's hard to believe we actually won the war. Tamarind said he was in hospital for a long time, and when he came to stay with them he was so thin she had to buy extra food on the Black Market...'

The waitress, a lank-haired, listless young woman, took their order. 'And tartare sauce,' said Elspeth. 'If you have any...'

The young woman's heavily blackened eyebrows rose slightly.

'I'll ask,' she said.

'And could you bring the wine now?' Elspeth said.

'I'm afraid the service is a bit slow,' she said. 'However, at least we can have a drink... As I was saying, Tamarind said Alistair was in a very bad way. So many people are finding it very hard to adapt to ordinary life — whatever ordinary life is.'

Catherine knew that Elspeth was trying to make Alistair's non-appearance more understandable, but she still wished she could speak to him.

The waitress brought the fish — quite decent portions — with bowls of mashed potato, carrot and broccoli, all balanced precariously on one tray. 'Sorry, madam, no tartare sauce.'

She put the dishes down on the table. 'Cook says they haven't had any for ages.'

Elspeth said, 'Never mind, I wasn't really expecting any.'

She told Catherine about going to visit Alison. 'I shall take Olive with me,' she said. 'Alison doesn't seem to mind Olive. Dr Phillips thinks she will be ready to come home at the end of the month.' She then explained about Heather moving into Alison's flat so that she would not be on her own. 'Such a nice young woman,' said Elspeth. 'And such a good friend. Very reliable.'

Catherine said she was so glad that everything seemed to be working out so well. She thought that temporary work sounded a really good idea, and hoped she would now be able to get on with life.

'Well,' said Elspeth, 'we are hoping she will be well enough to visit her sister in America for Christmas.' She filled their glasses. 'Let's have a toast,' she said. 'Good things for everyone.'

Elspeth telephoned Dr Phillips to arrange to come and see Alison. He sounded pleased, and suggested they lunch in their dining room. It would save time, and the food was very wholesome. Elspeth thanked him, and said that sounded a very good idea. She then telephoned Ladbroke Cars for a car, and the same driver — Mr Collins. A very steady driver...

She had enjoyed her evening with Catherine.

They had finished their meal with a rhubarb crumble, which was quite good, although the crumble had been rather soggy — and passable coffee.

She had insisted on Catherine having a taxi, which she also insisted on paying for, and said that she must come and have a meal soon, when the cleaning was all finished. She was sure Alistair would appear soon…

The flat looked much better with everything cleaned — much brighter, less weary.

She wrote a note to Mr Anderson to say how pleased she was.

Sybil phoned to say she had been dragooned into going to the opera with Cedric.

'I tried to get out of it,' she said. 'I told him I was not very keen on opera, but he said he had already reserved a box, and had invited his sister and her husband, and an old army friend and his wife to join us. Anyhow, it seems I can dress up, so I shall wear the silver grey, which is rather nice. Hopefully there will be plenty of champagne…'

Elspeth said she was sure she would have an enjoyable evening. Going to the Royal Opera House was always enjoyable.

Alison was in a class when they arrived.

The pretty young woman at the reception desk, very proper today in a black coat and skirt and strict white blouse, rang Dr Phillips. She said he would be a few minutes, and they could wait in his study. Leading the way, she remarked on what a nice day it was. 'So good to have some sunshine…'

He did not keep them long — smiling — shaking hands firmly — ringing for coffee — telling them that Alison would be there shortly. 'She is just finishing a session of meditation. Very calming,' he said. 'We try to make meditation part of the daily routine — it is most helpful…'

He said he had told Alison they were coming, and there had been no adverse reaction.

They did not embrace, Alison standing at a 'safe' distance, but she did manage a brief smile, and almost shook hands with Olive.

Dr Phillips said he hoped they would enjoy their lunch — 'We have some splendid cauliflowers at the moment' — and that he would see them afterwards. Alison led them away to the dining room.

She certainly looked better. She had some colour in her face, and her hair was clean and well brushed — she had always had trouble keeping her very fine hair tidy. She was also wearing a little pink lipstick, and was walking properly, instead of teetering about, even though she was wearing fairly high heels. Alison never wore flat shoes, except if she was walking in the country. She said they were frumpy and dull.

The dining room had a very pleasant atmosphere. It was light and airy, and there were little vases of flowers on all the tables.

Elspeth noticed that Alison had to sign a register as they came in.

The food was served at a long counter, so you could choose what you wanted. It all looked very appetising.

They all chose fishcakes and cauliflower in a white sauce, and found a table by the window overlooking the very well-kept garden, with long beds of Michaelmas daisies, a lovely mixture of pinks and mauves. The dining room was quite full, with people coming and going — mostly two or three people sitting together, some people eating on their own. Voices were raised at a table in the corner — somebody noisily pushing back a chair.

Alison said to take no notice. 'I don't know why they sit together. They always quarrel. Sometimes Martin — he's the short one — gets quite violent, and somebody has to remove him.'

This time he seemed to calm down, and sat down again. Alison said she expected he was hungry, and didn't want to spoil his lunch, and she gave a little laugh. Olive spluttered into her glass of water — Alison actually laughing was enough to make anyone splutter.

They talked about her coming home. How good it was that Heather was going to be with her. She seemed quite amenable, even though she did not actually say she was looking forward to it. In fact, she said very little, but at least there was no feeling of antagonism — no withdrawal.

They had a really excellent plum flan with homemade custard for dessert, and then Alison took them back to Dr Phillips' study.
She said she had to go — there was a talk on French cinema she did not want to miss.
It was all immensely encouraging.

15

Catherine had started to go for walks after work.

It seemed a shame to waste the long summer evenings sitting in her flat. The days were getting shorter and soon it would be autumn. Some of the leaves were already beginning to change colour.

She liked to walk in Hyde Park by the Serpentine, with the water gently lapping, and the woody sound of the rowing boats bumping each other on their moorings. Sometimes she would buy fish and chips on the way home.

Sometimes she just walked down to Marylebone High Street, looking in the shops, always hoping, perhaps, to see Alistair.

And then the summer was over, and by the time she reached the Serpentine the street lights were already coming on.

It was wonderful to have the street lights after years of intimidating blackout.

Sometimes she walked as far as the Albert Memorial, and caught a bus home, but tonight she was tired, and thought she would just walk up to the bridge.

And then she saw him, some way in front, the tall figure in the dark blue raincoat, walking slowly with the young woman who had greeted him so effusively at the Albert Hall. They stopped and faced each other — she was doing a lot of gesticulating, and he was just standing there. She was about to turn round and quickly retrace her steps when they started to walk towards her. Not knowing quite what she should do she stood quite still, ready to smile politely — 'Fancy seeing you,' when he saw her. He seemed completely taken aback, and then he smiled — a real smile — and came straight up to her and hugged her spontaneously. They stood there with his arms around her, and her face buried in his shoulder.

The young woman called out, quite angrily. 'For goodness sake, Alistair, do come on. We're already late...'

For a moment he did not respond. He released her, still keeping a firm grip on her arm. 'You'll have to make my excuses,' he said. 'I'll see them another time.'

'But they're expecting us,' she said. 'I said you would be coming...'
He said she would have to go without him.
She was really angry now. 'You can't just leave me here.'
He said she would easily get a taxi.
He had still not let go of her arm, and was starting to walk away, leaving the young woman standing there.
She shouted something that they couldn't hear, but Alistair kept leading her firmly away.

The traffic was very heavy in Park Lane, and they had to wait for the lights to change before crossing. She tried to think of something to say, but a tight ball of inarticulate feelings blocked her throat. If he had been here all the time, and seemed so pleased to see her, why had he not just come to see her — or phoned — or written — or something? If they had not had this unexpected meeting, would he still not have got in touch?
'We might as well just go in here,' he said. So they went into the Dorchester.

Catherine felt she was hardly dressed for the Dorchester, straight from work in her old coat and shoes.
They went into the lounge, and he ordered champagne cocktails, and they just sat and looked at each other. Somewhere in another room someone was playing nostalgic tunes on the piano, the music drifting in the air, like showers of coloured drops.
He said, 'That girl is one of a group of people I used to go round with — before all the ghastliness. She keeps turning up, trying to get me to go to parties, to bars, night clubs. False people in a false world. Sometimes I feel I should go, to try and fool myself that I am having a good time. She is very available — too available...' He stopped. 'I'm sorry for dragging you in here. I didn't even ask you if you wanted to be dragged...'
Catherine wanted to say she wouldn't mind being dragged anywhere with him, but she thought it was not really appropriate.
He summoned the waiter to order another drink.

'I thought I was getting better,' he said. 'Staying with Elspeth was very helpful — caring — practical — and not the slightest bit

sentimental. Aunt Tamarind was always fussing. And of course
there were Paula's great meals. And then moving into the flat, so
when they sent me back to Germany I thought I was strong enough
to deal with it. But of course I wasn't. I don't think anyone can ever
be strong enough to deal with it. Hamburg is a loathsome place.
People said things had improved, that everything was better now,
and I suppose in some ways that is true. There are not so many
displaced people now, but the ones who remain are the dregs — the
physically and mentally disabled — the ones with no surviving
families, no homes to go back to, the sick whose bodies will never
recover — ones who really cannot remember who they are — and
children, growing up with nothing. They have set up centres and
schools. Everybody does their best. I was supposed to be sorting out
administrative problems — trying to improve housing. They had put
up all these prefabricated buildings to house everyone. They are no
longer suitable. A lot of them are empty. People have gradually been
resettled — gone home, or at least, gone back to where they thought
they came from. It took a long time — so many sick and weak —
disorientated — skeletal creatures. It was unimaginably dreadful…
Now they have to decide what is to be done with all the furnishings
— all the bedding — hundreds of cheap bedsteads, blankets, pillows.
All have to be cleaned and documented and stored somewhere, in
case of some future disaster — floods, earthquakes…'

He drained his glass, and called for another.

'It is still a place that contaminates you. Contaminates you with
despair and anger — a kind of helpless rage. The horror will never
go away. There was this boy. He was dying when I arrived and died
whilst I was there. He had been found in a pile of dead bodies.
They thought he was dead — about six years old. He never really
recovered. He never spoke. In and out of hospital. We never found
out who he was.'

He stopped, as if it was too painful to continue.

'He was very well cared for. The nurses would get him special treats.
A Polish nurse read him stories. It was thought he might be Polish.

He never responded to anything — just watched silently. Most of the time he was very sick. He died. We took it in turns to sit with him, so he was never alone. Just sat and held his hand…'

Catherine didn't know what to say — what could she say? There was nothing to say. The monstrous things that had been done would always be there, lurking in the shadows, haunting sleepless nights.

There was a long silence.

He said, 'Well, I think we should be getting something to eat,' and he called the waiter to pay the bill. They got up and he helped her on with her coat.

It was dark now — a clear night with a sky full of stars.
He took her arm. 'What about fish and chips,' he said.

They went to the usual place in Marylebone High Street with its bright lights and white tiled walls, with paper cloths on the tables, and ate cod and chips. It was very busy and noisy, but it was a very friendly place.

Afterwards they walked slowly back to her flat holding hands.
They stood on the pavement outside the flat. He said he'd better not come in, and held her very tightly and kissed her, and the stars really seemed to dance. He started to walk away, and then came back and kissed her again, and said goodnight.

Sybil phoned to say she would come for tea after she had her hair done.
She always went to Antoine's in South Molton Street. 'Not French, of course, just a nice young man from the East End, but he has a marvellous accent, and does wonders for one's hair.'
She had been going there for years.
She said not to worry about tea, she would bring a cake from the French patisserie, which was almost next door to the salon.

Elspeth was pleased. It would make a diversion. She felt she needed a diversion.

There had been so many tedious things to do.

She was trying to sort out Alison's passport and visa for America. And information about flights. Countless telephone calls, and forms to fill in. The passport photograph would have to wait until Alison got back to London. She seemed quite keen to go — well, as keen as she was about anything — apparently even writing a letter to Rosemary.

Elspeth had had a very encouraging letter from Rosemary, saying she hoped Alison would be with them for Christmas, and that she had sent more photographs of the house and of Los Angeles, and said how lovely the weather was.

Everything was costing a great deal of money.

Elspeth thought she might have to sell some shares.

She had never had anything to do with shares. Jumbo had dealt with all that sort of thing. They did have a broker, Mr Atkins of Atkins & Carr. She found a file with a lot of papers and share certificates.

She would have to go and see Mr Green and ask his advice, and ask him to do whatever was necessary.

Heather had moved into Alison's flat. She was very pleased. She said it was so good to have somewhere so nice to live after years of miserable bedsits, having to share the nasty bathrooms with other people, who were sometimes quite unpleasant.

Elspeth said she was doing them a favour. 'We are very lucky that you are here,' she said. 'Otherwise I don't know what we would have done.'

Sybil arrived looking smarter than ever, carrying her hat, so she didn't mess up her hair, which did look really nice, and a pink cake box with pink ribbon.

Elspeth told Olive to go and see to the tea. It was Paula's afternoon off.

She hadn't seen Sybil since she had been to the opera. On the phone she had just said that it had been dull, dull, dull.

'I think I probably drank too much champagne,' she said, installing herself in her favourite chair. 'Cedric's sister was a totally dreadful woman, dressed like a floral settee — large — heavily jewelled — with a wretched fur stole — definitely not mink — something indeterminate — probably rabbit — looked me up and down as if I was a prize filly. I quite expected her to ask to see my teeth to check my pedigree. Asked a lot of impertinent questions. An absolutely dreadful woman. Cedric didn't seem to notice. I expect he is used to it. Seemed delighted with everything. His friend was very courteous, a man of the old school — unmistakably military — his wife an insignificant wispy woman, so used to being in the background she was hardly noticeable… The brother-in-law was a blustery, country gentleman type.'

She drank some tea, which Olive had managed to bring in on the trolley without spilling.
'He had actually encountered Pogo on some shoot or other — said he was a "first rate shot". It was quite strange, talking to someone who had known Pogo — well, very strange…'
She drank some more tea, and accepted a slice of cake.
'This is one of their best cakes,' she said. 'They only had one left…'

Elspeth said, 'That must have been rather…' She tried to think of an appropriate word. 'Off putting,' she added rather lamely, and wondered how she would react if she suddenly met someone who had known Jumbo. Of course all their mutual friends had known him, but somehow that was different.

Sybil said, 'Anyway, the opera had been really boring — Mozart — so many trills and twiddles. Seemed to go on forever. So I drank much too much champagne, and had quite a problem gracefully negotiating the grand staircase. Cedric had to take my arm. His sister was bristling with disapproval.' She laughed. 'Anyway, I have turned down all his subsequent invitations, and made it quite clear I am not interested.'

There had been no word from Alistair. No note. No phone call. Hoping he would come. Longing for him to come.

She thought a lot about what he had told her. Maybe he had had to go somewhere again. Maybe he had succumbed to the charms of the beautiful young woman.

She must go and get a new coat. At least she did not have to look so drab.

She had joined a French evening class.
She felt she had to do something positive. It would help to fill the long winter evenings. She had done French at school, so she was not a complete beginner.
She had always wanted to go to France.
She and Peter had talked a lot about going to France after all the 'rotten business' was over. He had wanted her to meet his friends who had the yacht. They had talked a lot about all the things they were going to do — sitting on the bench by the little river which flowed peacefully on the other side of the park — holding hands — snatching an occasional kiss — another world — gradually fading.
She had one small snapshot of him, which she kept in the drawer of her bedside table — sitting on the bench by the river, handsome and smiling. Looking at it filled her with a numbing emptiness, the terrible sense of loss now seeming increasingly unreal.
Now there was Alistair with his scars and his nightmares, and her longing to be with him, which was really stupid. It would never happen.

The Major said she looked tired — could do with a proper holiday — dear lady — somewhere in the sun — all this rain not good for anyone. He said he'd have a go at Wellington — not such a colourful chap as Napoleon, but still a national hero…

Mrs Turner came in, as bizarrely dressed as ever. Today she had a long cape in an unflattering shade of green — she was fond of green — a brown knitted hat — Catherine wondered whether she had knitted it herself — and black laced-up shoes.
She said Harold was having trouble with his chest again. 'All those nights firewatching in the freezing cold — he's had trouble with his chest ever since. It thought I'd get him something to cheer him up — he always enjoys a good adventure story…'

Catherine said she should try to get something by Eric Ambler. He wrote really good adventure stories. She could start with *Epitaph for a Spy*, and if he liked it, there were several others.

Mrs Turner said that sounded a good idea, and that she thought she might try *The Forsyte Saga*. 'My friend Edna really enjoyed it.' She said she'd better get on. She was hoping to get some onions — if she was lucky. She didn't know what they were coming to when one was worried about not being able to get any onions. She thought a nice onion soup would be good for Harold's chest.

Olive came to change the books.

Lady Thornton would like the third volume of Osbert Sitwell's autobiography — and she was thinking about reading the latest H. E. Bates. 'I think it is called *The Jacaranda Tree*, which sounds quite intriguing.' She said Lady Thornton was very pleased with all the cleaning. 'It does look very nice — much brighter...'

16

Elspeth went to see Mr Green about her money.

He was even frailer than when she had last seen him, his wrist bones protruding from the cuffs of his too large white shirt.

The photographs of his wife and son had been removed, as if by removing them he hoped his grief would become more bearable, but in fact it made their absence even more noticeable — drawing attention to the empty space where they had been.

He was as courteous as ever, making sure she was comfortably seated, and phoning his secretary to bring some coffee, remarking that it was 'quite chilly this morning'.

He said that at present there was no need to worry. 'You have a healthy bank account, and a substantial amount in your deposit account.' He then went on to add, 'Of course, if your outgoings continue at the present rate, there could be a problem...'

Elspeth said it was only temporary — her daughter had been unwell, and she had had a lot of expenses.

His secretary, a cheerful, solid, middle-aged woman with a rigid perm, sensibly dressed in a grey coat and skirt, with a slight hint of pink lipstick — she had been Mr Green's secretary as long as Elspeth could remember — brought in a tray of coffee, and a gold-rimmed plate of digestive biscuits.

Elspeth commented on the coffee which was very good. It was so difficult to get decent coffee. He said his wife had a friend who worked in the American Embassy and was always able to get proper coffee, which she kindly gave to his wife.

Elspeth asked politely about his wife, who she had only met once at a reception before the war.

'She is frail,' he said. 'Very frail. She finds things very hard,' and he trailed off, staring at the desk.

He showed her to the door of his office, where they shook hands. His hand was cold — skeletal — like shaking hands with a dead man.

'Just let me know if I can be of any further help,' he said. 'I hope your daughter will soon be well...'

As she went down to the street to find a taxi, she was overcome with the feelings of anger and the shame she always felt when confronted with someone else's pain — thinking of Alison, and all the effort and money spent on her miserable, self-inflicted problems. This kind man who had had to remove the picture of his son because he could not bear to look at it — to contemplate how he had suffered — to be reminded every day of what he had lost. She had put away any photographs of Jumbo that had been displayed in the flat for the same reason. She didn't need to be reminded that she did not know how or where he died. She tried to be positive, and think of all the good things about their life together. She was only one of so very many who had had to cope with losing someone they loved. She was lucky — they could have had a son as well.

Alison came home.
Heather and Olive had fetched her in Heather's boyfriend's car.
Elspeth was surprised. She didn't know Heather had a boyfriend — it was very pleasing. Heather was such a nice young woman. Her boyfriend was in the Civil Service. He lived at home with his parents in Putney. Heather explained that he had not seen active service because he had very poor eyesight, but had done something in the Ministry of Information.
He had been very helpful, carrying the cases, and offering to make tea. A tall young man with fair curly hair, a slight stoop, and thick-rimmed spectacles.
She had decided that it was better if she did not go with them, but stayed in the flat, ready to welcome them. Paula had made one of her Victoria sponges.
Alison looked quite well, with tidy hair, wearing the new coat they had bought in Dickens & Jones.
She went round the flat looking at everything, and then sat down on the sofa and burst into tears.
Colin hastily said he would go and make some tea, and disappeared into the kitchen, whilst Heather and Olive sat down beside her on the sofa. Heather put her arm around her, and Olive did a lot of patting. Elspeth was no use whatsoever in these sorts of situations. She just sat uncomfortably, pretending not to notice, feeling, as usual, profoundly irritated, wanting to say 'For goodness sake, pull

yourself together'. She had long ago given up any idea of having anything in common with her daughter. She found it almost impossible to feel any sympathy. She had become so pathetic.

As Nanny used to say, she had always been 'highly strung'. But now she was just a pathetic young woman…

She was relieved when Colin brought in the tea, and cut the cake in generous slices, and Alison's tears subsided into sniffles.

Elspeth made an effort at conversation, commenting that Putney was a really nice place to live, and was it anywhere near the lovely park?

It was all very stilted and polite.

As soon as possible after they had drunk their tea she said to Olive that they should go and let Alison settle in.

Colin offered to drive them, but Elspeth said it was quite alright, they would get a cab, and thanked him for all his help.

That night she hardly slept, thinking about Jumbo, and how different things might have been if he had not been killed — fitfully dreaming of trying to wade through vast expanses of sand, and getting nowhere.

Alistair telephoned to ask if he could come that evening to fetch the remainder of his things — a few shirts and books.

Elspeth was delighted. 'Of course, you must stay to supper. We were getting quite concerned not to have heard from you. It is so difficult when you still have no telephone.'

Alistair said he was sorry not to have been in touch sooner. He had been away. 'I was offered a party line, which might not have taken so long, but I don't want a party line, so I will just have to wait…'

He said he would love to come for supper. He had really missed Paula's cooking.

Elspeth told Olive to go and tell Paula that Alistair was going to join them for supper. 'I hope she can manage to stretch things. We are having hotpot, so it should be alright.'

Olive said Paula was very pleased Alistair was coming to supper, and that she would make herb dumplings to make the hotpot more substantial, and an apple crumble instead of plain baked apples.

Alistair looked thinner than ever — quite gaunt and pale.

Such a good-looking young man. Such a shame about the dreadful scar, which seemed even more prominent against the pallor of his skin.

It was a very pleasant evening.

The meal was a great success. Paula's hotpot was really splendid, and she had made real custard to go with the apple crumble.

Alistair relaxed. He said he had had to go away, and that everything had taken much longer than planned.

Elspeth told him about her visit to Scotland, and how it had rained all the time, and that Tamarind would really love to have some news from him. 'She said she was hoping that you like living in London, and was very pleased about the flat. I told her how nice it was.'

She couldn't think of a tactful way of asking if he had seen Catherine lately, so she just asked if he had managed to go to any concerts recently.

He said that unfortunately he had missed quite a few whilst he was away, but hoped to go to some soon. There were some really good ones this autumn.

Elspeth hesitated to ask where he had been, but Olive suddenly piped up and asked if had been somewhere interesting.

'Germany,' he said. 'Not nice at all,' and visibly shuddered.

Elspeth hastily changed the subject. The idea of Germany filled her with horror. No wonder he looked so pale and gaunt. The obscenities that had been committed there. The whole country polluted. Certainly not a place to go to for pleasure…

She said that Sybil might be wanting to use the box — she was having friends to stay who liked going to concerts.

It was arranged that he should let her have the tickets back, and then he could pick them up whenever he needed them.

They drank nearly two bottles of Bardolino and Alistair had a brandy with his coffee.

Elspeth said he should come more often. 'Paula really enjoys cooking for you.'

As she was waiting for Diana to relieve her so she could go to lunch, Alistair came through the door. She was so pleased to see him — she wanted to rush to meet him, but just stood quite still and smiled.

He came straight up to her, leant across the counter and kissed her. She put up her hand instinctively to touch his face, and he held it against his cheek. 'Can you come out now,' he said. She said she was just about to go to lunch. Diana was standing breathlessly behind her. 'Sorry I'm a bit late,' she said, and smiled at Alistair. 'It's quite nice now,' she said conversationally. 'A bit chilly though…'

He took her arm, and they went to the Italian café. Alistair said the minestrone sounded a good idea. It was a bit chilly, and they had such good rolls to go with the soup.

Catherine felt a feeling of immense contentment.

It was warm in the café, and they were always friendly, and their minestrone was very good.

She felt that he was wanting to tell her something. He had become quite tense. He had stopped eating, pushing back the lock of dark hair which always fell across his forehead with his badly scarred hand. He had long expressive hands — the hands of an artist — a musician's hands. She didn't think he played an instrument. He had never mentioned playing an instrument.

He said, 'I'm being sent to Paris.' He didn't look at her. 'A Central Bureau is being opened there to help with the repatriation of the remaining displaced people. There are still a lot of people in dire need. Often when they finally get "home" there is no home. There is no work, if they are capable of working. They are often ostracised. They have no money. They need continuing help. There will be small centres set up in most of the countries affected, which are pretty well the whole of Europe. There will be a permanent residence outside the Hague for people who will never be fit to go anywhere, and for the children — there are so many children — most of them perished — the remaining few often don't know where they came from, so we have to try and find out what nationality they are — sometimes from the language they speak — and then we have to find out if there is any family remaining. We circulate pictures in newspapers, that sort of thing… The main office will be in Paris, where all the records will be kept, and funding and assistance arranged. Some people need ongoing medical help — people trying to get to Israel…' He paused. 'I am being sent to organise it all.' He still didn't look at her, vaguely stirring the remains of his minestrone with his spoon.

She listened with a sense of despair — another crack of light extinguished — the warmth and pleasure of being with him abruptly dissipated.

She supposed she should be glad that he had actually told her, and not just gone away without a word. She tried to think of something to say — to be interested and casual.

'What about your flat?' she said.

He said the French Embassy was going to rent it to use for visiting staff. It was all being arranged.

'It will probably be for at least a year,' he said. 'Maybe more…'

She did not dare look at him in case her face betrayed her feelings — the sense of loss — the hopelessness…

He said, 'I want you to come with me.'

She was completely taken aback, almost choking on the spoonful of soup, which she was in the process of trying to swallow.

'I want you to come with me,' he said again. 'I don't think I can do it alone…'

She put the spoon down and looked at him.

They sat there looking at each other, and then he reached across the table and took her hand. He smiled a slightly crooked smile. 'Don't look so shocked,' he said. 'I've thought about it a lot, and I need you to come with me.'

Catherine was speechless. How could she go with him? What about her job? The flat? What if he didn't really mean it? Did he really want her to go with him? She couldn't believe it, and yet it seemed the most wonderful thing that could have happened — beyond anything she could have ever wished for.

He said, 'I realise it is a big step — a big decision— I'm not exactly an easy person…'

Catherine suddenly realised she was very late. 'Oh dear,' she said. 'I must get back to work…' She laughed for the first time in a very long time. 'I'm rather bowled over,' she said. 'I can't quite take it in…'

He kissed her again as they reached the library, and said he'd pick
her up later. 'You will have all afternoon to think about it,' he said. 'I
know it is a bit sudden…'

'Really Catherine,' said Miss Milburn, 'you're very late. I've had to
take over so Diana could go to lunch. It's a quarter to two…'

'I should have told you,' he said.
He was standing by the window, and moved to sit down in one of the
rather sagging armchairs.

She had spent the afternoon in a kind of daze, hardly noticing when
Diana brought her a cup of tea.
Of course she wanted to say yes.
She would be prepared to go with him anywhere at any time — there
was nothing that she wanted more — but what if it didn't work out, if
he decided he didn't want her after all, if he just went off?
He had not given any explanation why he had suddenly changed his
mind about coming to the garden party.
She could always keep on her flat — in case — so long as she was
paying the rent — and she supposed she could always get another
job.

A party of school children came in with their teacher. They came
quite regularly. They all had to choose a book. Catherine thought it
was an excellent idea. Usually she enjoyed their visits. It was always
interesting to see what they had chosen, but today she was too
distracted with her own thoughts.

He came just as the library was closing.
She said she must go home and change. 'I look such a scruffy mess.'
He put his hand out to touch her hair. 'You look fine to me,' he said.

He had gone into the sitting room whilst she went to change into her
good grey woollen dress.
He had hung his coat in the narrow hallway. They had not touched
— there was no need — they seemed so close.

'I should have told you,' he said. 'We were having a series of very long, very depressing meetings about all the reorganisation. They went on quite late. I couldn't face rushing to a concert. I should have come — seeing you would have made me feel better. But I just went with the others to the pub and drank too much. Then three of the poor, lost people committed suicide, and it was decided that I should go and try and sort things out. I felt completely alienated, unable to speak to anyone — and then, when I got back I should have got in touch straightaway, but I didn't know what to say. I was reluctant to admit that I needed you — that I needed anybody — so I will understand if you say that you don't want to come with me...'
Catherine said, 'But I do — I do want to come with you...'

They got up and put their arms round each other. Catherine held on to him very tightly, feeling the comforting warmth of his arms around her — thinking she could stay like that forever, and then he said, 'I suppose we better go and get something to eat.'

Later they lay still in the quiet glow from the street lamps in the square — throwing shadows of leaves onto the wall by the window. He said, 'I didn't mean to rush you — I don't want to rush you into anything...' And later, when the light from the lamps faded into the pink of dawn, 'Elspeth certainly had the very best beds...'

They had had a lovely evening.

They had gone to Gennaro's in Soho for a meal. Alistair said Elspeth had often mentioned that it was one of her and her husband's favourite restaurants. They had drunk champagne, and eaten saltimbocca with spinach. He had raised his glass. 'To us,' he said. And she said was he quite sure this is what he wanted — was he quite sure, and he said he was absolutely certain. 'I have thought about it a great deal,' he said. 'I have never contemplated living with anyone before. Never thought I would be able to live with anyone. It will probably be a bit strange at first.'

Catherine said she had been living alone for a long time, and had forgotten what it was like to live with anyone, and that had only been at home with her parents and Edward. 'You might find you don't like it at all,' she said. But he had laughed and shaken his head. 'I'm sure I shall like it,' he said.

17

Sybil had come to supper.
It was Francesca's day off.
She arrived with a large bunch of carnations, and a decorative box of fudge. She gave Olive the flowers to put in water, and said to give the fudge to Paula. 'More offerings,' she said. 'At least I am never without fresh flowers. Cedric is very impressed by my title… I was really surprised. I thought all that sort of thing had been obliterated by the war. Anyhow, he is taking me to a ball at Grosvenor House at the end of the month — some charity thing — so I shall be able to dress up again, with is rather fun, but I made it quite clear that I am not the slightly bit interested in taking the relationship any further.'

They had rolled fillets of plaice for supper, stuffed with shrimps and mushroom sauce, which were absolutely delicious.
Sybil said she was expecting the Carmichaels to come and stay quite soon.
'My first guests. Things are beginning to get back to normal…'

Elspeth was really pleased that Sybil was reestablishing her social life. Everything had been so gloomy for so long. If it wasn't for the continued, seemingly never-ending rationing, things were gradually improving. — even though there were still too many bomb sites and power cuts.

Things were better with Alison as well.
She had done a small amount of temporary work. There was a posh secretarial agency in Brook Street, which had a big demand for well qualified secretarial staff of a 'good class'. She had had a week at an estate agent's, which she had really seemed to enjoy, and a few days at a solicitor's which she said had been rather dull, but at least she was doing something, and living with Heather was working out very well.
They could now make serious plans about her trip to Los Angeles.

Sybil said she had sent the programme for the forthcoming concerts at the Albert Hall to the Carmichaels, so they could choose what they might like to go to. 'There is some Elgar which will probably do — he is English at least... I really have no idea what they would prefer...'
Sybil's knowledge of music was distressingly minimal, worse than her own. Elspeth was surprised that it had not been part of her very expensive education. She often wondered what finishing schools actually did. Sybil's French was pretty minimal too. She had no interest in literature or music, unless it was something to dance to.

Alistair had sent back the tickets with a note to thank her for supper and for a very good evening, and that he was having to go abroad again, but hoped to have some good news — very good news — when he came back.
She wondered again if he had seen Catherine. Olive had said she had seemed very sad the last time she had been to the library.
She must invite her for a meal...

Alistair had had to go to the Hague to inspect the new centre which was almost ready. It sounded very much like the clinic where Alison had been treated — large, comfortable bed-sitting rooms with private bathrooms, communal eating and living areas, various activities and classes would be available for those that were able, and a separate wing for the children.
He had shown her some photographs. It looked very impressive, and had lovely grounds with a great many trees. It had been a rather grand hotel before the war, and then had been used as an HQ for German officers. It had suffered quite extensive bomb damage, and had been left completely derelict, and had had to be almost entirely rebuilt.

He said there had been some fuss from the locals — various meetings had been held for them to voice their objections. They had had to convince everybody that it was only to be a convalescent home — no mention of displaced people or concentration camp survivors — and then he was to go to Paris to the new offices there, and to look at the apartment where they would live.

'We should be there by the New Year,' he had said. 'So you'll need to keep up the evening classes...'

They had joked about her choosing to do French. He said she must have had some kind of premonition. Anyhow, it was going to turn out to be very useful — for such an unexpectedly wonderful reason. She felt she was living some kind of dream.

Once or twice he phoned on a faint line to say he missed her, and she said she missed him too, and he said things were going fairly well, and everything was nearly ready and looking very good...

She telephoned Edward and told him she needed to talk to him about something important, and was it possible for him to come up to see her. She would ask for an extended lunch hour. He said that Harriet had to come up for a meeting at the Courtauld Institute in Woburn Square, and he had been thinking of coming as well and arranging to see her.

So that they could make the most of the rather short time, he came to meet her at the library, and they just went round to the Italian café.

He ordered spaghetti bolognaise, which came with a small bowl of grated parmesan, and she had a toasted cheese sandwich.

He sprinkled the spaghetti with the parmesan, which was hardly more than a spoonful, and said they had had a lot of super pasta in Italy.

'They didn't seem much bothered with rationing... There was always plenty of most things...'

She told him about Alistair, and that he wanted her to go with him to Paris.

'You must do what you want,' he said. 'As you said, you can keep the flat until you are really sure it is going to work... I'll help with the rent, and you will always be able to get another job...' He said he understood that Alistair had been severely damaged by his experiences during the war, but, hopefully, would gradually heal — her support would be invaluable — so much easier to cope if you know there is somebody there who cares about you. Everybody has dark places. 'I still find it difficult to think about what happened to Mum and Dad. That sort of thing will always be there. I still have nightmares. It is very good to have someone with you...'

They had never talked about that awful time.

When it was happening it was all they could do to manage to get through it — to do what had to be done — to keep going, and then to try to move on.

Catherine had always hoped that Edward, who was absorbed in his work — with his new life — his success — would have left the nightmares behind.

She felt a deep sadness as always, that their mother had not been alive to see how well Edward had done — living a life she could never have imagined. She would have been so proud.

She had not been in touch with Aunt May for some time. She had hoped to be able to visit them during the summer, but had used all her holiday going to Brighton. Both Aunt May and Uncle Charles were well, and now proud grandparents. Eric and his wife had had a baby girl, Clarissa. Aunt May had sent photographs — a lovely, jolly baby.

'You must come and see us soon,' she wrote. 'I am sending you some eggs, the hens are laying really well, and Charles is going to send you some onions — not in the same parcel. Hope the eggs don't break...'

Elspeth had just settled down in her favourite armchair with the *Evening News* — the curtains were already drawn, it was getting dark so early now, and Olive had taken the tea things out to the kitchen — when the doorbell rang. Who on earth could that be? They were not expecting anybody. Surely not Sybil, she always telephoned.

She was really tired out. The last week had been very difficult. Alison had had a setback, refusing to get out of bed, or sitting on the sofa in her nightclothes crying. Heather said she didn't like to leave her, but she had to go to work.

Elspeth sent Olive. There was no point in her going herself, it would only make matters worse. They had had to call Dr Myers, who had visited, made reassuring noises, and prescribed her a mild sedative. Heather had the excellent idea of getting some challenging jigsaw puzzles. Olive said they were very diverting — one of sailing ships particularly absorbing, so much pale blue sea and sky.

Alison had actually had a bath and eaten a little very belated lunch. Her flight to Los Angeles was now booked. She was to go on the 10th of December, to give her plenty of time to get settled before Christmas. Rosemary had written that there were lots of things going on over Christmas. 'They make a big thing of it over here.' There would be carols and parties and all the decorations to put up... She said not to bring many clothes. 'Everything here is incredibly cheap and there is masses of choice. No rationing. We have such a good life...'

They had also had a tediously long power cut, and had been without heating or light. They had had to wear overcoats. Trying rather unsuccessfully to read by candlelight. How on earth people managed without electricity. At least they had a gas cooker, so were able to have hot food. Even though Paula was complaining about the unpredictability of the gas pressure...

Now she was just looking forward to a quiet evening.

She heard Olive greeting somebody with a delighted surprise, and then she appeared in the doorway, visibly excited. 'It's Alistair and Catherine,' she said. And then they followed her into the room — holding hands — smiling — really smiling.
Alistair said, 'We wanted you to be the first to know that we are going to get married...'
Elspeth was stunned — momentarily lost for words. 'Oh my dears,' she said, getting up to greet them. 'Oh my dears, what absolutely splendid news... we must celebrate...'

Catherine was still in a complete daze — thing had moved so quickly — she still couldn't really believe what was happening.

Alistair had just turned up late one night from Victoria. He had arrived on the boat train, which had been very late. It had been a bad crossing...
He had come straight from the station. He would have telephoned, but there were queues at all the phone boxes.
She made some tea, and some toast for him. There was hardly any

of her butter ration left, but there was a fresh pot of homemade raspberry jam that Aunt May had sent. She was very good about sending her pots of homemade jam, and the fresh eggs, carefully double-wrapped in tough cardboard boxes labelled 'Fragile'.
He had so much to tell her. The flat they were to live in was in the 19th Arrondissement — north-west Paris — high up — near a really great park with a lake. High ceilings — tall windows — very light. 'The furnishing are rather heavy and old-fashioned, but it is all very comfortable.'

Catherine didn't care. She would be prepared to live with him in a shed if it was necessary.
He left in the early hours of the morning. He had to go home and sort his things out and get a clean shirt.

They had several blissful days. Meeting after work — talking about what they were going to do. He said he was sure she would be able to work at the centre. 'They desperately need organised people who could deal with all the files and records. There are so many — so much paper...' He teased her a little about the French class — she was getting on quite well, although her accent was pretty awful.
She made one of her stews which they ate in her little kitchen, and took fish and chips back to eat on Elspeth's breakfast room table. There was a full moon, so they didn't close the curtains, eating by the light of the candles Harriet had given her last Christmas — tall blue candles in elegant cut glass candlesticks.

And then he had to go away again. This time to Germany. He became still and withdrawn. 'I told them I didn't want to go back to Germany, but they said I was the most experienced, and they need me...'

She knew when he was due back, but there was no news. He did not arrive late and weary off the boat train. He did not phone. Perhaps things were not going to be so good after all — a life with him in Paris was not going to materialise. He had probably decided it was not a good idea.

And then he came. Just as the library was closing — pale and drawn — the scars even more noticeable. She was aware of Miss Milburn, silently disapproving behind her, and Diana, putting on her coat, stopping in mid sentence, as she was telling them about the film she and her boyfriend were going to see that evening.

He said 'good evening' to everyone and smiled the crooked smile, and said he was just in time before they closed…

They went round to the Italian café to have a cup of tea.
It had been quite amusing to see Miss Milburn's expression of bemused astonishment, and Diana had said she hoped it wasn't raining — she hadn't brought an umbrella.

He said Germany had been tough. So many blackened ruins — so many broken, distressed people, lost in some hellish limbo…
He stirred his tea.
'How do you feel about getting married?' he said, and when she didn't answer — totally astounded — he said, 'I feel it would be a really good idea…'
She said, 'Oh.' And then 'Oh' again, trying to take it in. Was he actually asking her to marry him? 'Oh yes,' she said. 'I think that would be an absolutely wonderful idea…'

Elspeth was delighted. It was not very often that anything so satisfactory happened. Two troubled souls who could now support each other. She told Olive to fetch a bottle of wine.
They talked of their plans. Olive got quite tearful.
'Paris,' said Elspeth. 'How exciting….' And Olive repeated, 'How exciting.' Elspeth said she couldn't really ask them to stay to supper tonight. 'We're having some sort of vegetable hotpot — we've used all our meat ration.'
They arranged to come for a proper celebratory meal the following Saturday.

Catherine had put off giving in her notice as long as possible.
She hoped she was not making a terrible mistake. What would happen if Alistair decided he didn't want to marry her after all?

The library was her refuge — somewhere she always felt comfortable and safe. The quiet solidity of the booklined walls, protecting her from the turbulent disarray of the world outside — distancing her from painful memories. Even during the last bleak year of the war, when the sinister juddering doodlebugs had been a daily threat, she had felt quite safe.

But now the wedding was, unbelievably, becoming a reality.
They had been to the Marylebone Registry Office to get a wedding license. They had filled in all the necessary forms, and decided on December 17th for the wedding. Alistair said that would give them a little time before going to Paris. They were supposed to be there for the New Year. Hugging each other in front of the Registrar, a dour little man with thinning hair, who coughed discreetly, and said she should apply for a passport. 'Better do it straight away,' he said. 'It will be issued in your married name, and will be here to collect after the ceremony.'
They hugged each other again, and wandered hand in hand, oblivious of the afternoon drizzle.

So now she must give in her notice, must tell Mr Simms she would be leaving. He had always been so kind and considerate.
She went to ask Miss Palmer to make her an appointment.
She hastily put away the copy of *Woman's Own* she was reading in the drawer of her desk, purposefully shuffling some papers.
'He's very busy,' she said. Catherine said it was important.
Miss Palmer tried to hide her curiosity, sighed, and opened the leather bound desk diary, smoothing the pages with her long red nails. Catherine wondered how she managed to do anything with such long nails. She was sure that Miss Palmer knew all the details of all Mr Simms' appointments for weeks ahead, and had no need whatsoever to look in the diary.
'I suppose he could fit you in just before lunch,' she said.

Elspeth had not felt so cheerful for a very long time.
She was so pleased about Alistair and Catherine. It was really splendid. Paula was going to cook something really special when they came for their celebratory dinner on Saturday.

And Alison was much better. She had accepted a job for a week at an advertising agency. Both Heather and Olive had said that it should be really fun. Heather had said she might meet some glamorous models, and Olive made encouraging noises. It had gone so well that Heather had phoned to say they had asked her to stay another week, and that one of the young men had asked her out.
'She got all dressed up and was really excited...'
Everything seemed to be going really well.
She had been buying presents for Rosemary and the boys. She didn't know what to get Don. She had no idea what he might like. She bought colouring books of London for the boys and doll-size models of soldiers — two each, one a Busby and another in Highland dress, with removable uniforms and appropriate weapons. She chose a pretty gold necklace and matching bracelet for Rosemary, and ordered personalised stationery and a very nice wallet for Don with his initials in gold leaf from Smythson's. A wallet was always useful, and the stationery would be nice for them both.

Sybil came to lunch.
She was going to spend Christmas and the New Year in Switzerland with American friends. 'Lots of parties,' she said. 'They're frighteningly rich.'
She had known Amy and Walter Hudson for a long time. Before the war they had always spent Christmas and New Year in Switzerland. This would be their first time in Europe since then. 'Walter likes to ski,' said Sybil. 'Amy likes to shop...'

They had grilled turbot with carrots and mashed potato for lunch, and tinned peaches. Elspeth really did not care for tinned fruit, however Paula had said she couldn't spare any of the sugar ration, and that it was lucky that tinned fruit was now available. She did not have time to make elaborate puddings at lunch time. She was not in a good mood. Sybil had not called until mid morning to say she was coming for lunch, and she had had to hurry to the fishmonger's in Paddington Street to get the turbot.
Elspeth said she was very sorry — 'I'm afraid Mrs Anstruther is rather inconsiderate...' — and she thanked Paula very much for all the trouble she had taken.

Sybil said there would be lots of parties. 'Amy loves parties, and there is all the beautiful snow. They always rent a sumptuously comfortable chalet.'
First, of course, there was the ball at Grosvenor House. She couldn't decide what to wear. She said Elspeth must come round one afternoon and help her choose. 'I don't know whether I will be able to remember how to dance — I haven't danced since before the war... I'll have to do a bit of practice. Dance around the sitting room to some old dance band records. I'm sure I've got some somewhere...'

Elspeth was not at all sure how she felt about charity balls. Why not just give the money directly to the charity? Much more money was spent on new outfits and beauty treatments than would be donated — not to mention the lavish food and entertainment.
She and Jumbo had never gone in for that kind of thing. The occasional fund-raising dance at the golf club had been quite sufficient, and it had certainly not been necessary to buy any new outfits for those. Jumbo had never liked dancing, reluctantly doing an obligatory quickstep with the president's wife, a dumpy little woman, who barely came to Jumbo's chest, always fussily dressed with too many bows and frills...

Sybil said, 'This fish is absolutely delicious. I'll have to ask Francesca to get some.'
Elspeth refrained from saying that the reason they were having turbot was because it was very expensive, and the only fish left that Paula was able to get at such short notice.

Sybil said everything was so expensive.
Mr Carver had got a really good price for the painting of the ugly man, but the supply of paintings was dwindling. 'The best ones were sold with the house,' she said. 'There are a few nymphs dancing around in the woods, which were in the small drawing room, and one or two dreary landscapes, but I don't think they will be worth much,' she sighed. 'I'll have to try and be more economical...'

The Carmichaels' visit had been very successful. 'They thought the flat was splendid. Lilian had done a lot of shopping, mostly handbags and bed linen, and Humphrey spent a lot of time at his club meeting friends. They had had lunch at Simpson's. 'I think they must have a special dispensation with the meat rationing. They still had quite large roasts, but there was no beef left when we got there, so we had to have lamb. They do marvellous roast potatoes…'

Francesca managed the meals very well. 'She is very good with vegetables, and pasta, of course. Do you think this dreadful rationing will ever end? Francesca has built up a very good relationship with the local shops, and, I'm afraid we do resort to a little involvement with the 'Marché Noir' now and again… We actually had some fillet steak…'

They had been to a concert — Mendelssohn, and something else she couldn't remember, but it had been very enjoyable.
She had brought back the Albert Hall tickets.
'I expect Alistair will be wanting to use them…'

Elspeth said, 'Alistair is getting married.'
Sybil was astounded. She stopped eating and put her fork down.
'Alistair? Getting married? For goodness sake — who is he going to marry?'
Elspeth said, 'The nice young woman from the library,' and Olive, who hardly ever joined in the conversation, said, 'Such a nice young woman…'
'A young woman from the library,' said Sybil. 'What young woman? What library?'
'The Marylebone Library,' said Elspeth.
She was aware that Sybil never went to libraries — really never read anything apart from *Vogue* and the *Woman's Journal*.
'She is, as Olive said, a very nice young woman. Ideal.'

In the safe comfort of the darkness, he said, 'I'm afraid some of the time it will be pretty grim. Maybe I should not have asked you to go with me.' And she said it would be less grim together. 'We can share the grim bits, and any good bits will be even better.'
They had been to a wonderful concert — Claudio Arrau playing Beethoven's Emperor Concerto, and the Fifth Symphony.

Their heads were full of music and stars.
The following day he had to go to the Hague.
A young woman, one of the new arrivals at the newly-opened Centre, had just committed suicide.
Everyone was very upset. One of the younger nurses said she couldn't stand it anymore and was going to leave.
The matron was in despair. She said it was such a beautiful place, and they had done everything they could to make it as nice as possible…
He was being sent to calm things down.

They had had a lovely celebratory supper with Elspeth and Olive.
There was champagne, and Paula had, as usual, produced a delicious meal with dover soul and meringues.
Elspeth had said she would be delighted to host a luncheon after the wedding, which was to be at 11 o'clock in the morning.
It would only be quite a small party. Alistair said he would invite Tamarind and Hugo, but did not think they would come, otherwise he had two friends he was going to ask, one, an old friend from Cambridge who would be his best man, and a French colleague from the Paris office. Catherine said that of course Edward and Harriet would be there, but she didn't think her aunt and uncle would come all the way from Yorkshire…
Elspeth said she hoped they would not mind if Sybil came. 'She has practically invited herself already.'
It had been such a very enjoyable evening.

Edward had sent a generous cheque as an early Christmas present.
He said he was sure she would need some new things for her new life in Paris, and that Harriet was absolutely thrilled.
'She says it will be a marvellous excuse to go to Paris a lot — to visit you — and she insisted you would need new clothes…'

She had bought a smart charcoal grey coat from Jaeger, a knife-pleated skirt in dark and light grey checks, some new shoes, and a warm dressing gown. Alistair said he thought the flat might be rather cold with such big windows — probably rather draughty — and with the money she had saved she bought a dark blue tweed coat and skirt, two blouses and a pale blue twinset.

Mr Simms said it was splendid news. 'Splendid — most pleasing,' particularly pleased that she was to marry Alistair. He had seemed such a caring, capable young man. So good that something so satisfactory had come from such a sad event. 'Life is full of surprises.'
He called Miss Palmer in to give her the news, and told her to bring the sherry they kept for visitors. 'We must have a toast…'
He said of course they would miss her. She had been invaluable, and he was very sorry that she was leaving, but she could hardly come from Paris every day to work in the library. Miss Palmer actually smiled and patted her arm. 'So pleased for you,' she said.
Miss Milburn's reaction was rather less enthusiastic.
'Well,' she said grudgingly, 'I hope you know what you are doing. It's a big step going to live in a foreign country. And what about the language?'
Diana was thrilled. 'Paris,' she said. 'How romantic. I wish I could go and live in Paris…'

Catherine was not concerned about living in a foreign country. In any case, France was hardly a 'foreign' country, not like Iraq or Libya, or even somewhere like Romania. And she was working hard on her French, which was improving.
She was concerned that this was what Alistair really wanted.
How would he manage actually living with someone?
He liked to be alone. He needed to be alone.
Spending every day trying to solve difficult and emotional problems for so many terribly, and often irreparably damaged people, haunted by faceless ghosts — the soundless screaming of lost souls.
Impossible to instantly distance oneself, to go home and have supper, and chat about mundane, everyday things.
Would he really want her there?

As soon as they had finished lunch — one of Paula's appetising vegetable soups — Elspeth wanted to lie down.
It had been a very stressful morning.
Alison was finally on her way to Los Angeles.
Despite her misgivings that Alison would react badly, she had gone with Olive and Heather to the airport to see her off — make sure she actually boarded the aircraft.

She had hired a car from Ladbroke Cars to pick them up at Alison's flat at 9.30, which would give them plenty of time.

The driver was short and dark. Elspeth thought he might be Greek. The man at Ladbroke Cars had said he was sorry Mr Collins was not available that morning, but that he was sure Lady Thornton would find Andreas an adequate substitute. He was extremely agreeable and very punctual.

Heather had helped Alison pack.

She was looking very smart in her new camelhair coat that Elspeth had bought her.

Heather had persuaded her to go to the hairdresser, and her fine fair hair was smooth and shiny with a slight wave.

She was even wearing a little makeup.

Dr Myers had again prescribed some mild tranquilisers, so she was quite calm.

Elspeth had invited Heather to come back to the flat and have some lunch, but she said she had to go to work.

Elspeth had been quite relieved. She did not feel like making polite conversation. She had a splitting headache. She had taken some aspirin before lunch, but it did not seem to have had much effect.

She was extremely weary, and somehow diminished.

Ever since the ghastly business of the abortion, there had been one problem after another, compounded by the fact they didn't really like one another — had never liked one another. She had to admit she had never felt close to Alison. Happy to let anyone else deal with her. Nanny. School. Darling Jumbo when he was alive. And Rosemary had always been good with her. At the airport Alison had hugged Heather, and shaken Olive's hand, but had avoided even looking at Elspeth. She did not really mind. She didn't want to be hugged by Alison.

She almost felt guilty about not feeling guilty at the intense feeling of relief when Alison finally disappeared through the departure gates — teetering on her much too high heels. She had done her best.

Trying to be sympathetic about the drinking — really considering her to be pathetic and contemptible — particularly as the shadow of the recent global slaughter and destruction still hung over so many lives.

She tried not to think how Jumbo had died. She would never know — obliterated by the choking Saharan sand.

She closed her eyes.
She must think about something nicer — be positive — put all the business with Alison out of her mind. After all she would be coming back soon, so she should make the most of the respite. There was only just over a week until Alistair and Catherine's wedding, and that was something extremely satisfactory to look forward to.
She had left the catering to Paula. It would not be a big party — easily accommodated in the dining room.
She must ask Olive to get out the large vases, and perhaps she could help Paula clean the silver. She must order the flowers.
Now she just needed to rest.

They were waiting for the taxi to take them to Victoria to catch the Golden Arrow to Paris.
Alistair was standing by the window with Monsieur Cendier from the French Embassy, who had come to fetch the keys of the flat.
Catherine had given the keys of her flat to both Edward and Elspeth.
Edward said that was great, he and Harriet would be able to stay there if they were doing something late in town.
Harriet was excited about everything, looking forward to frequent visits to Paris. 'Fantastic. The Champs Élysées, the Louvre, Montmartre, lots of beautiful clothes…'
Elspeth said she would get Olive to check everything was alright at least once a week.

The brand new suitcases were packed, labelled and ready.

Harriet had insisted they had new suitcases. She said Catherine could not possibly go to Paris with her old battered suitcases. They had been a wedding present from her and Edward. The rest of the luggage, including the wedding presents, had been sent on ahead. The French Embassy had been very helpful and efficient, and everything had gone very smoothly.

Everyone at the library had contributed towards a set of saucepans, chosen by Miss Palmer, and presented by Mr Simms at a little ceremony after work on her last day.
He made a little speech saying how sorry they all were that she was leaving, and joked again that it would not really be possible to come to work every day from Paris, and everyone laughed politely except Miss Milburn, who remained impassive. He then wished her every happiness and success in her new life, and made another little joke about all the cooking she would be able to do with the saucepans, and Miss Palmer handed round glasses of sherry.

Aunt May had sent a linen tablecloth and napkins, two jars of raspberry jam, and a cake plate with a pattern of roses. She had phoned to say she was so sorry, but they would not be able to come. Uncle Charles was having a lot of trouble with his hip, and couldn't manage the journey.

As they had thought, Tamarind and Hugo also regretted not being able to come. Tamarind said she couldn't get Hugo to do anything. He spent all his time at the golf club. And they also found the idea of the long journey intimidating. Tamarind said the trains were still so unreliable. She sent a Wedgwood coffee set, very smart, dark blue with gold rims, and said she envied them being able to drink French coffee in Paris, and was sorry not to have met Catherine.

Sybil gave them a set of silver teaspoons in a velvet-lined box. She said she hadn't actually bought them, they had been a gift years ago, and she had never used them.

Olive gave them towels, and Elspeth beautiful crystal tumblers and wine glasses.

Everybody had been so generous and kind.

Harriet had come up to London the week before the wedding, to help her choose a dress.
'You have to have a really nice dress,' she said. 'You can't wear just any old thing.'
They had gone to Liberty's and found a perfect dress, a Liberty print in blues and mauves, a small mauve satin hat with a veil, navy blue shoes and matching bag and gloves.
Harriet said she looked very chic. 'Très chic,' she said. 'A real Parisian…'

Alistair had arrived very late from the Hague.
He had travelled from the Hook of Holland, and the crossing had been very rough.
He went to sleep in a chair whilst she was making some tea, waking briefly to say it was good to be home, drank the tea, and went back to sleep stretched out on the sofa.
She covered him with a rug, tucking it around his feet.
After all, maybe, it was going to be alright — really alright.

Edward and Harriet had come up early on the morning of the wedding.
Harriet had brought her a lovely posy of pink roses and fern.
Everything had been very hectic.
The wedding had been joyous.
Elspeth gave her a brooch of amethysts and pearls, which was really beautiful. She said she would never wear it again, and it would be perfect with Catherine's dress.

Paula had prepared a sumptuous meal, with smoked salmon, coq au vin, and a glossy pyramid of profiteroles. Elspeth told Olive to fetch Paula, so that she could join in toasting the bride and groom, and to thank her for such an excellent lunch.

Everyone got on very well, and it was all very jolly.

Alistair's friends were really nice — relaxed and friendly.
Graham, his friend from Cambridge, extremely tall and thin, in a rather shabby brown suit, had a wry sense of humour,

making sharply funny remarks. Sybil, who was looking particularly glamorous, was really taken with him, and became quite flirtatious. His French colleague was suave and charming, saying how much he was looking forward to their being in Paris.

It had been a real success — a wonderful day — a truly wonderful day.

Now, waiting for the taxi, she tried to control her nerves — clutching her handbag and gloves — telling herself to breathe deeply.
It was all going to be alright.

She had slept fitfully, trying to keep as still as possible, so as not to disturb Alistair, who was sound asleep beside her. She was still not used to sharing a bed — to being so close to someone else all the time. After so many years of being on her own it was very strange. Everything was so new and so strange — embarking on a completely new life, far from her small, familiar world. She hoped she was going to be able to manage. She must work hard on her French.

Alistair said the taxi had arrived.
He came across the room with Monsieur Cendier to pick up the cases.
'Well, Mrs Sinclair,' he said, with a big smile. 'Here we go…'
And all her doubts and apprehension suddenly disappeared, and she put her coat on and followed them down the stairs.

18

Elspeth had never enjoyed New Year's Eve.

Before the war it was either a dismal dinner dance at the golf club, with people drinking too much and behaving badly — so much false jollity, disguising simmering resentments — the Christmas decorations beginning to look bedraggled, and a local band providing noisy music. Or a very grand evening, lavishly extravagant, in the chandeliered halls of their aristocratic friends' town houses, where people also drank too much and behaved badly. One year it had needed two footmen to carry a protesting Lavinia Carr — waving her arms and singing, with her dress half off — to another part of the house. The food was always excellent though, as were the dance bands, which was one of the reasons Jumbo agreed to go. He did not dance, but really enjoyed the music.

New Year's Eve 1939 was the last year they were all together.
The girls had travelled from their school, now safely evacuated to Cumbria, and had had a long and much delayed journey — transport was already being disrupted.
The blackout made everything very difficult and depressing.
Alison said it was really scary, but Rosemary thought it was rather exciting.

There were no parties — nearly everyone had left London, closing up their houses and moving to the country, or in some cases, leaving the country altogether.
They did manage to go to a matinee of Ivor Novello's *The Dancing Years*. Jumbo had had no trouble getting tickets — the theatre was half empty. On New Year's Eve the girls had gone to the cinema to see Fred Astaire and Ginger Rogers in *Carefree*, and had come back in good spirits.
Alison had done her impersonation of Ginger Rogers, and then they linked arms and sang 'Let's Call the Whole Thing Off'.
Martha had produced quite a decent meal.

There were so many shortages it was hard to find anything, and then, of course, there was the rationing.
It was hard to believe that there had now been rationing for over ten years, and no end yet in sight.

She took her tea to the window and looked down onto the street. There were sounds of singing and cheerful shouting. A line of people were doing an uncertain conga down the pavement opposite, and there were several couples arm in arm wearing funny hats.

During the war it was not possible to celebrate New Year, or really anything at all for that matter. With the blackout and the air raids, the rationing, the endlessly grim news, and most of the men serving somewhere, one never knew where, it was hardly the time for celebration. Jumbo's assurance that the whole wretched business would soon be over, becoming less and less likely.

The terrible New Year's Eve of 1943 was something one really wanted to forget.
After the shattering, heartbreaking news of Jumbo's death, she was hardly able to function at all. Rosemary was in the Wrens, and already going out with Don, and Alison had moved into a flat with friends, and had a job as a secretary at the Ministry of Agriculture. It was a relief to be on her own, not having to try to be cheerful, or even normal.
She had not gone to bed. Just sat in her chair, embracing the overwhelming grief and loss.
Martha had appeared in the doorway in her dressing gown at about 2 o'clock in the morning. She had seen the light was still on. She had quietly brought a tray of tea and some precious chocolate digestives, asking if there was anything else she could do.
Elspeth had thanked her, shaking her head.
Martha had been so good.
She stayed there until dawn, when she could turn off the light, and draw back the claustrophobic blackout curtains to let in the dim, wet dawn of 1944.
Since then she had never felt able to celebrate — going through the motions — doing the right thing — always doing the right thing.

Things were brightened briefly with Rosemary's wedding. That had been a very successful, happy occasion, but a very brief respite, when after the excitement of the D-Day landings everything slowed down to an agonising crawl, and their lives were overshadowed by the menace of the new V-1s and the silent horror of the V-2s.

Martha became almost too scared to go shopping.

People were weary — weighted down with weariness — of being stoical — of making do — of dreading the arrival of life-stopping telegrams.

The hysterical euphoria of VE Day had soon been dampened down. There was still the awful war in the Far East — still more casualties. By New Year's Eve 1945 they were settled back into grim austerity — food shortages — rationing — the shocking sight of the corpse-like figures of men returning from Japanese prisoner-of-war camps.

Elspeth thought that most people would have been pleased if there had been more atomic bombs dropped on Japan.

'Savages,' Maisie Burton had said at a jumble sale to raise money to help the returning troops. 'All savages.'

She had managed to collect quite a lot of classy jumble from her wealthy friends, some of whom were selling up and moving abroad to avoid the extortionate taxes.

She said they couldn't be bothered to leave the country — they were just going to move to Kent. They were tired of London, and Osbert could easily commute to the City.

She tried to sell Elspeth a large, extremely ugly vase.

'It's rather heavy,' she said. 'But you can always get what's-her-name to come and carry it for you...'

Just before Christmas she had encountered Jasmine Campbell-Brown in the Food Hall at Harrods.

She had gone to Harrods to buy Olive a Christmas present.

It was their usual habit to exchange small gifts — diaries or boxes of handkerchiefs, but this year Elspeth really thought she deserved a better, 'proper' present. She had had to admit that she could not possibly have managed all the awful business with Alison without her, and what was more she managed to get on with her — Alison had even seemed to like her — so she decided to get her a really nice silk scarf and some Roger & Gallet soap, and, of course, she would give her her usual Christmas bonus.

She had been very pleased with what she had bought — beautifully wrapped, in a smart Harrods bag — and decided to go out through the Food Hall, where, despite the many shortages, they always seemed to be able to put on an appetising display — and then she saw Jasmine at the fish counter, leaning on the glass, hardly recognisable — no hat, her glossy, expensively-coiffed hair a frazzled greying mess, tied back with a ragged scarf. She was wearing an ankle-length mink coat, with what looked like pink bedroom slippers. Her chauffeur, Guthrie, who looked just the same as he always had — hardly changed at all — was standing at a safe distance holding a shopping bag.
Jasmine was berating the young woman behind the counter.
'How can you have a fish counter with no dover soles?' she was saying. 'It is really disgraceful. Why don't you have any dover soles?' The young woman started to reply, but Jasmine turned away.

Elspeth was shocked at her ravaged appearance.

This supremely confident and sophisticated woman, who had given the most lavish parties, and hosted so many select social gatherings that everyone wanted to be invited to — so beautiful — so elegant — sponsoring musical and artistic talent. Elspeth had endured many musical evenings and dubious art exhibitions. Inherited wealth — Hamish's father had amassed several fortunes in various businesses. Jumbo had always thought them frightfully pretentious — the sort of people who bought books by the yard — which was a little unkind. This woman was now a bedraggled wreck — grey faced — badly smudged scarlet lipstick — thick black crooked eyebrows — giving her the look of an aged, dying clown. She staggered slightly and Guthrie quickly stepped forward to take her arm. 'Now, now, my lady,' he said quietly. 'We'll go home now…' He nodded to Elspeth. Jasmine was still muttering about there being no dover soles when she noticed Elspeth, and made an effort to smile. 'Good heavens,' she said. 'Elspeth! Such a long time. You must come to tea… I'm afraid

I don't entertain much anymore — no staff,' she gave a little laugh. 'Not much to entertain with. Not even enough cheese ration to make cheese straws…' She gave another little laugh. 'Tea sometime — perhaps — do get in touch.' And she made her way unsteadily, being carefully guided by Guthrie.

Elspeth remembered Sybil had told her that her eldest son had been killed in the first days after the D-Day landings, and that she had never recovered.

Elspeth thought of Mr Green — the photographs he could not bear to look at — and herself with Jumbo's medals hidden in the back of a drawer.

She sat down in her chair and poured another cup of tea.

Paula had gone to spend New Year's Eve with her Italian friends, and would stay overnight.

She and Olive had listened to the announcement of the New Year on the wireless, and then Olive had gone to bed.

It was quiet now on the street — the revellers had also gone.

Christmas had been very dull — grey, cold and damp.

Everything after Alistair and Catherine's joyous wedding seemed rather dull.

She was so glad it had been such a success. Everybody got on so well and Paula had surpassed herself with the wonderful meal.

She had been so pleased to meet Catherine's brother — so much like Catherine — tall, good-looking, with the same gravity and stillness — and his very lovely girlfriend. Alistair's friends had been very easy to get on with, and everybody had really enjoyed themselves, including Sybil who was looking amazing, and got rather tipsy.

She had gone to Switzerland, laden with luggage. 'Its so difficult to know what to take…' Cedric had been very disappointed. He was hoping to persuade her to spend Christmas with him and his family. Sybil said that was a positively ghastly thought — his children were probably as insufferable as his sister. He had given her a rather pretty opal necklace and matching earrings for a Christmas present. She supposed she could give him the ivory cigarette box Pogo had had in his study. She had always found it very unattractive — carved with entwined elephants — very unattractive elephants. She said Pogo had liked it. He said it reminded him of his father, but in what way she wasn't sure. He had never got on with his father.

Alistair and Catherine had come to say goodbye, and to thank her for all her help, and for making their wedding day so perfect.
It was very pleasing to see them so happy.
They said she must come and visit them in Paris.
Catherine said it was supposed to be especially lovely in spring.
Perhaps she would go. It was many, many years since she had been to Paris — another life — another world. It had been one of her and Jumbo's favourite places. They had like to walk along the banks of the Seine and sit in little cafés under the chestnut trees on the Champs Élysées.
Yes, maybe she would go. She would take Olive. She didn't think she could manage the journey on her own. She was no longer used to journeys, and she had always had Jumbo with her.
It would be nice to see where Alistair and Catherine were living. They had already sent her a card of the Arc de Triomphe.

The Colberts had already invited her to stay with them.
They were finally reinstalled in their house in Paris.
Thérèse said they were very thankful it had not been trashed — just stripped of everything. Jean-Jacques said they had been lucky to have had officers billeted there. All the same, everything that was in any way portable had been taken — the silver — Jean-Jacques' wonderful collection of paintings, which had included a precious Bonnard and a small, perfect Sisley — linen — the Chinese silk rugs and the antique chairs from the dining room — lamps — the contents of the wine cellar — even clothes… But there had been no graffiti or wanton destruction.
It had taken some time to put everything in order.
Thérèse said there were quite a lot of things still to do — redecoration and refurnishing. It was sad to have lost so many things, but it could have been a lot worse.

They were deeply saddened and distressed by the disappearance of so many of their friends.

Thérèse had shuddered when she told Elspeth — a close friend, Oliver Cohen, a gifted cellist and all his family — her pretty young hairdresser and her mother and sister — her dressmaker — the wealthy banking family, Marc and Emilie Kahn, with the magnificent house in the Bois de Boulogne — all gone — the house now a burnt-out shell. All gone. To unimaginable deaths. So many. And the children. And not knowing who, among all their many acquaintances had silently acquiesced to the monstrous evil of the deportations. And she had buried her head in her hands, whispering almost inaudibly, 'and all the children — all the children.' Jean-Jacques had tried to comfort her.

They were sitting in the calm comfort of the lounge at the Savoy, a tray of tea with plates of brightly iced little cakes and neat squares of assorted sandwiches on a small table in front of them.
Thérèse and Jean-Jacques were in London for a few days. Jean-Jacques had some business to attend to.
Elspeth sat stiffly — would these terrible shadows ever fade?
She felt an all-pervading sense of loss and impotence — a helpless fury that these appalling horrors had been allowed to happen.
Thérèse made an effort to control herself.
She drank some tea, chose a little cake with her beautifully manicured hands, her nails a gleaming scarlet, and tried to smile. 'We like to come to London,' she said. 'But we are so very glad to be back in Paris.'
She said Elspeth must come to stay with them and Jean-Jacques said she would always be welcome.

Now there were other concerns.
She had to face Alison's return from America.
Rosemary had telephoned at Christmas to say everything was fine.
The line was particularly bad — very faint with a lot of interference.
Conversation had been very difficult. She managed to gather that Alison was enjoying herself — the boys had loved their presents and that there were a lot of parties.
She had exchanged cards with Heather, enclosing a generous gift token from Harrods. She had so much to thank her for.
She had hoped, somewhat vainly, that Alison might meet some nice

American and decide to stay — perhaps never come back.
She had decided she must distance herself from the whole thing.
Alison would just have to manage on her own. She had had enough.
Silently she apologised to Jumbo — she had done all she could.

The tea had gone cold.
The room was cold.
She should go to bed. Olive would have seen to the hot water bottles.
She did not have much expectation that this new year would be any
better — she just hoped it would not be any worse.